WALKING ON NATHAN'S GRAVE

A TALE TRAVERSING HEAVEN AND HELL

A Novel by

R. LUCE

ISBN: 979-8-9922202-3-0 (Hardback)
ISBN: 979-8-9922202-4-7 (Paperback)
ISBN: 979-8-9922202-5-4 (Digital)

Cover design and layout by Veronica Scott
Cover art from *Adobe Stock* images.

*To all those who accept
and welcome diversity*

Acknowledgements

I am indebted to my editor, Don Weise, Veronica Scott for her cover and interior design, and Rodney Hatfield for his wisdom and advice about promotion and marketing.

A special thank you to John Cunningham for his love, support, and encouragement.

PART 1

1

Looking back at it now, I am amazed by how quickly rational thought escaped me. Dust in a windstorm. Of course, the world didn't end when the relationship died, but for a while it sure as hell felt like it was going to. And while I was in the midst of it, there were times when I wished it would, times when I said to myself, "I want out"—the big *out*." I didn't, of course, but I played the part well. People who knew me then would probably have said I worked damned hard at acting like I meant it. They would have been right.

Friends tried to help, fed me on clichés of new beginnings and all the other well-meaning, but useless, one-liners people dream up for people who are in a state of emotional turmoil. My response was to fake smiles and words, "Thanks. I know you're right," before leaving them as quickly as possible to dive deeper into the cesspool of self-destructive behaviors. This hadn't been my first go-round.

There I was, forty years old, feeling beaten up by life, and despairing about myself as a lover and a mate, someone able to hold a relationship together. In that state of mind, I couldn't write, couldn't muster the will, told myself I was as lousy at being a professional writer as I was a worthy lover, as lousy an example of maturity as a broken-hearted teenager. For four long months, I engaged in daily self-flagellation via alcohol, drugs, and sexual carelessness ... all the cliches of a hijacked mind. It took that long for the seed of desire—the hope to survive—to begin to plant its roots once again. It took two months more before I took the first steps back into life that would lead me to the adventures and experiences that would become this book.

Over the month or so prior to Matt's booting me out of his life, I had felt a cooling in the ways he responded to me, but when I tried to talk about it with him, he would say everything was fine, or I was imagining things, or he had had a bad day or week but didn't want to discuss it. Other than the feeling I had that he was struggling with something he wouldn't or couldn't share, we functioned as we always had, went places together, enjoyed mutual friends, spent alone time like any other romantic couple. Yet, beneath that normalcy lay a question mark like the proverbial pea placed under the mattress. After a while, I stopped asking what was going on with him, just went to him when he became sullen or depressed, touched him, took his hand, did whatever felt like a declaration of my concern and willingness to help if I could. And I waited.

It was a Friday night when the bomb dropped. He came into the apartment at his usual time after work and put his briefcase against the wall just inside the door as he always did. He didn't say anything when he saw me. Until that minute, he had always at least said "Hey!" or "Hi" or called me some silly name he made up for me. His eyes looked saggy, tired. His face—the way he was controlling his eyes, mouth and clamped-tight jaw made him look a little fierce, as if he were going to confront a client who was three months overdue in paying his bill. He took a couple of steps into the room and planted himself like a warrior taking on a space he was ready to fight for. As he did this, I was walking toward him saying, "Hello" more like a question than a statement and asked what was wrong. He put his hand out like a traffic cop to stop me. Though he had looked at me briefly as he said, "No! Stop," he seemed to have found a way to look *through* me when he spoke again. "Rob. Stay where you are. I need to tell you this ... make it as painless as possible ... get it over with. I've decided I can't do this anymore: You and me. I need to move on."

That was it. Surprise! Two years into what I had thought was making a life together, he wanted out. In a handful of explosive words, he had made a crater of our lives and pushed me in. I remember with the first shock wave, my heart began pumping rapidly, a tingling sensation took over my body. It was difficult to think, to frame the word, "Why?" It was all I could come up with. I was like some B-movie actor who couldn't be trusted with an intelligent line and flubbed the one he was given. My brain was reeling and further attempts to find words, failing. The only word for a while was the repetition of "Why?" He said nothing as I slowly began to fight back tears. I tried to take a step forward again only to have the palm of his hand in front of my face. I turned, looked around the living room for some consolation, some awareness of what to do. Then, staring at Matt's unforgiving facial features, I was walking backward away from him until I fell into a chair still asking my question over and over. He finally broke through my mantra of *why* with a stone-faced offer of a month to clear out my things and find another place to live. There was to be no, "I'm sorry," or "I wish it had worked out." It was as if all kindness and memories of our lives together turned off inside him like a burned-out switch he did not want repaired. Moments into my attempts to grasp what was happening, he turned away from me, picked up his briefcase, and walked out of the apartment, the door closing ever so gently behind him as he went like a thief who has burglarized a home and doesn't want to awaken the owners.

"Don't do this, Matt! Please!" I yelled as I pushed myself up out of the chair, got my legs to hold me upright in the room that was spinning around me in a gray confusion about depth of field, perspective, and how to negotiate my way. Then the door was in front of me, open, letting me out in search of him and answers. I could hear the self-propelled begging—the emotional cliché—that came out of my mouth hideously like a high school drama queen trying to humiliate her football jock boyfriend in front of an audience of her peers. By the time I got down the hall to the exit, he was nearing his car. I shouted again loudly in clumsy, begging words. He quickly opened the car door, jumped in, and drove off. All sound died as I sat down on the curb and watched him go out of sight. I folded my arms over my knees as cushions for my head. An actor in a 1950s melodrama couldn't have given a better performance.

In the heat of the initial blast, there had been no time to analyze, reflect ... intellectualize the experience as I might have done in preparation for one of my stories. Instead, I had been overpowered by the storm winds of the useless "Why?" and my imaginings of Matt having fallen for someone else, and the fear I had not been good enough. It took a while to get into the reality of my suddenly altered situation and begin to think, or at least, my best version of thinking at the time.

When I got back into the apartment, my thoughts and feelings were spinning still. But now they were more like slots in a roulette wheel where the ball lands randomly as it must on spaces labeled "anger," "hurt," "frustration," or any of my personal insecurities about "worthiness," "questioned masculinity," and desirability as a "lover." I went to a shelf in the kitchen where we kept a stash of whiskey, took a long drink straight from the bottle of Johnny Walker Red hoping it would calm me down. After another drink, thoughts of vindictiveness, multiple vulgarities— each dosey doed around an overwhelming sense of loss. At some point, in a fit of anger, I tried to call Matt on his cell phone to vent. He did not answer. Between attempts to reach him, I sat staring at the walls and tried to think of what I was going to do: Stay? Fight? Run? After four or five tries, I called my friend David and asked if I could spend a few nights at his place.

Before leaving, I put a note on the kitchen table: "Will need several days to sort my stuff and clear out. Will pack each day between ten and four. Will be out by Friday." It seemed so inadequate, nothing in it to make him feel guilty or to express my anger; so goddamned polite to inform him so he could avoid me. I thought about using my skills as a writer, knowing all I knew about him, to make words punch him in the face, humiliate him, kick him in the groin once he fell. In the end, I just couldn't make myself do it.

When I pulled into the parking lot that Friday—the last day of packing and loading—I sat in the small U-Haul I had rented and fantasized that Matt would be waiting for me, meet me at the door, beg me to come back, say he was sorry, make up some kind of excuse for what he had done. If not that, maybe he would at least talk to me, give me some clue as to what had happened between us and why we couldn't have talked through it or gone for some counseling. He hadn't done it for the past several days; why I thought he might change his mind on the last day before I was officially "out," I don't know. I remember walking to the door balancing hope and dread like two buckets of water hanging from each side of a long wooden yoke on my shoulders. After a moment's hesitation, I turned the doorknob and entered. He wasn't there, of course. In his stead was a sheet of paper on the table telling me to leave the key. Not even a "please." A knocking at the door, pulled my attention away from my thoughts. The young man I had hired to help me load had arrived, and we went about the task of filling the truck with my many boxes of books, book-cases, clothes, and miscellaneous objects I had collected. Everything else—furniture, appliances, carpets, drapes, dinnerware—was all Matt's. Other than bookcases loaded with books, the apartment seemed not much different for my having been there. When we were done, I asked my helper to wait for me in the truck while I took one last look around. It wasn't so much that I expected to find some-thing we'd missed as much as it was a recognition that the moment had arrived when I had no choice but to let go of Matt. For the most part, looking around was quick. Going into the bedroom for the last time was not. Nostalgia waft-ed in the air, got sucked into my lungs as I lay on the bed and pulled Matt's pillow against my face and chest, held it there and wept briefly before rising.

It was over. No magical reprieve; no "happily ever-af-ter" was in sight. When I got up from the bed, I went to the table and picked up the pen. I drew an arrow to the word "key" and wrote in the space where the arrow start-ed, "This is just to say ... Go fuck yourself!" Silly as it now seems, I drew a big smiley face with sharp teeth after the words. I dropped the key down into the mouth of the gar-bage disposal, and then walked out and closed the locked door behind me.

2

It took nearly three months, gallons of alcohol, a few escapades with Ecstasy, as much anonymous sex as I could find, and a freight truck load of remorse before I admitted to myself I might have a problem. I hadn't written anything worthwhile since the break-up. Every time I sat down at my journal and tried to create words I could care about, they—those hyena fanged attempts at saying anything worthwhile—growled at me, laughed hideously, told me I was done, told me I'd been fooling myself about being a real writer. Most of all, I hated their sneering. Most days, the best I could do was make bullet-point notes in my journal when I could remember whatever I had said, done, or seen in the day or evening before. Over time I had little more than a handful of scribblings and potentially useable ideas, but mostly emotional blather that attempted to mask my self-loathing for being an emasculated fool.

Self-destruction came so easily to me. What saved me from starvation and homelessness during this time were my friends, two thousand dollars I had received for royalties from one of my books, and the part-time job I had worked for the past ten or eleven years. Though I hated the work, I knew I had been fortunate to link up with a few agencies to write copy for brochures, pamphlets, and training materials, and occasionally I did some copy editing for a small publisher. It was centered around writing, but it was writing that meant nothing to me other than a way to gain some income I needed to pay expenses. During the post-Matt period, it paid for storage of my things, for helping friends out while I was couch surfing amongst them, and for paying my nightly expenses in the clubs, bars, or wherever else I might end up.

Finding my way back into life, leaving Chicago, and writing this book came about slowly and largely by chance. It started getting better when David Grayson, one of the people who had put up with me during my self-destructive phase stopped putting up with me. He was fifteen years my senior but a good friend. He was the person who had taken me in that first night when Matt and I split, and I stayed with him often over the next several months. One evening, I stopped at his house when I was still sober. He asked me to sit. I tried to make some small talk, but it was clear that he wasn't interested in that, that something else was going on. For a moment, I could feel my emotional reactions to Matt's dumping me transferring to David when he said he didn't want to talk about whatever it was I was babbling about. I did my best to control my agitation with him for seemingly being uninterested and taking control of the discussion. As it turned out, he had been looking for an occasion to talk and wasn't going to lose the opportunity. His face gained a grim seriousness I wasn't used to seeing in him. His voice was lower than usual. Stronger too. His eyes were intensely focused on mine as though to hold me in a spell. He told me that he was worried about me; that other friends were worried about me; and that he felt like I needed some straight talk, and he hoped I would "take it in the way he meant it"—the phrase for "This is going to be painful."

"I'm concerned about you, Rob. You are drunk or high nearly every day now. You keep going like you are, you're going to kill yourself. You hear me? Is that what you want: to kill yourself?" He didn't wait for a reply and continued emphatically, "You need some help. You've got to do something to get out of this terrible state of mind you're in. Anything but what you're doing."

I responded angrily with something like, "Do what? I can't write. Can't sleep. Can't think straight. I'm spent, David! Forty years old. Got nobody. Going nowhere. Sometimes I feel like ..."

He cut me off and roared, "I don't want to hear that bullshit! You're already trying to kill yourself. You're just doing it over a period of time." He continued speaking angrily, paternally. "You're feeling sorry for yourself, that's what you are. Matt is over! History! He isn't worthy of you giving up on yourself! Never was worthy of you in the first place as far as I'm concerned. Your life isn't over. Now, I'm going to say this straight: If you need a shrink, go see one, and if you don't need a shrink, get the hell off your ass, and do something. You've wallowed long enough. If you're not going to write, you need to go get yourself a job doing something else."

"Writing *is* a job. I'm a writer, goddamn it!" I was shouting

"Then write, goddamn it!" He matched my level of intensity. "You're *not* doing your job! All you are doing is throwing away your life." His echo of my own words about being a writer rattled my rib cage. Had he been of a religious bent, what David gave me as he went on would have been his "Come-to-Jesus Talk"—where somebody tells the unvarnished truth to somebody who is obviously not seeing it for himself. Had he been a father, this would have been his "Dad Talk" to a recalcitrant son. And like that son or the recipient of the "Come-to-Jesus Talk," I wanted to be resentful about interference in my life. I just wanted to down another glass of whiskey, add it to the swollen river of hurt I had been floating on for the past few months. When he was done telling me how much it pained him to see me like I was and that he cared about me, he stopped and asked, "What are you going to do with the rest of your life, Rob?" Then, his eyes fixed determinedly on my face. He wasn't going to let me run out of the house or avoid responding. He waited patiently as I processed my reactions to having a "problem."

In the moment between the question and my response, I realized I had no idea of how to respond, that I had been dodging the question, hiding in a bottle, and relying upon an illusion of escape to get through my days. In that realization, I lost the desire to be angry and admitted in a subdued voice that I was afraid. "I don't want to spend my life alone," the words fell out almost in a whisper from my lips finally giving my feelings a semblance of life.

"You're not dead for Christ's sake," he said sarcastically, then as if my previous response finally sunk into his consciousness, his pace slowed and his voice softened as he abandoned the confrontational tone. "You're still a good-looking guy, you've got brains, talent. Did you ever take a minute to think it wasn't your fault ... that he was the problem ... not you ... that maybe you're just a better person than he was? Is he really worthy of losing yourself over?"

As he continued to talk, I knew he was going to be right. I didn't want him to be. Had he been anyone else, I probably would have asserted my right to declare myself a grown man who could deal with my own problems, gotten up from the chair and walked out, and, maybe, asserted my right to destroy myself if I so chose, could, in other words, have acted like I was sixteen instead of forty. David didn't deserve that. I knew every word, phrase, sentence he delivered—sometimes awkwardly, sometimes rambling, sometimes more prescriptive than helpful—was delivered out of love for me as an unwavering friend. He had been good to me, put up with me, nursed me when I got out of the hospital after taking the unidentified drugs I paid $40 for to some random guy when I was drunk, checked up on me, fed me, and so much more. And there I was, wanting to lash out at him—knowing full well it wasn't him that I was angry with, knowing full well that what I really wanted was to cling to him, ask him for help. I sat there trying to come up with something to say, and knowing I had nothing of any substance for defending my behavior. When my hands finally came up to wipe the tears leaking down my face, he was in front of me and taking me in his arms as the torrential rains of grief flowed into the space hope and self-confidence had seemingly abandoned.

3

L anding in Emberland, Ohio, where I now live wasn't quite as weird as throwing a dart at a map and going wherever it landed, but almost. It was a place I had remembered passing through as a bored teenager traveling with my parents. Though I would never have expressed it to them then, I thought it was a beauty of a town, quaint, brick streets, brick buildings, a university, young people everywhere, something that felt like an old well-loved book that sat comfortably on the shelf alongside a new and eagerly anticipated work I had not yet read. Why it came back into my mind, I don't know. Maybe it had dropped out of my mouth in one of my sessions with the psychologist I was seeing shortly after David's talk with me. Or maybe it came from the many discussions that David and I had as he helped me through my efforts to regain some control over my emotional state. Regardless of the when and how, it got into my head and stayed there. After doing some research, I decided it was as good a place as any to start fresh. My contract work could be done anywhere and would keep me alive financially, and the cost of living in rural Ohio would have to be less than living in a big city like Chicago. After weeks of thought, talking to David and the psychologist, I made the decision to go and treat the going as an adventure ... as it eventually proved to be. I found an apartment online, said goodbye to my friends, packed up a U-Haul with my car in tow and drove off with excitement and fear randomly taking turns riding shotgun.

As I got to the outskirts of Chicago on I-90, somewhere near the sad rust-covered city of Gary, Indiana, I thought of Matt, of disappointment and self-doubt ... anger ... what I had told the psychiatrist about carrying the weight for the relationship and its demise ... and what I had done in my attempts at self-destruction ... thoughts and images played like the long talkers on an FM radio station ... they talked across many miles of perfectly aligned northern Ohio windmills. Their gigantic turbines turned slowly like hoping for hope until the image came into my head of stopping briefly along the roadside—Matt, now on the bench seat of the truck—reaching across his body to the passenger-side door latch, opening it and pushing him onto the roadside's gravel, and then driving away as the swinging door closed itself with an acceleration the actual truck didn't have. Matt's flailing body faded from the rearview mirror like an end shot in a clichéd romance comedy.

4

Red and gold leaves came down from old trees that whole first month. Snow fell the second and stayed long beyond its welcome. Long, dark days took their toll on my attempts to stay positive about my new life. As a result, I started seeing a psychologist who tried to pick up where the last one left off. Unfortunately for me, his cure-all for anything and everything I was dealing with was what he called "mindfulness": mindless breathing techniques that did nothing for me other than remove some of the weight from my wallet. Maybe I just wasn't doing it right. At any rate, I stopped seeing him, focused on doing the work I had to do for money, and spent much of my time trying to find something I cared enough to write about.

"Ant tracks!" I called them: the words I was able to create during the first two months in my new home, words that seemed to meander pointlessly on the pages of my computer journal where they often disappeared behind the "delete" button. The ants didn't appear to be interacting well with one another most of the time. Occasionally, a few words started to become people, places, and ideas, but not enough to carry me into that space where time and ego fall away, and transmogrification lets words write themselves into art.

Much of my time early on was spent being frustrated, doubting I could get back to where I had been as a writer before Matt's execution of our relationship, but I committed to writing every day and called David when I needed someone to talk to. Sometimes we would talk for an hour or more, and I always felt better after the talk. To my delight, he and his boyfriend, Max, came for a visit at Christmas and spent several days with me ... all of us joking, laughing, and reveling in whatever pleasures we could find. David insisted on spending lavishly for meals, a wild night out in Columbus, and a present of a Quince Italian overcoat for Christmas.

An added bonus for me was that these men were educated and loved to read and talk about what they read. Preparing for the visit, they had obviously taken time to read some of my published works and wanted to discuss them with me. Mostly they talked about a novel I had written that they had particularly liked—a novel that hadn't sold particularly well. I had known when I wrote it that it wouldn't make me rich. It required a high level of interaction with sophisticated readers. It was a book I had felt the need to write whether the critics liked it or not. They didn't, but my guests did.

"You know what I say about critics, Rob," David said.

"Yes, but it's anatomically impossible."

"Well, they screwed up on that book. I can tell you that."

My guests were complimentary and talked knowledge-ably about specifics of the book and were eager to know about my thinking at the time I wrote it. Though they quib-bled about a few minor differences of opinion with things I had written, they made excellent points about where a few of the critics had missed the mark in their evaluations. They also talked about a few of my short stories, asked questions, picked up on some of the intersections within the stories and the novel. If they had had their way, I would have put together a collection on the spot and sent it off to a publisher, and that publisher "had goddamned well bet-ter snatch it up before someone else has the chance." They were great ego boosters. By the time they left, I was feeling good about myself and was eager to get back to writing.

Unfortunately, my financial condition made that diffi-cult. Though I was still doing contract work when it was available, it was coming in sporadically, making it difficult for me to pay my bills on time. The application I had put into the university's personnel department for an adjunct teaching position shortly after I arrived in the city—a po-sition I was well qualified for—obviously had fallen into a black hole, and no amount of my checking on its status produced results other than to learn it was somewhere in the system. That same black hole must have eaten the ma-jority of the applications I sent elsewhere. There weren't many options in the city or nearby towns for a person with a master's degree in English who would work part time only, preferably no more than twenty hours per week.

In January, I took a part-time job at Fannon's—a local-ly-owned grocery and mini department store. It was a job that that didn't require lots of brain power, and it gave me enough money to survive within my bare bones budget while I transitioned away from the irregularity of freelance work. It allowed me to do what I had set out to do when I first came to the city: find space and time to write.

Surprisingly, the quality of my manuscripts began to improve shortly after I started working. Perhaps it had to do with being less concerned about money. Perhaps it was just the right time. Whatever the reasons, coherent thoughts, more elaborate characters, complicated story lines, and effective language seemed to come more easily without causing me to lose the underlying poetics that I loved so much. Short stories I had nearly finished before the breakup with Matt found their way back into my heart. The revisions I made went smoothly, and I sent each of them off to potential publishers. One of them was picked up shortly after I sent it and was scheduled to be included in the fall issue of the magazine. The other was in that lim-bo that is every author's frustration: waiting for a response that could happen in days, weeks, months, even a year or more. In the meantime, a couple of book reviews and es-says put a few dollars in my coffers while I wrote in search of the elusive next project.

By spring, I was feeling like I had stumbled past the hell of the previous year, and I was ready for something to trigger a new writing adventure. While I spent my time searching for it amidst my scribblings and lists of possible topics and partially developed plot lines, the story creeped up on me from behind, followed me like a cat among shadows flexing its claws as it studies an oblivious mouse that has wandered into the kitchen. It waited ever-so-patiently to catch me.

5

It was May. Students were vacating the university and the city to return to their lives as children of their parents, social butterflies sucking the nectar of their parents' wealth, or wage earners trying to make enough money to help pay for their educations. By the end of the month, Emberland, like other college towns where the university is the primary employer, slowed to a crawl. As for me, I had been writing stories based on newspaper articles I read, people I met, overhearing talk as I hung out in coffee shops or bars. And I was gaining pride in my commitment to writing and my ability to avoid things that might trigger the disappointment and sadness that had turned into self-loathing at several points in my life. For a year, I had kept relationships superficial and had avoided committing to anything other than my work, making enough money to survive, and taking care of my physical and mental health. I worked at looking good and staying in shape so that when loneliness got to me I could go out occasionally and compete for dates. Unfortunately for me, I found the men

I dated to be intellectually challenged and uninterested in anything resembling meaningful discussion. Most thought from below their beltlines, which was okay by me once in a while, but after a date or two without anything between us other than sex, I lost interest, just felt cheap and lonelier than I had been before meeting them.

When I got the message that a Jake Davidson called me at Fannon's, I couldn't imagine who he was and what he wanted. The scribbled note from the helpdesk worker provided the name, a phone number, and a message to call. At the time, I was too busy moving items along the conveyor belt and punching data into the cash register to do more than stuff the note into my apron pocket. As I did so, the overly officious clerk, ten years younger than I am, who had delivered the message made a condescending comment about receiving private calls on company time. I looked straight into his eyes and smiled at his prickish manner and sneering face, watched his face shrivel at my stare.

As he abruptly turned and walked away, I mentally flipped him the bird and smiled at what an accomplishment it had been to let his behavior remain his problem, not mine. I continued chatting with the elderly woman in front of me as I scanned and pushed her groceries onto the conveyor belt. She was the most important customer we had ever had! That was the attitude I tried to take with her as I would with the next person and the one after that until my shift ended. Cashiering wasn't a job I loved doing. It wasn't work I had gained two degrees for. It was a source of needed income. However, since I was doing it, I took pride in performing the role I was given: servant. The customers seemed to like me and the way I treated them. My boss seemed to like and appreciate me as well.

When I finally got Jake Davidson on the phone later in the day, I expected he was going to try to sell me something I didn't want or couldn't afford: insurance, membership, magazines. That, or maybe he was one of those guys I had dated, and he had somehow tracked me down even though I never told any of them where I worked. Initially, I thought I would probably just skip making the call, but then I was afraid whoever this guy was might call Fannon's again. When I pressed the call button on my cell phone, I prepared myself to tell him not to call me at work and then hang up on him the minute he broke into the sales pitch. After he identified himself and started talking, I still wished for a moment that I had not returned his call, or that I could get past his polite approach and hang up the phone. But there was a respectful kindliness to his voice that disarmed me; it was apologetic about having "bothered" me; there was what Scott Fitzgerald would have called "vitality" behind it. The thought of hanging up on him just felt wrong.

He had called wanting to talk about a story he thought might be worth writing. He was eager to learn what it would take to do it, and he was hungry for validation of his idea even though it turned out he didn't quite know what he wanted to do with it. I suppose he tapped into my basic tendency to be kind when he said he would like to meet me even if I wasn't interested in writing it; he would like to talk to a real writer—whatever that meant to him—and would be grateful if I just listened to the idea and gave him some feedback.

When he told me he wanted to resurrect an unsolved murder story from the 1870s referred to locally as "the Trent Murders," I stepped into teacher mode, speaking as kindly as possible without giving away the negative reaction my face was expressing to the cell phone screen. What kept me involved was him telling me he loved the ways that Hemingway and Faulkner wrote and that he wished he could write like that. Though I wondered if he understood that they were writers coming at language from two different and opposing ends of a spectrum of style and wondered which one he thought was most clearly in line with his own ideas of effective language and why. However, I kept the inner teacher from jumping into the conversation. He started talking about specific books and what he liked and didn't like about them. To my surprise, he was a reader and thought about the ways books make meaning, and how styles of writing worked on him. He talked about what he liked and didn't like about the each of the writers and some of their works without committing to either of them as "the best." That nailed it for me. Talking about a story, even a bad one would be more interesting than being alone all of the time. It would be a diversion from picking at the carcass of a college town devoid of students for ideas. At least the meeting would be an escape from looking at my apartment walls and chasing the ants that still came into my work. Worst case scenario, if he pressed me to write something I didn't want to write, I knew how to say "no" as gently as it can be said.

6

I walked into the Hot Spot Café wearing the striped shirt and black jeans I told Jake Davidson I would be wearing so he could recognize me. When I got through the door, a strikingly handsome, late twenty-something man backed away from a table where he was sitting, stood up and asked, "Mr. Wilson?" Inwardly, I was amused at his formality since I had no status in the world other than his assumption that a writer gets a "mister" from strangers and we had stated our informal names to one another on the phone the previous evening.

"Rob, please," I said as we shook hands and my eyes took in his stunning visual appearance. As he went to buy me a cup of coffee, I had the pleasure of watching that powerful, confident body in motion, and then leaning on the counter like a model doing a commercial as he waited. Looking at him was even better as he came back to the table like an unavoidable tidal wave of good looks and masculinity. My imagination put him on the cover of *Instinct* magazine. Definitely not an image I conjured from talking with him on the phone. Subduing my desire to just look at him, I took the warm cup from his hand, sat down, and gave my best performance of a professional.

As professional men often do, we passed back and forth what are often meaningless pleasantries about the weather, the coffee shop, and the city. When I asked what he did for a living, he told me he was a police officer, which surprised me—all of my stereotyped images came into play as I tried to fit the previous night's phone discussion with the biases that suddenly arose like a heavy fog between us. As he made his response to my question, he sat up a bit straighter, added a bit more authority into his voice as if he were speaking on behalf of the entire police department as I asked questions and he explained the variety of demands upon his time working in a college town where he dealt with the common hijinks of late adolescents and the misbehaviors of older people who should know better. However, within a few sentences, he had relaxed again and began joking and laughing about the foolishness he encountered. The fog lifted as I found myself laughing out loud. After a few moments, he turned the conversation back to me and asked me questions about me and my work.

He was smart, articulate, and funny, and I quickly found myself interacting with him as though we had been friends for a long time. Twenty minutes passed like two before we reminded one another that we hadn't talked about the point of the meeting. It turned out that Jake was fascinated with the story of a young man hanged long ago by a lynch mob on the property he—Jake—now owned.

Apparently, the young man was going through a trial, but a mob hadn't been willing to take a chance on the courts getting to the *right* verdict, so they took it upon themselves to make sure that the *right* punishment was applied. Jake, speaking with enthusiasm and passion, was certain that, if the details could be dug out, this would make a great story. My original fears rose to the level of consciousness. I expected him at any moment to propose that I do what he couldn't or wouldn't do and wasn't able to pay for.

I was already plotting the means to say "no" as I listened to the sketchy details, only some of which he was sure about: Nathan Sanders—a young man—was thought to have murdered a seventeen-year-old girl and the girl's mother with a club or an ax and killed a farmhand with a gun, but it was never proven that he actually did any of the murders. Many people believed there was an accomplice, but the most notable suspect had an alibi. Obviously, the boy was either not too bright or had an overwhelming need for attention because he told the sheriff and others that he had been at the murder site at the time it happened, but he was just watching, not taking part. That was enough information for the majority of people in the community to decide a hanging was in order; the only question was whether or not they would do it before the trial or afterward if the court failed them.

When Jake finished—despite my instinct to just say I wasn't interested—I found myself taking pleasure in his exuberance for the story and his naivete about the world of publishing. There was an innocence and vulnerability

about him that made me happy to be with him. It didn't
hurt that he was also beautiful and exploded with vitality
like the debris of firecrackers going off between us. Pure
joy came out of my open lips in the form of laughter before
I could stop it. Jake caught it like a baseball thrown forcefully at his glove, stopped talking and looked at me with
some embarrassment, and said, "You think this is a stupid
idea?"

"It's not stupid, Jake; I wasn't you I was laughing at. I
was laughing at how ridiculously difficult it is to get anything published." I said it as I tried to maintain a façade of
professionalism to cover the attraction I was experiencing. "It's not the topic that's a problem; it's about the work
involved in doing it. It's difficult to get a story published,
even a good one. What you are talking about is an ugly incident from so long ago that it might not connect with the
world people know today. It would likely be a hard sell to a
publisher. People have seen all kinds of TV programs and
movies where people get murdered, and guys get hanged
by vigilantes even for crimes they didn't commit. The questions will be, 'How is this different from other stories like
it? What makes this matter to modern readers?'"

I could see the weight of my words pressing on his
shoulders, the turning downward of his lips as he began
to realize all he hadn't thought about. I was preparing him
for the inevitable disappointment as I asked him why, from
his perspective, this story was worth telling 150 years after it happened. I expected I would hear something about
his just wanting to know what had occurred on his land

or about it just being "interesting," but that wasn't what he said.

"A name and a personal history are all we have in this world. I can't change what happened back then. I know that, but maybe there's a way to give him a fair trial. Don't you think there are people who still care about truth and justice? Doing right things? Isn't that worth going after? To make sure a man's name is recorded for who he actually was and what he actually did or didn't do?"

I was surprised by the response, thought it old-fashioned and, yet, a surprisingly appealing sentiment, a sentiment that touched some of my own perceptions of a moral world that would be so much better than the apocalypse of the present in which truth has been replaced by alternative "truth," where people are destroyed by innuendo without any factual support whatsoever, where presidents attempt coups when they can't win elections by fair voting, where people are killed for the sin of being black and their murderers are excused for their crimes.

"Here's the deal for me, Jake. Even if I had all the facts, I wouldn't want to write a simple rehashing of the story—something for the record ("Here are the facts!)—unless, of course, you want to pay me," I joked. "I do that kind of work for clients, but what I publish under my name are short stories, poems, and novels." Perhaps I got a little lost in trying to explain to him what makes me write—particularly in my writing of a novel or a short story—how I need to feel the story behind the story before I create a plot line, and how I imagine the thoughts and feelings of the people involved, and how I use whatever I have at my disposal as a writer to drive toward creating an experience for readers that becomes *the* truth inherent to the world created within the novel or short story.

Everything about Jake's facial expressions and body control suggested that he was listening intently, trying to understand. There was a moment of silence in which I tried to catch whatever I was feeling as I took in the composite parts of his face, the boyish innocence of his smile, his intellect trying to wrestle with the complexities involved in creating meaning from a writer's point of view.

"I get it," he said. "I'd a whole lot rather read a novel than a textbook, but it sure would be good to know what actually happened. I guess I should have done more research about what might be done with the story before I wasted your time."

"You haven't wasted my time. I've really enjoyed meeting you and talking about Nathan Sanders. And I don't want to shoot your idea down. I like what you said about why you want to see the story written. That could be a story in and of itself."

"Where do I go from here?" he asked.

"Home with me." The thought came out of nowhere and caught me by surprise as if I had said it out loud. But I hadn't said it. My lips had clamped down on the potential disaster of blurting out the desire. Instead, I told him it seemed to me he really needed facts to begin with. Did he want to tell the facts or make a story based on facts? He would need to understand the time period, the main characters, details of the crime: anything and everything he could find that would inform him whether or not there was enough foundation to work with. I suggested that facts could be difficult to find, that it would require research, particularly if he wanted it to be a historical piece. Any facts he found could be organized and written as a valuable part of local history, or maybe a non-fiction publication for local historians. If he wanted to make his own story out of it and wasn't hung up on historical accuracy, the facts were still a great place to start. Because I wanted to see him again, I found myself offering to do what I called "some down and dirty research" to get a better feel for what historical materials might be available and get back to him when I felt I had enough to share.

A soft redness of appreciation rose up into his face like sunlight.

As we pushed our coffee cups aside and prepared to leave, he put his hand on my arm, held it there as he said how much he had enjoyed our time. His hand still in place, he asked if we could meet sooner than whenever I had found enough material ... if I wasn't too busy.

7

When I left Chicago back in October, eight months earlier, I had vowed not to get involved with anyone again, and here I was getting all hot and bothered about a guy I had met over coffee. It was not the kind of feeling that had propelled me into the one-night stands I had experienced since Matt. The attraction was different, something more like a genuine desire to know his thoughts about the world we shared. In the course of an hour and a half of talking, I had come to like him, wanted to know things about him: who he was, what he believed, thought, felt, what I might learn in the "next time" of our interactions. Yes, there was the physical part as well; he was a beautiful man, and I wondered how he might be as a desirable sex partner, but that didn't feel like the most important part of my thoughts. In the space between parting from him and getting back to my apartment, I rolled the possibilities around in my head. The joy of attraction had been exhilarating until images of Matt and Chicago crawled into my consciousness. Then an entire chorus of self-doubt and fears started singing—Matt singing the solo baritone parts—and suddenly I was frightened.

Back at my apartment, I sat down to write, found myself writing everything I could recall of our conversation, everything I could remember about him, his body, his eyes, his mannerisms, and my responses to him. When I couldn't recall exact words, I made them up in an attempt to capture the gist of the experience. As I wrote, I found that words fell onto the page, took on a life different from those making the ant tracks across my computer screen over the past months. That day, words walked in line as though they knew exactly where they were going--even if I couldn't know where that was. Feeling freer than I had in a long time, I was comfortable with the notion that the words would let me know when they had arrived. They were pushing me past my fears, and I was like a teenager after a first kiss, I couldn't stop writing about him, the joy I had experienced in his presence.

At a break from the writing, I happened to look at myself in a mirror. My face and body appeared to be different from those I had seen that morning as I shaved and prepared to go out. The skin and muscles of my face appeared tighter, my upper torso was more muscular and gave more body definition. If I had been trying to take notes for a story, I would have said it was the body of "a well-kept thirty-year-old man in a forty-one-year-old man. Full head of brown lively hair neatly cut. A playful mischief in the eyes.

That night, I allowed erotic images to dance on the pages of my consciousness and keep me awake long after

I climbed into my bed. The following morning, I awakened and reread what I had written the previous day and thought about this thing Jake seemed to have for the Sanders story and how much I admired his desire to right an old wrong. I decided to see what I might find in a quick search of the online *Newspaper Archives* and the Library of Congress's *Chronicling America* about Nathan Sanders. Surprisingly, a few badly written, and somewhat confusing, articles were fairly easy to find and gave me at least a sense of the story line.

Apparently, much of the story of the "Trent Murders"— as the newspapers referred to them—came from Sanders himself as he told it after he was caught and put in a cell. It seems visitors were able to walk in and out of the jailhouse individually or in clusters and question him as they saw fit; among them were reporters who prodded him or listened in as others questioned him and attempted to record Sanders' every word.

In my first efforts to piece the story together, it seemed fairly clear that 19-year-old Nathan Sanders and a friend, 21-year-old Alf Carson had spent the night prior to the murders drinking. Though they didn't have a nickel between them, they had somehow persuaded others to buy them drinks and got very drunk. Sometime in the late morning of the following day, both men were out wandering around, looking for something to do to fill their time. Part of their conversation must have focused on money and trying to figure out who they could borrow from so they could get whiskey. According to Sanders, somewhere along the walk, he suggested they go see what he called an "old lady" who lived up on the ridge above where they were at that time. She had loaned him money in the past, and though he currently owed her five dollars, he thought she might consider loaning him a couple more.

The articles mentioned there being a path up to the woman's farm through the woods—a shortcut— that Sanders and many town people knew about; so, they used it to make their way to the top of a ridge and into her meadows. His story was that once they got to the top of the hill, Alf Carson started asking about the widow and who else might be around the farm. Nathan responded by saying that a man, Everett Parsons, was working the land for the widow and the widow had a daughter, Rosie, who was about sixteen. He claimed to have asked Alf what difference it made who else might be there.

"I intend to get the money and just wanted to know who might be around the place," Carson responded ... or, at least the newspaper articles *said* he responded. Sanders interpreted the meaning as being that Carson was going to rob the Trents of the money, and he didn't want to have any part in robbing people but continued walking with him into the meadows and toward the house.

Before the men got far across the first fenced-in meadow (there seemed to have been three they had to cross) they saw a man walking toward them. When they got up close, Everett Parsons greeted them. Nathan claimed to have asked Parsons how he was doing and where he was heading. The man responded by saying he was taking the path down to the road and was going into town. As Parsons ended his sentence, Carson pulled out a gun, shot Parsons between the eyes, and stepped over his body like it was a clump of weeds and continued walking toward the house. Nathan, tagging along like a kid brother asked, "Why did ya kill 'im?"—the newspaper's version of the way Nathan talked. As I read this paragraph, I spoke out loud to the space of my apartment, "Asked? Why not, 'yelled' or 'cried' or 'in a state of shock, fell to his knees beside the body in disbelief'?" *Asked*, sounded like a chit-chat, like seeing someone shot was an everyday occurrence. He was "asking" while he too was walking away from the body. And he went right on walking with the guy who just killed a man. And the answer to the Sanders' question? Alf didn't want anybody to be a witness against him.

Nathan was reported to have said that when he and Alf got to the barns and outbuildings that stood between the two men and the house, Alf went into the main barn. Nathan stood outside and waited. Eventually, Carson came out with an axe handle. Sanders claimed he had no idea at the time as to what Carson was planning to do; however, again he continued along with Alf toward the house where they could hear a woman's voice singing something somewhere in one of the rooms and an occasional clunk or clink of what sounded like kitchen dishes, pots and pans being put on a stove or counter. Seemingly clueless as to how his own storytelling made him look, Sanders kept on talking, saying that Carson, whispering, asked if there was a back door to the house, and he (Nathan) pointed it out. Again, he innocently waited outside the house.

Repeatedly, Sanders said he didn't want to be any part of what he now suspected Alf was going to do, so he sat down on a stump in the side yard and refused to go in. After a few minutes, out came the "old lady" (who, as it turns out was in her late 40s) from the back door "walking like she was coming out to enjoy the sunshine and chat with him," and right behind her came Alf who swung that axe handle like a sharpened ax into a tree. When she fell, Alf continued with crushing blows to the woman's head. Then he turned around as if nothing of any importance had happened and went back into the house in no particular hurry.

Five or ten minutes later the girl, Rosie, came running out the front door with Alf right behind her. He swung the bloody handle again and "dropped the girl like an old worn-out cow"—the reporter's countrified way of talking to his readers. When the killing was done, Carson released the axe handle there beside the body and returned to the house. Sanders said he could hear doors and dresser drawers opening and closing. When Carson finally came out again, he said, "Let's go!" Nathan then—and only then—got up off his stump and followed. Somewhere down the hillside, not far off the path, some water had accumulated, and Carson took his clothes off and washed the blood off his body in the pool of water and then soaked his clothes, wrung them out and put the wet pants on, slipped into his shoes, and carried his wet shirt as the two of them descended. According to Sanders, when he and Carson arrived at the bottom of the hill, they simply said goodbye, and each went his own way.

The fact that the young girl had been sexually assaulted was something Sanders claimed to know nothing about.

When Sanders was asked by various people why he didn't stop the carnage, he said he just didn't as if to say, "It was no business of mine!" He adamantly insisted that he never got off the stump he was sitting on. Just waited for his buddy to finish whatever he was going to do.

The few articles I read that day were filled with grizzly descriptions of the wounds on the bodies of the dead. Reporters used cascades of adjectives to promote the horror of a "little girl's"—she was 17—sexual *assault* without once using the word *sexual*: "Horror," "shocking," "heinous" "despicable," "fiendish," "monstrous," and any other words they could think of to attract the eyes of their readers with implied sexual perversion and mold readers' opinions and, coincidentally, sell more newspapers and subscriptions. Nathan's telling of the story only added to the notion that he and Alf Carson lacked guilt, shame, embarrassment, or, even, sadness about the deaths of three people. In the articles I had read, the suspects were stripped of any status as human and were effectively recreated as demons from hell. Reporters were adamant about the just outcome, openly advocating for "Judge Lynch" to take the case.

8

The gun, badge, and the electronic equipment hanging from the belt walked into the diner ahead of Jake with an authority that demanded some kind of attention as if they were, in fact, the law and the man carrying them was but a vehicle for getting them from one place to another. It took a moment for me to assimilate them and attach the uniform with the man I had spent time with previously. The face, the form on which the clothes hung were his, but it took a few moments for me to get back to the reality that paraphernalia had no life of its own. He walked up and stood at my side, maybe sensing what was going on in my head about the nature of law and order, power, and control. He didn't speak; he waited.

"Are you here to arrest me, officer?" I asked, trying to be playful.

That mischievous smile crawled up onto his face as he asked, "Have you committed a crime, sir?"

"Yes, sir! I have."

"Are you going to tell me what the crime is."

"No, sir, I am not."

"Do I need to take you to the station for questioning."

"I'm not into handcuffs, sir." The double entendre hung in the space between us for a moment until his snicker evaporated in our awareness that others might be listening. Quietly, as I sat down, I promised jokingly that I wouldn't make a scene if he would sit down with me. "We'll talk handcuffs later."

A teenaged girl came to the table to take our orders, smiled at me and referred to Jake as her "buddy." He greeted her by name, asked how she was and how she was doing with her GED classes. They chatted for a moment, her telling him about coursework, things getting better at home, and staying away from people who are "trouble." When she turned and walked away with the order, he looked at me and said, "Poor kid. She's had a rough time of it."

"She seems to like you."

He smiled, then asked what I'd been up to. I told him about how good it felt to write over the past few days to be writing and doing some research. Then I launched into what I had found about Nathan Sanders and listened to the many comments and questions Jake was interjecting. I had to remind him that I had only read a few articles. "With what you originally told me about their being an attempted lynching and Alf Carson having an alibi, and a trial almost completed at the time of the lynching, there're likely to be many other articles ... maybe some court records to uncover ... if they can be found."

After a couple sips of coffee, I said, "It's hard not to think he committed the murders, at least judging by what I've read so far. He sure as hell comes across as a cold-hearted son of a bitch in the papers. They did a number on him. It'll be interesting to see how it all played out."

That last sentence caught me by surprise as it jumped out of me, raced across the space between us, slipped into Jake's consciousness and deposited itself in the sparkle of his eyes. Neither of us went forward with the notion that I had just set myself up to continue the research. After that, we talked of nothing in particular as we engaged in a bit of repartee that men do as a substitute for wrestling in the grass of their boyhood, each of us dueling for prizes neither of us thought to name, but which brought pleasure like stars pasted on the heads of kindergartners: stickers to wear home, show to Mom and Dad, and sleep with for as long as the glossy-paper's glue held and the stars fell off in the night.

During a pause in the back and forth of our banter and questions about one another, Jake took a long draw on his cup of coffee. When he spoke again, it was more serious.

"I kind of dumped this murder story thing on you."

"I can only be dumped on if I let you do it, my friend. Right now, I am doing this as much for me as for you." As I said this, I thought it was the healthiest thing I had said to myself in a long time.

His appreciation for the work I had done was obvious. His schoolboy politeness and concern for my time were ingratiating ... different from the "let's just screw" attitude of the men I had dealt with since Chicago.

"If you point me in the right direction, I can do some of the legwork on this thing. I just didn't know that old newspapers were available or how to get at them." When he said it, I thought, "Any good librarian should have been able to help with getting at some of the archived newspaper sources." My instincts as a teacher were to embolden him to do his own research, my instincts as a lonely man said, "Let this slide. Research keeps you in his life ... at least for now."

We talked non-stop until he checked his watch, said his allotted lunch time was running out, and asked when he would see me again. As much as I wanted to leap at the opportunity of saying, "How about when you get off work?" the words got boggled up with the residue of fear I carried around with me, mistrust from my past, my sometimes-debilitating sense of inadequacy. My hesitation created a momentary dead space between us that led Jake to say in his generous and thoughtful way, "I'm sorry. I don't want you to feel pressured. If you're not into it, just say so." His voice dropped to a whisper as he leaned toward me and said, "I like you. And just in case it needs saying, I want to see you even if you never do anything with the Sanders story and you never want to talk about it again."

Our remaining time was too short to tell him the story of my life in Chicago, the months of grieving and self-destruction afterward. "I like you too," I whispered. "It's not you. It's me. Just a little 'gun shy.' Story for another day."

I could see recognition in his eyes. "I get it. Got burned, huh?"

"Yeah, big time." I felt a chill run up my spine as Matt's face came into my consciousness. "I've got to tell you, I'm scared."

"Me too."

Jake's face, the sincerity with which he spoke, the kindness that radiated from him made me want to trust him, but I had trusted before. I figured I might as well lay it all on the line and find out what he was willing to accept. "You know I've got some years on you. I'm forty-one. Is that an issue? I'm probably never going to be rich or famous."

As if expecting my concern, he responded without hesitation, "So, you've got thirteen years on me. So what? I'm interested in you, not how long you've been on the planet or how much money you make."

Pleased by what he had to say and the evident sincerity behind it, I asked, "What did you have in mind?"

"I was just wondering if you'd like to come out to my place on Sunday to spend the day, go swimming at the quarry, have a few drinks." He made sure to tell me I could call the shots on anything beyond that.

The "Yes" I heard myself firing from my throat scattered particles of my earlier hesitation burning like gunpowder behind it.

9

By the time I figured out that what my GPS told me was a "road" was not a road but an unpaved opening in a field, I had driven past it at least twice. Though my city boy upbringing hadn't prepared me for the notion that people lived where there wasn't pavement, lived at the ends of lanes that run up through meadows and woods, I decided to make an adventure of it and hope my GPS hadn't gone haywire. I gulped, and turned my five-year-old, slightly dented, red Toyota Corolla onto what I was sure was a cow path and followed it for what seemed a long distance until I came to the only house at the end of the rutted and ruinous path ending at the huge sliding barn door.

Jake must have been waiting to hear the crunching of what crushed stone remained on what he called a road, must have heard the pinball-like pings of my car-hurled rock chunks against the tires and chassis. Immediately, he came out of the house wearing his toothy smile and waving in greeting. I rolled down my window and asked where I should park. "Up by the barn there anywhere," he said.

Then he walked alongside my car as I took it up the slight rise and cut the engine to let the poor beast rest in front of the barn door.

I grabbed my rolled-up towel and stepped out to take Jake's extended hand and was surprised when he held onto it and pulled me into him, wrapped his arms around me, patted me on the back. His body was hard muscled, and yet there was a gentleness and a warmth in the way his arms enveloped me and gently squeezed me against him like family. After he told me how glad he was to see me, he released me. Reluctantly, I let my arms fall from their hold on his back.

"What do you think?" he asked as his hand and arm gestured across the landscape: the carefully mowed and trimmed yard that spread hundreds of feet from the woods, flowed around several very old and gigantic trees up to the flower gardens artfully planted and bespectacled with reds, purples, oranges, and yellows jutting out of the luscious greenery that rose above the black mulch around the two-story farmhouse. The house's first-floor porch spanned the entire front of the house and then wrapped around the east side in an arc rather than making a right-angle turn, softening the entire appearance of the structure. I liked the way the landscaping followed that arced corner like a skirt that follows the line of a girl's hips.

"It's art, Jake!" I told him I liked that there was no backdrop of traffic to distract the eye from the beauty of the lawn and the trees and the sky. Though I probably didn't say it out loud, there was something about the house that seemed to be standing shyly like a country girl waiting for her first love at the end of the inconspicuous final turn in the long curvaceous pathway through the woods.

As we neared the house, I turned back, used my hand like a visor to look at the barn, its roof with all its old slate shingles in place as firmly as they had probably been when they were first nailed to the cross boards—their gray, blue, and black discolorations holding memories of thousands of days, the onslaught of winters past laying their heaps of snow upon them; the onslaught of summer suns beating upon them like men beating a stake with sledgehammers; and the cascades of rains determined to do nature's work of destroying what humans have imposed upon it. I wrote the thought of inherent destruction of all things into my brain, repressed the saying of it out loud for Jake's sake as well as for my own so that each of us could cling to that something that allows us to endure one more weathering of a storm and the courage to write one more story for posterity.

Jake broke through my lost-in-thought-time, invited me to come into the house. He had made sandwiches in the old kitchen with its green-painted wood cabinets, put some chips on the table, handed me a bottle of beer, directed me to sit, and said he thought we should eat before making the hike to the quarry or we wouldn't be able to stay out as long as we might like. We drank the cold beer slowly while we ate and while we talked about the house and about the work it would take to renovate it. He was determined, he said, to make it more his own rather than his mother's, as he still thought it. He joked about the too-many feminine touches she had imposed upon it. The flowered wallpaper on the kitchen walls had to go for sure, we joked.

I joked that I hoped he wouldn't go overboard and put in faux-leopard skin covered chairs and cheap shag carpeting on the floor, put a bar in the middle of the living room or mirrors on the bedroom ceiling.

"No, man! Where's your class, Rob? I'm painting all the walls black and putting black lights in every room. I'm putting a pool table in the middle of the living room. The bar's going in where the dining room is now! And I'm decorating all the walls with Elvis paintings on velvet canvas, except for the wall where I put the dart board! I *am* going to put mirrors above the bed, and I plan to have a mirror ball and colored strobe lights in the room too!"

I laughed and told him never to invite me back after he made the changes, although I had to admit that the mirrors above the bed might be a nice touch.

When we finished lunch, Jake picked up both sandwich plates from the table, took them to the old porcelain-coated cast iron sink, rinsed them, and set them down as if they were Haviland or Limoge, easily broken and precious. He picked up the bag of chips and placed a chip clip on it like the exclamation mark at the end of a sentence and put the bag in the cupboard above the sink. He filled a gallon water jug—a plastic milk bottle he had washed clean—with cold water to take with us. He carried it in his left hand as he walked over and picked up a medium gray bath towel that was rolled up and waiting on the chair by the kitchen door, tucked it into his armpit. Just before we were ready to walk out, he went to a cupboard and pulled down a pint bottle of Jack Daniels Whiskey, and said, "Let's do it."

As we walked out the door, I picked up the striped beach towel I had brought with me, its red and blue stripes dulled by many washings. My black spandex swimsuit with the torn mesh liner was rolled up inside it.

When I asked if I could help somehow with carrying the jug or the towels, Jake assigned me the role of whiskey packer and handed me the bottle. I pushed it into the back pocket of my jeans, and we set off for the quarry.

About ten minutes into the walk, we got to what Jake called "the path." He stopped, put his hand on my arm to hold me in place, and reached into my back pocket for the bottle.

"You'll need fortification to handle the walk, city slicker," Jake teased as he motioned for me to take the first drink.

After I swallowed, I handed the bottle over to him, and as he drank, I told him, his so-called path looked to me like little more than a tamped-down furrow the width of a skinny rabbit who had run it just enough times that the weeds hadn't had a chance to stand up again. Jake almost lost control of the whiskey just beginning to slide down his throat as he laughed at the long-winded writerly description I made of something most people would just ignore.

Then, like a hunter—from one of those 1950s B-westerns—trying to keep up with the herd of roaming buffalo, Jake pushed the pint bottle at me and took off at a good pace using the jug of drinking water like a phalanx to push aside overgrown grasses and weeds that flexed their muscles as they rushed at him—us—reaching for our pant legs and punching ineffectively at our bodies as we made our way down the narrow slit in the green field and stirring the mosquitoes that lay waiting there. We swatted at them as they attacked kamikaze-like from all directions. I probably said something pointless like, "Get away, blood suckers" as though words could somehow dissuade insects. Maybe I just hoped I was feeding the connection I was making with Jake, showing him I was good humored for being a city slicker as he had labeled me earlier. He stopped momentarily, quickly pulled up a couple of feathery weeds, handed one to me, and showed me how to use it like a horse or cow uses its tail to keep the dive bombing bugs at bay.

Jake led. I followed and watched his muscled torso riding above the Queen Anne's Lace, thistles and Pig Weed, watched his control of the mosquito switch, watched the way he marched forward sure-footed and cocky without looking down and the way he lifted his arms above the grasp of the thistle pins and turned sideways to give them a wide berth. My role of the initiate here following the experienced trail scout across this strange new land was fine with me.

We walked over what I learned were old meadows desperately in need of cows to clear them. It was at least two miles or more of rough ground that we covered—or, at least, that's what it felt like to me at the time—before we came to anything that resembled a serious change in the experience of walking "the path." It was a wooded area, and I remember thinking I hoped the woods would be a respite from the man-mangling weeds and scrub brush, insect assaults, and the ache in my legs from stumbling over tufts of grass that I hadn't learned to foresee before they caught the toes of my shoes. I took pride in the fact I'd survived, kept up, and hadn't fallen like a feeble old man who has tripped over his own cane.

When we entered the woods and walked in maybe twenty-five feet or so, we stopped. Jake turned and looked at me and asked, "You doing alright, man?" He put his hand on the back of my shoulder, rubbed his palm over it in a circular motion. There was something healing in that touch, or, at least, something comforting, and I was sorry when he stopped.

"The quarry isn't too far beyond the other side of the woods. Have I taken the city slicker out of you yet, pardner?" Jake's voice had turned to his interpretation of a Texas drawl, and the gleam in his eye was that of a little boy who has just played a prank on his best friend.

"Let's just say, you're getting there!"

"You hot?" he asked.

"Well, some people think I am," I said. "Why do you ask?" As I said it, I felt my face flush, took pleasure in watching Jake chuckle.

As I looked into the cerulean blue of his eyes, I thought about what he had asked me about being hot and realized that I had been so involved in the walk that I hadn't thought much about the sun beating on my body. But now that Jake had called attention to it, I was suddenly aware of just how warm I was and realized my T-shirt was wet and sticky. Sweat was falling from my forehead, face and neck, my pants were damp under the belt and in the crotch where the sweat had leaked through my undershorts and into the denim.

"Guess I am! Didn't realize until now. You're sweating too, man," I said.

"Damn straight I am," he said, and set the jug down, pulled his shirt over his head and stood bare to the waist. He flipped it outward with his right hand to flap in the drying air. Many shades of gold, brown, and tan of his body played in the tree-filtered light on his pecs, biceps, triceps, and lats, all of them toned like the muscles of a younger man.

He was right. He was *hot!* Even his slightly receding hairline and the tiny time-wrinkles encroaching upon his eyes didn't detract from the overall effect. Sweat ran profusely down through the top of my jeans to the tensing flesh below.

All the pieces fit: the muscled upper torso; the broad shoulders making their graceful curve up to his neck; the neck muscles rising to the strong jawline and dimpled chin perfectly proportionate to his mouth, nose, and his piercing blue eyes. He wore it all so well and unconsciously—his masculinity. In a millisecond of thought, I knew what great sculptors felt as they built the complex minds and souls of the men who modeled for them, chiseling into the materials that would encompass them and their souls through the centuries. Looking at Jake, I understood what it meant to find the breath that lives within the stone.

I couldn't find words. "Unfuckingbelievable," crossed my mind, almost pushed its way out of my throat. Anything more profound simply escaped me as I stared at that body.

Jake spoke and pulled me out of my brain's ability to get lost within itself as I try to frame a reaction.

"Take off your shirt, Rob. Relax."

I became self-conscious immediately and felt woefully inadequate, knew my own body paled by comparison. Most bodies would, I thought. My physique was far from the Greek ideal of proportions. I had been called handsome by a few people over the years, but I was never sure why, and I regularly questioned their judgment when I looked in a mirror at my face. I didn't see it... I wanted to believe it sometimes, but I guess I had learned to accept that I was, at best, stunningly average. Despite the piddling money I was making from my writing and working in the store, I managed to keep a gym membership and to slow the inevitable deterioration that time imposes on all of us. Like Jake, I had reached the point at which no one would mistake me for being in my early twenties, and no amount of working out or wishing to be different was going to change that. I accepted my age and all that came with it. However, I thought about keeping my shirt on to withhold the inferiority of my physical credentials as compared to his magnificence, and then I remembered that we were going swimming, and he was going to see me shirtless soon no matter what I did now. I looked at Jake and said, "When I look at you, I feel kind of puny, you know."

At that, Jake walked over to me, took hold of the bottom of my shirt with both hands, and pulled it up and off me and held it in his left hand like a trophy. Then he took it with his right like a magician readying to say his magic words and laid it on my neck, stood directly in front of me and put his hands on my shoulders. He looked me in the eyes and said, "You look good, man. Let go of whatever is going on with you. Let's not get into that macho comparison crap. Okay?"

I felt my chest swell a bit as I looked straight into the blue crystal balls of his eyes and realized that I felt safe in his presence, something I didn't feel around many men.

He pulled his hands from my shoulders and asked, "How about some water after that hike across the prairie?"

Before I could respond, he pulled the cap off the jug, took a short swallow, handed it to me as if the only response any sane person could give to him was, "Sure. I'll take some!"

"We'll save the whiskey for a bit. I've still got a buzz going. You okay, man?"

I nodded yes while I still had the water jug up to my lips, allowed the water to gurgle its way down my throat as I looked at him. When I finished, he took the bottle, capped it, picked up his shirt from the sapling he had thrown it on, and we set off again through the trees and the shade.

The floor of the woods was soft with pine needles and years of fallen leaves. The spongy ground was like carpet in a rich man's house under sunlit chandeliers.

"Sound changed here; did you notice?"

"It's part of why I come here," he said. "It's not *there*—the city. It's my other world. Other worlds."

"Other worlds," he had said, adding the "s" as if reading my mind: "other worlds," like the arts, like being so lost in the creation of a thing—a representation of an artist's thoughts and feelings and spiritual motivations—that time becomes merely an inconvenience quietly eating away at the flesh, inevitably removing it from a culture that chooses not to understand what it means to create, even when the artist's creations are everywhere in museums and galleries, and in books like mausoleums. And even there, the works themselves slowly give way to time and tastes. Everything all too human waiting to disintegrate among the worms, insects, microscopic beings beneath the surface of the earth eating slowly, steadfastly and irrevocably. And, still, there is a "value in doing it anyway!" My thought had made itself verbal before I could stop it.

Jake turned and looked at me, asked, "Value in doing what?"

"I was lost in my head, and the thought slipped out," I said. "I do that sometimes. I was thinking art. I'll tell you about it another time."

"Aren't you supposed to be getting away from that today and relaxing?"

I thought about trying to explain the difference between doing the physical and thought work of writing versus living the art. Then, I realized that I didn't want to explain it. I wanted to laugh and enjoy his company, and that, too, was living the art!

"You're right. Lead on, McDuff!" As soon as I said it, I realized that I sounded like a college professor and Jake might not know the illusion.

He turned around, looked at me with a slight smirk on his face, and responded with, "Damned be him that first cries 'Hold,'" I was stunned. He wasn't only beautiful to look at, he knew something about literature ... or at least had a good memory for one-liners.

Seeing the stunned look on my face, he said with a smirk, "What? A cop can't love literature? Think you got a corner on Shakespeare, buddy?" Laughing at my surprise, he chuckled as he turned.

Jake halted a few times to listen to the various calls of birds and to see if he could find them in the trees. When he stopped like that, he looked at me, made sure he had my attention, put his pointer finger up to his lips—the non-verbal "Shhh!" He walked ever so quietly to me and stood close, put his hand on my shoulder, and pointed toward the sounds he heard and whispered the birds' specie name.

At one point along the way, Jake suggested we sit on a fallen tree trunk and just listen for a moment to the chittering of chipmunks and squirrels, the endless variations of bird songs, the incessant jackhammering of the woodpeckers on the trunks of trees. I sat down first, glad to give my legs a few moments of rest. Then, he sat down beside me close enough for our knees to touch, close enough to hear and feel the rub of our jeans as if they were talking to one another, asking and answering the question of what waits at the end of the trek.

After a short while, I heard the rapid ticking clatter of a woodpecker on a tree and asked, "Wouldn't you think they'd get a headache?"

"Who?" Jake looked confused.

"Woodpeckers," I said. "Woodpeckers, using their heads like jackhammers!"

"What in the hell made you come up with that? Must be a wild place up there inside your head!"

As he made the comment, his face muscles pulled his jaws tight, raised the left side of his lips into a tight exaggerated half smile with his bottom lip pulled behind his upper set of teeth; he scrunched his left eye closed and made a screwball face for my entertainment, causing me to all but fall off the log with laughter until we were both laughing like schoolboys. After a couple more face contortions now coming from each of us–each trying to outdo the other—we finally reached a point of getting ourselves under control enough for Jake to blurt out, "Man, you are goofy!... and I like it. Haven't laughed like that for a while ... Anyhow, in response to your question..." at which point, I burst out laughing again and said I had forgotten the question, to which Jake used his own powerful shoulder and musculature to push me off the log, both of us again laughing as I got up, brushed the leaves off my backside and sat down again.

"You asked if woodpeckers get headaches! How the hell would I know? Do I look like a woodpecker to you? Maybe it's because a woodpecker has a brain the size of a BB! No room in there for too many pain receptors."

"True," I said. "I guess it's all in what you've been programmed to do! An unfortunate name, by the way: Woodpecker."

He turned his head and looked at me again as if I were a three-headed, wart-covered, six-armed alien creature that had just fallen out of the tree in front of him. He was grinning like a pre-teen boy discovering sexual innuendo for the first time in his life. His eyes suddenly shifted to staring at the ground. I thought for a moment he was embarrassed by the notion of talking about sex.

When he raised his eyes again, he looked at me and said with a deadpan face, "I don't think the woodpeckers would get the joke. I seriously doubt that's what they would call themselves if they had any say in the matter." Then he broke and laughed out loud. "You are one crazy dude! And just in case you didn't know it, the 'pecker' part of their name refers to using their beaks to peck for insects in the wood."

"So, you're saying a better name would be 'Pecker Head.'"

Again, he knocked me off the log as he laughed out loud. Then, he stood up, offered his hand to pull me up. When I took it, I was lifted as easily as if I had been that bag of potato chips he removed from the table after lunch earlier. As he turned to walk on, I heard him mutter rhythmically, "How much wood will a woodpecker peck when a woodpecker pecks on wood, Pecker Wood? Pecker Head?" He turned just enough to engage his peripheral vision in checking to see if I was in tow and to allow me to see the uplifted jaw carrying the weight of his grin.

Having fun hanging out with a cop was not something I had ever imagined for myself. But there I was. Perhaps part of the joy of it all was that he was refreshingly more than one of those guys who has trained himself to talk only about such things as repairing a carburetor or which team won a game, or which team was likely to make it to the series or playoffs, or how many women he had banged. It was difficult for me to imagine Jake, gun-in-hand, standing over an escaped killer sprawled face down in the dirt, or imagine the sound of Jake's command voice demanding the escapee's hands move slowly behind his back so Jake could slap the cuffs on him and lift the guy up off the ground like a potato chip bag. He was a not-cop in my head. But, if he was a "not-cop," what had I determined a cop was? That would have to be a topic to ponder another day, I decided. And yet, my brain did not retreat from free-ranging thoughts, and I got lost in the adventure of my own thinking, the kinds of attachments my brain was making to assess what I meant by what I allowed myself to say within my own head and what I had said in the past for others to hear. And should I have to explain that I am just a man who is trying to make sense of what comes at him in this world? I was glad to be pulled back from the madness by Jake's voice.

"Not far now! Hang in there, Slick!" Jake pointed up ahead and said, "See! There's a clearing coming up. The quarry is just beyond it over that rise."

"I think I'm doing pretty well, for a 'city slicker,' Scout."

As Jake turned and looked at me, he pumped his arm muscle into a weightlifter pose, and said, "Don't you mean, Mighty Scout, Slick?"

"No. I like 'Scout,' as in 'Boy Scout' or 'Cub Scout.' It knocks you down to size."

"I liked 'Mighty Scout' better."

"Too bad! I guess you'll have to live with it, or I'll start calling you Gertrude."

"You're a weird dude, man," he said as he turned away chuckling.

"Been told that before!

As I slogged on, I looked out beyond the trees to the open space before us and thought about the sun's rays readying to paw savagely at our bare skin as we trekked the distance to this mystical place that Jake had spoken of in superlatives: clearest, cleanest, most refreshing, most beautiful. If it's only half that good, I thought, it still sounds great. I could hear Jake's voice and his enthusiastic descriptors crawling out of my memory bank and clinging to my ears. His joy had embedded a feeling for the place that I had not yet seen and now longed to experience; I found myself hoping I could meet whatever expectations he might have for bringing me here, hoping I could meet my own growing expectations of the day.

"Not many people know about this place anymore," he said matter-of-factly. "And I don't tell many people about it. Don't want them coming out when I don't know about it. Don't need anybody drowning, and me getting hit with a lawsuit... like it should be my fault somebody sneaked in and died. I've got posted signs up all over the place."

"So, I shouldn't be expecting I'll have to fight anybody for a space to put my ass on?"

"Not unless you want to fight me, buddy!" Jake turned and started walking backward pumping his arm muscles to impressive bulges and making fists that looked like they could easily KO any opponent. He flashed his toothy grin.

"No fight from me, officer! I don't want to get arrested or beaten to smithereens!"

When we reached the open space, Jake stepped out into it like a deer surveying the field before going too far beyond the safety of the woods. Then I stepped out into the open like his totally feckless faun taking its first jaunt out into the world. I had no idea why we were doing these maneuvers or what there was to present a danger. Maybe Jake didn't either. Maybe it was the animal in us that has learned not to trust much of anything until we've checked it out. The sun was blistering hot as I had suspected it would be, but the rise was not far, and we moved forward determinedly, swatting away mosquitoes with the still-wet shirts we carried, now using them as substitutes for the insect swishers we had dropped on the floor of the woods earlier after escaping the first barrages of the bug squads. When we got over the knoll, we stopped once more. Jake put his arm around my shoulders and said as if showing an original and magnificent work of art that had not been seen in public for a century or more. "There it is. The Quarry." It was downhill from where we stood and only a short distance from us. The land in front of it was mostly flat as if graded for the sole purpose of enhancing the theatre made by the immense chiseled walls that surrounded three sides of the space.

"Before we go down to it, though, I want you to look over to your left. You see that tree?" He pointed to it over top of my shoulder. "That lone tree standing there in the open space where you can still see a partial stone wall? That's the tree! That's where it happened."

The tree was one deserving of the term *majestic*. That was it. It was a majestic tree rising high into the sky, laying its leaves out in sprays like hands praising Jesus in a Baptist church. Massive branches jutted off the trunk in gentle curves skyward, with the exception of one lone thick branch at least ten or twelve feet up and pushing outward almost perpendicular for seven or eight feet before bending toward the sky to join its siblings there. It was an arm flexing its powerful muscles.

"How do you know it's the one, Jake."

"I only know what my dad told me. Where he got his information from, I don't really know. He grew up here when there were still some old timers around. Maybe they told him. I don't know how anyone could prove it is or isn't. It sure looks like a hanging tree, though, doesn't it? And it's been standing there a long, long time."

I stared at the tree and pictured Nathan Sanders with his hands tied behind his back, his corpse swinging there after the fall from whatever had been used to prop him in place until the hangmen pulled, kicked, or whipped it from beneath him. I could imagine the kicking of his legs trying to find something solid in those nanoseconds to stop his fall, I could hear the crunch of the knot at the back of his head, the silence when the mob knew it was over, and they were left staring at the work they had done before heading home to supper.

After the shutter of my body reacting to the images in my head, I found myself wondering if any of the mob came to regret what they had done. I wondered if there are people incapable of feeling any regret for anything they've done, if it's possible for whole swaths of people to be soulless.

Whether or not it was *the* tree, I had now seen it and given it meaning, given ownership for the hanging to it as Jake had done. "What an awful thing that must have been to see," I said out loud.

"I wanted you to see it—the tree, not the hanging itself," Jake said. "Sometimes I come out here and climb it and sit on that big outright branch and think about it all. Can't get it out of my head. I keep trying to understand why it matters to me. Maybe it's just a boyhood thing. You know? One of those memories that keeps a part of my childhood alive. I always kind of felt sorry for Nathan even if he did the murders or helped with them somehow. I mean, if he did it, I don't forgive it, but somehow what happened to him shouldn't be forgiven either."

He started walking again. I started after him, stopped, turned, and looked once more at the tree, saw the swinging corpse in my mind's eye. I, too, might need to come back someday to climb out onto that branch and look down from there into the last seconds of a young man's life lost and feel the nothingness between the limb and the ground. Then I turned away, determined to let the image of the broken-necked man slip somehow into some far reach of my brain for a while. I tried at first to walk slowly in homage to the dead, but the insects would have nothing of it and started goading me to play the game of trying to outrun them.

As I came up to Jake's side and set my pace to his, I saw the water. Trees stretched out over it ... all of them juveniles by comparison with the hanging tree. Many, mostly maples, stood atop the back and side walls of the chiseled space that had become a quarry. The side walls dropped on a slow angle from the back wall's height to the front of the quarry pond. At the front edge of the pond, several flat hewn stones lay about like chairs in a ransacked house, dividing the terrain between the fields and the pool. Elsewhere, stones lay randomly about where cottonwoods, redbuds, and various scrub bush species and time had cast them so as to filter some of the sunlight that fell into the water.

A multiplicity of colors was splayed on the remaining walls of the quarry as light and shade played on the textures and sheens depending on whether surfaces were wet or dry. I could see obvious places where the water leached through and fed the quarry, allowing cool water in and pushing the warmer surface-level water to evaporate. My eyes were drawn to the greenery that grew freely on the wet sections of the carved walls where it clung to crevices and climbed like ivy on an English manner house. Whatever it was, lichen or moss or something else I knew nothing of, it was a dark green—a forest green, I thought, but then it changed as the tree-filtered light shifted in the slight movements of the leaves, leaves that moved ever so slowly in the slightest of feather-soft breeze that trees can decipher and humans can't. At those moments, there came momentary hints of yellow and chartreuse, and emerald on the forest-green base, teasing, like multi-colored butterfly wings the eye's ability to differentiate colors as it flexes in the sun. I thought a painter would be hard pressed to decide at any given moment, which colors belonged where over the hours of painting the picture that caught his eye and triggered the desire to capture it on canvas while fighting the reality that what he could see was changing second by second in shifting light that moves shadows and tricks the eye.

There was a beautiful sadness to the place, I thought. Perhaps solemnity would be a better word. Perhaps serenity. But none of those words fit exactly. I wasn't sad, didn't feel like being solemn, and I was enjoying being with someone who made me feel whole and alive. And yet, those thoughts rolled over one another in my brain, living simultaneously. I liked the feeling of taking it all in, absorbing complexity upon complexity. I could feel stories held somehow in some cryptic code in the molecules that made up the stone, the landscape, the air … stories that could never be adequately transcribed, and, at the same time, as real as anything I had ever written or lived. As I told Jake about the feelings I was having, he listened intently, he touched my arm and spoke.

"I had a feeling you might like it. What you are saying is how I've always felt here. Sometimes I try to imagine the people who came here: the men who worked here, did the cutting and carving of stone, loaded it in wagons and hauled it to wherever they took it. I like thinking that people once came out here to swim, feel peace—men, women, children. I guess, I've always felt like the place holds lots of lost lives. Doesn't make much sense, I guess."

"It does, Jake. Places like this hold lives, just like the rooms of old houses do. History doesn't die. It just waits to be heard." I heard my voice and thought how comfortable it was to say the words to Jake, wondered how many people I could have said that to in that particular way without embarrassment.

"You know, Rob, I imagine sometimes I can hear them, their voices, their jokes, their secrets. I wish I were a writer, like you, and could get my thoughts and feelings down on paper. I wish I could capture time, step back and forth in it, and meet the people who are long gone and those who will come along after I'm dead and gone. I know when I think I hear them talking, it's just my imagination working, but it doesn't change that I feel them here. It's like we carry our own and other people's past inside us, and we connect with that in places like this."

He was a writer, I thought, though his words were written into the air like the words of those who once stood in this space. Our words mostly come and go as nameless ghosts like so many people who came and went before us, our genomic predecessors of clans long since devoid of first and middle names, devoid of their histories of having lived, loved, interacted with one another and struggled against the impositions of would-be conquerors and politicians and even their own community members as each of them tried to figure out the meaning of meaning.

As we reached the water's edge, we set down the water bottle, the whiskey bottle, and our towels, and I got down on my knees and put my hands in the cool water and said how good it felt, scooped up a handful and rubbed it into my face, scooped again and spilled it on the top of my head as best I could, felt the cool wetness roll down my face to my chin and slide down my neck and chest. Jake knelt beside me and did the same; for a moment, we were two priests asking blessings at the baptismal until Jake's eyes sparkled with mischief like a pre-adolescent; he looked at me, scooped another handful of the holy water and threw it, catching me on the chest. I returned the favor, and we splashed one another, laughing while each tried to get more water in his hands to soak the other.

After a moment, Jake pushed me playfully, as he had done on the log in the woods, and announced it was time to get in. He got up, picked up his towel, unrolled it and laid it on a flat rock slab and then started taking off his shoes.

When I stood up, I looked over at Jake, the rock, the towel, there were no trunks. I thought perhaps he would be wearing them under his jeans. I also realized that the thought of skinny dipping hadn't crossed my mind until this moment. I picked up my towel and unrolled it, laid my trunks next to it, hesitated, sat down and started taking off my shoes and socks, all the time keeping an eye on Jake, waiting to figure out what I was to do or not do next. He was in the process of getting out of his pants right there in front of me face-to-face no more than three feet away, and with no hint of shyness, undid his belt, released the button above the fly, unzipped the zipper and slid the pants down over his hips and muscled thighs. There were no trunks, no underwear. And now I could see the entire magnificent sculpture: every part of him perfectly proportioned, a stunning study of proportions.

"I hope you're not planning to wear those trunks," Jake said.

I stood up, looked into Jake's eyes, and tried to say something—something about Jake's being a good-looking man, about admiring his body, the pleasure I was having in studying his musculature, his skin, the way all the parts fit together with his comfort in being naked in front of me. While I was chattering to subdue my desire to touch him,

I felt myself releasing my belt buckle, unzipping my pants, pausing, feeling them falling down as Jake watched patiently, never taking his eyes off me as blood rushed into my penis. And then, I pulled at the waistband of my shorts and slid them down my legs and stepped out of them and felt the cooler air on the uncovered skin.

"Now, that's over!" Jake said nonchalantly, "No big secrets, so we can enjoy the day as we are—whatever we are at any given moment."

"I don't know about that secret stuff. Seems like you were keeping a pretty big secret there, Jake," I joked.

Jake stepped in close and said, "You too! We're *both* just fine. Quit worrying about that stuff, man. You seem to think you're not great looking in your own right. Anybody ever tell you that you look a lot like the actor Julian Morris? He's about your age and hot as hell."

Julian Morris wasn't a name I knew, but I made a mental note to look him up when I got back to my computer.

"You're not going to arrest me for indecent exposure, are you?" I asked.

"If I did, you could do a citizen's arrest on me, and we'd both have to explain ourselves to a judge."

It felt good to be free of all clothing, standing in the open air, feeling the sun on my entire body and enjoying that feeling with another human being who was so comfortable with it all. In the water, we alternated between swimming, floating, splashing, laughing, and climbing out to rest. Out of the water, we sat on our towels and talked as we lay face up looking into the crowns of the trees. At first, I chose my own flat rock to lay upon, but after a while we were lying side by side, shoulders touching, hips and thighs touching... Jake laying his hand on my body and saying, "It's okay, man. Just be! Enjoy!" He turned on his side at times facing me, his eyes scanning my body like a painting, as if following the flow of the lines that created my being from my head to my neck to my chest, to my belly and genitalia, to my thighs, shins, and feet and back again, the lines sliding under me and into me and out in infinite numbers of undulating motions. "You are a double helix," he said almost as a proclamation that rattled like multiple tin cans hanging by strings from a tree branch in the wind clunking one against the other.

I rolled to my side, face to face with him and whispered, "I'm having one of the best days of my life, Jake!"

He laid his hand on my chest and rubbed the thick hair there, let his hand rest a moment, then allowed it to slide down onto my belly and penis, lingered a moment before he rolled onto his back and let his left hand lay over his right at his belly. "Me too," he said.

After a short time of lying on the hard stone bed we had made, we got up to swim again. At Jake's command, we swam to the high-walled side of the quarry to see where people of long-gone generations had carved their initials into the stones. It was difficult to look carefully at the carvings while treading water, and there weren't many places where the stone jutted out to get a handhold on them or for our feet to step, but we managed to find a few such places so I could look more closely at what Jake had seen many times. Some of the carvings were simply pairs of initials set inside heart shapes. There were others with no hearts, using only plus signs to link one to another, and there were symbols that had once meant something to someone, but we could not decipher them.

Looking at the dozens of carvings we could see, we talked about what it must have taken to carve the stone and tried to guess how so many names had been made with so little space to stand, how a swimmer might carry tools to cut into the surface of the stone: hammers, chisels, sharp rocks.

"Maybe the pond and the stones weren't always like they are now," I said. "Maybe they did have something to stand on back then. Maybe people brought a boat."

I thought about the Lascaux caves and asked Jake if he knew about them. When he said he did, he said he hadn't thought about anything like that when he looked at the quarry walls. Nothing here was magnificent or pictorial. And yet, the fact was people had felt the need to keep something of themselves alive, not even their full names, just fragments of themselves.

"These are the people you hear, Jake." They're speaking to us right now, even if we can't understand them."

"It's kind of like stepping into a crowded room where everyone is talking and you can hear the noise but none of the words," Jake said.

"Maybe we're just not ready to hear what they have to say."

"Not many men interested in stuff like this, Rob," his voice absorbing the loneliness that comes with being gay in a culture dominated by straight white men who have not been allowed to feel the range of their emotions.

"Which stuff? The hanging out naked? Or the talk?"

"Both, actually."

"Most of the men I work with are really hung up on whatever the hell they think 'real men' are. They're afraid of anything that doesn't fit with their notions of *straight* or *masculine*; they hide behind talking shop, or sports, or cars... stuff like that. I just find most of it to be boring. Always have. I mean, I get along, enjoy being with the guys I trust, but I get tired of living on the surface all of the time."

There was disappointment in Jake's voice, the same disappointment I have felt in the presence of many men— men like my father who never seemed to feel anything unless he was drunk, and who brushed away all meaningful reflection upon the world with the discarded carcasses of beer cans left laying wherever he had been.

"Is the gay thing an issue for them?" I asked.

"Most of them don't know. I don't talk about it when I'm around them. I just don't want that to be an issue for the 'phobes.' The job is tough enough. The chief knows. A friend there knows. Most don't, and those who know don't tell. Lots of the guys have tried to fix me up with their sisters or cousins, get me married off. Probably, some have wondered what's wrong with me that I don't leap at the opportunities to take up their offers."

"You're not like any image of 'cop' I've ever thought about ... by the way, that's a good thing."

"We're not all the same, Rob, no matter what the TV shows try to make us out to be. And the work isn't all compacted into getting the bad guy every hour or half hour of the day."

He paused for a moment, splashed water on the insect trying to land on his skin. Sunk down so that only his head was above the water.

"Police work's no different from other kinds of work, I suppose. Good days, bad days, busy and dull days, exciting and boring. You have to kiss a lot of asses, and you're supposed to know when you need to look the other way when the 'right' people do the wrong things. I've kissed ass, but I'm not good at looking the other way. Hasn't made me popular."

"Made some enemies?"

"For sure. Including some of the cops I work with." As he said it, I saw a shift in his brow, heard a slight alteration of his tone, a brief pause showing he had gone inward momentarily to something painful, pushed it into a closet somewhere in his brain.

"Anybody else on the force gay?"

"None that are open about it. I suspect some are or are bi. You probably know this, but you get a bunch of naked men in a shower room and watch where their eyes go, and you kind of know. Only one of them ever hit on me, a guy who made a big deal out of being straight, tough, a manly man. It was when I first got onto the force, and we were doing patrol together. Kept laying his hand on my leg when he talked. At first, I just tried to ignore it, thought it a quirk. When his hand came over onto my balls and squeezed, I was shocked. I bent his fingers backward, made him squeal, and told him to back off or I'd file charges. I didn't want any part of that."

Joking, I asked, "Not your type? Ugly?"

"It wouldn't have mattered either way. I just don't want to mix my work life with my private life. And I wouldn't put up with that in my personal life if it was unwanted. There was nothing about him that interested me other than that he was a cop and was assigned to be my trainer through my rookie phase. After I practically broke his fingers, he tried to pretend that what happened hadn't. For a while, after he made his move on me, he turned up next to me in the men's room at the urinals a little too regularly ... you get the picture. I told him I wasn't interested and that I'd file a sexual harassment complaint if he didn't back off."

"How could you work with him after that?"

"I asked to be placed with a different trainer. Just said we weren't compatible. Chief asked him about it. When he realized I hadn't reported him for sexual harassment, he agreed to the change. He turned into a real prick after that, doing everything in his power to undermine me and make life miserable. Bad mouthed me to other cops. Tried to make me look bad to the chief. Hated everything about me. I guess he thought I'd get discouraged and quit; then I wouldn't be a daily reminder of my being a threat to his cover of heterosexual masculinity."

"You had the goods on him."

"Yeah, except that I didn't. I hadn't reported it. Didn't want to out the guy. I just wanted him to leave me alone. Anyway, I had no evidence. It would have come down to my word against his, and then too much time passed for it to be taken seriously."

"Still, it must have eaten at him that he knew you knew," I said.

"He worked hard at appearing a 'manly man'. He regularly made a point of bragging about all of the women he was supposedly fucking. And maybe he was. But when he knew I was in hearing range, he would get a little quieter and then change the subject and glare at me if he could see me."

"He sounds like a dick," I said lightheartedly.

With a hint of injustice behind the words, Jake said, "Still blames me for his getting fired last year."

"For hitting on you?"

"No. Like I said, I've never told anybody about that ... except you. I found out he was on the take, and I turned him in. As far as I'm concerned he screwed himself; but in cop world, that makes me a rat ... I got him fired ... and whether or not he deserved it, I'm the bad guy. He was popular with some of the men in the department—women mostly hated him—and still has buddies who make it clear I'm not to be trusted. Told you I wasn't popular."

"So, I'm hanging out with a marked man," I quipped.

"I try to be careful."

When I asked him how he had come to the decision to do police work, he suggested we get out of the water and dry off, have a drink before getting into his story. When we got to the stones where our towels lay, we sat down, side by side. Jake picked up the bottle of Jack Daniels, took a quick drink, handed it to me, and then lay down face up.

The whiskey burned my throat as it slid down, felt good when it reached my belly. I sat down beside him, looked up into the sky and waited for him to talk.

There was a bit of the storyteller in him that liked to dramatize for effect. When he said, "I think I decided to be a cop when I was really young," It had a quality of "once upon a time," then he launched into the background equivalent to "there was a little boy who...."

"I probably read too many comic books about superheroes. Always wanted to be somebody who helped people—somebody who'd 'fight for the right'! I thought rules were actually rules, and answers came only in black and white. There were only good guys and bad guys in the world. It took me a long time to learn about gray."

He took another short drink and went on, "After I did a three-year hitch in the military, I got into the police academy. Wanted to work in Emberland if possible. Didn't want to move. Lucky enough to get in. Been here ever since. Most days it's all right, but sure as hell isn't like I imagined when I was a kid. The longer I stay in the cop racket, the more I realize how naïve I was when I thought I could somehow fix some of the world's ugliest problems, at least make some inroads. It's all so much easier in the land of make believe when you're a kid and you don't know enough to see the holes in your dreams."

For a moment, I stepped into teacher mode—or maybe it was writer's mode—saying, "Doesn't change the fact that the dream is a good one, Jake. The holes aren't in the dream; they're in the society we live in." I wanted to go on and explain that nobody can do big things all on their own. So much depends on who's got power and how they use it, how much greed powerful people have got going for them or working against them and remind him there's a whole lot of stupid everywhere in the world that kills dreams. But I had said enough, and without thinking, I placed my hand on his belly, felt his warm skin beneath the soft blond and brown hairs that grew there, told him, I'd like to know him, his work, his story, whatever he wanted to share. He stood up, taking my arm with him and raised me from the sitting position to him rib cage to rib cage, touching his lips to mine as trees moaned almost inaudibly beneath the late afternoon sun.

10

The following morning, I awakened to the sunlight that had already filled the bedroom. Pictures on the dresser were staring at me: people who I suspected had been Jake's parents and a picture of Jake in his military uniform. The house was quiet in the ways that old houses have of being quiet but not silent, like the sighs and groans of old people who have said many times over all they have to say of their lives and have gone into themselves to say or feel what they would never have said out loud of their passions, pride, sorrows and regrets—the things that would lay beside them in their graves. Jake's side of the bed was empty. I tried to hear the sound of his moving about the house, maybe the creaking of old boards, or the closing or opening of a door, or perhaps a whistle or hum. Nothing.

When I lifted myself off the bed, I walked to the window where I watched light splaying on the huge maple poised on the lawn. I played with the notion that it was a voyeur with ten-thousand eyes staring back at me, recording my body, adding it to all it had taken in over the years.

It looked proud as it played sentry over the yard humans had made of its forest, recorded the infinitesimal changes of the landscape over its own long life multiplied as it watched the world from different heights in different lights and from its own changing perspectives, faithfully encrypting them in its many, many memory rings.

At last, its leaves flapped a wave at me as if it was dismissing me for my being too inquisitive, waving me away like a sometime lover at a bus or train station or airport wishing to get the goodbyes done so he could get away, perhaps to something more interesting or to catch up on all the day's work to be done.

I opened the bedroom door and called out, "Jake! You there?" My voice was absorbed in the hollows of old walls—a melancholy response. I walked down the hall, past the open door of the bathroom, to the creaky stairwell. Beside the kitchen door that opened onto the porch the clothes I had carelessly tossed aside the night before lay neatly folded on the old well-worn wooden chair. My cellphone was on top of them serving as a paperweight for the piece of yellow, ruled paper that Jake had used to leave me a note. As I picked it up, I felt the clunk of my brain as I remembered the ways men dumped one another. I felt the shudder in my chest as Matt's face intruded on my thoughts.

Rob,

I got called into work. There's food in the pantry and in the fridge. Coffee in the coffee maker. Just press "start." Help yourself!

*If you manage to get your lazy butt out of bed before
noon and want to meet me for lunch, I'll be at the diner.*

*When you leave, make sure the coffee maker is off and
lock the door behind you.*

Great time with you, Slick!

Jake

While the coffee was brewing, I walked around the
house, looked at Jake's careful placement of pictures and
mementos, the placement of furniture, the way he made
his space comfortably masculine, despite the ugly flowered wallpaper in the kitchen. For a few minutes, I sat in
the deep leather chair in the living room looking out of the
windows to watch the sun dance on the lawn. At the beep
of the coffee maker, I poured myself a cup and carried it
to the porch where I went back over the previous day, the
pleasures, the freedom, the feelings of being young again.
I was comfortable in ways I hadn't been for a long time.

Though I was enjoying being in Jake's home and the
feeling of belonging there, it was time for me to dress and
head back to town to my apartment to shower and get
ready to meet him for lunch. All the way home I thought
about the day and night I had just stepped out of, the feelings I was experiencing, and the images in my head of our
time at the quarry, in his home, in his bed. As I thought
about Jake, I couldn't help but think of him as a Rodin
sculpture come alive that, at least for a night, loved me
and was mine.

11

It had taken me only minutes into my first visit at the courthouse to fully appreciate that I would be dealing with over-worked, underpaid, and mostly unenthusiastic records staff, who listlessly stated there *might* be court records, but they didn't know for sure and had no way to look it up, and I would have to go to the Court Records Annex if there was to be any hope of finding anything.

The following day, on my second attempt to call the number I had been given, the phone was picked up. "Annex. Tina speaking." It was the voice of disinterest hiding behind well-rehearsed, but lifeless, responses to my questions: "You need to make an appointment to use the resources here at the Annex." So, I asked for an appointment.

"And what is it that you are looking for in particular, sir?"

To my surprise, when I told her, she sounded a bit more cheerful, or at least a little more willing to believe I wasn't just going to be wasting her time. She told me she thought she remembered finding the records for someone in the past, was "pretty sure" she had something on the Sanders case, and that if I wanted to come over right then it would be fine. I wasn't about to ask the point of being required to make an appointment if I could come right over.

The building itself looked like a factory. Inside were rows upon rows of steel shelves holding many years of records stuffed in boxes, placed in hole-punched binders set willy-nilly on shelves where they awaited processing, and hundreds of heavy, oversized books where the writing of judges and their clerks and scribes was entered by hand.

"You can look at any of the volumes you want," she said, "but you'll have to take them back to the table to open them. It hurts my back to lift them down." By 'the table,' as I would soon learn, she meant the one—and only—available flat space in the room other than her own desk or the front counter.

In many ways I found it all to be rather comical: "an experience," I told myself. Between clearing the table debris, searching for and lugging four or five heavy, over-sized books, and learning that many of those writers of yesteryear hadn't taken classes in penmanship and had used ink that faded over time and disappeared altogether in some cases, I was questioning whether or not I was willing to go any further with trying to be helpful to Jake. Initially, I found almost nothing of any value, and realized I was going to have little or no help from the clerk, who could only say she thought there was a book "somewhere back there" that dealt with the case. I was doing my last walk through the shelves that held the ledgers from the 1870s when I happened to notice a journal marked on its spine in faded magic marker with "Murder Trial, 1873." It had been filed with 1875 journals; given my observations of the Annex operation, I wasn't surprised, but I was glad I had taken the time to move beyond accepting the notion that official records are always put where they belong. When I got the ledger to the table and opened it up, I realized I had hit pay dirt. Nearly four hundred pages of court recordings related to the case. In it were handwritten duplications of lengthy newspaper articles and court procedure reports: coroner's inquest records, a preliminary hearing report, recording of the jury selection process, and trial records, including testimony and contested decisions filed by the attorney for the defense against the court's handling of the case. Now I knew that what was likely the only extant, semi-reliable material was available, but it would need to be read and studied, and it was only available in the courthouse and only at the whim of the clerk.

12

Jake and I saw one another as often as we could around our work schedules. Jake's in particular was difficult. He was working too many hours filling in for the summer shortage of officers, many of whom were taking vacation time. Apparently, his cop buddies had learned over the years, probably with the help of Jake's generosity, that they could count on him to fill in so they could spend time with their wives and children, take leaves of absence for medical problems, and various other life situations that pulled them away from work. However, it was clear to me that he needed a break from the too-many-hours and the stress of dealing with the people he had interacted with, helped, caught, fought, jailed or testified for or against. He was exhausted.

One evening when I arrived, Jake had been at home only a short time and was removing his uniform and all the accoutrements that went with it. He had met me at the door in his unbuttoned shirt, invited me to grab a beer while I waited for him. He came downstairs and joined me in the living room where I was looking at his bookshelves that were largely filled with novels: every Hemingway novel, much of Faulkner's work, Steinbeck, Fitzgerald, Proust, Sandra Cisneros, Arturo Islas, Scott Momaday—a veritable convention of literary luminaries.

After a few comments about his library, we went to the living room where he sat in his overstuffed cordovan leather chair just off to the side of the two large, four-panel windows that framed a silhouetted tree line beneath a three-quarter moon. Between Jake and the windows was a warm, walnut brown sophistication of a table holding a Tiffany lamp, his neatly stacked magazines and whatever book he was reading at the time. I sat within an arm's reach of his chair, off to his left where I could watch the shape of his face in the diminishing light of the sun's falling and the moon readying to come into the room like the aroma of baking apple pie with cinnamon.

We sipped beers slowly and talked. He wanted to hear what I had been working on. After talking about a couple of short stories I was readying for submissions, I started talking about my research into the Trent Murders. He wanted to know what I had found, every detail I could remember. I approached the telling, as best I could, chronologically, but tried not to rehash the basics we had talked about in the past. The many disparate facts led to side discussions and occasional trips down the rabbit holes of conjecture.

We continued in the kitchen as I pulled dinner together from what I had brought and what he had available. He was excited as I shared that I had found the coroner's inquest, pre-trial investigation, and the trial transcripts, though I had only had time to read portions of them. I told him I was piecing the timeline and storyline together and writing thoughts and questions in my journal. The eagerness to hear anything I had to say showed in his face like a husband waiting to hear an announcement from his wife as to whether or not they were going to have a child. He wanted to hear it all. Despite being tired, he was unable to subdue his questions and interrupted the story often as I was weaving it.

"So, was Parsons killed first?"

"Would it make any difference?" I asked.

"I don't know for sure. Maybe. Couldn't he have been last to die just as easily? That would challenge Sanders' story at least. And the women? Same thing. How did the prosecutors think they were going to *prove* a case when morons walked all over the scene of the crime?"

"Judging from what I've looked at so far, the prosecution came down to trying to weave a bunch of assumptions into a story. Guilt by fiction based on a stupid boy's jailhouse confession!"

"Did anybody explain how one man, a not-very-bright man, orchestrated three murders single-handedly, particularly with an ax handle? ...."

"Hold it, detective! Let's remember that if I could answer your questions, we wouldn't be talking about this: it would have been solved way back then. I've only taken a quick look at hundreds of pages of court records. I've got a lot of work to do to get at specific facts. Reading testimony takes time. What little I've read can be mind-numbing."

I explained the problems of reading almost illegible handwriting, run-on sentences, chaotic punctuation and spelling, and just downright ludicrous statements that some people made and having to go over the lines many times just to figure out which words went with which sentence.

Again, I reminded Jake that a whole lot of the trial centered around what Sanders supposedly said. And that came largely from newspaper reporters. Early on, the vast majority of community members believed Sanders and Carson had committed the crime. After Carson was released, based on his alibi, the newspapers spent the better part of a year convincing the community to believe Sanders was *the* monster and obviously guilty, whether or not he had help with the murders. Many continued to believe Carson was involved but had gamed the system and was smart enough to get out of town as soon as he was released and head for parts unknown. Case closed! They had *the* killer they wanted to kill. Initially, it seemed all that had to be decided by the court was when Sanders would get his comeuppance. And the reporters' not-well-hidden message was clearly *Why wait for the courts to waste taxpayers' dollars when a rope would take care of everything?* As far as I was concerned, I had read more than enough articles to think the newspapers should have gone to trial for murdering Sanders.

"The whole thing was wild," I said. "It took ninety-eight interviews to find twelve supposed fair-minded people to sit on the jury; most had decided in advance that Sanders was guilty and deserved to hang. Then there were the witnesses! It looks to me like some witnesses came to the trial convinced that their only task was to tell their stories in ways that were most destructive to Nathan Sanders' chances of beating the rap, even if they had to lie or alter their previous statements to make it happen."

"He set himself up with a dumb defense," Jake said.

"Everything about Nathan's story is just plain dumb. Bizarre, really! But I think maybe, by some twisted logic, he thought he was outwitting the legal system by building a defense that went something like this: He did nothing wrong, he only watched a crime, and that shouldn't count ... by the way, his attorney later tried to make that exact case. It went nowhere with the public or the judge."

I explained that my impression was that it was the clear callousness of Sanders' published statement that signed his death warrant. He offered no logical reason for ignoring the bloodshed. The best he had to offer was an emotionally vacant statement: "I feel bad about what happened to those people who died. It was horrible to see." No tears. No regrets about doing nothing to help the victims. No sense of horror; he felt "bad"—no further explanation of what the word meant to him. "The only smart thing he did was to keep his story fairly consistent each time he told it," I said.

As he listened, Jake often leaned forward and looked me in the eye like an overworked, over-tired, coffee-drugged detective questioning a suspect—a suspect who was about to break after twenty-four hours of being under the harsh lights of the interrogation room in an improbable detective story. He was patient as I shared a story about a "high-priced" investigator brought down from Cleveland who didn't seem to come up with much in the way of any meaningful evidence but had plenty of suppositions. Then there was some local guy—not a cop or qualified investigator—who had been allowed to go back over the grounds and see if he could find clues that others hadn't seen; he had found some "evidence" of crushed grass near the location where Parsons died that he was certain was an indication of a struggle, though nothing in his testimony explained how he came to that determination. He had also reported that he followed two sets of footprints (one set barefoot) over the terrain. Unfortunately, the explanation of where the footprints went was so convoluted that people trying to follow a map would be totally confused by his explanations. I doubted his report was of any value in the trial. And no one seemed to be able to learn whether either Sanders or Carson wore shoes or were barefooted that day. The foot tracks could easily have been those of the many people who went to the farm to investigate for themselves. Worst of all, from my perspective, was that the so-called sheriff who had taken Sanders into custody was caught lying during the trial about what Sanders had said and about what he had said to Sanders.

"I don't get the impression that anyone knew what the hell they were doing," I said.

"Sure sounds that way."

"The only thing that seems to be consistent in all of it was that lack of evidence didn't seem to have been a matter of consideration for anyone other than Sanders' lawyers."

Jake had been yawning for a while though he was trying to stay focused. His cop brain was studying the story for more questions and clues. It seemed that he was determined to go on, but I had had enough. The grimaces and head shaking he had done through much of the discussion said he was horrified by everything about the way the case was handled.

I stood up and pulled him out of his chair saying, "Come on, Jake. Off to bed. We can talk about this another time."

His face was that of a little boy having just heard a scary story told around a campfire that blazed in the night. The boy was pretending not to be afraid of the dark. But he would be afraid when the bogeymen who lurked in the shadows came out of the woods or the closet or out from under his bed.

You need some rest."

"I need you more," he said, and laid his hand gently on my chest.

"I don't think you're up to that tonight."

Taking him by the hand, I could feel the pulse of his blood flowing against my palm and fingers, rhythmically adjusting to my own. We left the living room behind us to its shadows and silence as we made our way up the steps in the light of the moon fading behind a passing cloud. He fell asleep in my arms like dead Jesus in Michelangelo's "Pietà."

***

The first time I awakened, it was to pull my arm out from under Jake's weight on my bicep and shoulder where he had fallen asleep. As I lay there, feeling him next to me, listening to his breathing and exhalation, my brain played with the desire to be his empath, magically absorbing the work-related stress he was under, knowing I was already doing the best I could do with my all-too-human limitations. He was in a deep sleep, oblivious to the extrication of my arm and my lowering of his head to the pillow. Once I was free to move, I rolled to my side and put my hand on his chest, felt it rise and fall, and felt the pulsations of his heartbeat against my palm. I kissed the skin on his shoulder.

Sometime after that, I reawakened, realizing that I had rolled away from him, wondering why I was awake, why I felt so strangely alone even though Jake was beside me. There was a pleasant breeze-rustling-leaves sound coming from outside, calling me to it. I rose from the bed and looked out upon the maple, heard it speak in whispers against the window glass. I felt its eyes on me. This is that god that people talk about, I thought: a god I could love. Its only demand of me: patience as it recorded my existence to be held until all of its time runs out. There was holiness involved, and it lasted for several minutes.

The second time I woke up, I didn't get out of bed. I lay there, feeling my head filling with thoughts good and bad, hope and disappointment, successes and failures—rumination. The breathing and focusing exercises I had learned in therapy came to mind; for five minutes I tried, found it as annoying as I had remembered but soon, thereafter, fell asleep.

The third time I woke, I was on Jake's shoulder, and he was wiping my wet face.

"Are you alright?" he asked in a whisper.

"I must have had a bad dream," I said.

"You were crying."

"I was trying to protect us from something and couldn't do it. I'm sorry I woke you up. Go back to sleep. I'll be fine," I lied.

"I'll protect you."

"You can't," I wanted to say but didn't.

My free hand wiped the renewed wetness from my eyes, and then I waited to feel him slip beneath the skin of the night like a saturated leaf falling through the surface of a pond. I lay there looking up into the ceiling's darkness and the small gray blocks of light upon it made by the moonlight coming in from two sides of the house through old weather-worn windows. I tried to think of what I could say about why I had wept, what I couldn't remember of a dream now gone, or what I didn't want to remember that had slipped into my brain without naming itself, without showing its face, leaving behind it the feelings of whatever it had been, what I had done, not done, or had done to me

... so many potentials. And yet when I tried to think my way into answers, my thoughts were kaleidoscopic, shifting and reshaping. Rage, violence, anger, cruelty, images of my father, drunkenness, begging kindness of strangers, dead soldiers, dead cops, riots, dead people guilty of being black, hundreds of thousands of people railing against the sky, betrayals, petty bickering, pecking to death of wounded chicks, slaughter of hogs screaming to be saved from mass executions, the destruction of children, long nights, the stomping of a guitar, the stabbing of the knife, a childhood eaten by the obscenities of adults, thoughts of killing, thoughts of being killed, the effect of pills, the siren of the ambulance, Fascism, Capitalism, the earth and the air and the water. I covered my mouth and stifled the blurting horror of knowing there was little or nothing to do but weep for us all, let the tears run between my fingers and onto my chest until all that was left was the damp muddy remembrance of that which has been, and the need to face it all again and again until I die.

With my fist stuffed into my mouth, I tried to stop my desire to scream until consciousness eventually overtook the murderous spree of irregulated thought. Perhaps I should have just called it a dream, a bad dream, and pretended such things only happen in the night and that I could bear them. Perhaps I should have focused my energy on something positive like Jake's breathing, the soft sound that rode the air from his lungs into the room like a chant in a cathedral where I might be granted sanctuary.

Perhaps I slept again. I can't remember. But I was up long before Jake made his way down to the kitchen where I had made coffee. He poured himself a cup and came out onto the porch where I was sitting on the rocker sipping at my own cup, feeling the morning air on my naked skin. He sat beside me, laid his hand on my inner thigh and wished me a good morning.

"Are you alright?"

"I'm better now," I said.

"You want to talk about it?"

"No. I've suffered and survived the night. I don't want to go through it again."

13

"You up for the quarry today, Slick?" Apparently, that moniker was going to be sustained at least for a while. And I didn't mind. It sounded like a compliment coming out of Jake's mouth.

"Whenever you're ready!" I said enthusiastically. "I brought some insect repellant with me this time. You can keep your country swisher if you want, but I'm not going without using this bug stuff."

Jake smiled, and, though his head was held as if looking out into the horizon, I could see his eyes shift toward me sparkling with mischief, as he said, "I'll take some if you'll rub it on me."

When I came out of the house with the bottle, the liquid felt cool in my hand, but warmed as I spread it over him as I told him, I had never known anyone like him and how much I liked him, being with him, experiencing him.

"I feel the same about you, Slick. I'm not as good as you are about saying what I mean, but you make me feel good, make me feel alive ... like there's more to me than a job and a plot of land."

"Oh, man! There's so much more to you. So much more. And so much more for both of us to learn about."

"You mean the good, bad, and the ugly of me? The ugly might scare you off."

"We've all got ugly in us. It's just a matter of deciding to tame it, keep it caged, or let it out to destroy you." The words fell out too easily. Platitudinal. As though every ill is controlled by choice; as though each person decides moment by moment what responses will be in their best interests, in the interests of those around them, and for humankind as a whole, when a thousand times a day each of us acts out of anger or self-loathing, jealousy, hatreds bred into us by the lives we have lived up to each of those moments ... all without reflective consideration. No choice. Reaction. Reaction incomprehensible to those who live by it and fight the consequences that go with it. I thought about trying to retract my statement, but Jake had already moved on.

"Did the ugly get you last night?"

"It broke out of its cage, turned on me and attacked."

As I was saying it, I was caught off guard as a pang of shame passed through my body. A ghost perhaps reminding me that manly men don't cry or tell other men their fears ... all of clichés I and men like me have been force-fed about what a man *should* be. Typical of me, I started to apologize for being weak, being unable to conquer my emotions, but Jake cut me off.

"Rob, one of the things I like most about you is that you're *not* one of those guys who has to play macho games all of the time! I love that you feel life, that you don't keep your feelings on the back burner all of the time. Don't apologize to me for being who you are, man. Ever. I don't want to be with a phony. Let's agree to be ourselves, whatever that might be."

It felt good to hear the words, and I knew intellectually he was right, but then there were those goddamned feelings that come with the myths of culture that deny the intellect and reaffirm the predominant "truths" that culture imposes. In this case, intellect won, and I told Jake about the mishmash of thoughts I had as I tried to figure out how to deal with a world I didn't always understand, sometimes hated, and often feared. Through much of what I said, I could hear myself talking about the helplessness I sometimes feel, about myself as a man as a writer, and as a part of American culture negotiating the chaos of living.

As I went through the litany of the thoughts and feelings that led to my difficult night's sleep, I ended up saying, "I want to do or say something to make it all better. I find the world too ugly, lives too stupidly managed, good things ruined, and I get overwhelmed and just want to scream out: 'Just stop! Give me a fucking break!'"

"You too, huh? For whatever it's worth, you're not alone. I can't tell you the number of times I've laid awake at night feeling beaten up by the world. The things I see every day, the death and destruction I saw in the military, the ugliness of people hating people like us, or hating people who look different from them, or killing others so they can reach their delusions of power and wealth ... There are times when I'm sitting here in this house, and I let the rest of the world into my head. Sometimes I just want to do a primal scream or punch something that would take the hate out of the world. More than once, I've stepped outside and done it ... screamed, that is. It kept me from breaking my hand. Do what you've got to do with other people to get along in the world. Put on the masks you think you need to, Rob, but not with me, and I'll do the same with you. Okay?"

He was looking intently into my face, leaning toward me, radiating sincerity like hot sun, laying its copper and bronze and gold light on my skin. His eyes were the human equivalent of the feelings I had had during the night as I went to the window at my first awakening.

"You're good for my soul, Jake. More than you know."

"You're a writer. You have a gift to give. Not just to me, but to others when they read your work. Write it all! Tell the world what it needs to hear, man!"

"That's a heavy load to carry."

"You don't have to carry it all alone."

Feeling somewhat overwhelmed by his passion, I said, "You think I can write, or I have anything worthwhile to say, or I have a mammoth audience? You've never even read any of my stuff!"

When he shot back with an abrupt, "Actually, I have," he totally surprised me. I just looked at him, probably with my lower jaw hanging open like that of an old man who has lost the facial musculature to pull his chin up from the look of "duh" to the look of "I see!

"When we first met, I went to the library and got a librarian to help me figure out where your stuff was and how I could get my hands on it. I've read four or five short stories, one of your novels, and an article you wrote. Even I know how to use interlibrary loan, Slick. For a few bucks, I managed to get some of your things directly from the people who published them. Your stuff is good, and you say lots of things that I think are important ... I mean, I'm not a critic, but, you know, I think you're *really* good."

The words hit me like a jolt of electricity. I could feel my chest tighten with pride. When words found their way up from my lungs to my mouth, I asked, "When were you going to tell me you had read my stuff? I could have given you anything you wanted to read!"

He looked at me calmly and said, "I'm telling you now ... I think I waited because I was afraid of sounding dumb. I didn't want to sound like some groupie or one of those people who says, 'Wow! You're a writer—a celebrity' when they hadn't read or thought about your work or didn't know what they were talking about or were just talking out of some half-assed sense of obligation to you or just trying to be polite—or, at least, what they think is polite ... all the things you complained about in that essay you did for that journal, uh ..."

Woodruff, I filled in.

"You say stuff that matters, Rob." Then he went on to talk to me about the stories he had read—which of them he liked best and why. And I marveled at his ability to see beyond the words to the ideas and to remember details. Other than David and Gus's feedback at Christmas, it had been a long time since anyone had given me the kind of feedback that suggested my work had the depth I worked so hard to create. He had actually read like the reader I tried to write for: intelligence, ability to pick up on nuance, ability to hold ideas from one page to the next; and ability to piece the parts into a whole as a reading experience that broke through the boundaries of book covers, binding, print, stitching and glue.

Listening to him talk about my work felt intimate like making love. I didn't want it to stop. But even love making has to stop at some point if for no other reason than to recuperate for a few moments before beginning anew. In this instance, I had become conscious that we had talked about me for a long time. That was not the way the world was supposed to work according to the warning signals emanating from my brain. From somewhere out of my past, I heard the words, "selfish," "it's not all about you," and "get over yourself" ... in other words, try playing the selfless, kindly priest who keeps secrets, including his own. After a moment's pause, I asked Jake how he had come to be such a sharp reader. Unlike any image I had ever had of him, he looked at me with dead-serious cold eyes and said dramatically as if entering into a serious argument, "What? You think because I'm a cop I didn't go to college? I'm stupid? You think I've just spent my life eating donuts?"

My first reaction was one of surprise and confusion. I stuttered through a response: "I didn't mean to piss you off."

Images of his diplomas hung on his bedroom walls raced through my brain; he must have known I had seen them. I had never questioned his intelligence; it had never been an issue from the first few moments I talked with him at the beginning of this adventure we were having. When he saw my look of embarrassment for what I assumed was my haphazard encroachment on his feelings, his lip quivered and gave way to his playful smile like a fine actor playing Lear and coming off stage after the fifth act making a Jerry Lewis funny face at the stage crew before returning to take his bow. He put his arms around me and hugged me tight.

"I read a lot!" He laughed. Had you there for a minute though, didn't I?"

"Remind me never to piss you off for real," I responded. In an attempt to buy time to adjust to the shift in humors, I tried to duplicate his dramatic performance, trying to sound abrupt and angry, "So, why the hell do you have me doing all this work on the Sanders case, Mister Reads-a-Lot?" I couldn't sustain the tone and laughed before I finished the line. But he wasn't laughing.

"As a kid, I spent some time being afraid of Nathan Sanders; imagined his ghost walking around on our land looking for the people who killed him. I think I knew that I was being ridiculous, but that didn't stop the feeling that something of him was waiting for me." My dad told me the basics—everybody around here knew the story—but I always felt like he knew something about it he wouldn't tell. Carried whatever it was to his grave. Maybe he thought I was better off not knowing."

"Did you ever try to do any real research into it?"

"Yeah, I did. Didn't get far. Just couldn't figure out how to get at whatever might be out there. After a while I started feeling like local history is more difficult than digging up ancient history."

He went on to tell me about his frustration with trying to find records in the university and public libraries and at the local community history center. When he asked at the courthouse about records, no one seemed to know where they might be kept and who could help him, and he didn't have the knowledge he needed about how to research specialized resources like genealogical records and newspaper collections. My suspicion was that, like most people, he found the time commitment and hassles to be more than he could deal with.

"Sounds kind of lame," he said. "I guess you are the research I did best."

"And don't you ever forget it, buddy," I joked. "But we still don't know much of anything for sure. I've still got a lot to do to make my way through the court records. There will be lots to talk about, but I want to remind you that, in the end, we might not be any closer to the truth than we were when we started."

"You're right. I know that up here," he pointed to his head. "But something in here" (pointing to the space at the bottom of his rib cage) "says something's there to learn." Sometimes I feel like Nathan's a part of who I am, who my father was, who my great grandfathers were."

"From what I'm seeing, you're nothing like him or the people who would join a lynch mob and hang a man. I'm just not seeing how you are connecting with this other than that you know a piece of it took place on the land you now own, and your dad made you afraid of something that had nothing to do with you."

After a brief hesitation, he said, "Maybe what I really want is to know my dad. Whatever he knew ate at him."

He explained that his father had often made vague references to Sanders and the Trent Murders, but when he—Jake—began asking questions, his father refused to explain other than to say, "It don't matter no more."

"Insisting that something doesn't matter, but constantly referring to it, tells me it mattered," Jake said as if analyzing a crime case. "So, he set me up to know there's a mystery and gave me nothing to go on but his unhappy life and 'It don't matter no more.' My father was the son of an unhappy and secretive man, who was probably the son of an unhappy man, or at least that's the image my mother put into my head. I guess I'd like to let my dad rest in peace, like killing the ghosts of whatever happened way back then would somehow do it. But, when it's all said and done, I don't know if that would have made any difference to him, even if I had managed to figure it all out before he died."

"Do you think your family was involved in the lynching?"

"I guess I think maybe they were connected somehow, but ..."

"And if they were, would that make a difference in who you are?"

"Probably not, but it feels a little creepy to me."

"Before you ask," I said, "the articles about the lynching don't give any names or details about anyone at the scene of the lynching other than Sanders. Somebody unnamed who had been at the hanging fed the reporters some details about Sanders' placid acceptance of his fate, his denial of responsibility, the reaction of his body as the noose broke his neck. Hell, the editors and reporters might have been in the mob for all I know. Chances of getting names would be nearly impossible."

My fingers interlaced with his as I told him I would stand between him and the ghosts as best I could, "But ghosts can't be killed, my friend; they can only be made impotent." Where that bit of wisdom came from in my brain, I had no idea, and it sounded humorously pontifical coming out of my mouth, causing me to blush and him to laugh.

"Impotent apparitions," he said.

"Important impotence," I countered.

After a few moments, Jake said, "I want to know more about you, Rob."

"You mean my life story?"

"How about telling me what happened that had made you afraid of me at first."

I told him the story of growing up with an alcoholic father, coming to terms with being gay, my fears and insecurities, the work I had done to get past the trauma of my childhood and how the arts saved me, writing in particular. I told him of Matt, how I had loved him, the unexpected shock and self-destruction I experienced, the struggles I went through to restore my desire to live, and how I had come to Emberland to escape that self I had become in Chicago.

"The world's a god damned lonely place, Jake, when you feel like you don't have anyone to turn to." My statement called up the images of being a teenager and lying in bed listening to my parents arguing about my father's drinking. I had become accustomed to readying myself to intervene, take over as the parent in the situation when the loud battle of words shifted to physical combat. I remember wishing I'd been born to someone else. The world is a lonely place ... the words reminded me of the aftermath of Matt's declaration of independence.

"You've got that straight," Jake said softly, empathetically. "We share that part of your experience—the loneliness, the feeling that making it on your own would be better than living with the family you're stuck with." He took my hand, held it, squeezed it gently as I responded.

"I grew up feeling disconnected ... like I didn't belong anywhere. Didn't fit in with other human beings. Still do sometimes." It sounded strange to my ear to say the words in a setting that wasn't a therapist's office. More real.

"You didn't deserve that life," he said, his compassion coming not only from his words, but his body and his mind, everything that was him invested in the moment, in listening to understand me. Unlike so many people, he didn't spend time looking for the moment to take control of the discussion, didn't leap in to make it about himself. He waited for me to finish, waited for me to ask him about his own struggles to find himself.

Apparently, his upbringing wasn't particularly great either. He shared that his mother was heavily into control and was severe in handing out punishment. Initially, he gave information out in a matter-of-fact voice like laying facts in a row. His interpretation was that his mother hated men, both him and his father. Because he was male, he was expected to spend much of his time working with his father or doing chores his mother wanted done; there was little room for play or pleasure. His father was quiet, even secretive; interactions with Jake were largely task-oriented—getting the job done. As Jake shifted his explanation from his mother to his father, I heard a slight shift of tone. . . sad maybe ... disappointed ... as if he could see his father's face, felt the suffering of the man who lost himself—his hopes and dreams—for the woman he married. As he neared the end of his story, Jake's face was pained, the reflecting difficult.

Touching him, wanting to be consoling, I said, "It must have been difficult for you; doesn't sound like there was much to be happy about." After a pause, in an attempt to lighten the tone a bit, I said, "You seem pretty well-adjusted for having come out of that kind of parenting."

Attempting to rise to the uptick in the conversation, Jake responded with "I think it was school that saved me—the interactions with a few teachers who treated me like a person capable of thought. You know, most kids think that whatever their parents do and how the family gets along is normal. For whatever reason, early on, I figured out that my normal was not normal. It was just what I was given, and I learned early on to expect little to nothing from my parents. So, I guess I just decided to hang out and put up with them until I was old enough to walk away. They knew nothing about me really. I told them only what I had to and never asked anything of them. What's the point when you know what the answers are before you ask?"

14

By the time Jake and I had another day together, I had gathered a great deal of information from my readings of court records. Unfortunately, I waited to tell him about it until we were leaving the house to make the trek to the quarry. The questions started almost immediately.

"How about we wait until I'm not worrying about falling on my ass after tripping over the weed clumps and stones and crap along the path? I promise I'll give you everything I've got once we get past walking!"

"Got you, Slick! Can't talk and walk at the same time," he teased.

"Yeah. Can't chew gum and walk at the same time either! Guess I'm just not very bright."

We walked largely in silence except for an occasional stop to sip the whiskey or water or to rest my city slicker legs, which gave Jake many opportunities to amuse himself with making comments about my stamina—or lack thereof. Sometimes, he just stopped, walked up to me, touched me, or hugged me... often without words, and then turned and set off again in the direction of the quarry.

As we neared, and as though he knew I had wanted to go there, Jake took a turn off the trail and led me to the 'hanging tree' where we stood under the elbow-bend of the infamous limb. Jake did a 180-degree sweep of the area with his body, making a gesture with his hand to reinforce the power of his gaze.

"My dad told me he believed Nathan was buried somewhere around here, but he didn't know where. I've always wondered if maybe I wasn't walking right on top of him."

"I always thought a mob leaves a body hanging as a warning to others."

"Me too, but who knows? When I was a kid, I thought Nathan might come out of the grave and chase me if I ever stepped on him. Funny, when you think about it! Though I didn't know it for a long time, I must have stepped on him at some point because he's been chasing me for a while. Can't seem to escape him."

It occurred to me as Jake told me of his childhood fears that Faulkner would have had a field day with the Trent Murders story if it had happened somewhere in the South. Add in a family curse or a tragic flaw, and layer upon layer of complexity; after that, the only thing missing would be some miscegenation and the unrelenting waiting of Black folks for their time of freedom to come sometime in the far distant future. Hemingway, on the other hand, would have everybody get drunk, wallow in some decadence, talk about it before getting into some kind of brawl, and then move the characters to another country and rotate eternally through them as war booms in the background and meaning hides in the spaces between words where profound loneliness lingers. Henry James would still be describing the wallpaper in the kitchen two-hundred pages into the story. I just let Jake talk when he wished and interjected my "hmms" and "yeahs?" and chuckles and the many other verbal and non-verbal markers I could pull out of myself to say in shorthand, "I'm with you, man! Keep talking! I want to understand who you are!"—things people say to one another to touch one another's skin, love them, with the vibrations emanating from their throats.

"Of course," Jake said, "he might have been buried somewhere else, and the stories my dad told me were just stuff that was told to him by his parents or grandparents or other people who pass stories along. How would you ever know where it might be after all these years even if it is out here somewhere? It's not like somebody put a marker on it. But it could be true. I doubt the lynch mob would have taken time to cart him far away. When I was still a kid, I walked all over this ground around the tree trying to find something that might give me a clue. Don't know what I was going to do if I did find it."

In that pause that happens in human interchanges— his pause—I knew it was time for me to give him something more than my repertoire of listening cues: "Sometimes it's all about doing the finding, and you don't have to do anything with what you found except say you found it. It's kind of like writing a story. There's something you want to say, something that makes it worth writing but you don't know what it is until you write it. And once you've found it, you know you're done with it. And if you don't find it, you have to put the story in a drawer and hope you'll find it somewhere in the future when you've honed your skills more and trained your brain to see things you couldn't see back when you first started to write."

"This one's been in the drawer for a long time," he said.

We looked up into the tree as if it would somehow make sense of what Jake and I had said beneath it and would deliver a proclamation about the meaning of it all. However, like time, it merely took in our existence and ignored the rest of my attempts to imbue it with power it didn't have. In the awkward moment of the silence that comes after destroying a metaphor, I mentioned ground penetrating radar and aerial mapping that I had read about somewhere and the possibility of locating where Nathan was after all these years, assuming, of course, that his remains hadn't been accounted for by someone long before us, moved, or never buried here in the first place. And we both came around to the idea that wherever Sanders's bones lay, it didn't help us know anything more about him than where he lay. Interesting. Challenging. But not essential.

I had stopped thinking about the potential value of writing about Sanders' case other than Jake wanted to know the truth and I had found pleasure in writing about him and writing about the quest for truth. I had concluded that the story wasn't just about justice as he had originally suggested back when I first met him. It was about his sense of connection to the world. If it had been purely about justice for Nathan Sanders, we already knew there probably wasn't going to be any. If it had been about justice in the larger sense, there were, undoubtedly, contemporary cases that could more easily and readily be used to make the case that justice isn't always fair. But there was something in Jake that needed this story, this part of history that walked this land he had known all his life, invaded his thoughts, crying like an inconsolable child within him and I wanted to somehow be a part of helping him find whatever it was he was looking for.

As we walked away, leaving the tree and its prolific foliage behind us in the sun that was eating the diminishing limb and leaf shadows—the gallows—splayed on the ground around its braces, side by side, we talked. oblivious of the heat, immunized against dive-bombing pests, and lost in the thicket of memories and recollections of what we were learning about Nathan Sanders and the Trent murders.

"The lawman," I said, " ... can't remember his name ... who nabbed Nathan, got him to tell the story a couple hours after Nathan was dragged out of a saloon "drunk as a skunk" according to a story I read. That's important, I think. Nathan later said that he told the lawman 'the truth,' because, now get this: he was told that, if he did, he could get out of jail and go home. If that's true, sounds like coercion to me. Once he told it—the so-called 'truth', that is—he was smart enough to know that he would have to stick to it, no matter what."

"So, the lawman played him ... but I don't know if that was okay to do back then," Jake inserted with a boyish enthusiasm.

"Apparently not," I said. "At trial, the officer dodged the attorney who was trying to pin him down for making false promises. The cop denied that he made any; but then he was caught in lies about other parts of his testimony."

With a bit of anger behind the words, Jake blurted, "I hope they nailed his ass."

"The cop's ass?"

"Yeah. I hate crooked cops." He was eager to remind me that he was dealing with one, suspected some others on the force. Realizing that he had stopped the flow of the story, he said almost apologetically, "Sorry ... at any rate, go on with what you've got." As he spoke, I felt myself taking in his reactions with pleasure, as though his reactions were my own.

Smiling at him, I went on and talked of the many contradictions I had found. According to some articles, Nathan was out drinking in the evening of the murders. Another one claimed that Nathan went to his parents' house. Supposedly all his family members were asleep when he got there. He took his clothes off and hung them up on a nail on the wall. Then he crawled into bed and slept all night. He woke up the next day, got into some other clothes and went out and chopped some wood for his mother.

"Wait. He left his clothes—possibly blood stained— hanging on the wall?"

Feeling like I had a key to his solving the case, I took pleasure in being able to feed him information and being able to call up explanations. "Cops found them still hanging there two days after he'd been arrested."

"Blood stained?"

"They thought they saw some stain, but not much."

"If he hadn't changed his clothes, wouldn't somebody have noticed some blood or figured out that his pants were wet from trying to wash the blood off?" Jake asked.

Trying to hang onto the threads of the story and respond to the interruptions, I found myself struggling to answer my own internal question: "Now, where was I?"

"Next morning—day after the murders—he was reportedly being a 'good son' and helping his mother with chores around the farm." According to the stories and testimony I had read Nathan supposedly had something to eat, and then, a little later, went into town where he was paying cash at the bar and buying drinks for himself and his buddies. "Now, the rest of what I'm going to tell you about how he got caught is kind of pieced together between what Nathan said, what the lawman said, and what the newspapers said they said and what some of the bar crowd told the reporters." Pulling together fragments of the many versions, I explained that somewhere in the midst of the drinking and carrying on, Nathan took a time out to go down to the general store where he bought some bullets for his pistol that he apparently always carried in his pocket. He put some bullets in the gun and then went back to the bar and got into a fight with one of the men there. He pulled the gun but didn't fire it. Somebody ran and got the lawman to come in, take Nathan's gun away, and take him out of the bar. Another story had it that he just put the gun back in his pocket and walked outside and started talking to the cop. "Either way... he was totally wasted by this time ... he started talking about the murders and what a terrible thing it was." The lawman was supposedly surprised at Nathan knowing about the killings since he, the lawman, had only just learned about them a short time before being called to the saloon.

At that moment in the story I was telling, I expected an interruption, a barrage of questions that didn't come, took a pause to look at Jake's face and see the processing going on there. When he noticed that I wasn't moving forward, he laughed and told me what I already knew: he was listening for clues. I chuckled.

"What?" he asked innocently.

"Nothing. I like looking at you." And then I went on.

Jake leaned forward as I told him that sometime that day, according to the newspapers, Everett Parsons's wife, a neighbor of the Trents, was trying to find out where her husband was and why he hadn't come home the previous night. "Why she waited so long is anyone's guess," I interjected in anticipation of the question I expected from Jake. Sometime in the afternoon, the wife sent her fifteen-year-old son up to the farm to see if he was at the farm or to ask the widow what she knew; the boy found Mrs. Trent's body outside the house. Newspapers said he didn't look any further, just ran back home, told his mother, and was sent into town to find a lawman while she went to other neighbors to find men who would go up to the farm with her. Nobody in town could have known about a murder until the "little" boy—as newspaper reporters referred to him—came into town yelling for help only an hour or so prior to Nathan's arrest. One officer got saddled up and went back with the boy, another—the one who later arrested Sanders—stayed behind.

"Do you have their names?" Jake asked like a good editor or a good cop trying to be as clear as possible about the details. I laughed and told him I thought I had done well to tell the story line and he would have to wait for details.

"The officer—the one who stayed in town ... whatever his name was—obviously was kind of like you at first. He wanted to know how Nathan knew about the murders already." The drunken suspect told the cop that somebody at the saloon told him. Later, the lawman claimed to have taken note of what Nathan said in his drunken state, and he (Nathan) was saying murders (plural) and how 'awful' they were. "What I find interesting is that the lawman never disclosed all these recollections about what Nathan supposedly said and how he said it until a year later at Nathan's trial when he claimed to remember it all word for word." As I said it, I realized that I too was looking for clues and trying to impress Jake with my sleuthing. As I looked at him, he had a cheshire cat smile on his face.

When I returned to the narrative, I covered what I had gleaned from the newspapers about the interactions of the lawman and his prisoner. When the lawman checked

Nathan's pockets at the courthouse, he found a box of bullets and a wad of cash ... eleven dollars (a five with what
looked like a blood stain on it and six ones) all of which he
turned into the court's clerk. The cop asked Nathan where
he got the money for all the alcohol he had been drinking.
"Obviously, eleven dollars seemed to the officer a huge
amount of money for a non-working, drunk, street bum in
1873." Nathan mumbled something about having some
cash hidden away in his bedroom that he had been saving
to move away from the area. One of his claims was that he
and another guy were planning to go out west somewhere
to live. The officer asked Nathan who the man was that
Nathan was going to run away with, and Nathan said it
was Alf Carson. From the way all of this was reported, it
seemed pretty obvious that the lawman figured he already
had at least one guilty party in hand and could guess who
another guilty party might be.

"Did they find any more money at his house?"

Trying to sound like an attorney, I responded with "No
corroborating evidence, Detective ... at least none that the
papers I read reported. I couldn't find any mention of it in
the court records I gone through so far."

I tried to describe the confusion of co-occurring stories
of Sanders being tossed into a cell to sleep off his drunkenness so that he could be interrogated more effectively
later, while simultaneously other people reported that the
officer got a confession from Sanders before he let him go
to sleep.

At some point, the lawman set out to see the murder scene for himself. Before he could get saddled up, people had been going out to the widow's farm 'by the wagon loads' for at least half an hour ... or so the papers said; it seemed to me it would have taken longer than that to deal with Sanders, get him in jail, get his testimony, saddle up, etc. When he—the lawman—arrived at the farm (whatever happened to the first lawman who went out ahead of him wasn't reported) ... the towns people who went out 'by the wagon loads' had already found the three bodies. They had walked all over any readable footprints that might have been present. They had shifted the corpses to get a better look at the gruesome destruction. They had tramped through the Trent house as they played amateur detectives.

"It doesn't surprise me," Jake said with some annoyance within his voice. "People aren't any different now. So goddamned stupid about crime scenes. They get some kind of pleasure out of being first to see the blood and gore: the more gruesome it is, the more people want to see it. Others seem to think that they've got special insights for finding clues that us stupid cops wouldn't look for. Sounds like a real mess for anybody to sort out, even a really good detective."

"It gets worse," I said.

I told Jake about the two doctors who were summoned to look at the bodies before they could be taken away for burial. They found that Everett Parsons had been in a brutal fight before he died and had been seriously injured by what looked like a corn knife cut across his brow before he was shot in the head. Margaret Trent was hit with such force multiple times that the back of her skull was shattered, and her body had been beaten as well. Then they found that the girl had been 'violated.' Some of the pseudo detectives amongst the crowd decided that at least two people had to have done the crimes, that no one person could have managed killing all three and raping the girl. They informed the lawman of their opinion, and he concurred, having no evidence whatsoever other than he believed it, and he believed he already knew who the two were. Meanwhile, others were so enraged by the rape of the girl to begin demanding somebody pay with getting lynched.

The day after Sanders' arrest, Alf Carson was found and brought to the jail. He had been told he was there under suspicion of murder, and he was furiously protesting and proclaiming his innocence. When he saw Nathan in a nearby cell, he screamed at him and asked him why he had accused him of such a thing and proclaimed his innocence.

In the meantime, word got out that Nathan and Alf were suspects, and talk of lynching was out in the open, loud, and insistent. Fueled by alcohol, a mob formed. "Probably lots of bravado. Each man in the group thinking himself 'the manliest of men', the rightful protagonist of a story of 'good destroying evil.'" Apparently, the lawmen picked up on the growing anger and decided to cart the two men off on a train to a jail in Lancaster thirty miles north of the town and left them there for a week until tempers cooled down a bit. Then, they brought them back for a preliminary trial. "And that's where Nathan Sanders learned how he had screwed himself with his story!"

Jake was a buzzsaw chewing question after question and talking about all the holes in the reporting and things he wished he could find out about. I couldn't keep up with him, couldn't provide him with the specifics he wanted—specifics I wished I had—as I realized we were both now on a quest to make sense of a senseless crime. We reviewed what I had shared up to that point, went back and forth with our perceptions and with theories based on experiences Jake had had as a law officer. We were still talking about it as we floated on the quarry's cool water in the afternoon sunshine.

After a pause, Jake spoke decidedly as if his thought could reach back in time and resolve at least something about the case, "So, what I get out of what you've been saying is that it was going to be almost impossible to get a guilty verdict against the kid if he had kept his mouth shut. It's probably also true that the most he could get was a reprimand for not doing anything to help the people that Alf Carson supposedly killed."

It was supposition based on flawed source material, but it was all we had and it matched my own perceptions. As I thought about what he had to say, I realized that Jake's intensity was based in a genuine desire for truth. Though I too would have liked finding that truth, my own growing enthusiasm was based in him, his ability to look at an injustice and believe that it could never be too late to at least try to understand the motivations of people and give them a fair and unbiased hearing. My own truth was based in providing him what could be known one hundred and fifty years after the event based on the remnants to be studied and use my skills in parsing written language and making sense or declaring nonsense of it and recognizing how much nonsense lay behind the supposition

As if it needed saying, I reminded him that I wasn't an attorney and that he knew more about the law than I did, but my guess was that with the lack of tools they had back then to get around some of the destruction of evidence, Sanders would have been likely to get off if he had just kept his mouth shut, denied everything and hadn't tried to set his buddy up as the perpetrator of the crime. Based on my research, Sanders wasn't what anybody would call 'real sharp.' It struck me as sad that the reporting of the case suggested that he thought he was, and if he could tell a story that he could stick to, he could somehow convince people he would be set free. It seems he believed that right up to the point where vigilantes pulled him out of the jail.

"But, you know, Jake, I can't help but wonder if maybe his version of the story wasn't the real story, crazy as it must have sounded back then. He never admitted to committing the crime to anyone as far as I know. The newspapers said people who were at the hanging claimed he refused to admit the 'truth' that he did the work of killing and insisted it was Carson who was responsible."

Ever listening for clues, Jake jumped on my statement with "I'd like to know how people knew what happened at the hanging. Somebody was there and reported it and yet,

I haven't heard you say that anyone in the mob was ever named. Somebody covered for whoever did the telling."

We had talked for a long time, and even in that, I had slid over top of the endlessly contradictory or outlandish details the papers were pumping out, the intricacies of conversations and postulations, the names of the people involved, pieces of so-called evidence that I'd read about but couldn't put into any kind of clear narrative about who found the other bodies, who moved them, or when they were found. It was a lot to take in and depressing as hell. I needed time away from Nathan Sanders, the Trents, and Mr. Parsons.

It wasn't them I had come to the quarry for. I had come for Jake, for the us we were becoming; I had come to help him relax and to be relaxed and to take in the here and the now of our shared existence in that place—that Eden—to enjoy our time together while we could before it would be taken from us by the demands of our lives for food and sleep and work. We agreed to release ourselves temporarily from the responsibility of that so-long-ago-time and the intricacies involved in the case. We spent the next two hours determinedly avoiding talk of the world we would inevitably return to. We frolicked like schoolboys, laughed like fools, pretended to be innocents like creatures of the wild for whom the only moment is now ... all "was" and "will be" removed from our consciousness. We did not verbalize those things that could not be put aside by men. We ignored them, consciously left them preying in the shadows, waiting for our return to a dangerous world.

When we got back to the house, dusk was pulling shadows up under its chin. We were hungry. Together, we made salads, steaks, and baked potatoes layered with butter, sour cream, and a good dose of pepper; and we ate like ranch hands after a hard day's work. After dinner, we washed the dishes, cleaned up the kitchen, and were ready to move to the living room when Jake's phone rang.

"It's the dispatcher," he said as he pressed the button. He listened for a few moments, said, "Okay, I understand," and pressed the stop button.

"Seems they're down a cop again. Somebody couldn't show up for some reason, and I'm going to have to go in at least until the bars close and we've made sure there isn't any after-hours stupidity. I'm sorry, Rob."

My mother's voice came into my head for a split-second belittling my father for not taking enough interest in her and us and always trying to get away from his responsibilities, making excuses to escape. The thought flickered in and out of my brain just long enough to trigger some shift in my face that Jake immediately picked up on as if I had screamed it at him.

"I'm really sorry, man. You're welcome to stay here. Or if you want to go back to your place, I can come there when I get off work."

Neither choice was great from my standpoint, but he didn't need stress coming from me. He wasn't my father escaping my mother, and I wasn't a child.

"Shit happens!" I pulled my face into a probably-phony-looking-grin. "I hate that you've had to work so many hours. You need rest, man!" Then, I told him I'd decide about where I was going to sleep by the time he was ready to leave. I followed him upstairs so I could talk while he transformed himself from the playful boy-like man I had spent the day with into my version of him as superman disguised as a police officer.

As I watched him hurriedly remove his clothes and slip into his uniform, he told me that one of the other police officers called in sick. "Only got two experienced cops, George Ballard and Mickey Etcher, out there tonight with a couple of newbies, and let's just say, that none of them is what anyone would call a 'ball of fire' when it comes to handling the drunks if they get out of control."

"You need a break, Jake! Couldn't they find somebody else?"

"Captain has called in the University Police, but that's about as helpful as calling in the Girl Scouts."

As he was slipping on his shoes and mechanically tying the laces, he looked up at me and smiled. "Like I told you, we're really short-staffed right now. I appreciate you worrying about me. I really do! I haven't had anybody worry about me for a long time. I'm careful when I'm out there and pretty good at my job. All of the guys on vacation will be back over the next few weeks, then I can take some time off. I'm sorry, but I've got to go."

He pulled out his keys, unlocked his top dresser drawer, and removed his gun and placed it in his holster. "What do you want to do, Rob? Stay? Or go home?"

"Stay," I said emphatically. He came up to me, wrapped his arms around me, and pulled me into him, squeezing me uncomfortably against all the hardware he wore, and whispered in my ear, "I'm loving being with you." And then he turned and walked quickly to the stairwell and made his way down to the living room, through the kitchen, and out of the house as I tailed him uselessly all the way out onto the porch, not knowing what to do but say, "Be safe." I stood under the porchlight looking out into the blackness that had swallowed him until the engine of his pick-up growled into action. Headlights awakened like cat's eyes against the barn wall, then glared at the barn as he began backing out. Gravel spun noisily away from the tires like popping corn as he revved the engine to gain speed. Jake made a hard turn in front of me as if to force the slight skid to say goodbye. In seconds, the truck found the lane, its rear red lights fading fast and, finally, disappearing behind the trees and dragging all sound away from my ears.

Many levels of lonesome splattered themselves on me like mud thrown from the heels of a man running in the rain a few feet in front of me. After a moment, I stepped back into the house and took in, almost as if for the first time, the space that was Jake's, felt his presence as I walked from room to room and wished he would manifest from out of a corner and break the devastating silence.

***

Being in Jake's house alone made me think of what had brought us together, all that I had learned about the Trent murders through the research I had done, and the frustrations I experienced with the confusion available materials created for me. As if speaking to Jake, I thought about the reality that *the* "truth" could not yet be written; but a coherent story as a creative act could become a truth onto itself.

Before writing I made notes at the top of my laptop screen: Nathan Sanders = Jimmy Chambers; Alf Carson = Mike Larson, Rosie and Grace Trent = Molly and Margaret Taylor. Below this, I wrote, "Names have been changed to protect the innocent" – a fun, but silly thought considering all concerned were long dead. I wrote for a long time:

Jimmy Chambers had once been a sweet little boy, the youngest of three siblings, the only male born to David and Mary Chambers. He grew up alongside his older sisters in the ramshackle home his parents provided on the hilly and rocky farmland they owned in Bethlehem, Ohio, a hamlet a mile and a half outside of Emberland.

His father had always been an old man, feeble, sickly, often unable to work. He was not old in the sense of age, but in spirit; the wounds he had received in the Civil War, the sickness he had endured in a deep-South prison camp, and the horrors he saw on the battlefield ... they had stolen the man-fire from him, made him overly reliant on Nathan's mother and his children.

Mary adored her little boy. She tried to teach him manners, encouraged him to work hard in school, and make something of his life. But she also worried about him, his strange behaviors that showed themselves shortly after he started attending the schoolhouse in their little community.

The teacher made the trek to the Chambers' farm on several occasions to complain that Jimmy would get up in the middle of lessons, walk out the door, and go sit in the nearby woods where he would talk to himself as he pushed dry leaves around with his hands and the scissor actions of his legs. The teacher could see him through the window, watch him, and finally stop class, open the door and call for him to come back in. He ignored her; so, she sent older and bigger boys out to drag him back inside. No amount of paddling him changed his behaviors. He seemed to be oblivious to the pain she inflicted, just bent over her desk and took it while the other children looked on.

When it came to learning how to read and write, Jimmy tried at first, became easily frustrated and insisted he couldn't do it. After a while, he stopped trying altogether and his teacher did too. Mary had scolded the boy, tried to work with him at home, only to find that she was getting the same responses as the teacher got. After a while, it seemed pointless to send him where he was a constant disruption. She decided her boy would just have to learn to be a farmhand or a day laborer of some kind ... whatever he chose as long as he chose to be a good and honest man. When he could work, David made Jimmy work beside him and tried to teach him about farming, farm tools, farm animals, seasons for planting and harvesting, and about what men must know.

By the time Jimmy was fourteen, he was already a very handsome boy: strikingly handsome. His almost coal-black hair capped his suntanned face, deep-set dark-brown-almost-black eyes—bedroom eyes—beneath pronounced man-like brows. He had perfect, shiny, boy-skin-fleshed cheekbones, jaws and chin that were sprouting the first stubble of manhood beneath his slightly-thicker-than-normal lips—the kind of lips that would make a lover crave them constantly. His was the chiseled body carved out of the hard work he was doing to help his father who could not do the farm work for himself. There was no denying that he was a beautiful young man to look at. What was going on inside him, however, was not so beautiful.

At sixteen, Jimmy came to terms with the things that would shape the remainder of his short life: his body was powerful and could be used to intimidate others; alcohol gave him freedom to escape the rigid structure of being a farmhand; women provided pleasure like nothing else he had ever experienced prior to his first sexual encounter; and working at hard labor was not something he intended to do any longer. Alcohol gave him the courage to make the decisions that pleased him and provided him with a sense of belonging amongst his rough and tumble friends—comradery, something he obviously needed and couldn't get enough of to make up for his years of self-exile. He aligned with a cadre of young men who were also making alcohol the connection to all kinds of excitement and mischief: fights, gunplay, taking on the town whores. Jimmy quickly dominated and became the captain among them, fighting and destroying anyone who challenged him for the position.

By the age of eighteen, Jimmy had become one of the town's problems: a drunk, a gambler, a bully, and a nuisance, and he was no longer controllable in any way by his parents. He had learned how to turn on charm when it suited him and how to turn it off when he got what he wanted; that included interacting with his mother, for whom he would occasionally assist by doing a small chore that didn't require much time commitment and would often ignore when she tried to talk to him about how he was spending his life amongst a "bad element."

When he first met Mike Larson, Jimmy found the brother he never had, another male who could be intimate with him, who could share in his activities, who could sleep beside him in a hay mow and be trusted never to share his secrets with the world outside of them.

I had been writing for several hours, busily revising and rewriting paragraphs as I went, making up facts to cover the holes in the real story. It was late and I had begun losing my ability to focus. My mind started wandering, drifting ahead of where I was in the story. Pleased with what I had written, I knew it was time to stop and be glad I had put words on paper—impressions—all of which could be far from the "truth" I was trying to help Jake find. And that was okay. I had something to cling to, add to, play with as I wished, and most importantly, I had a clear idea of what was coming next in the story, something to begin with the next day or whenever I might return to it.

I had had enough writing for one day, but I wasn't ready to sleep, kept wondering when Jake would return, stared at my cellphone thinking somehow it would tell me what to do next. It didn't. Scrolling through the internet on my small phone window, I suddenly had a desire to look once again at images of Julian Morris and try to figure out what Jake—who had now mentioned the resemblance a couple of times—saw in my face and body that I couldn't see. Yes, I kept a short beard like some of his images, still had good hair ... maybe it was the brown/green of his eyes, the same color as mine. I liked the kinship of our eyes, felt they were our best features: thoughtful and caring with a bit of a saggy ripple beneath them that carried sadness within them. Morris's pupils counterbalanced that sadness by radiating a rich imagination and intelligence I could only hope mine equaled. My lips were straight like his, not too full, but whether or not they met the test of sensuousness like his, I couldn't guess with any objectivity. What connected for me was not so much that I might somehow resemble Julian Morris—though that would be great if it were true—but that I felt, based on nothing other than my looking at his image, like we (Julian and I) shared a knowing about the world that showed in our faces. Whether that was what Jake saw, I didn't know. Whatever it was that Jake might have perceived beyond that, I couldn't see for myself, but the more I stared at the actor's image, the more flattered I was. Julian was a good looking man.

When I grew tired of looking at the cellphone images, checking messages, reading email, and anything else that distracted me for a while, I turned it off and went to Jake's book collection and pulled down one of my favorite novels and began to read, certain that at any moment Jake's truck would come up the drive scattering crushed stone in its wake. Somewhere in my attempts to focus, I fell asleep.

A Farewell to Arms fell off my lap. Fell flat on the floor with a bang. A bullet leaving no pain. No blood. Just an exaggerated pulsing within my chest as I oriented myself to the room. It was after 3 a.m. I got up and went to the kitchen door, stepped out under the porch light thinking somehow my doing so would bring Jake home. But there was only the great darkness beyond me extending into forever.

I was too tired to think I was going to be able to stay awake any longer. When I had stumbled my way to the side of the bed, I slipped out of my clothes—dropping them to the floor like peanut shells in a steakhouse franchise—climbed in and put the side of my face on Jake's pillow, and hoped he would awaken me when he came in. And then I slept holding that hope tight against my torso. Little did I know then that I wouldn't see Jake again until he was released from the hospital.

15

When Jake hadn't come home by the time I awakened, I tried to call him, left a message on his cell phone, sat outside on the porch staring into the morning over coffee, hoping for a return call that didn't come. After an hour, I had had enough of waiting. Dressed. Drove into town not sure of what I was going to do once I got there.

The lobby of the police station was essentially a cell without bars. Florescent lights flickered white to yellow to white over the scarred, faux-wood laminated panel walls and well-worn vinyl floor. A camera protruded into the space above the door, its eye watching over the forlorn parlor that encouraged anyone entering to leave as quickly as possible.

Left of the entrance there was a small counterspace waist-high protruding from a framed space in the wall— the only point of contact with the living creatures who worked there. Beyond the glass I could see a fat man sitting at a desk looking at a clipboard of papers that had been clamped with no particular care. I waited for him to notice me. He looked up at me once and returned to whatever it was he was doing. I thought of Tina in the Records Annex and controlled my desire to tell him to get his ass up off the chair and help me.

As kindly as I could muster, I asked, "Sir?"

"Be with you in a minute," he muttered. He put the clipboard down, shuffled a few papers around on his desk and slowly pulled himself to a standing position, slug-like made his way over to the window, looked through the glass at me and asked, "What is it I can do for you, bud?"

"I'd like to talk with Jake Davidson if he's around."

He gave me the visual once-over and asked, "And who are you?"

"I'm a friend of his. Name's Rob Wilson. I won't take up much of his time. Can I see him?"

He gave me another scan as if I might be trying to put one over on him. "Why do you want to talk to him?" he asked.

"I was with Jake out at his place last night when he got called out. He told me he'd call me when he got finished with whatever he was doing, and he never did. I was out at his house this morning and he wasn't there. I just want to be sure he's all right."

The fat man's eyes focused on the counter that stopped his belly and kept his upper torso well back from the window. The muscles of his body sagged minutely as he leaned forward and relinquished his cop demeanor, briefly exposing the man he probably was in his off hours.

"I'm sorry to tell you, buddy. He's in the hospital. He got beaten up pretty badly by some guys last night. I understand he's in pretty bad shape."

Though I had heard the words fall out sequentially, the jumble of thoughts and feelings they produced were roiling within me as I tried to make sense not only of what was being said but as to what I should do: run to the car and head to the hospital, ask more questions, cry, rant, go hunt down whoever hurt him, kill. I could feel the heat rising out of the boiler system my body was becoming, feel it rise up into my face, feel the stinging of my skin as my brain was shutting down, translating all rational thought to that of panic.

I heard myself saying, "I've got to get to the hospital!" as if I had spoken it in a windstorm, my garbling words flying from me faster than the speed of sound. An afterthought.

"Get hold of yourself, buddy," the cop said. "You can't go there. Not letting nobody in right now ... COVID and all.."

He was right, of course, about me needing to calm down. I managed to say that I needed to get some air. The bench outside the door became my respite as I breathed the morning in as deeply as I could and waited for something resembling rational thought to return. I had been sitting there tapping the ground with my toes, shaking my legs up and down on the balls of my feet, trying to decide what to do for maybe five minutes or so when that same cop came out a side door, walked over near the bench and asked if I had had the vaccination. I nodded that I had. He came forward and sat down beside me with some effort, put his hand on my shoulder and asked if I was going to be all right. His name tag was now close enough for me to read: Angelino.

"We're all worried about Jake," this Angelino said, "One of our best officers! Chief's been calling the hospital for updates, but they're so busy over there it's hard to get someone to talk to who knows anything." There was a slight pause before he asked, "How do you know Jake?"

I did the standard half-truth routine—that performance so many of us do to keep the audience with us without having to deal with their biases. Smoke and mirrors! I told him I had met Jake over a writing project I was involved in, and Jake was helping me with the story, and we had become friends in the process. He accepted what I said but asked questions about the project (I think for a moment he feared Jake might be telling tales about the department). The Trent Murders story didn't seem to interest him much, I gave the synopsis badly, just wanting to get past the small talk and on to Jake.

Leaning toward me as if telling a secret, he kept his voice low and said, "Here's what I've heard, but you can't quote me on. We haven't talked with Jake. He was unconscious when he got to the hospital, and far as I know still is." Angelino's large body was awkward as he tried to shift himself on the bench so he could see me. Telling me what he knew, he made it clear that everything he said was based on what others had told him and he had no first-hand knowledge. When he finished, I had the impression that Jake had been beaten by a gang of people and that Angelino believed Jake would never let himself get into a situation like that unless he knew someone or got caught by surprise ... not that that was terribly insightful. Apparently, Jake's gun was holstered when he was found behind a building unconscious. He's being checked for internal injuries ..."

Interrupting him, speaking overly fast and probably too intensely, I asked, "So, you don't know anything about his condition since he went into the hospital?"

The officer didn't try to match my speed or volume. "I only know what the chief passes down and what I hear from the guys ... other officers. You know how hospitals are. Don't give real information out. We've just got to wait until he wakes up." He tapped my shoulder gently with his huge hand and said like an old friend, "I'm glad you're here though, bud! We didn't have nobody to call and tell about him. No family I know of."

"I don't think he has any," I responded abruptly. I remember asking at some point whether he thought they— the police—were going to catch whoever did this to him. It was one of those questions that arose more out of a desire for retribution than a concern about stopping future crimes. Had I been thinking more clearly, I would have avoided asking it. The obvious answer was sure to be something to the effect of "We're doing everything we can,": a non-answer that is supposed to be somehow comforting. Certainly, an experienced cop would be picking up on the tension in my voice, the nervousness, the blurting of unanswerable questions. Reverting back to more typically cop-like behavior, he gave me the standard line I expected and added that everyone at the department was hoping Jake got a look at somebody or recognized a voice or something like that. He believed detectives had been sent to the scene to look for clues, but added for reasons all his own that even if he had known what they found, he wouldn't or couldn't share the information.

"Was he out there alone?" I said too loudly, perhaps argumentatively. "Don't the officers work in pairs?" I started firing questions at him, wanting him to give me something he didn't have to give: access to Jake, a way to understand the confusion and concern I was feeling. I probably didn't sound appreciative enough for what Angelino had shared in his attempt to be friendly and helpful. His voice became a bit defensive as he turned his body forward on the bench, dropped his hands to his knees, and said, "Look, we don't like sending a guy out alone." As if trying to cover for an error in judgment by telling me what he had, he explained that sending someone out alone is not all that uncommon, particularly when the office is short-staffed, or the situation doesn't appear to be a dangerous one. He emphasized that Jake had a radio and was supposed to call in if he needed help.

He said matter-of-factly, "We knew his location, and when he didn't call in, the dispatcher sent someone out as quickly as he could. That's how we found him."

It was obvious when Officer Angelino started repeating himself, he had given all he had or all that he was allowed to tell. I suspected that because of my response to him, he might have felt he had gone too far already. Recognizing that I wasn't responding to his kindness appropriately, I stumbled through thanking him for taking the time to talk to me and asked him to call me if he learned anything more about Jake's condition. He wrote my phone number on the back of a business card he pulled out of his pocket and then tucked it back into the same pocket.

After Angelino walked away and returned to his job, I was shaking with frustration over not being able to get to Jake or find a way to at least let him know I was trying. Perhaps I just wanted to prove to myself that Angelino was wrong about visitation rules. I called the hospital.

"Can you tell me his condition or when he might be able to see anyone?" I asked it, even though I knew what the answer would be, and it was: couldn't divulge information without the patient's consent; he was being well-cared for; he's listed as "stable"; only immediate family are allowed to visit; no calls unless the patient gives permission.

"Can I at least leave a message for him for when he gains consciousness?"

The response was an explanation of the problems with assuring delivery of messages. I left one anyway.

The following morning, I received a call.

"Mr. Wilson, this is Jenny McIntyre. I'm a nurse at Riversedge Hospital. Mr. Davidson gave me your phone number and asked me to call you on his behalf. He has given me permission to discuss his case."

"How is he?" I blurted out. "I haven't been able to get anything from anyone at the phone desk other than he's listed as stable."

"I understand that can be frustrating ..." She was *managing* me. "He was brought in during the early morning hours yesterday with multiple injuries. He was unconscious when he arrived. He has had a considerable shock to his body; however, today, he appears to be responding normally in terms of his ability to process information and make decisions. He has multiple bruises and cuts over much of his body from being beaten with a blunt object of some kind as well as being kicked a number of times and punched. His right eye received a significant blow and will need to be further evaluated by an ophthalmologist to make sure there hasn't been a retinal tear. He lost a front tooth and will require dental care once he is able to move around comfortably. Fortunately, there are no indications of any internal organ damage. He has three cracked ribs and will be in considerable pain for a while, but they will heal if he rests and doesn't do anything to damage them further. He is in a lot of pain and has been prescribed medication that should help with that. We have advised that when he leaves, he should have someone with him for at least a day or two, preferably more; he is going to be sore, and the meds will make him drowsy. He shouldn't drive right away, particularly while taking the meds. We recommend that he contact his own physician as soon as possible to decide what he can and can't do and when he can return to work. I think that covers everything ... unless you have questions."

I had lots of questions, but not about what she had said, and I knew she wouldn't be able to tell me who had beaten him or why. I'd been around enough to know Jake would be released with a packet of paperwork going over his care. And, besides, I was just too eager to get him the hell out of the hospital and home where I could be with him. I told her I understood what she was saying and would stay with him.

"We plan to release him this afternoon if someone can pick him up. He asked specifically for you if you are available."

After locking in a time and assuring her of my intention to be at the door at that time, we ended the call. I tapped the phone link to Nancy Tryger, the store manager at Fannon's. She wasn't thrilled that I wouldn't be able to cover my work hours for a few days while I cared for Jake. However, she was understanding and said she would find ways to cover for me. What that meant was most likely that she would personally cover more hours on the cash register than usual and would have less time to manage the younger workers who needed someone to ride roughshod over them to keep them focused and working.

When I arrived at the hospital, I had to press a buzzer and tell the disembodied voice through a speaker who I was and who I came for and then wait. After about five minutes, Jake was wheeled out of the hospital door by a mask-covered nurse who looked much too small to be pushing the weight of a man like Jake. She had to lean forward and push with her legs like she was trying to push a car out of a ditch all by herself. But she kept moving him toward me. I asked if she wanted help.

"Nope! Hospital regs. But thanks! You can help him get into the car though!" The way she said it convinced me she might be little but tough, knew her job, and wasn't going to have any man suggesting a woman wasn't just as capable as any man of doing the job.

When she stopped, Jake put his right hand out to me. He squeezed his hand against mine, looked up trying to shape a smile onto his battered and swollen face and showing the open space of the missing tooth on the upper middle of his mouth. Without thinking, I leaned over him, put my left hand to his neck, and let my face touch his for a brief second before I remembered the nurse. As I rose, I looked up into her expressionless face.

He tried to stand on his own, winced with pain, and emitted a groan he couldn't hold. The scrappy little nurse took his right arm. I took his left and lifted him to a standing position to take the one step forward he needed in order to be at the door opening and the seat. Standing as close as I could in case he needed help, I let him turn slowly so his back was to the car, and I held his arms as he lowered himself painfully into the leather seat and pulled his legs—first the left, and then the right—into place as though each foot weighed two-hundred pounds and was wired directly to his cracked rib cage.

Before turning the chair around and leaving, the nurse said over the open door, "You take care of yourself now, Mr. Davidson. I hope you feel better soon." He nodded, tried to raise his hand as if to wave. She wished me a good day and was gone, walking upright behind the light metal frame on wheels that now allowed it to move like a grocery cart.

"I am so sorry this happened to you, Jake. I wanted to be with you, but they wouldn't let me. I'm sorry." I said as I leaned in across him with the seatbelt and snapped it into place. As I began to pull back, I felt the back of his hand on my chest. I looked at him, saw the tear roll off the corner of his eye.

He pointed to his own chest and mumbled in a whisper, "You were here."

The sound of the car door closing against the frame had a discomforting quality to it like a chapter break in a book, a space between acts in a play, the surprise in Haydn's Symphony. For me, everything would be different now. Something about who we had been had slipped into our history like people ravaged by war going back to homes forever marked by the bullets that blew away huge pieces of stone from their positions within the once immaculate walls of beautiful homes.

Once I made the dash around the car to my door, opened it and got in, I found myself—ignition key in hand— with no desire to use it and with an overwhelming desire to lash out. I was pressing the back of my head against the headrest, at first staring forward through the windshield, and, eventually, looking at Jake and saying angrily, "I *hate*

whoever did this to you! I would love to kick their miserable fucking asses and let them have a taste of what they've
done to you! The sons o' bitches!" As the last syllable fell
out, I realized in that moment that I was thinking vigilante justice a desire to do something outside the law to get
revenge. I understood why somebody could at least think
about stringing somebody up for murdering someone ...
for even less than that.

Jake just moved his left hand to my thigh, laid it there,
turned his face slightly toward me and whispered through
clenched teeth, "I know" with no malice in his voice. The
sound of those two words elegantly diminished my own
crude rant and left me embarrassed for having said the
unnecessary words and allowing myself to hate.

After leaving the hospital, I drove to the mall and pulled
into the least busy of the two drive-up window lanes of the
pharmacy where I was to obtain Jake's medications. After
the three cars ahead of mine finally moved on, the voice
on the speaker told me that the prescriptions hadn't been
filled yet and "I'm sorry for your wait; we'll get it ready as
quickly as possible." She—the female voice, the person behind that voice—shouldn't have had to take my mini-rant
as I stated that the prescriptions had been ordered from
the hospital at least "a god-damned hour earlier." Then,
I sputtered some words about incompetence. Had Jake
not put his hand on my leg, I would have carried on with
something like, "That's part of the problem with the world:
The incompetents are always shielded by layers of innocents who have to take the crap for them. How the hell are

things ever going to get better when people in power are untouchable?"

Jake pushed the words, "Patience, Slick," past his teeth.

Again, he had caught me overreacting and called me on it. And, again, I became aware that I was acting out of anger and a desire to make somebody pay for Jake's condition. I had gone the easy route of being angry with someone totally disconnected from what had triggered my response and had added that anger to my frustrations of dealing with everyday life: corporate greed, poor customer service, broken agreements, lies.

"You're right. I'm being an ass ... You don't need this. I'm sorry. I'm just frustrated. Just want to get you home. I'll apologize when she gets back on."

It was a bit startling when the voice came back on the speaker and said, "I understand your frustration, sir! I don't take it personally. I will let you know as soon as the order is filled."

"Well, now I really feel like a horse's ass," I said as I looked over at Jake and laughed out loud. I turned back to the microphone and said, "If you're still listening, thank you for putting up with jerks like me." There was no response.

As we continued to wait, I wished Jake could talk and tell me what had happened to him. As though he could read my thoughts, he put his left hand on my thigh, rubbed the palm of his hand on it, then pulled his hand back, laid it on his own, and let his head drop to his right against the window and closed his eyes. When we finally received the drugs, it was not the female voice to which I had intended to apologize once more. Instead, it was an abrupt male who lectured me about using the drugs only as prescribed. Then he asked if I had any questions; he asked it in one of those voices that suggested the only response he wanted to hear was "No." I gave him what he asked for, said my autonomic "thanks," and moved away from the machinery that mediated customer service, wondered if everyone in the pharmacy had heard my rant or would hear the rants of all those behind me who could very well be saying the same things, and maybe those people who were listening bore resentment for the neural pathways carved into their brains by the thousands of rants of people who had pulled up to the soulless machinery day after day for many years prior to my arrival expecting the humans behind them to meet impossible expectations for instantaneous service.

When we pulled out of the parking lot, we were within two miles of County Route 36, the road that would take us to Jake's place. As we turned onto it and left the better-maintained pavement of Emberland's main thoroughfare, Jake sat up to keep his head from bouncing against the glass with each dip in the road, the rough edges of cuttings and patching upon the pavement, and the occasional pothole that I didn't see in time to avoid. I hadn't taken much notice of how many discomforts the badly abused pavement created until I heard the winces and groans Jake let slip from him. As the driver, all I could do was drive as slowly and as carefully as possible and deal with the passing cars—their drivers throwing me the bird for holding them up from getting to wherever they were heading and whatever seemingly essential thing they had to do once they got there. Whatever those things were, drivers were obviously late and desperate to get me out of their way. We had been in a no-passing section of the road for a short stretch as we neared our turnoff, and the driver behind me was inching up to my bumper, and he was leading a pack of three others riding his and one another's bumpers like male dogs on a female in heat. I could almost feel the man's relief as I pressed my turn signal. Tires screeched. Once we ever-so-slowly made the turn and dropped from the six-inches of the highway's cracked and broken pavement onto the rut-ridden path that led to the house, I could imagine the blue air of cussing going on in the cars behind me and actually heard the voice of the lead car's driver as he rolled down his window and screamed an obscenity at me before hitting the gas and roaring on down the road with the other two cars behind him just as determined to get him out of their way. The clunk of the car as it dropped from the pavement to the lane was simply the preamble to the remaining half mile of misery that I would have to make Jake endure. And there was nothing to be done about any of it unless, of course, I just simply stopped. The car bucked and kicked, trying to find any kind of stability in the earth beneath it. Even at a crawl, pain shot up from the tires, through the chassis, and into Jake's seat where it climbed cat-like and clawing into his nervous system. And all I could do was say over and over, "I'm sorry."

At the house, there was still the matter of getting Jake out of the car and up the stairs to the bedroom. This, too, would be a long and painful process. When it was finally done, I helped him undress and gave him his medications, and I was exhausted. I had now seen the discernable boot prints on his body, as well as numerous welts and bruises of various shapes and colors—splashes of blue, black, red and orange all over him. And there was nothing I could think to do about any of it except swallow my anger and be with him.

As I laid the sheet over him and pulled it up to his neck, he looked at me with that look I remember from my own life as a boy wanting to become a man and realizing for the first time that it was better to have been a child.

"Favor, Slick?" He asked, struggling to get above a whisper, clearly in pain.

"As long as you don't ask me for a loan," I joked.

"Hold me," he said.

"I don't want to hurt you." Trying to be as gentle as I could, I laid my hand on the mattress just beyond him and lowered my upper torso to his chest, holding back as much of my weight as I could while still making contact. He slid his arm slowly out from under the sheet and maneuvered his hand to lay it on mine. For only a moment, he wept.

Jake slept much of that first day. The drugs were powerful, and he could only handle staying awake long enough to sip water and eat a few spoonsful of soup. In the evening, he was able to sit up in bed for a short while and eat small bites of soft foods. But even yogurt hurt his swollen and bruised jaw muscles and the interior of his mouth with its many cuts, the open gap where a front tooth had been, and loosened and aching teeth that remained. But even then, he was trying unsuccessfully to flex and stretch some of the pain out of his arms and legs.

Watching Jake suffer was difficult for me. Knowing that I was doing everything I could do came from the rational part of my brain. The irrational part wanted to take the pain away, make it stop crawling all over him, lift it like an errant insect and flip it off my finger to the floor and step on it, hear its exoskeleton crunch and ooze out its life under my shoe. But there was no insect. Nothing but the waiting. My brain was flooded with all of the stereotyping that had been bred into me: A man has to do something, fix things, make everything okay, stand up and punch the bully. Something! Anything other than bearing the frustration that there is nothing to do but wait, like the ultimate waiting of all of humanity for the answer to "Why?" Of course, there was going to be the work of helping Jake move about the house, keeping track of his meds, helping him rise, helping him lie down and rest, and there was the cooking, cleaning up, sitting with him, lying with him ... but somehow in little moments of reflection they seemed unimportant things, the things that didn't match the male ego—my ego—that wanted to do great things and expect others to take note of my deeds for posterity. And when I saw the word ego rise up on my brain screen, turn and then exit in an explosion of light, I realized that I was making Jake's pain mine, not to help him, but to feed some perverted notion that the world was about me.

Of course, as I often do when I've gotten lost in my attempts to understand why I do some of the things I do, I pawed back through the blither of my thoughts—thoughts about my thinking—to determine that this—what I was able to do—had to be enough. He needed me right then. And, whether or not that need would or could continue, was something I couldn't control. And if he ceased to want me after all that, that should not affect the value of what I was doing in that moment ... at least, that's what I wanted to believe. There was time enough to contemplate his— our—new reality as we tried to fathom the how's and the why's of what had happened and how it might affect our future.

Myriad thoughts rattled around in my brain like marbles in a shaken glass jar, clinking and clunking against the feelings trapped in the air between its base and its hand-tight lid.

PART 2

16

Two days later, Jake was able to talk to me with less pain. Without any recognizable transition into the topic, he started telling me the story of what had happened to him as though he was picking up mid-sentence after a brief interruption. It took me a minute to catch up with him and connect with the subject matter. With the pain he experienced when he tried to talk, he must have wanted to avoid any unnecessary movement of his mouth. He struggled, but he was determined like a boxer who knows he's winning on points, trying to get through the tenth round with a broken wrist and trying to avoid getting knocked out. He was trying to punch the space between us with words that would sustain him until he could rest. His words were occasionally damaged by the needle-like jolts of agony in his face and his inability to open his mouth fully. Much of what he said was devoid of all the connecting words we expect in written language, but his meaning came through. Later, as he slept, I tried to capture the essence of what I had

heard and write it down as if ideas hadn't been truncated
or telegraphed by gestures:

*At the station, the dispatcher sent him out on call:
something was going on at the old abandoned Black Baptist Church on Seventh Street. Anonymous caller said a
cop was needed as quickly as possible ... The dispatcher
didn't seem to know what the problem was. For all Jake
knew, it could have been anything from a bothersome noise
to a murder. His first thoughts were that maybe somebody
broke in, kids were breaking windows, there had been a
car accident on the street in front of the building, or maybe it would just turn out to be a hoax and there would be
nothing there. He got into the cruiser, drove over to Seventh Street. At first, he didn't hear or see anything amiss.
Then, from somewhere behind the building he heard
somebody—female—yelling, "Help me!" The voice sounded fake, like a cartoon. He called the dispatcher and told
him what was happening and reported that he was going
to investigate at the back of the church. He asked to have
somebody come back him up. Jake had his flashlight on,
gun pulled—just in case—and went alongside the building,
hugging the wall so he wasn't out in the open. When he got
to the back corner, he peeked around it and saw a woman
lying in weeds next to a shed maybe twenty feet behind the
church. She was still calling for help in that same strange
voice. He did a quick look around with the flashlight but
didn't see anybody."*

*"Are you hurt?' he called out, but there was no re-
sponse other than another call for help. 'Are you alone?'*

Again, no response. He kept the flashlight on and did a visual sweep of the area as he walked over to her.

"I should have waited for backup, but I didn't know how badly the woman was hurt," he told me. He felt he needed to take the risk in case the woman was seriously injured. First, he took another sweep with the flashlight and saw nothing other than the woman who was moaning as if in pain. When he got to her, he bent down to check the woman out. Next thing he knew, he was in the hospital feeling like he'd been trampled by an elephant. "Whoever did it must've been in or behind that outbuilding that he had his back to, or they were laying on top of it. Couldn't have been far from me; got me too quickly."

The last thing he said was, "When I woke up at the hospital, no one knew anything about anything. And if the chief is counting on our detectives to solve this crime, the whole case is screwed. I'd rather have no investigation than to let those Bozos fuck it up."

As the day went on, Jake's ability to speak improved with his determination to get past the pain of stretching his facial muscles, the pain in his teeth as his tongue searched for new pathways around the inside of his mouth to avoid them. As he spoke, he seemed at times to be looking past me, rather that at me. At times he stopped altogether as if he saw it all as pointless—a symptom of depression I knew far too well. Then he would start again in a voice that was subdued and too often self-critical. Trying to retrace the events that led to his current state, he talked about what had happened to him, his sense of failure at figuring out that he had walked into a trap. As I looked at the hole in his mouth where the tooth had been, I felt an intense desire to know everything I could about what had happened to him as if knowing would give me the opportunity to exact some kind of revenge that I could not yet articulate.

But it was more than that. It was about building our relationship and creating what would become this book. He didn't get too far before I realized it might be a good idea for me to have a notepad at hand. I asked if he minded. He had no objections, even tried to smile as he said it and called me "Shakespeare." When I had retrieved the pen and paper, I picked up where we had left off speaking of his perceived failure.

"You couldn't have known it was a trap going in," I said as gently and soothingly as I could. "You were trying to help someone. Were you supposed to ignore the woman's yelling for help?" Then I was quietly pleading, "You've been beaten up enough, don't beat yourself up on top of that."

Picking up on my concern for him and the implications of my notetaking, he shifted his tone slightly: "They did a number on me for sure," he whispered and turned his head away from me.

Trying to think of ways to keep him from turning too far inward and shutting me out, I asked "Do you think cops were in on it?"

"They were!" he said, suddenly louder and more determined in his response than he had been. The clear emphatic statement suggested he thought it should have been obvious to me as well; and then realizing he might have come across as critical of me, he moved his hand toward my arm and touched it like an apology and went on. He had clearly decided the issue well ahead of my question. He tried to clarify that there was no doubt in his mind that Aaron Weller had conveniently become 'sick' as part of a plan to get Jake in that night. He had seen Weller the night before. Weller, who had never shown anything but contempt for Jake and rarely spoke to him, on that particular night asked what Jake was going to be doing on his night off and if he was going out or staying at home.

"I asked him if he was planning to drop in for a visit." Jake's voice feigned sarcasm.

According to Jake, that was the way Weller talked to him when the two of them had to interact. Apparently, Weller didn't take the bait, didn't act angry or tell Jake where to get off as he sometimes did. He said he was just trying to be friendly and hoped Jake didn't get called in on his day off to cover for somebody. Given the sudden shift in Weller's behavior, Jake seemed to think he should have known something was in the works and he should have been more careful than he was the following evening when he came in to cover for Weller's absence.

"But that's not proof of anything; it could have been what he said: an attempt to change how he got along with you."

"Not likely," he said in a harsher voice. "I should have put the pieces together," he grumbled through his clenched jaws, showing his interior struggle through the tightening of his body into a painful rigidity expressed in his tightened neck and chest muscles and the sudden whiteness of his knuckles protruding from his fists.

As I took hold of his hands and manually pulled his fingers out of his palms and told him to ease up on himself, he appeared to realize how much the thought process was magnifying the pain already radiating from his battered body. It took him a couple of sighs, verbal renditions of "I'm sorry," and sips from the water glass I had brought him for his muscles to begin relaxing. He closed his eyes for a moment as he went to some space in his mind to find and repair control switches and dials. When his eyes opened, he seemed more carefully in command of what he was going to say, how he was going to say it, and how he would appear as he said it. When he was ready to continue, he shifted his approach to explaining himself like a teacher helping a thick-headed student understand how a cop thinks. As he saw it, there was a list of points to consider: 1) the conversation happened the night before Weller called off; 2)Weller specifically wanted to know whether Jake was going to be in town; 3) he wanted to know whether or not Jake would be available to come in; 4) the minute Jake got into the station and clocked in, a conveniently anonymous incident occurred; and finally, 5) Jake just happened to be the only person available because others had been sent out on other calls or to do "drive-arounds."

"When there are lots of 'coincidences' going on around a crime, it's a good idea to check them out," he said.

It all made sense, but I still couldn't understand why he was so determined to think of himself as having failed. All of his "points" seemed to me to be hindsight details that anyone could have missed.

As he tried to explain it to me, his voice became less focused on what he called his "screw-ups" and more focused on helping me to understand the complexities of the situation. There were other components to the story I hadn't known or hadn't considered. Weller was a friend of Mike Harridan, the guy Jake had told me he had reported for being on the take and had been fired. As far as men like Weller were concerned, Jake had "ratted out" a fellow cop. Jake surmised that since Harridan was facing a trial in the near future and maybe a prison sentence, he might be getting a bit desperate to make sure Jake changed his mind about being a witness against him. But it was more than that for Harridan, Jake said. His perception was that Harridan needed to assert dominance over him, keep feeding the lie that he was tougher than Jake was—more *man*— the man that fit the image Harridan consistently tried to sell about himself about being macho, heterosexual, dominant, the envy of other men.

"I'm sure he would like to see me cower and say I lied about him." Jake paused as if weighing his next line especially carefully, dropping his head for his eyes to be staring downward like a guilty man, and speaking quietly of what only he, Harridan, and I knew: "He's afraid of what I might say about him and who I might say it to." He paused as if seeking a way to deflect the feelings associated with the earlier statement. "He's got a wolf-pack of lawyers gnawing at witness statements and saying I've got a vendetta against their 'innocent' client." Jake's perspective was clear: Harridan was behind his beating, and Weller was Harridan's inside man who put pressure on other cops to help prove Jake wasn't credible as a witness or a cop.

Though I offered several times to postpone further talk about his ordeal, Jake insisted on continuing; and I already knew he was going to process it whether or not I engaged with him or not, so I continued. Staying calm, listening carefully, and speaking quietly, I tried to help him think rationally and not jump to conclusions.

"But you don't know for a fact that what happened was a message to you from Harridan?"

"You're right. His voice trailed off for a moment then slowly increased in volume. "I can't *prove* any of it ... yet." The word "yet" carried a wealth of information about Jake's eventual ability to stop blaming himself and get busy being proactive in his recovery.

During the discussion there had been several long pauses between us as Jake wrestled with his desire to speak and the pain it caused and the effort it took. Despite my attempts to spare him talking further, he looked at me with determination that said he needed his thoughts said, recorded in someone else's consciousness as if he were fearful that those thoughts would somehow be lost if he didn't put them in a lock box at once.

"I told you I pulled my gun. When I was found, the gun was in my holster!"

"Why would somebody take the time to put your gun in your holster? Why not steal it or just let it lay wherever it was dropped? "Wouldn't they have left fingerprints if they touched it?"

"It's part of the reason I suspect cops. It makes me look stupid ... or guilty if the gun was used for something while I was unconscious. Lots of ways to avoid fingerprints. Wear gloves. Wipe the gun down and wrap my limp hand around the grip. It will have to be checked to see if it was fired. I don't know whether the woman was a decoy or a victim— somebody they wanted to tie me to for some reason. If she's a victim, and the goal is to tie me to her, she would be found fairly quickly. I told you she sounded phony. She was either a plant or she's dead."

"You're way beyond me, Jake. I never thought of anything like that."

"I've got a couple of things going for me that might help the investigation. Boot prints on my body. Two different sizes and patterns. Photos were taken at the hospital of the damage that was done. Our dispatcher was supposed to record every call: who called, what time they called, and what the call was about. Same thing when I called to tell him I was going to investigate and needed backup. There should be recordings of those calls."

"You think Harridan did this? If this was cops, wouldn't they know how to cover their tracks?"

With an attempted smirk, he said, "Cops can be dumb as shit ... just like the people they make fun of for being stupid enough to get caught. Even the best con—even a cop— makes mistakes, can't control everything. Smart ones are harder to catch. Problem is figuring out what the mistakes were."

After all the talking, Jake was drowsy again, and I suggested he rest. Though he said he wasn't sleepy, it didn't take him long lying in silence before he fell asleep. When he did, I went downstairs to write what he had said. When I had captured as much as I could remember and glean from my notes, I still wanted to write under the influence of my thoughts about what had happened to him, but I needed a break from standard prose and found myself laying down a different way of expressing the disappointment I was feeling about my fellow humans:

Geese sing discordant songs: the rite of flight—same refrains sung in Xanadu. The lead in the "V" that is their brand shifts amongst them as each tires of piercing countercurrents of sky.

Rude bellows and blasts of motors and horns below. Drivers soar down the homestretches of their lives trying to outrun the gods who never come to save them from themselves.

Just off the roadway, beyond the vituperative rage that is humanity, they glide into a pond to breed the assault of humanity into the genes of coming spring's goslings.

And for it all, geese, sounding and seeming the same, will never be what they ever so briefly were.

When I finished working through changes, corrections, eliminations and adding in of words and thoughts, it was five o'clock in the morning, and I wasn't sure of why it had written itself as it did. "It has reasons of its own," I said out loud. It was an "is," and I was fine with letting it live at least for as long it could sustain its own life free of me to explain it.

I sat a few minutes longer staring at what I had written. In that time, the words were alive, breathing, standing on their own, and all I could feel for them was sadness. They had nowhere to go in the domain of current editors of poetry who seem to enjoy only words that slither around one another like bait worms in tin cans going nowhere before the coming of the hook, words that lose their way two lines into a stanza then lay atop one another as obfuscation of the fact that few contemporary poets have anything worthwhile to say. But I supposed they would say the same of this thing I had made. Once a poem—or any other written piece—leaves the writer's hand, it is a freed dove that rises high above the cage that held her and becomes vulnerable to the elements and can be easily ripped from the sky by a peregrine, hawk, eagle, other birds of prey or by the mercilessness of guns and of human judgement fired like cannons from the lungs of the critics who determine art, taste and refinement for those who can't think for themselves.

I could hear the voice of a former therapist asking, "Does someone's opinion of your work define you? The essential you?" I knew what he wanted me to say, but, at the time, the honest response was "Unfortunately, yes."

Exhaustion was trying to close in on me, but I couldn't sleep. I thought again of the poem as light rose slowly on the horizon. I had spent too much time grinding through words about human ugliness, and I was tired enough to have lost perspective. I needed to escape myself, get up out of the chair and move.

I twisted the handle of the kitchen door and pulled it back abruptly, stepped quickly outside, pulling the heavy door shut as if somehow making it impossible for something to escape or get in. I stood in July's warmth and let it hold me. As I lowered myself into the porch chair, it sat down beside me and held my hand until I became calm.

In that embrace, I thought about Jake and how my life had changed in such a short time, how I had taken up a piece of his life as my own, how I felt at ease with him in ways I had rarely ever experienced in the presence of other people. As I held Jake's image there, my mind flashed to the many occasions when I had not felt safe with anyone ... times when I felt like an unwanted foster child, a motherless child, the child who bears the parents. The age-old image came up in my head again: My father, William... his drunken "you're a fucking faggot" screwing into my head with an electric drill of disdain—a drill that I eventually owned and used on myself for a number of years: the self-destruction that had coursed through my veins as I fought the image of William, fought the truth that I was a man who found only loneliness in the arms of women, joy in the arts, and hope in kindly men, and no amount of wishing or pretending I was something else was going to make me so.

As the morning sun started making its trek across the hills, I held the kaleidoscopic thoughts of that night now printed metaphorically upon a single sheet of paper in small type that I folded into quarters and then pushed carefully into my father's pocket before pointing him back to his grave and telling him not to visit again.

Jake's image—always smiling—was waiting patiently in my brain for me to think my thoughts before calling me to him. With that image in my head, I returned to the house and tried to go quietly upstairs and down the hall's wood plank floor. When I got to the bedroom, Jake was sitting on the side of the bed, his feet on the floor, his face red from the exertion to get into that position without help. When he saw me, he dragged up a half-smile from beyond the pain.

"I woke up a while ago. I heard you downstairs, assumed you were writing. I won't mention you banging on the stairs and walls when you came up. Why didn't you turn a light on?"

Of course, I could see how silly it was to say, "I didn't want to wake you," after it was obvious that I probably would have awakened the dead without turning on the light, especially when I misjudged the last step and fell forward catching the wall with my left arm.

I sat down beside him on the bed. "So much for my stealth skills. I wish I could sleep as easily as you seem to."

"You're a thinker! It's who you are. One of the things I love about you."

"It's as much a curse as it is a blessing. Believe me."

"It's how things get better. People like you figure it out for the rest of us."

"I'm not sure how I'm making it any better! All I do is roll around in it, put some words to it, and put it out there in some form for publication. Arrogance. Who in the hell am I to tell anyone else anything about what life's about?"

Jake turned his head slowly to face me. We were practically nose-to-nose. He touched my cheek and let his hand slide down my face to my neck and held it there as he said, "You seem to have the notion that you're responsible for it all, Rob! You're not! You can't make the world okay for other folks. You can give them things to think about a little differently if they're open to it. You can entertain while you do it. You can make them feel they have experienced another person's life. But you can't make them okay if they choose not to be or if they can't or won't help themselves. Just be who you are! That's enough work for anyone to get done in a lifetime. Now, turn off that fucking brain of yours for a few hours and get some rest!"

I wished I could do as he commanded. Instead, I fumbled for a response, and the best I could come up with was, "Why couldn't I have met you a long time ago?"

"Didn't happen then. It's happening now! That's all that matters," he said while wincing at the pain shooting through him.

He admitted needing one of the pain pills. I got it and a glass of water and brought them to him. When he had drunk the water, he set the glass on his nightstand on top of a magazine that lay there and decided he should rest a bit more. We lay together face-to-face for a while until I heard the sound of his sleep-breathing, the consistent in and out sound of air crossing over his lips and tongue carrying a slight whistle beneath it. I rolled over and stared at the tree standing between the house and the dawn framed by the shadow-covered wall that held the window firmly in its place.

When he awoke again it was 8:30 a.m., I still had not slept and knew that I wouldn't for a long while.

"I'm going to start moving around, stretching out muscles," he asserted. "I can't do another day of staying in bed. I need to get outside for a bit. But I might need help getting down the stairs."

By now, I should have known the answer I'd get, but I asked anyway: "Do you want to get dressed first?"

"Hell, no," he said.

17

Four days after I had brought Jake home from the hospital, I had to return to work or risk getting fired. I hated that I had to leave him alone. He insisted he would be able to function well enough for the short periods of time I would be away. Nancy Tryger, had been very kind in agreeing not to schedule me for more than four hours on any given day until Jake was further along in his recovery.

Though he needed help getting up and down the stairs, moved ever so slowly, and was obviously experiencing pain, Jake was able to negotiate the first floor of the house, get to the kitchen and the downstairs bathroom, and get to his meds if he needed them. I made sure he was on the first floor before I went to work each day so he could get out of the house if the need arose. I made meals for him requiring nothing more than the microwave to ready them for eating, and I made sure he had his phone readily available and was as comfortable as possible before I left.

A couple more days into the healing process, the swelling in his face receded, and he could talk normally again.

His many bruises had turned to dark blue and black but would undoubtedly linger for weeks to come. I noticed that he was becoming self-conscious about his missing tooth, and he often moved his hand up in front of his face when he talked. Seeing him do that several times, I took his arm and pulled his hand away, telling him I accepted him just the way he was, and reminded him that the gap in his mouth would be repaired as soon as he could get an appointment with the dentist.

It was at that point that he asked me, "How much longer are you going to hang out here with me?"

"For as long as you need me or want me," I responded almost mechanically, and then, I heard the question echoing through my neural networks, my thoughts rattling like the seeds in a maraca given to a rhythmless hyperactive child. My Chicago experience raced back into my head, Matt's face staring coldly at me: maybe Jake had had enough, maybe I hadn't been enough, maybe we were too deep into one another's lives too fast and he was frightened.

As if reading my mind, he said, "I don't want you tied to nurse duty. I want you to be able to do the things you want to do; I'm tying you down with all this caretaking."

Giving away my insecurities, I reacted defensively and probably had some sarcasm in my voice when I said, "I haven't complained, have I? But, if you need some time to yourself—if that's what you're getting at—I can go whenever you feel ready to go it alone here. I don't want you to feel like you're stuck with me."

Even through the bruising around his right eye, I could see the eyelids dimming his vision like putting a light under murky water as he realized that he hadn't meant for his words to come across as a three-legged horse making its way out of a starting gate for a race it couldn't win. For a moment, he held in place the wrinkling of his forehead, the rise of his brow, the lift of his chin and jaw muscles that froze in carved-marble confusion. Then all at once the muscles returned and his face sagged like water off a rock wall.

"Whoa, man! You've got it all wrong! I'm not trying to push you out! In fact, if I had my way, you'd just move in! I just don't want you to lose yourself in nurse duty. I didn't want *you* to feel stuck!"

Strange, the games of parry and weave we play with words as they race through our hearing into the cells of our brains, process and mean, cause our bodies, our feelings, our renovated thoughts to react. I had whacked hack-like at Jake with my dulled saber tongue—an *avertissement* rising out of my misreading of his attempt to make a caring gesture. How unlike a sabreur I was at that moment as I came to the awareness that I had already grown so attached to him that I had to put up a wall against a potential rejection—a hurt I had unleashed upon myself and that he had never intended. I had fallen prey once again to my own incessant need to analyze the why and the how of my life as they made their journey out of the past and stepped into wherever they were headed. But first, I had to own the now and the reaction I had dumped on him.

"I over-reacted. Jake. Stupid on my part. I'm sorry! I've been happy being here. Helping you out ... and thought maybe you were getting sick of me ... Did you mean what you just said? I mean, move in?"

"I've never felt so good about anyone, and I want you with me if you're willing. But it's not just about what I want! What do you want?"

In the short time we had been together, we had talked about our pasts, what we wanted out of life, our desires, our strengths and our foibles. But there was still so much to learn. I knew I wasn't his first love, and he knew that he wasn't mine. Mine had been a fake, an actor who grew tired of his role and walked offstage forever. Jake's had been a narcissist who liked having a good-looking man as a boy toy, not as someone to share a life with. Neither of us was eager to get into anything resembling those kinds of relationships again. It was kind of crazy to think about jumping into this relationship as if it were a "done deal." We hadn't even said the magic words to one another. The closest we had come was to say, "One of the things I love *about* you ..." or "I love *that* you ...," etc. I wanted to say it, could have said it right then. The question wasn't "Could I?" It was, "Should I?" And I suspect he struggled with the same questions. How does anyone know it's the right thing to do and the right moment to do it? And how can anyone know it will last? People fall in and out of love all of the time. It's all a game of chance, isn't it? And yet at that moment, the idea of being with Jake on a daily basis felt right.

When I told him how my mind was racing, he said in his thoughtful way, "Rob, I already know I've loved you since the first time we met. And maybe it's reckless to jump into living together after such a short time; but you know what? Even if you said you didn't want to be with me, I'd love you. I might work at trying to get along in my life without you, but I'm never going to be the same now that you've come into it." He went on in his soft, romantic voice to say that he had changed forever just by knowing me for the short time we had been together. Then he shifted to his attempt to make a rational argument about the idea that we could end up deciding the relationship might not work for reasons neither of us could foresee, but that happens to people who have dated for years before living together too. "There aren't any guarantees in anything. All I know is that I wake up every morning thinking about you even when you're not here and looking forward to seeing you and being with you. I just like having you in my space."

"I didn't know you were going to be so fucking handsome and charming when I agreed to meet you for the first time," I said. "And I didn't think a guy like you could ever see anything in somebody like me. By the second day when we had lunch together, I was ready right then and there to give you anything you wanted from me. But that was the sexually starved me making that decision. I really fell in love with you at the quarry. Not because of your body—though that was a huge bonus—but because of your intellect and your humor and your kindness. You are either one of the most genuine people I've ever known or a phenomenal actor. I've never felt as safe and as free as I am with you. I love you too."

18

As Jake improved, I was able to find opportunities to get him out of the house for short periods of time. We tracked down and visited the gravesites of the Trents. We tried to get to the site where the Trent house once stood. We got as far as a fence blocking the entrance to the overgrown path beside a ramshackle mobile home with a big hand-painted sign stating, "Stay out! We will shoot to kill! No exceptions." Looking toward the trailer's window, I saw a curtain fall into place behind the window. With that, I backed up into a flat spot in the weeds, turned around and headed home listening to Jake going on about people making threats and claiming a perverse belief in redneck "justice."

Jake went with me sometimes when I went into town to run errands or to visit the Annex. I had resumed doing research, reading and copying the story of Nathan Sanders' interactions with the law. He waited in the diner sometimes, met some of his cop buddies there to chat and get a feel for what was happening at the department. At other times, he went with me to the annex where he tried to read some of the journal entries I pointed out to him: the coroner's inquest, the pre-trial hearing, and the actual trial, including seating the jury, and we were learning just how awful the legal system got for a guy like Sanders. Justice had already flown out of the courtroom windows before Nathan Sanders stepped into it, flown out as if on the wings of a hapless bird that had mistakenly breached an open door or window and then was chased out by a posse of broom-bearing cops who had been ordered by a bellicose judge to remove the distraction.

A careful reading of the record suggested to me that a case could have been made for the bias of the judge and manipulation by the prosecution. As far as I was concerned, the only positive for Sanders was that his defense team did a good job of calling circumstantial evidence into question and creating doubt about whether anyone could have done the murders without the help of at least one other person. Using Sanders poor mother (recently widowed) as a witness, defense attorneys worked hard to portray Sanders as a troubled young man who was not very bright and, therefore, probably not capable of plotting and executing such a crime by himself. Looking to soften the verdict if Sanders was found guilty, they worked at making him worthy of some compassion. By putting his mother on the stand, they made *her* worthy of consideration for her grief in losing a husband a few months earlier and now facing the loss of her only son as well.

For some, the defense team was doing too well. Though it had appeared quite obvious at the beginning of the trial that the jury was stacked in favor of a guilty conviction, the newspapers started suggesting that jury members had been listening intently to the defense attorneys' arguments and appeared to be receptive to their arguments. As the trial neared its end, town wags, fearing that the defense team might be successful in creating reasonable doubt, began plotting a way to get to the "right decision."

In the late evening after final arguments between the prosecution and defense attorneys readying the jury to deliberate, a mob formed. The following day's newspaper editions provided variations of the story of what happened, none of them with any significant details.

> Dissatisfied with the tenor of the trial of Nathan Sanders, a group of citizens stormed the jail last evening. Strong men overwhelmed the sheriff and locked him in a jail cell. They then pulled the murderer out of his cell and drove him off into the night to be lynched. We are told that Sanders refused to admit responsibility for the murders and would not beg for mercy, which would have been denied. He is said to be buried somewhere in the county in an unmarked grave. Had Judge Lynch taken the case earlier, much public money could have been saved.

Neither Jake nor I could understand how the mob could break into the jail without someone being recognized by the sheriff who was conveniently locked behind bars by the mob while they carted Sanders off. There was nothing to suggest he ever named names or even came up with a good excuse for not recognizing his assailants. For all we knew, this same god-damned lawman that lied on the stand had invited the mob, handed them the keys, and locked himself behind bars to provide himself with a way to avoid responsibility for stopping the lynching.

"Probably where the son-of-a-bitch should have stayed," Jake said.

If anyone's name was ever reported as being part of the mob, I couldn't find any mention of it. If there was any kind of investigation into the lynching, I had not been able to find any mention of it. After the report of the hanging and sickeningly sappy reminiscences of the murder victims' souls finally laying at rest, newspaper reporters moved on to other stories. Their work has served its purpose: the essential story they concocted had become engrained in the minds of the community's members and became mythological as it was handed down from one generation to the next.

As far as Jake and I could see from the records, the case should have been tried in a different venue given that it took going through ninety-six potential jurors to find twelve "acceptable" people approved by the judge and prosecutors despite what seemed to us to be reasonable objections and evidence of bias presented by Sanders' attorneys. Of course, all we had to work with was the words in the journal—transcriptions by a clerk of all that was said, implied, and manipulated by the attorneys—and words in old newspapers—which often opted for sensationalism over factual reporting. Though we found some allusions to others who might have committed the crimes, including Alf Carson, there appeared to be nothing that suggested a willingness on the part of the judge or prosecutor to give any credence to the names proposed. And nothing in the testimony suggested that even the defense questioned the coroner's statement as to the time of death of the victims, essentially taking away Sander's only defense that he saw Carson do it.

The circumstantial evidence against Sanders was flimsy at best. Jake and I both agreed that the State's argument based on their perceptions of that evidence provided a logical *story*, but the prosecutors didn't do anything to prove it, and in the end, it was no more reasonable than the defense's narrative of what happened, including Nathan's insistence that Carson was the actual murderer.

"Don't you think," I asked, "that if the prosecution created a story based on speculation and it was a completely different story from what Nathan said in his confession, that would invalidate the confession and make Nathan a liar rather than a murderer? The confession he made was what the prosecution lawyers used to pin Nathan to the wall, but it didn't fit with their own pieced-together rendition, so his confession would be a lie, right? Just a different version of the circumstantial evidence, right? If they were invalidating his story, how could they allow the jury to use the confession in their decisions? And since they couldn't prove their version to be any truer than Sanders' version, how could a jury believe anything it heard?"

Then there were all of the unmistakable screw-ups of the people who provided testimony that helped convict Sanders. The law officer who took Nathan to jail and collected his statement, clearly lied about what he heard from Nathan and how he remembered it. He lied about gathering evidence. On the day he was to take the stand, he was caught, prior to giving his testimony, reading newspaper articles written about the case a year earlier. It seemed he needed to prepare what he was going to say so it matched the records, and, even then, made statements that were inconsistent with what he said at the coroner's inquest. Others clearly lied in their renditions of what they had seen or done. Whenever Nathan's attorney objected, the judge shut him down. It was the classic example of "a bird in hand." And that bird was already plucked.

Nathan was no angel by any stretch of the imagination. Any number of witnesses made that obvious. It was possible, of course, that Nathan had killed Mrs. Trent to get her out of the way so he could rape the refined young girl he would never have been allowed to touch otherwise. Based on what we read about him, his upbringing, his proclivities for gambling, drinking, and carousing, it wasn't impossible to believe that he killed the girl to keep her from being a witness against him, and then, he ransacked the house for money. It was possible that Nathan raped and killed the girl while Mrs. Trent was out of the house, and she returned and found him, so he had to kill her so she couldn't testify against him. It was impossible to know whether Everett Parsons, the man who was working the property for Mrs. Trent was the first victim or the last, depending on who was telling the tale. It was also possible someone else committed the murders just as Nathan said. Nathan had said clearly in every interview that Alf Carson was responsible for the murders even though he knew Carson had an alibi for the time established by the coroner.

Nothing we could find explained how a coroner in the 1870's could accurately judge a specific time of a crime based on the condition of the bodies or how to interpret fly larvae that might have been present or by calculating ambient temperatures over twenty-four hours or how these factors and others might have affected the rate of body decomposition. It seemed to me that "guesstimation" might have been substituted for science, but since the issue went unchallenged in the courtroom, all concerned must have found the coroner's assessment acceptable and, therefore, removed all attempts at linking Carson to back up Sanders' story.

"Whether he did it or not, Sanders was screwed from the start," I said. "Maybe he could have appealed the case if he had lived."

"It's looking like there's not much hope of ever knowing for sure whether or not he did it," Jake said.

"You're probably right. But we know he sure as hell didn't get a fair trial."

"What he did get was a miserable way to die."

"But why on your land, Jake? They could have hanged him anywhere. But they came way out here. What was there about this place that was worth the time and effort?

"I wish I had the answer to that. This whole thing is just weird. It's like everything about it is so screwed up, that the minute you start to get a handle on it, the story twists, and, instead of answers, you get more questions."

"Maybe it's about who was out there in the mob. Or maybe it was about what the place offered that couldn't be found anywhere else. Or maybe it was just a place away from the town where people could gather without attracting busybodies who might squeal on them. Who knows? We might just have to accept that truth died with the people of that generation. Maybe we just need to lay out the facts, what was said in the records and in the newspapers and be satisfied with that. At least it will be easier for other people to get at the material than it has been for us. Maybe that's enough."

Jake was quiet for a moment and then half-whispered. "It won't be enough, but it may be all there is, and I might have to accept that."

***

As time passed, Jake's muscles began to loosen from the stretching he insisted upon doing each day; we joked that they—his muscles--awakened each morning moving like shiftless employees who had to be reminded of how they earn their keep and who they were working for; they cursed his name for moving them and rebelled, and yet, they finally gave in and worked to the extent Jake could bear the pain in his slowly healing rib cage. However, no amount of force on Jake's part was going to make his body heal as quickly as he wanted. Grudgingly, he came to accept he had to deal with whatever time it took, and he would have to find the patience for it. However, he had no intention of lying around more than was necessary. Ultimately, it took six weeks for Jake to recover and be cleared medically for returning to work. During that time, I moved in, his dental work was completed, the bruises were gone, and we became comfortable sharing space within the old farmhouse.

19

The night before Jake returned to work, I awoke about 2 a.m. I lay in the bed thinking about Jake returning to work, fears I had for him, fears I had that he might be working side by side with some of the people who put him in the hospital.. From there, my brain leaped from image to image and idea to idea. Then, for whatever reason a mind focuses, mine began to ponder the question of why a mob might have chosen this land for lynching Nathan Carson. As I lay there, it dawned on me that neither Jake nor I had thought about doing any checking on who actually owned the land at the time of the murders, who might have been living in the house, and whether or not there were any obvious connections to the murders. Strange, how things that seem so obvious once you think them can hide for long periods of time in the recesses of consciousness, and once they've been found, demand an immediate reaction. Had the Auditor's Office been open in the middle of the night, I would have had to get up, get dressed, and get there. The rational part of my mind settled for making it a primary task for the following day and then disappeared ... another leap ... the abyss ... that goddamned thinking that leads to unnamable fears about past, present, and future— the value of my work, the desire for acceptance, my place in this thing that is life swirling into a state of chaos gaining in strength, becoming monstrous. I wanted to wake Jake and say, "I'm scared! I'm scared that my having been won't have been for anything, and our time together will disappear." I was like a hellfire and brimstone preacher having a crisis of doubt and demanding his god come up to the altar in an antiquated New England church and assure him he was going to be able to withstand this world's next inevitable step toward devolution.

Had I done it—woke him—I knew Jake would have comforted me, asked questions to understand, looked at me with patience and understanding, tried to get me to say what would help. And when I said the truth about not knowing, he would have said with absolute sincerity something like, "For me, it's all about living honestly and freely, learning everything I can about who I am and how I can be better and how you and I can live what time we have. That's enough for me. All we have is *now* and what we can carry along with us about the past—all of it." It was a common sense view of existence, and I wished I could own it for myself, let up on the notion that there is more to it, more awareness of where we as a species are headed, how my contributions fit into the big scheme of things ... whether or not there is a scheme ... whether or not anyone actually contributes anything worth anything to the whole of human existence.

I envied his ability to focus his energies and avoid distractions. Unlike me, he didn't dance around every human problem like a person doing the St. Vitus dance. He didn't fool himself about the complications of life, but he seemed to be able to find ways to deal with the messiness of it all—ways that didn't keep him awake at night staring at what would have been the ceiling if it could be seen; he accepted it was ceiling. He slept untroubled by the need to write his thoughts into memory or on paper or screen for later use or to debate whether such things could or *should* be remembered as they connected, disconnected, started and stopped like the paint on one of Pollock's canvases making some kind of sense for the future as I came up with statements like,

Abstractions in black and white, the extreme ends of the entire spectrum of gray dust covering the landscape of time. Ego. Id. Why? Reductio ad absurdum.

Words beat against the rock wall of my skull, mixing the existential questions with the reality of the here and now: my world with Jake and all that it had brought into my life: a murder mystery, a crime story, a love story, a sudden awareness of the history that lay like pottery fragments ground to powder where my feet fell on the earth. It was the sound of Jake's breathing that touched me, made me get up and dress and do what needed to be done: go downstairs and write for a while, find some way to avoid the recklessness of my brain fluttering in the dark.

When I finally stumbled around enough to find my way downstairs, I walked into two different chairs and fumbled for the table lamp and turned it on. In the light I realized I had my T-shirt on inside out, and boldly determined that I would leave it that way as an act of defiance against my internal need to make it "right," made this decision as an act of rebellion against the darkness of the bedroom that had made me grope my way to my clothes like a blindman placed in an unfamiliar space without his cane. I took my laptop from the bookshelf where I had left it earlier in the day, laid it on the coffee table in front of the sofa and wrote without concern for what I might do with the words that fell out there.

I wrote for a long time, adding and removing words and sentences, rethinking and rewriting my way into a fiction loosely tied to the Trent Murders.

Seventeen-year-old Molly Taylor was a beauty: milky white skin on a perfectly proportioned and curvaceous body; a petite heart-shaped face; brown eyes with long lashes that fluttered seductively and made men want to fall into her spell; a small, red-lipped, mouth that puckered slightly as she smiled; the small nose of a fairytale princess. Her pert breasts held proudly forth under the seamstress-like creations she and her mother made.

She had no conscious intention of diminishing other women in her presence or being overly provocative with men; she did so simply by being herself in her vibrant youth. She would have done so had she been wearing rags. There wasn't a person who'd ever seen her who hadn't taken notice of her beauty, including her mother, Margaret, who knew well what her daughter had become and how carefully she would have to be guided past the many men who eyed her.

Margaret Taylor fully intended that her daughter would be a virgin at her marriage; she made it her mission to ensure it even when she couldn't watch Molly's every movement, largely by preaching morals and values. She also worked to keep young men at bay for as long as possible. When that approach eventually stopped working, she gave in and allowed Molly to be courted by those men that she, Margaret, pre-approved. Pre-approval included learning about the man's character and the breeding and financial well-being of his family.

Ellery Curtis of Zanesville, Ohio, and his family— owners of a large clay-product manufacturing company— somehow passed Margaret's rigorous review process. He had been allowed to visit and to take Molly out on buggy rides into town and back when he arrived for his once per month weekend visit after Margaret made clear to both Ellery and her daughter that propriety was of the utmost importance. Arrangements were made for Ellery to sleep at a neighbor's house, sharing a room with one of sons who lived there. Molly had to leave her own bedroom and share her mother's bed both nights.

Despite her mother's controlling nature, Molly and Ellery wrote long letters. When he visited, he and Molly found occasions to talk, hold hands, walk in the fields, ride in the buggy away from the house, kiss, fall in love, and become engaged.

Ellery was not inexperienced with women, and he had done everything he knew—without violating his vow to be a gentleman—to convince Molly that, since they were getting married, they should enjoy the full meaning of love; however, she made it clear that she was not planning to give in to him until they were married.

Four months before the wedding was to take place, Ellery had come for his regular visit, and he and Molly were taking a buggy ride on a long straight road where they could see anyone coming either direction from a long distance. There couldn't be any surprises, he was certain. He stopped the buggy, put his arm around Molly and pulled her to him, tilted her head and torso back and placed his lips over hers, kissing her with such passion that she simply sank into him. He took the liberty of putting his free hand on her breasts; he felt the weight of each of them, the softness of them, the stiffening of the flower-blossom nipples. He could feel his own body responding to the pleasure of touching her, the feeling of his muscles flexing and pleasure of the blood rushing into his groin, racing inside him in all directions, reaching to his brain and removing inhibition, taking him into a state of sweet intoxication that a man wants to have go on forever. And Molly wasn't resisting. As he kissed her again, his hand began to move down her body when, as if suddenly awakened from dream, she pushed him away from her and sat up straight.

"I can't! I'm sorry. I just can't."

"But, Molly, this is part of what people in love do. They share their bodies, all parts of their bodies, with one another. Molly, you're a woman now! I want you so badly. Please? I know you want it too. I can feel it in you. I feel it in your kisses, in your breasts, in the ways you touch me. Couldn't we? Just this once?"

Molly wanted to say yes. She wanted to know more about Ellery's body, wanted to know what it felt like to have a man's body intermingling with hers, and yet, her mother's voice was in her head. "When we're married, I'll do whatever I can to make myself a good wife for you, give you my body completely, take your body to mine, but not until then. I want to, but I can't. Please be patient." He wasn't happy about having to wait, but he did.

Molly satisfied herself with the promise of the upcoming marriage and with the dream of what it would be like when Ellery took her into their marriage bed. She created pictures in her mind of every contour in his beautiful young muscular body. In the night in her bedroom, she would imagine touching every part of him, feel him inside her as they shared that most intimate human connection.

Jake came down the stairs at 6 a.m. and sat down beside me. He touched my leg, asked as if something in the air suggested he should be concerned, "Are you okay?"

"Yeah." I lied. I didn't tell him of my wrestling with demons before coming downstairs to write. "Just tired. Didn't sleep well. ... Are you happy to be getting back to work today?" It was a pointless question, a deflection.

We drank some of the coffee I had made earlier and chatted about some of the things he would likely face at work. his expectations for the day, and his desire to get back to the work he loved. He accepted the faked cheerfulness I spewed into the air like cigarette smoke. After a few minutes, he got up, made himself some breakfast, then went upstairs to get ready for work. I went back over what I had written earlier, made some changes and corrections, and tried to focus on what was to come and how to say it.

It was a hot June day. She and her mother had been at the pine kitchen table eating their lunch and talking about whatever flitted into their heads: the weather, the farm, their neighbors, the upcoming marriage; books or articles they had read. They both loved to read, decipher meaning, figure out what was said between the lines. Margaret had a large collection of books accumulated over many years and was constantly adding to them. She also had books she had carried with her from teaching school in her younger years. She subscribed to two different newspapers and a couple of journals that were piled on a table in the sitting room. She had loved teaching Molly to read and to think about what she had read, and she enjoyed having someone to talk to about her own joy in reading. They particularly loved to talk about the works of Charles Dickens and what they considered to be his many well-drawn characters. They would quote lines or read them out loud to one another. Sometimes they would try to talk with British accents about their daily activities and, occasionally, try to apply the roles of the characters they liked most to "get their opinions" about issues the women found amusing or concerning. As they played the roles, Molly had learned to look at issues from multiple perspectives and become respectful of ideas that did not fit her own.

Jake came down the stairs half an hour or so later dressed in his uniform, wearing all of his cop paraphernalia. I had forgotten how formidable he appeared in the outfit and told him so, tried to sound cheerful as we said our goodbyes. There was a moment's hesitation as he headed for the door. He stopped briefly, turned and looked at me smiling. It was a knowing look that said, "I'll be fine. I'll be careful. I'll come home." When the door closed behind him, the house felt suddenly hollowed and lonely. So, I wrote.

On that last day of their lives, they had David Copperfield on the table and were talking about the Micawber family and Uriah Heep. Looking out the window as Molly talked, Margaret saw Jimmy Chambers and a young man they didn't know coming across the field toward the house.

Mrs. Taylor, who was usually patient and kind with neighbors was not pleased by the sight of the men, "Here comes that Chambers boy. Always trying to get me to loan him some money. Twice this month already. You pick up the dishes and stay inside, I'll try to head him off."

"Mama, he's just a poor boy. I don't think he means any harm."

"He wouldn't be a poor boy if he was willing to work and didn't spend all his money on whiskey. You just do as I say and put those dishes away."

Mrs. Taylor wiped her hands on the apron she was wearing, untied it, and hung it on a nail in the kitchen wall. By the time she had gotten out the door, Chambers and the man with him were in the dooryard.

"Howdy, Mrs. Taylor," Chambers said, dropping his eyes quickly from her to the dirt path that led beyond the flower beds to where the woman stood.

"Hello, Jimmy. Who's your friend here? Don't think I've met him."

"This here's Mike Larson. We're just out walkin.' Jest tryin' to figure out what to do with the day when we ain't got no money. We ain't had nothin' to eat since yestidy mornin', and I don't know's we can handle this heat all the way back to town without something in our stomachs. We was kind of hopin' you might be able to spare a bite to eat seein's how you know my family and all."

"Won't your family feed you, boy?"

"They's havin' a hard time right now. I'm livin' 'way from home so's not to be a burden."

"What are you planning to do with that axe handle, there, Mike," she asked. "If you put an axe on it, somebody might want to hire you boys to do a little work so you can afford to eat."

"Yes, ma'am," Mike said "Jes' brought it along. Thought somebody might buy it, give us a quarter for it or somethin' so's we could buy some food."

Margaret looked at the two young men in their dirty, thread-bare clothing, their bare feet, the sunburns on their faces, and felt pity for them, felt badly that she had spoken ill of Jimmy from within the house. She told them to go over to the hand pump and wash themselves off best they could before entering the house and carrying all of their dirt along with them. She turned and went inside, leaving the door partially open as a neighborly invitation. As the men were at the well, she started pulling out cornmeal and eggs and leftovers from lunch. Margaret turned to her daughter who was standing off to one side of the room and barked at her to get a couple of bowls down off the shelf, get some eating spoons, and pour two cups of buttermilk and set them on the table.

The men came in, looked sheepish as they greeted Molly standing before them in a neatly pressed dress and store-bought shoes. But sheepishness didn't last more than a moment after the girl turned to the counter to pick up a serving spoon to hand to her mother. The men looked at one another with those lewd looks that unsophisticated men use when in the presence of a beautiful woman, those looks that say without words their shared fantasy of what it would be like to possess such beauty, be the first with her, make her cry out and writhe with pleasure. Without words, they boasted that each had what every woman wants but which only the most beautiful can have. What they didn't say was that each of them was keenly aware that a beauty like Molly would never want to be touched by either of them.

When Mrs. Taylor spoke, the communication between the men was momentarily broken. She invited them to sit down and relax while she got some food together. The man called Mike, said, "Ma'am, I think we might jest need to hol' up on the vittles and sittin' down. I think I like the view from up here." Without any attempt to cloak his thoughts, he looked Molly up and down and up again and then at Jimmy and said deliberately and forcefully, "Yup!"

They took steps forward; Mrs. Taylor turned toward them in shock at what she read in their faces and in the way they were moving toward her and Molly. She grabbed the cast iron pan from the wood-burner, raised it in her right hand and prepared to wage war on these invaders; and, suddenly, stopped as she saw the pistol Chambers had pulled from his pocket aimed directly at her. Molly screamed, and the man named Mike ran at her, grabbed her, and wrapped himself around her to stop the flailing arms and twisting of her body as she attempted to make her escape or protect her mother or whatever it was a terrified person might do in a moment of panic.

Mike spoke menacingly to Molly, demanding she calm down, "or we're gonna hurt your ol' mama real bad. You got it?" Molly stopped resisting. "Now, that's a good girl," and turned toward her mother, "Got any money in the house?"

Mrs. Taylor responded nervously, "A little. I'll give it to you if you get out of here and leave us alone."

"I think you're gonna give it to us whether we leave or not," Mike said to her. "Because, if you don't, I'm gonna find it if I have to pull this here house apart one board at

a time until it ain't nothin' more 'n a pile of kindlin'. Now where is it?"

"It's up there on that shelf." She pointed it out. "It's twenty-six dollars. It's all we've got. You take it and get on out of here. And you—turning to Jimmy—I've known you and your family almost your whole life. You should be ashamed of yourself. Your mother and father would just die if they knew what you were up to right now."

Young Chambers just looked at her dead eyed. Said nothing, just kept his hand on the pistol and his trigger finger extended and ready.

Larson spoke: "We've got us some business to do before we'll be moseyin' on out o' here, Ma'am. You and me, we're going out for a walk so's we can git some fresh air." Then, tilting his head toward Jimmy, he said, "Unless you wanna take her out and let me watch over this pretty little girl. Which you wanna do, boy?

Jimmy spoke out of the side of his mouth, never flinching, "I already said I'd take care o' Miss Molly afore we even come in here."

"I'm not leaving my daughter in here with either of you," the woman asserted as if her determination could somehow stop what was happening.

Larson released his right arm from around Molly, telling her not to move or her mama was going to get hurt. Then he reached into his right-hand pocket and pulled out a pistol of his own and pointed it at Molly's temple. Then he looked back at the woman, "I think you'll do what I tell ya ta do or this pretty little girl's gonna be layin' in a pool o' blood. Now get that money down."

The woman, now shaking and crying, reached up to the shelf, pulled down a clay pot and took out a ten, three fives and a one. As she was reaching up to the shelf, Larson told Chambers to cover the girl. In an instant, the guns had shifted their targets as Chambers grabbed Molly by the arm and pulled her over to him and he put the barrel against her back and his left arm around her shoulder and pulled her up against him. Mike walked over to the older woman, grabbed the money from her hand, took the clay pot, looked in it before smashing it against the hard surface of the wood-burner. He stuffed the money into his pocket, walked over to the wall where he had left the axe handle and told the woman to walk out the back door with him. Both she and the girl were sobbing and begging to be set free and were told to shut up. The mother was being pushed out the back door at the end of the axe handle and ordered to keep walking and not look back. Chambers, moving the girl forward with the hard-edged ridge of his gun barrel, pushed her into the spare bedroom. Through her sobs, Molly blubbered out many pleas, "Don't do this, Jimmy. You know me. Don't do this to me."

Beyond the walls of the house came several dull thud sounds like those of smashing pumpkins that Chambers chose not to hear, and Molly missed for the raging fear beating against the inside of her skull. Her own voice and the chant of "No! No!" and "Please" became distant, receding like a last echo across a valley; all rational thought escaping her like milk from a fallen and broken jar.

When he was done, Jimmy stepped into his pants and pulled them up quickly, stuffing himself inside them. Mike, watching from the doorway, was removing his blood-soaked clothes. After a few moments with the girl, Jimmy rolled to his side, pulled himself up from the bed, shook his body as if casting off water from a cold swim. He looked at Jimmy, smiled and winked.

Molly lay still, more like corpse than living flesh. She was staring into that emptiness that is the promise beyond life. Though Larson shook her violently, she didn't respond, nor did she fight as the men lifted her to a standing position and wrapped her arms over their shoulders and worked her body toward the door where Larson used his free hand to pick up the blood-covered axe handle that he had set aside when he came in. Together, the men took the girl outside to a place no more than twenty feet from where her mother's body lay in a pool of gore. Larson released the girl from him, shifting her weight onto Chambers, who held her in place until Mike gave a signal for him to step away quickly while he swung the axe handle with all the force he could create, laying the handle like a sword slashing against the side of her face over her left ear. Again, there was the sound of smashing pumpkin. And he didn't stop after she fell, couldn't stop until the face was gone. And when it was, he walked calmly to the pump, took off his clothes and soaked them in water, wrung them out and soaked and wrung them again. Then, he lay down

*under the spout and ordered Chambers to pump the water
all over his naked, blood-covered body.*

I had reimagined the brutality in technicolor, seeing it
as an accidental witness looking through the window of
150 years ago and much too late to intervene. But maybe its ugliness, my revulsion at what I had created, was
the point. As the draft of a story ended, I could feel anger
within my chest—anger about wasted lives, inadequate
information for building a true history I could present to
Jake, anger about my inability to find answers to seemingly
unanswerable questions.

I suddenly recognized that I could have accepted that
Sanders was or wasn't a cold-blooded killer. I had made
him one in my story because that was the easy thing to
do, and it was fine for a work of fiction where I had no obligation to provide facts beyond my own imagination. As I
thought about it, I realized that my anger came from what
had been set in motion by Sanders' jailhouse statements
that he had been sitting off to one side uninterested, unin-
volved while Alf—the devil incarnate, if Nathan's version
of the story was true—destroyed the lives of two women
and the Parsons family. The best he could muster well
after the murders was that he "felt bad about it" (people
being killed). It was his refusal to engage, his lifeless claim
that he was there, watched the murders happen, and neither helped nor hindered the horror that had simmered
into anger at last. "Indifference is far more deadly in the
world than a million armed forces united in an evil cause,"
I handwrote on the printout I had made of the story.

Needing to escape myself for a while before going into Fannon's later in the day, I turned on the TV, flipped through the cartoons, reruns of *The Waltons* and *Golden Girls,* endless commercials, and settled on news. After an hour or so, when I was sufficiently depressed by the blood, guts and gore left lying about by politicians, corporate entities, and religious fanatics, I thought about the massive indifference of the American people to the horrors of our own time.

My thoughts stared back at me, making a phalanx of words in a foreign alphabet meaningless beyond their myriad colors: unreadable hieroglyphics. Had they been printable, I would have collected them from the machine and torn their pages violently, crushed them, hurled them into the trash as statements against a world closing in on itself and cannibalizing its own flesh. ... With that, I had created a metaphor—a monster—to haunt me many nights as I lay in the dark wishing prayer somehow worked.

***

By 4 o'clock, I was sick of staring at computer and TV screens, sick of listening to myself think, tired of trying to lose myself in the inanity of what passes for entertainment, being depressed by shallow news reporting. I was almost happy with the thought that I had to get ready and go into work and do something that needed little more than staying awake and trying to be pleasant with customers and co-workers.

Just before I made the trek from the employee parking lot into the store, Jake called to say he would have to stay on until midnight to deal with some event downtown. In my sleep-deprived state, I complained that he was working overtime hours on his first day back at work, knowing full well he had probably volunteered. I didn't like it, told him I was worried about him, and then accepted his assurance that he would be fine. At work, I stayed busy at the cash register most of the evening and only had time to think about being tired in brief lulls in customer flow and during my break.

Back home shortly after 10 p.m., I was moving mechanically, going through the motions of washing a few dishes, and wiping the counter. I had left the house with drafts from my earlier writing still lying around and felt the need to clean up before heading off to bed. At first, I started crumpling up useless printouts and shooting them at the wastebasket. The majority of paper balls missed the target despite what should have been clean shots as I pretended to be giving my best efforts to emulate a great basketball player. Too tired to play out the fantasy, I picked up the scrunched balls of ink-splatted paper around the basket and dropped them carefully so as not to embarrass myself by missing again, watched each of them fall amongst their discarded and soon-to-be-forgotten peers. Then I went to bed and passed out.

It was well after two a.m. when Jake came into the room and woke me with the clunking of his miscellaneous pieces of equipment as he pulled them off his body and put them on the dresser. When I whispered that I had missed him, he apologized for the noise. "I saw the heap of paper downstairs. Have you solved all the world's problems yet?" I could hear the smile behind the words.

"Not all. Maybe got a little closer on a couple of them," I said in gest as he slid between the sheets to hold me.

20

Chief Cooper had told Jake to stay out of the investigations into former policeman Mike Harridan. Jake knew it was the right thing to do, but the cop in him wanted to get into the hunt. Though he didn't violate his agreement with the chief, he didn't ignore opportunities to pick up clues about what was happening with the case. He had a few friends in the department who would allude to the fact that investigations were ongoing, but they couldn't give any details without risking the chief's wrath or giving Jake some kind of false hope that the case was near completion.

"He's a 'by-the-book' kind of guy, and Cooper is not going to tell me anything about what's happening until he gets all of the evidence he needs," Jake told me. "I know him well enough to know that he's throwing all the resources he has at figuring it out. What I don't know is whether or not he's close to having enough evidence for the city prosecutor."

Cooper knew Harridan was the kind of guy who could have been plotting vengeance, and he wasn't particularly surprised by Jake's belief that Harridan was behind what happened the night of the attack. He probably suspected it from the moment he first heard that Jake had been taken to the hospital. The chief also knew that Harridan, if he was behind it, was smart enough to think his way through almost anything that might link him to the crime.

Jake was very matter of fact in his analysis of Cooper and seemed to admire him and to trust that he would get to the bottom of the case if there was a bottom to be found, and he expressed appreciation for the fact that he had Cooper to work with and not his former chief who seemed to think Mike Harridan could do no wrong.. Cooper had come to the department when the previous chief decided to retire. Two years in, Cooper seemed to be doing a good job of overseeing the operation given that he had inherited a department with problems: problem employees, lack of resources, and a long history of lax leadership. Not only had he inherited the problems of handling officers used to a loose structure and lax leadership, but he had also inherited a previously negotiated union contract that made it nearly impossible to fire anyone for any reason other than blatant crime, dereliction of duty, or acts of violence or sexual harassment. My take on what Jake said was that Cooper's task was not dissimilar from that of a one-legged, one-armed aerialist trying to cross a gorge on a tightrope.

Since I didn't know Cooper, I lacked the confidence Jake had. Doubt and frustration leaked through my question, "Is it realistic that Harridan or whoever gave you the beating is going to get caught?"

"It could happen if somebody rats somebody else out, I suppose." The words "I suppose" registered with me as a recognition that he wasn't all that much more confident than I was, but he wanted to be. Jake was, to my way of thinking, a cop's cop ... always thinking ahead, thinking about how he would handle things if he had to make decisions. He was certain that the chief would be looking at the call logs in the office, grilling the dispatcher, questioning Aaron Weller about his calling in sick that night. The dispatcher would be a key figure the chief would want to lean on, try to figure out his connections with Harridan and why he would go along with the scheme ... as Jake was certain he had.

As we talked, I couldn't help but wonder if Jake's confidence in the chief was justified. What he said Cooper would likely be looking into sounded right, but was he in fact looking at anything? When I asked Jake if he had any way of knowing what was actually being done, he referred to Tony Angelino, the officer I had met when I went to the station looking for Jake and learned he had been beaten. He referred to Angelino as a good man and a friend; "not the best cop in the world, but a good guy" who would give what information he could. There were a couple of others on the force who would drop tidbits every once in a while that helped Jake keep faith that his case wasn't being ignored.

As a story writer, I wanted all of the pieces that I was getting from Jake and reactions to my own thinking about potential holes in the plotline. Like a reporter, I wanted to challenge assumptions, check facts, make sure I wasn't going "down a rabbit hole" based on my negativity about Harridan. As a result, I questioned again the assumption that Harridan had to be behind the attack. After all, Jake was a police officer, had gotten into altercations with people who were out of control due to drug use and alcohol or dealing with anger issues, and people committing any number of other crimes, any one of whom might carry a desire for revenge. It seemed worthwhile to at least pursue the idea that he might have enemies other than Harridan. Though he acknowledged my concern, he said he assumed the chief would have thought of that, but no one had more reason to hate Jake than Mike Harridan, and, as far as Jake was concerned, there was every reason to suspect him.

"It's the clues, Rob! They all start at the station house. If it's not Harridan, it's somebody else on the inside working for him. Whoever it was, specifically targeted me." Jake was in full cop mode saying in a matter-of-fact way what he was thinking. He reiterated the coincidences ... something he'd learned to think about in his early education about investigating crimes along with the other maxim, "follow the money." He was also keenly aware of the gun; for him there was significance in its being re-holstered. He was convinced that putting the gun back in his holster was meant to make him look careless or stupid when going into a dark place with a woman's voice calling for help, and him not knowing what might be going on when he stepped into an open space with no protection. It could also attract suspicion that he knew what he was walking into and had no fear of a bad outcome because he was involved in something shady himself. Setting him up for these scenarios was not something the average person would think of as an added perk to beating him senseless. As far as he was concerned, the one person who wanted to frighten him, get revenge, and wanted him to look bad in the department was Harridan. Knowing that the investigation into racketeering was closing in on him, Harridan would want Jake to know that he knew who turned him in and was upping the ante on Jake's going forward with testifying against him.

"What's kind of funny, he said, is that I never had 'evidence.' If I had, I would have run him in myself. I just expressed a suspicion. If there is evidence, it came from the detectives or the chief." His point was that Harridan knew police procedures for dealing with suspicion of crimes, and police officers who expressed suspicion and had to know that Jake was far less a threat than the people he was shaking down or the prime investigators. Jake was convinced that Harridan was looking for revenge that had little to do with his criminal activities.

"Revenge for your not letting him screw you?" As I said it, I heard the restrained jealousy I felt for the notion of Harridan touching Jake, having his body. Jake did not play into my momentary overdramatic response. He maintained his plain-spoken, analytical examination of the situation and agreed that what I suggested was part of it, but he suspected that more important to Harridan would be his fear of Jake telling other people what he was and how he had propositioned Jake. Jake and I both had known so-called "straight men who wanted a man on the side but were terrified of anyone finding out: men who cannot accept that there is a significant fluidity to masculinity that ranges between gay and straight, and many men hang out near the middle of the scale despite what they proclaim to their friends and relatives.

As Jake and I talked, I tried to put a face and a life to Harridan. My image became that of a man in his mid-forties, edging toward stockiness, but still in good physical shape, muscular, swaggering, and dangerous. He was the face of a failed Marine, strong-jawed, war-scarred skin, dark eyes beneath a dark brow recessed in the dark caves between his wide nose and weathered cheeks. He was the brute taking his own life's disappointments out on weaker men. He was wifeless, a man desiring power and money more than love, the kind of man who paid for sex, got it over with, and walked away without leaving a tip. No responsibilities to anyone but himself. I imagined him as the force that propelled the main characters in some of my stories to find their courage, act and overcome. Were he a character in one of my plays, I probably would have made sure he got his comeuppance ... maybe even killed in the final scene—the cliché for dealing with life's brutes.

After listening to Jake talk for a while, I concluded that many officers on the force were afraid of Harridan, though most of them would never admit to being afraid of anyone.

However, it was clear that he had made himself *the* lead cop on the force by creating fear in those who worked with and around him. For sycophants, his decisions were always to be considered correct decisions. Any lies he told became the truth and any truth he disagreed with became a lie not only for him but for those under his spell.

As a rookie cop, Jake had learned much from Harridan: where the action was in the city, the types of cases Jake could expect, and how to handle citizens according to 'the rules' mandated by the laws and monitored by the chief. Toward the end of Jake's training period and before the groping incident, Harridan started talking about the "real rules"—the ones that make life easier, and he started asking questions about Jake's finances and how he was going to survive on a cop's pay. Harridan ran through a litany of grievances about the money, the commitment police work takes, the problems coming at cops from both sides: the public and the expectations of the chief, City Council, city prosecutor, and judges. When he assumed he had Jake under his spell, he said, "You know, cops have ways of getting bennies that can add to the 'bottom line,' if you know what I mean."

First time around, Jake didn't respond or ask questions; they were rushed to a call. It was a few days afterward that Harridan made his move on Jake and had his hand nearly broken by Jake's hold on his fingers. Before leaving the car that day, Jake made the mistake of announcing, that if what Harridan and his buddies were doing for 'bennies' was illegal, they all should go to jail right along with all other crooks."

Harridan yelled back at him, "Fuck you! I didn't say anything about *illegal*." Jake knew instinctively that Harridan was dirty.

Later, Jake remembered that oftentimes, Harridan wouldn't arrest people who probably should have been arrested, would let them off with warnings after he talked with them privately. When Jake asked him what happened in those conversations to make him give people a break, Harridan would just say, "I scared the shit out of him, and I don't think he'll be a problem anymore." He liked to "scare the shit" out of hookers too, and then cut them loose as if to say, "You owe me one." And there were the many occasions when Harridan would demand that Jake stop the car while he, Harridan, ran into one business or another for purposes that were never explained, sometimes making four or five stops a day at various locations.

When Jake got transferred to ride along with another experienced cop, he tried to talk about his suspicions with his new partner but was told, "Best not to ask questions and just do what you're told." Within a few days, he was suddenly somebody some cops were leery of trusting or talking to for anything other than necessary business. And, even among the officers who liked Jake, joked with him, took him into their confidence, there was a dead spot in their interactions like the sound of a deflated tennis ball whacked in a powerful backhand when any talk of Harridan and his activities came into play. Apparently, it was as far as they were willing to go to call Harridan a 'miserable son of a bitch" behind his back and let it go at that.

Only Tony Angelino was able to say in confidence to Jake, "He's on the take. I know it as sure as I know my own name. I only wish I could prove it." When Jake asked him if the chief (the chief prior to Cooper) knew about Harridan, Tony said he probably did, but wasn't likely to do anything about it because he was—according to Angelino—as dirty as Harridan was."

When Mark Cooper took over, and Jake got to know him as a fair man and a good boss, Jake decided to lay out his suspicions, knowing full well that without concrete evidence he could end up looking like a troublemaker. He accepted the dangers and hoped the chief would see his concern as something worth looking into. Cooper grilled him, wanted to know who in the department had shared concerns and why no one had come to him previously. From the way Jake described the situation, it seemed to me that the chief was trying to be sure there was no personal vendetta hidden within the telling about Harridan. Jake must have done a good job of laying out the reasons for concerns not only about Harridan, but about the way the previous chief created an atmosphere where it seemed dangerous to buck the system, particularly when it came to anything about Harridan.

A week or two later, Cooper gave Jake a limited amount of time and authority to do a preliminary look at the issue with the understanding that anything Jake found, or thought might be worth knowing, be provided to him

before taking any action beyond asking some basic questions of store owners. He made it clear that he didn't want
to go too far down the road without something more than
a few officers' "beliefs" and "feelings."

"Shouldn't that have been done by detectives?" I asked.

"Probably, but you have to remember the chief was
struggling with many problems. I suspect he wasn't sure
he could trust those boneheads to keep their mouths shut."

"Wow! Just like that, you became a detective. Sherlock,
how about from this point on, I become your Dr. Watson,
the bumbling but erstwhile companion who marvels at
your brilliant mind. When you close the case, I'll write
'The Case of the Crooked Cop.'"

Jake picked up the newspaper from the table beside
the sofa and rolled it up. He looked at me as though I were
out of my mind and swung the role gently toward the back
of my head and then wrapped his arm around my neck
and pulled me toward him on the sofa, the two of us struggling against one another like pre-adolescent boys. After
we settled down and stopped laughing, he began telling
me about his foray into detective work as I listened and
tried to lock in details as they came at me.

Jake's first stop was at Lidon's Uptown Grocery—one of
the places Harridan had stopped many times during Jake's
early training, always leaving Jake to wait in the car while
he went in. He couldn't remember Harridan ever having
returned to the cruiser with anything visible that he might
have bought. For all Jake knew at the time, Harridan might
have been buying gum or needed to use the bathroom, or

any number of other possibilities that could have been devoid of any underlying illegal activity.

The shop was run by an elderly couple that had started the store in the early '80s and made it profitable by focusing sales on beer and cigarettes, lottery tickets, and quick-buy items, selling largely to the people walking the Main Street of Emberland. The Lidons lived above the store in an apartment, rarely left the building, and worked from 8 a.m. to 10 p.m. six days a week and from noon to six on Sundays. If they had a life outside the store, children, friends, other family members, they kept it to themselves. When they had time to spend, and what they spent it on, was anyone's guess. By the appearance of the building, both inside and out, it was obviously not being spent on fixing up the exterior of the building or painting the interior or doing thorough cleaning of the store where dust-covered shelves were often canvases for jokes, comments, initials, and vulgar drawings.

During the months I had lived in Emberland, I had gone into the store several times for a six-pack of beer or a soft drink and knew what Jake had seen. Everything about the store was old, tired, on the verge of death. The floor's antiquated tiles—those that had not succumbed to time and been thrown in the trash, had holes in them from the constant wear of harsh boots and shoes that ground at them constantly under the heavy bodies of drunken or obese patrons—often students who staggered around the streets pre-loading for or unloading from their drunk fests or other debaucheries and who came in day after day and year after year to make their way to the coolers, up to the cash register, and out into the street again in sun, rain, snow, heat, cold, wind or stifling stillness any given day could offer.

It's doubtful Jake would have taken the time to notice expiration dates on canned goods, meager frozen goods, or hanging bags of Beef Jerky. Clearly, the Lidons didn't spend their time rotating their minimal stock. The profitable products rotated themselves via the many hands of students and street people who would come in for their beer supplies or to buy their habitual need to keep their lungs full of warm smoke. On the other hand, the Lidons probably had to be told by the more astute customers that the sell-dates had expired. Maybe at one time or another they thought about throwing items out; however, apparently, they decided to rely upon the ignorance of customers who didn't know to look for "sell-by" dates—people who just paid and walked out the door and wouldn't have time or the wherewithal to return and demand a refund.

The Lidon's were friendly enough to all who came in, but rarely engaged in more than the "Welcome," "Thank you," "Anything else I can get you?" and "Come again!" courtesies expected of all small businesses around the country if they wanted people to continue buying from them.

Jake knew them because of the street activities in the late evenings when he was on duty: fights taking place where someone's body hit the thick glass of the storefront or attempted thefts where drugged-out-would-be thieves demanded money of the couple but were too stupid to know the Lidons had a panic button directly linked to a call service that would inform the police immediately that they were needed at the store. Jake learned at some point that the Lidons always asked for Mike Harridan to come if he was available when they called in for aid. But Harridan wasn't always available, and sometimes Jake or others would take the calls and learn for themselves that the Lidons had strange reactions to officers in general. The old man and woman often seemed as afraid of the officers as they were of the brawlers who were fighting on the streets or the occasional out-of-control customer who needed to be dealt with.

As usual, Jake was good at giving the facts related to his first time visiting the Lidons as he began his investigation. Specific details that would spice up the story weren't his forte. I listened to get basic facts as he perceived them and later tried to make them into a story which provides the essence of what he told me, making up dialog and action that might become useful at some point in the future.

On the day that Jake went to the store for the first time as an investigator, the old man and woman stood at the counter watching him enter. Their faces were ravaged by the effects of gravity. Skin hung from their faces in clumps gathering beneath their eyes, in folds about their jowls, and waddles under their chins, and yet, they could not hide the fear that rose like last whiffs of smoke rising from a slow burning and near-dead fire at the sight of his uniform. Jake tried to relax his body to appear non-threatening as he walked up to the counter and made a few comments about the weather, asked if they remembered him from those occasions when he came to deal with various problem customers, reminded them of one of the funnier incidents they had called in.

"Don't remember. Nope. Can't remember any of that. Sorry." The old man looked to his wife, who agreed that she couldn't remember Jake or the incident. He suspected they were lying but pretended to take them at their word. He tried to make a joke about being unforgettable, but it fell flat. Finally, he looked into the face of the old man standing behind the counter—that proverbial wall between them. In his peripheral vision he saw the old woman who had been standing off to one side reach for a broom. He didn't speak, let the couple struggle with his presence for a moment. The old man looked out at Jake through his droopy and reddened bloodhound eyes as Jake finally asked, "Curiosity. Has Officer Harridan been in here in the last couple of days?" Jake knew when he asked that he needed to watch the faces of the Lidons as they reacted to his question.

Mr. Lidon quickly looked down at the floor. Mrs. Lidon turned to one side and frowned. The old man spoke quietly to the floor before lifting his head up on the last word and tried to fake being comfortable with his response: "We don't talk about who comes or goes here."

The old man dropped his gaze to the countertop as Jake said, "Mr. Lidon, I'm asking a simple question. I've seen him come in here many times in the past. I just want to know if he's been in lately—the last few weeks. Simple question. You're not in any trouble if that's what you are concerned about."

There was a quick "yes" response that dribbled out of the side of the old man's mouth and ran down his chin. It was followed by a lifeless, "We don't tell no one they can't come in ... unless they try to steal." Again attempting to perform the role of casual conversationalist, he asked, What difference does it make he comes in here?"

The old lady turned away with a look of disapproval, went to a space just out of Jake's line of sight. The sound of broom bristles pawing at the dirt and dust flying in every direction diminished as she made her move away from the men toward a back room where she quickly—as quickly as an eighty-something-year-old woman can move—drifted out of sight.

"If it makes no difference, why are you so uncomfortable answering my questions?"

Jake's eyes fixed on the old man's eyes. Lidon hesitated, then said, "What you want to know?"

"I'd like to know what your relationship is with Officer Harridan."

Still not looking up at Jake, he said, "He comes in. Gets what he came for and leaves. That's all."

Then he looked up at Jake as if to assert some kind of honesty about what he was saying as Jake asked, "That's all?"

"That's all!" Lidon was trying to maintain eye contact and sound convincing.

"What is it he takes with him usually?"

"Why are you asking?" As he finished the question, he projected the impression that an idea had struck him. He paused, and the asked quietly, hesitatingly, "Did he send you to test me?"

Picking up on the man's phrasing, Jake said, "I was just asking, Mr. Lidon. Chief's just doing a check on records. Seems like Harridan comes in here quite often." He paused hoping that the old man would think of the questions as trivial. After a brief pause, Jake smiled and asked as if it were an unimportant question, "What did you mean when you asked if he sent me to test you?"

"I don't wanna get caught in middle of anything," Lidon reacted abruptly.

"Why do you think you're in the middle of anything?" Jake asked still trying to keep a nonchalant voice and knowing he had just stuck his toe in the doorway of Lidon's secret, but he had to follow it up quickly if he was going to get through the door. "You said a couple of minutes ago that he just came in to get things. I'm trying to understand how that gets you in the middle of anything."

Rattled, Lidon became defensive, and announced, "I should talk to Harridan before I answer any more questions. You got a beef, go talk to him. I don't want no problems."

"Are you afraid of him for some reason, Mr. Lidon?"

"I'm afraid of all police," the old man said through quivering lips.

"Mr. Lidon, I am not here to make life difficult for you, but you seem afraid to talk about Harridan. Why is that?"

The old man's face started turning red. He gasped, then said, "I'm a stupid old man. Shouldn't have said nothing... You go now." As the man's voice got louder, his wife came out from the back room shuffling as quickly as she could to her husband. She was shaking her head as if saying "no" many times without making a sound, as if denial would eat the responses he had given me.

Speaking sharply to Jake, she said "Don't believe anything he says."

Maintaining his calm demeanor, Jake said, "He didn't say much of anything, Mrs. Lidon, but he sure seems afraid of talking about the officer. Is there a reason for fearing Harridan?"

"My husband is losing his mind. Crazy. Does all kinds of crazy things. It's not true whatever you think. Officer Harridan is a good customer. One of our best. Please, you go now!"

The old man put his arm over his wife's shoulder as if she could somehow carry him away from his blunder. "I'm sorry about bad impression!" he said. "You're nice young man. Go home now. Everything is fine here."

Jake gave the couple a business card with his name and the station number and told them if they had any problems, they should call him.

"We don't need help," the old woman said. "We just want to be left alone."

Jake left knowing full well they were afraid and were covering for Harridan, but they would need a lot of coaxing before they would divulge the truth. He also knew that they would likely tell Harridan about his visit.

Jake managed to get bits and pieces of information from several other business owners, most of whom reacted similarly to the Lidons. It didn't take long for him to conclude that no one was willing to take the step of exposing Harridan, giving a statement, or being a witness against him. What Harridan had over them, by what means he was able to threaten them, why they feared him ... would have to be discovered through more aggressive investigation.

21

According to Jake, when he and Chief Cooper went to talk to Prosecuting Attorney Carolyn Boyle about their suspicions, he had been warned that he would be dealing with a hard-nosed politician, experienced litigator, and too-busy prosecutor who would have little time for them, and she was going to nail them to the wall if they hadn't prepared effectively to lay out the story of how a long-term police officer was strong-arming merchants for weekly payoffs. Behind her back, officers, clerks, and community leaders called her "Hard Boyle" because she could be quite abrupt in her interactions with people if she felt her time was being wasted or she was being bothered with issues that could have been handled by any competent attorney; however, despite her demeanor, her reputation for getting convictions was more than enough to keep her in office for as long as she wanted it or until she died—whichever came first.

Of course, I wasn't there to hear what was said and how it was said, had no idea whatsoever what Carolyn

Boyle looked like, what her mannerisms were. So, when Jake finished telling me his interpretations of the meeting, I had to ask lots of questions and piece together what he said based on my own impressions of the people involved as he described them. Then I wrote my way into the ongoing story I had been creating.

The chief did most of the talking. Prosecuting Attorney Carolyn Boyle sat behind her desk slowly moving her body from side to side in her black leather swivel chair, elbows on the arms. Her folded hands rested just under her bottom lip as she listened. When Chief Cooper was done presenting his case, Boyle dropped her arms to the armrests and said she agreed there was every reason to suspect Harridan.

"However," her voice was the equivalent of pointing a finger at Cooper's face, "suspicion doesn't get him into a courtroom. Get me some solid evidence. But you'd better be goddamn sure you're right about what you're doing before you take him into custody. If he's dirty, any case he's ever worked is likely to become a major pain in the ass for me. And if you're wrong, he's probably going to sue everybody in a fifty-mile radius of here."

Boyle hadn't reacted well to Jake interjecting his belief that some of the merchants might be turned to testify, particularly if sophisticated surveillance techniques could be applied. She stared at him, said nothing, the darkening of her eyes conveying all of the humiliating disapproval anyone could handle; they were the eyes of his mother when he had displeased her.

The prosecutor turned her head away from Jake and spoke to Cooper, "Mark, did you just promote this young man to detective? I think this case will require someone more capable than a street cop doing the investigating, don't you?" She used a pause in her response like a powerful workman's sledgehammer making its final swing before a wall falls. "I'll work out surveillance issues with you if you think you can find a cooperating business owner, but I want detectives on this. And you keep me posted on what's happening. I want to see anything and everything you get on film and audio. Unless you can catch him red-handed with incontrovertible evidence, do not arrest Harridan until I tell you to do it! You hear me?"

Before releasing the men from her office, Boyle clarified where she stood with both Jake and the chief. Speaking to Jake, she said, "You did some good work, but you are not to do any more. It comes across like you've got some kind of personal stake in this. This isn't a TV show, and you are not a movie star. If you muck up this case, I'm going to kick your ass. You got it?"

"Yes, Ma'am," he responded politely, not wanting to react to the tongue lashing and the sense of disappointment he was feeling.

As he and the chief started toward the door, Boyle's voice stopped them. "One more thing!" Then it was the chief's turn. She said that he should have known better than to bypass the work that detectives were supposed to be doing. Cooper made the mistake of trying to explain the issue of not trusting his own detectives because of their known association with Harridan.

"Then you should have come to me! Trust the goddamned system, Mark!"

When Cooper pulled the door closed behind them, and they started down the hall, Cooper whispered, "I feel like I'm ten years old and just got an ass-whoopin.' How about you?" Then, he reminded Jake that those in power want their own rear-ends covered at all times, and if anything were to go wrong, someone other than them was going to take the hit or, at a minimum, go down with them. Only half joking, he said, "That means you and me, buddy."

22

The detectives took over, and Jake was relegated to providing statements about who he had talked with and what he saw and heard. He told them everything he knew, but he made clear that he hoped they would keep confidentiality to protect people like the Lidons. Then all he could do was wait and hope. He had accepted the chain of command and Cooper's order that he stay out of the case.

A couple of months later,

Jake was in the station house at the end of a shift where some of the officers were talking, as usual, about "stopping for a cold one" on the way home or getting to the ballfields to watch their children play, or some other routine part of their day when Mike Harridan came storming out of the chief's office. Jake noticed that Harridan's shield was no longer on his shirt and his gun and holster were missing. Harridan was already ranting before he got through the doorway. Clearly, he needed an audience.

"This is what you get in this fucking place, folks! Fired for nothing!" He started moving toward Jake. "Davidson,

you rat-faced bastard ... you set me up! Got me fired! I'm going to kill you, you son-of-a-bitch, motherfucker. It's a fucking frame up! When I'm done with you, you'll wish you were never born! Don't think you're getting away with anything, motherfucker. You will pay!" His blood-red face was merely inches from Jake's. The veins in his neck had swollen, his muscles were taut. Jake readied himself for taking the first blow.

The chief heard the yelling, came out of his office, and spoke with authority: *"Mike, get out of here. Walk out the door right now, or I'll have you thrown out."*

Harridan turned toward the voice, *"You and what fucking army? I'm not afraid of you, motherfucker!"* He started toward the chief but stopped short and punched the wall, puncturing the gypsum board with enough ferocity to leave an impact hole like a small cannon had fired upon it.

Speaking authoritatively to the group of officers standing around, the chief said, *"Get him out of here or I'll have him in jail for destruction of public property and any other goddamned charge I can come up with, and don't let him drive until he calms down."* At that, a group of Harridan's acolytes surrounded the man, tried to calm him down, encourage him to go home, think through the next steps before he got himself arrested. Harridan finally gave way, spewed a few more epitaphs of rage, and went outside followed by the officers who had tried to control him. Jake could hear the ravings outside as Harridan screamed at the sky, the officers, the people driving down the street

or walking on the sidewalk. And then it stopped, and the
street was quiet, and the officers and Harridan were gone.

Speaking to Jake, the chief said, "You can press charg-
es for the threats if you want. It's up to you."

"What's the point? You heard him. The whole depart-
ment heard him. You know where to look if anything hap-
pens to me."

At least, what I had written was more interesting than
the pure factual information I got from Jake: Harridan was
pissed; he came out of the chief's office ranting and making threats, mostly against Jake; he thought he and Harridan were going to have a fist fight right there in the station; then Harridan went after the chief, thought better of
it and punched a wall; Cooper threw him out, threatened
to arrest him; Harridan's buddies managed to get him out
before he could cause more trouble.

When Jake finished reading the draft and giving me his
feedback, I asked him, "Why is it when somebody like that
jerk punches a wall, he always hits the spot between the
studs? Can't they ever connect with a stud, break a knuckle
or something? Might not be so apt to bully people if they
found out that every time they punch something, they hurt
themselves."

Jake just looked at me with his quizzical scrunching of
the brow and sucking in of his bottom lip, and then releasing it to say, "You are one weird dude, Slick, with the things
you think about."

"Tell me something new," I said, as he grabbed me and
put me in a headlock under his left arm and messed my

hair with his right hand's knuckles rubbing hard against my scalp. I started laughing and yelling into the earless hollows of the house and miles of distance between us and the nearest neighbors, "Somebody help me! He's giving me a "noogie"! The sound of the long-forgotten word of my childhood just amped up the hilarity of the moment. He had me, and I wanted to make some attempt to react to his powerful body. So, I tried to talk him into submission. It was kind of like trying to wrestle a boulder, and all I could do was continue laughing as he released his grip and attempted to push my disheveled hair back into something resembling what a comb or brush might have done.

23

Jake liked that I was following the story of his police work, particularly as it related to Harridan. He was eager to read whatever I wrote about the case, offer praise for the fictions of dialog and character, and challenge me when the basic facts got lost or became murky. He joked that he wanted half of the royalties if I published whatever came of telling strangers about was going on in our lives.

"I'm just making notes at this point," I said. "I don't know that it's going to become ... if anything. I'm making it up as I go, Buddy."

Trying to sound like a cagey businessman, Jake responded with, "So, you're saying you're not going to cut me in after you steal my life? You're cutting me out of the royalties? I'll sue."

After a while of playful banter in which I promised to give him a cut, we talked about his work, Harridan, threats, and investigations. At some point he told me old Mr. Lidon had called the station the day after Harridan was fired and asked specifically for Jake.

When Jake got to the phone, and before he could ask what he could do for the old man, he was hit by a hammer-fisted wave of panic at high volume:

"Why did you do this to us?"

"Why did I do what, Mr. Lidon?" He asked the question even though he suspected he knew the reason for the call.

"He thinks—"

"Who thinks what, Mr. Lidon?"

"Officer Harridan... he thinks we told. I didn't tell! You can't use what I said. He's going to hurt us, my wife, my business. It's your fault."

"Mr. Lidon, if you have been threatened, we can protect you."

"Protect me? You can't protect me? Nobody can. I won't testify. I'll say I lied. You tell him I didn't do it. You did it. YOU did it!"

"Mr. Lidon, I'm sorry if he is threatening you. Let us help... Mr. Lidon? Mr. Lidon?" The phone was dead. And all Jake could do was write a report about the call, tell his chief, answer the questions of the detectives on the case, and listen as the chief played the recording of the conversation that had been logged into the station-house phone.

The poor old man didn't even know that cameras and audio recordings had probably been made in other locations, and that what he had hinted about Harridan on that day Jake had questioned him was likely a Post-it Note in the ongoing development of the case. Jake wished he could have explained to Lidon the reasons Harridan was fired, that he (Lidon) wasn't the center of the investigation, that Harridan was fired due to incontrovertible proof from some other source that he was a crook ... but then, Jake didn't know what the chief used as grounds for giving Harridan the boot. Whatever the reasons, that was between Harridan and the chief, and the chief wasn't sharing any information.

As Jake talked with me about the old man's anger and palpable fear, the sound of regret was in Jake's voice and he had a sadness in his eyes as if he were talking about a close family member, as though he should have been able to make the old man's fears go away, protect him and his wife, not only from Harridan, but from both the power and the powerlessness of the law.

24

November crawled into December and died. But I was feeling as well as I had in a long time and was working diligently. I had a good short story going that I built around the dilemma of a gay actor getting a so-called "gift" of a call girl from a friend who didn't know he was gay. To make matters worse, the friend wanted to stay in the actor's dressing room while the call girl tried to seduce the actor. It seemed like a good situation to try to write my way out of. I knew it was unlikely to sell. It conjured the notion that there are all kinds of sexual pleasures in the world and would fly in the face of readers who think there are "right" and "wrong" sex acts between consenting adults. I was okay with that. More interesting to me was the relationship between the two men who were able to get real with one another without the hangups of labels "gay" or "straight." The call girl was the real problem. I felt bad for her as just another pawn for a guy with money, and I hadn't resolved how I could turn that stereotype on its ear.

There was also a play I was working on that showed a lot of promise as well, but it only revealed itself in fits and starts and would not be rushed. I continued to write about my relationship with Jake and the conversations we had about his work. I finished some short stories that dealt with corporate greed and abuse of workers and managed to place them into some paying publications. Often, when I looked up from any of these pieces, there was the ghost-like specter of Nathan Sanders standing in the corner of the room watching me. He often followed me out onto the porch when I took a break from writing, sat on the railing to watch me think. He was persistent in his staring, his question obvious:

"When are you going to deal with me?"

"Soon," I would say to him, "if for no other reason than to get you off my back."

I had read as much about the Trent murders and Sanders as there was available in old newspapers, court records, and summaries written by people who had tried to make sense of his case, some, apparently, without having looked at those same newspapers and court records I had. I had typed and compiled all the written materials I could find and had organized them in chronological order on my computer. At the press of a button, I could drop them into a book-length collection of articles that would tell a powerful story—assuming a reader was willing to read through the seemingly endless repetition and the overwhelming verbiage of sensationalism. The story was within the mass of paper littered with unsolvable contradictions. A faithful rendition of facts was not.

There was no question that the story itself had all the potential of a novel: In 1873, an uneducated, good-looking young man was determined to be the killer of three people, all for a few dollars and a sexual event he could never have without resorting to violence. It had not mattered that he claimed innocence or that there was only circumstantial evidence against him. Community members lynched him— their murder of him was righteous, his murder of others a horror. It was a story about mayhem, intrigue, brutality, poverty, lust, vengeance, retribution, justice, the duality of human nature and the essential question: "Why?"

Embedded in the story was a powerful character that would serve much like the father's picture in Tennessee Williams' play, *The Glass Menagerie*—a constant remind-er of a pervasive force watching over everything that happened. In the Trent Murders, the force was the news. Newspapers had done the lynching long before the literal lynching took place. The people who made their livings selling ads and subscriptions had created and pontificated on the meaning of justice and constantly focused and re-focused their readers' attentions to monstrous murders at the hands of fiends. Horror! Brutality beyond human com-prehension! The constant escalation of the good of those who died and the soulless brutality of the monster who committed the crimes raised the actions and characters to mythological proportions—a myth that was highly lucra-tive for papers for many months. Without much concern for actual fact-finding, pages of fantasy were filed in the community's history; words had been freed from the confines of reports and thrown into the air of a common lore to be passed from one generation to the next regardless of truth into the present.

And, then there was Nathan Sanders himself: A villain? A sociopath? A dupe? A child's mind in a grown man's body? At a minimum, he was someone who relished attention—even if it was negative attention—and because he wasn't smart enough to know better, he gave the community every reason to hate him as they read his every word interpreted by reporters who had already found him guilty.

I tried to imagine that I could have made a version of the story as if painting words with a brush on a huge canvas meant to depict the imminent destruction by hanging of a saintly-looking man/boy surrounded by a furious mob, each mob member dressed in brilliant-colored clothing totally inappropriate to the reality of common people of the time, but which made for striking contrasts in dark and light like a crucifixion scene by an Italian master of fifteenth century chiaroscuro—a painting where the viewers' eyes take in the whole of the painting but are drawn relentlessly to the central figure... an artist's trick to make viewers think *they* are doing the work of seeing. And had I painted the agony on young Sanders' face just one-second after the support being pulled from him as he fell before the mob's hate-filled eyes, I would have painted his bulging eyes staring straight into the image of one innocent young girl kneeling off to one side of the picture. She would be looking up into the heavens, her hands folded in prayer for the condemned man/boy's soul while the light of her god cascades from the heavens through the dark of night onto her pure white face. . . had I painted that canvas, it might have made me happy were I a fifteenth century artist, but I wasn't and it didn't, and I found myself thinking it merely derivative and myself a master of now-ancient attempts to assemble a pathos in the heart of those who looked upon the monstrous, technically-masterful, but artistically bereft image of the human condition. How much more interesting it would be to paint a Picassoesque image of a bulging-eyed judge with a noose around his fat neck and his bloated swollen face pushing out his green-bile-covered tongue while the laughing spirits of those he sent to their deaths looked on.

The court records weren't all that much better than the newspapers. The testimony of various people was recorded as best a scribe could scribble by hand his interpretations of what people said on the stand, their words racing ahead of him and running out of his memory. Using the recorder's words for whatever represented accuracy in 1873, it was obvious that many of those who testified had their own agendas, as many witnesses do: avoiding getting called out for their own mistakes, lies, and biases; trying to make sure the villain got the comeuppance the witness wanted him to get; or wanting to cover for friends who might be guilty of distorting truth; or lying outright to put the defendant in the best or worst possible light.

At times, I worked from home typing out the pages of the handwritten court records I had photocopied; it cost me time and money to make those copies, but having the copies allowed me the freedom to work beyond the Annex's limited open hours and around my work schedule. So, I was working with reduced-sized pages of handwritten records and had to become my own version of the ancient scribe meticulously trying to create an exact replica of the words placed on the pages despite the words' abilities to disappear, get up and walk away mid-sentence or run up my arm and laugh into my ear, making fun of my inability to follow their confusion of tenses, their rat races of run-on sentences, their taunting *nah, nah, na nahh-nah* of seemingly endless variations of spellings of names, and smirking illegibility of various scribes' scrawls.

The spare bedroom had become my monk's cell, providing me a desk, a light and an electrical outlet for my computer and printer and a floorspace. Paper lay everywhere, covering almost every inch of the floor boarding except for the path in and out and immediately below my feet when I was sitting at the desk; originally, the laying of paper in little stacks served my need for sorting all of the materials I had printed out of old newspapers and court records. I had copies of county maps of the period, made drawings of the Trent property lines, the footpath into town, the location of the house in relationship to the meadows and woods. I followed the movements of various investigators as they walked the property looking for clues and later described their every step in the court records.

I made timelines for reported activities and cross-refer-
enced the rat-maze of details reported in local newspapers
with documents and testimony in the court records and
noted the many contradictions and misrepresentations.

It was a productive time for me. Not only was I doing
something for Jake, but I was also enjoying the research
and organizing. I was writing every day about things Jake
and I talked about—things I just felt like writing. When
Jake wasn't working and we had time for one another, I
was young again, playful, and often happy.

25

Nancy Tryger, the manager at Fannon's, had scheduled me for a four-hour stint at the store. After my final visit to the Annex, I barely had enough time to run through the McDonald's drive-thru, choke down a sandwich, a few fries, and a cup of coffee before my shift started. When I got to the store, the parking lot was nearly full, and I could imagine Nancy trying to juggle her many responsibilities for managing the stockers and two cashiers and jumping into either position as needed for employee breaks, mistakes, and customer complaints. She had been at her job for many years and knew every aspect of it. She was a whirlwind who probably could have performed the work of any three employees without perspiring. Though she was now in her fifties, she moved like a young woman, darting from place to place with an athletic agility and a sense of joyful purpose, keeping the entire operation running smoothly despite the inadequacy and tomfoolery of some of her staff composed largely of teenaged workers.

When she saw me come through the door, our eyes met; a stranger would have seen nothing more than Nancy's acknowledgement of my entrance. I, on the other hand, saw the "thank-God-you're-here-I'm-going crazy" look that sent me to the back room to get into my company uniform—a dark blue apron with "Fannon's" written in script across the width of the bib. Just below the script was the narrow pocket where employees are supposed to keep pens for customers who inevitably needed to write checks but hadn't brought a writing utensil. Pens are like gold amongst grocery clerks; every loan of the sacred pen has to be followed by a reminder that the pen needs to be returned, or the customer walks off with it, leaving the clerk to hunt all over hell to find a replacement for the next customer that wants to write a check. I kept two extras in my pants pocket, tucked two others in the apron pocket just for such inevitable experiences. I tied the apron behind me as quickly as possible, clocked in, and walked rapidly out to the registers.

As the lady she was serving pushed her cart away, Nancy punched a couple of buttons on the cash register, told me to take over, told the waiting customers they were in good hands, and stepped away to take care of whatever was next in her many tasks.

After checking out the groceries of three or four female customers, a man was standing in front of me. He had piled his various items on the back end of the conveyor belt right behind the previous customer's items, essentially pushing her and me to move along. He had intermixed groceries and liquors, ammo and a camouflage jacket that had come out of the store's small "Outdoor Department." He looked somehow familiar to me though I couldn't have said at the time how I might have known him. He was one of those guys that looked like he'd been weight-lifting most of his life—broad muscular chest, thick neck, wearing a tee shirt that stretched tight over his sculptured chest and abs and over his arms that swelled against the sleeves as if with a flex of his muscles the cloth would split. He had a thick head of black hair and a day's growth of stiff, black beard, and eyes that hid themselves under the ledge of his brow as if looking at me from within a cave. I didn't know a lot of people that looked like that, but I'd been in Emberland long enough to have seen many people. I thought perhaps he was just someone I had run into at the gym or anywhere around town at one time or another in the past. Something about his appearance niggled at me, made me feel like I should know him, made me feel like he expected me to know him. I didn't like the awkwardness I was feeling, and I didn't want to insult this powerhouse of a man by my not remembering him. As he handed me his credit card, I said, "You look familiar to me, but I'm embarrassed to say that I'm drawing a blank. Have we met before?"

"I doubt it. But I know who you are," he said.

My first thought was that maybe he knew something about me as a writer, but then almost no one in the city knew anything about me other than being an employee in the store and just another guy who moves about getting haircuts, going to the post office, going to the library, occasionally eating in restaurants. Other than that, my life took place largely in the confines of my living spaces.

I ran the card's strip through the credit card scanner, saw it was accepted and handed it back to him. When the white and yellow copies of the signature tape rolled out of the machine, I separated them and put the white one down on the stand and placed a pen beside it. As he signed and handed the slip and the pen back to me, he said almost as if whispering a secret to me, "I understand you're Jake Davidson's girlfriend."

At first, I hoped I had just heard incorrectly, but as I looked at his face and saw the smirk that had placed itself on his lips. I responded as straight-forwardly, unemotionally, and as quietly as possible while trying to suppress the tension that was racing back and forth between my stomach and my head, "What exactly is your problem?" Catecholamines were speeding to my defense making it more difficult for me to squelch the anger that was taking control of my face like a week's worth of whiskers bursting forth in three seconds or less.

The man was still leaning toward me over the counter and speaking softly enough that others couldn't hear him, and yet with an intensity of controlled threat that reverberated in my ears like standing at the speakers in a rock concert. "You can tell your pansy-assed butt-buddy that I'm sorry to hear he got himself beat up a while back. I'm sorry that whoever did it didn't kill the son-of-a-bitch, which is what the faggot actually deserved."

"Look, you asshole," I heard myself saying too loudly, "I don't know who you are and what your problem is, but you need to get out of here, and if you say another fucking word, I'm going to punch your stupid, fucking face in."

The man looked at me and laughed, unfazed by my threat, and spoke again with that slightly-more-than-a-whisper, but powerful, voice. "I wish you would come at me, you little prick. I'd love to have an excuse to stomp your skinny little ass into the ground."

Suddenly, Nancy was at the register and the people who had lined up behind this guy had retreated to the second cashier's lane or gone back into the aisles to listen while avoiding being in the direct line of action if a fight was about to happen.

"What is the problem here?" Nancy's voice had taken on an authoritative tone to it.

"No problem, missy," the man said. "Just having a friendly little chat with this fag here, and he got mad, that's all. It was him who did all the yelling."

Placing herself in front of him as though she were ready to break him in half, if necessary, Nancy declared in her controlled, matter-of-fact voice, "There is no need for you to call my employee names like that! You need to leave!"

The man looked at Nancy and then at me and smiled as if he had carried out a coup. He casually took hold of his shopping cart and pushed it out the door in front of him.

Nancy pulled me farther from the registers and half-whispered, "What in the hell is going on? I want to know what possessed you to talk like that to a customer in front of other customers! And you'd better have a god-damned good explanation other than his stupid name calling."

After I told her what he had said to me and explained in general terms the threat he posed to Jake, she softened some. She knew me well enough to see that I was genu-inely sorry for the incident, but she still felt the need to give me a brief recitation on controlling my anger in the face of a bullying experience and warned me she wouldn't accept another incidence of using foul language in front of customers even if the customer deserved it. When she was done declaring what she would and would not tolerate, she asked me who the guy was who had riled me enough to become that angry because she would make sure he was not welcomed in the store again. I started to say I didn't know; but that wasn't true; I had known who he was after his first statement to me, but I hadn't allowed myself to say his name.

Nancy told me to cool off before getting on the regis-ter again; she stepped back into the role of cashier. As I started to walk away feeling the guilt of imposing on her, I realized I was still holding in my left hand and turned to hand it to her, but before I could release it, I stopped long enough to read the printed name and signature to verify what I already knew. I had just met Mike Harridan, and he was everything I knew he would be.

***

After work, I drove over to the police station and entered the depressing room they called a lobby where I walked up to the window that looked in on Tony Angelino or other clerks who might be on duty. The room was empty, but there was a sign taped onto the inside of the window glass saying, "Press BUZZER for service." Then I started looking for it. There was nothing that resembled a buzzer on the counter, around the window, under the counter lip, the walls, or the door to the inner sanctum. As I stood in that gloomy space wondering if I was simply blind to the obvious, I thought about what it might feel like if this were an updated episode of *The Twilight Zone* in which a man walks into a room and the doors disappear behind him. He has nothing on him but a wallet and a cellphone that is within seconds of having a dead battery. Out of nowhere, hideously ugly men appear initially as ghost-like forms coming through the walls into the inescapable room, materializing as flesh and blood men with cudgels in hand that they have raised against the man armed with nothing but his adrenaline and a cellphone. The man, having no other option, paws at his phone, punches in 9-1-1 with the desperation a man has at knowing he is about to die while realizing the screen that was his consciousness is fading to black as the brutish men come at him one at a time, the first laying a single blow and then the others coming on, each laying a stronger blow than the man before him and returning to a cue line to await round two and three and four of striking the man's head and shoulders, arms and legs, desecrating the body until it oozed into the floor leaving only his useless cellphone still in the grip of his useless hand.

Finally, I had to accept the fact that if there was a buzzer anywhere in that room, I was incapable of finding it. So, like a sheepish child finding the courage to risk getting scolded, I went to the inner door, tried the handle first, knowing it wasn't going to open, and then knocked lightly, hoping someone would be standing on the other side of it so I didn't have to disrupt the whole operation and everybody in the building. After a moment of waiting and getting no response, I became increasingly more aggressive and ended up yelling behind my pounding on the door, "Hello! Anybody there?"

Shortly after my little tirade, an officer entered the office space and looked out at me from the glass and said, "What can I do for you, sir?"

The officer didn't seem much interested in my explanation about the buzzer and my explanation of looking all over the room for one. When I finished, he simply said, "It's outside to the right of the front door." Looking at him, I could sense that launching into an explanation about why the sign didn't explain that and how people could easily be confused just didn't seem worth the effort. He stood rigidly straight, his right hand resting on his gun handle protruding from its holster and his left hand gripped around his baton handle attached to his left hip. He was staring through me or beyond me like a problem he didn't want to have, as if waiting to get an annoyance removed so he could move on to something more interesting. It was the

cop stance that some officers have that says, "I'm pretending to be listening to you, but unless you say something
that triggers a cop response—something I need to write
down or take action on: murder, theft, or bar fight—you are
wasting my time, but, I'm smart enough to know the game
of 'if-I'm-not-as-polite-as-the-public-thinks-I-should-be,-I'll-
have-to-put-up-with-some-bullshit-complaint-and-waste-
more-time!'"

He repeated, "What is it I can do for you, sir?" over-em-
phasizing the word *sir*. I told him I was looking for Jake
if he was available. Instantaneously, he responded with,
"He's not.

"How about Chief Cooper? Is he around?"

"Nope! If you've got a problem, I'm capable of dealing
with it. What can I do for you?"

"Well, I guess I need to report an incident I had with a
former police officer today."

He pulled out a notepad and asked for the name and
what happened. When I said, "Harridan," his eyebrows
tightened, and his eyes came up from the pad, but his head
didn't come up with them. He wrote something on the pad,
and asked, "So, what did Mr. Harridan do that got you
lathered up." I realized that I couldn't talk about Jake's involvement or "out" him if this cop didn't know. I couldn't let
on that I knew anything about the ongoing investigation of
Harridan or Jake's involvement. Essentially, all I could say
was that I felt threatened by Harridan for his homophobic
remarks. All I could say was, "He harassed me."

"Was he violent?" "Did he touch you in any way?" "Did anybody get hurt?" "Did he break anything?" The questions came fast, and he wasn't interested in discussing my reasons for making a complaint or thinking about verbal abuse, hate speech, or disruptive behavior. If it wasn't physical, it, apparently, didn't count.

It wasn't just his demeanor or lack of compassion that got to me. My reaction was coming out of what a previous therapist told me was my own deep-seated sense of inadequacy that made me feel like he was stealing the emotional half of my being, clanging the cell door shut on my thoughts and feelings, proclaiming me less masculine than a male human is supposed to be, and I was feeling frustration because I wanted to prove to myself that gay doesn't have to equate with weak. Men like that officer seemed to have a preference for the physical, would have respected me more had I leaped over the grocery belt, taken a swing at Harridan, sent customers running to hide, had the boss call the cops who might—if they were lucky—arrive in time to get into the fray, whap somebody over the head with a baton, cart him off to a jail cell. Then, when he was completely under their control as a result of the beating, and after charging him with any number of crimes against the state, they would kibbitz with him through the bars. "It wasn't personal." But, of course, it was.

I suppose I just should have walked out and tried to call Jake on his cell phone or waited to tell him later in the evening when he got home from work. The notion of inadvertently outing him was making it difficult for me to explain the background that would have helped a good cop understand why I was so upset. Jake and I had been relegated to a parallel universe by people like this officer.

"So, a guy comes in, calls you a couple of names and pisses you off and you two yell at each other. There's no case here! Two guys shooting off their mouths. Sounds like free speech to me. You got your feathers ruffled, and now you want to make a federal case out of it."

"Look, I'm not saying this is a federal case! I'm saying I don't trust the guy, and I want a record of what he did."

"It doesn't sound like he did anything worth putting on the record. If your boss wants to put a no-trespassing complaint on him, have him call. Otherwise, you just need to get over it. Go home and cool down and forget about it."

"The boss is a *her*," I said as if that somehow undercut the way he dismissed my concerns. He shrugged it off with a "Whatever."

"Officer, I'd like to have your name please."

"What for?"

"I have a right to know who it is I'm interacting with. That's all."

"Officer Weller. You want my badge number too?"

It hadn't registered with me at that moment who Officer Weller was or why his name resonated once it was given to me. I wouldn't put the pieces together until I was halfway home.

***

Jake came home shortly after I arrived. We had a beer and sat out on the porch looking out over the gold and red and browns of the trees preparing to drop their colors. I told him what had happened at the store. He reacted in typical Jake ways. First, he wanted to know that I was all right, and then that I didn't get into a fist fight with Harridan.

"If I'd gotten into an actual fight with that gorilla, you'd probably be at my bedside in the hospital or at my gravesite," I said. "There was a minute there, when I thought I would, and I didn't care if he had killed me; I was ready to try to get at least a punch in. Nancy saved my ass, actually."

"You let him get to you, Rob. He wanted you to get angry; he wanted you to make the scene for him."

Of course, Jake was right, and I would eventually see how I'd been played, but I wanted Jake to know that it wasn't Harridan's words to me that had set me off; what had made me most angry was the thug's hatred of Jake, his total disdain for Jake's very existence because Jake had the ethical courage to act when he caught Harridan doing what others had overlooked.

"I understand, Rob. I really do. I'm glad you or Nancy had the good sense to de-escalate the situation. No offense, but he could break you in half if he got angry enough."

As I thought about How I had been played it dawned on me that Harridan had focused his attention on me because he was jealous of my being with Jake. As I expressed the thought to Jake, he agreed that I might be right, but more importantly, I was now a means for Harridan to get to Jake and, therefore, a target.

We slid into the second phase of Jakeness as if he had choreographed a dance routine making the transition from the role of lover, friend, confidant into cop all in four beats of a musical bar in 4/4 time; then it was like moving from ballet to jazz—syncopation, freestyle going after the particulars, eking out the facts, trying to lock into my memory what happened in what sequence and differentiating what actually happened from what I might have imposed on my telling of it. He wanted to hear the exact words Harridan used with me like he was studying the notes of an improvisation to figure out how the musician had made that high-pitched squeal of the trumpet fit. He wanted to know what I had said, how I said it and how angry I came across, what witnesses may have heard, and whether or not there were any surveillance cameras in the store. My responses were slow and deliberate, his questions came in staccato notes that clashed with the whole notes I was trying to give him. As we talked and played off one another, I finally realized that I looked far worse to the other customers than Harridan did. In reality, they probably saw me as the villain in our little play because they could hear me and not him, and he never tensed his body, raised a fist, or raised his voice beyond a loud whisper.

Then Jake stepped into the role of information synthesizer and rationalist and said what we both knew but I didn't want to accept: There was little anyone could do about what Harridan did and said that day; he had accomplished exactly what he wanted to accomplish: get a message to Jake that he knew how to hurt him through me. Jake admitted Harridan was good at what he did: playing on the fringes of the law and doing his damnedest to avoid getting caught when he made his surprise raids behind enemy lines.

When I mentioned Weller, Jake winced, and I thought I saw a flicker of anger pass across his eyes. Again, he wanted to know everything about what had gone on at the police station, what had been said and how it had been said. It was as if he were collecting psychological traits of the enemy, filing them away in some compartment of his brain. He reminded me that Weller was the man who had called in sick the night Jake was lured into the beating he took at the church. A bit impatiently, he expressed his frustration:

"Why didn't you wait until you could reach me? You can't trust some of those guys at the station. I've told you that!"

"I was coming in to tell you! Then I felt like I needed to have something important to make it worth his while to come out of the back area after I pounded on the door and yelled."

Rather abruptly, Jake said, "You didn't owe him anything, Slick! When he said you couldn't talk to me or the chief, you should have walked out!"

I suppose he saw the startled reaction I had to his way of implying that I had somehow failed to be as attuned to the internal operations of the police department as he was.

And in those seconds of reading one another's body, eye focus, stance, and tone, he tried to snatch the words that had
escaped him as if they still floated in the air between us,
wishing he could stuff them into his pocket and pretend I
hadn't reacted as I did.

"Look! It's okay. You tried to do the right thing," he said
quietly as his face reddened slightly and his head lowered.
"You didn't do anything wrong."

"Did he know who I was somehow?

The momentary stare coming out of Jake's eyes told
me what he was about to confirm after his eyelids blinked,
lashes swatting away the pain that had entered like wind-
swept dust.

"If Harridan found out I'm gay, chances are they all
know. Angelino knows. My friend Jim Lanning knows, the
chief knows. It wouldn't take a rocket scientist to figure it
out if anybody cared enough to look beyond their noses;
and, if anybody had asked me, I wouldn't have lied about
it. I'm not ashamed of it; I just didn't want it to become a
big deal. But that's not what I'm worried about right now."

He put his arm around me. We sat staring at the window without speaking for what seemed a long time before
he spoke again:

"I don't like it when I think this way, but sometimes I
think about how much better the world would be if somebody took Harridan out of it."

He hadn't said it so much for my sake, but as if he was
speaking to the gods and demons that possess the human
mind as though the words themselves expressed the anger

and frustration and the feeling of powerlessness, the feeling of being chained to a wall and being told that evil is coming and all that could be done was to wait. It was coming. It was going to do what it was going to do, and the only option was going to be to bear whatever it was that was going to be done and hope that somehow at the last minute there will be the *deus ex* machina—that absurd fantasy that once satisfied the Greeks sitting in their cold stone seats even though they knew full well it was a trick, what we call today "smoke and mirrors" or religion.

When we got into bed, Jake pulled me to him and said, "They know who you are."

"So, what? I don't care that they know. I don't care if the whole world knows. I love you, Jake."

"You don't understand. They know who you are, and they're using you to get to me, and I'm afraid for you."

"I'm not going to live in fear of people like Harridan. It just feeds his delusion that he's controlling us. I'm not afraid of him *or* his minions." I said that last line with as much commitment as I could muster, knowing Jake and I both knew I was lying.

"You should be, Slick. You, at least, better be goddamned careful."

26

On the cover were the serifed words, "The Trent Murders," and just below it, "1873." In the lower right corner were, "for Jake," in a complimentary, sans serif font. The leather binder was a custom-made, hand-carved masterpiece executed by a local artisan: leaves and blossoms woven amongst background tweed, and curved lines moving the eye of the beholder to follow the undulations into and out of the words and designs and wrapping around the side edge onto the back cover where leaves and dahlia's and daisies and phlox intermingled orgiastically—an homage to Jake's gardens and his revelry in them.

It was late October when I had the Trent Murder documents assembled and ready to place in the binder. The compilation and editing work I had done on the pages resulted in over four hundred pages of typed copy done in laser-jet print on acid-free off-white vellum. As I placed the stack of hole-punched pages in the binder, I had the feeling of seeing one of my stories or plays come out in print form. The work was an entity unto itself now, a thing to be taken up, read, studied, or set aside and ignored, a thing that may or may not hold a tiny place in local history. Though I had determined I was essentially done with Nathan Sanders and the Trent murders, holding all that material in my hand in that beautiful binder gave me pause. It felt like a precious object that needed to be passed on, but one I didn't want to release from my hands. I held it to my chest ritualistically, looked around as if a stranger might see me—laugh at me—felt a flicker of guilt for my sentimentality and set the manuscript gently into the tissue-lined box that would be wrapped and presented to Jake for his birthday.

A few days later, we were eating large pieces of cake after dinner—a cake I had special ordered from Fannon's bakery with "Happy Birthday, Jake" scrawled across the top. Beneath the words was a sugar-frosted design of red, yellow, and orange buildings with local well-known business names on them... all set along a green-gray sidewalk beside a lime-green street with yellow "no-passing stripes" down the middle. A Hot Wheels police cruiser was placed on the street with little puffs of smoke coming out of the exhaust pipe that the decorator had added to suggest the vehicle was moving past the buildings, perhaps in pursuit of some speeder imagined beyond the cliff edges of the cake. A side-street quickly became a circle around a single six-inch tall slim candle I'd bought.

We sat at the worn oak kitchen table drinking wine, joking about Jake's getting old, reminiscing about our time together and laughing at his renditions of my first hiking adventure to the pond. We now had a history together, a time that was us, a time to be carried forward for as long as there was at least one of us still alive to hold it. Jake exaggerated my responses to mosquitoes and heat and my initial surprise at getting naked to skinny dip. He was playing me like a stereotyped sissy boy as he vamped around the kitchen laughing as much at himself as at the scene he was playing out for my amusement.

When he had had his laughs and felt he'd gotten the better of me, I told him it wasn't easy trailing behind a wannabe Vin Diesel and dealing with a hardcore nudist on the first date; then I went into my own schtick:

"Out thaah in the will-da-ness amongst the heeaathens and wald animals, ah had to relai on mah man! Mah big brute of a maan! Howevah, did ah get along in this scaaary ol' warald befoah I met you, mah big hunk o' maanflesh? Thank goodness I haave you ta take caah of me, ta saave me from those awaful hayang-nayls ah get aend the wind messin' my be-u-ti-ful haih! Whay, ah doo declah: yo' my Rhett Butlah! Ah do so hope yo' goin ta stai soba tonaght so yo' caan pehfo'm yo' maanly dutae befoah this eve-nin's ovah, Rhett!"

Jake's face had turned a pleasant shade of rose-red behind that broad goofy smile of his while I was doing my performance.

"Frankly," he retorted, "Miss Scarlett, I do give a damn! I shall do my best!" Then, he looked into my eyes and said, "You are one strange dude, Slick! And I love you for it. I can't think of a happier birthday."

That's when I got up and went to the cupboard where I had hidden the present behind some pots and pans. I brought the carefully wrapped package to the table, set it in front of him and watched. At first, he just looked at it as if I had brought him something he feared he might break just by getting too close; then, he touched the wrapping like a four-year-old who is as dazzled by the shiny paper and the big orange ribbon and the size of the box as he was by the thought of what might be in it.

"What are you waiting for? Open it up!"

"Let me savor it for a minute. This is a new experience for me.

"What? You've never had a birthday before? I'm living with a one-year-old."

"We didn't do birthdays when I was a kid. No parties, no gifts."

He told me that his mother would make a cake and set it on the table after she cleared away the supper dishes, and she'd say something like, "So, Jake, you are nine years old today" (or whatever age he was in any given year). You can have a big piece of cake to celebrate." His father never said a word. He just ate his piece of cake in silence. That was it!

"I didn't expect anything else until I got old enough to become jealous of my friends. When I got old enough to get out from under my parents' control, I didn't have anybody who knew me well enough to care about or think about my birthday."

"Well, you do now, buddy!"

He waited a moment longer and began trying to undo the tape as if he was going to save the paper for some future use. It was strange to watch another man—particularly one who could easily pass as heterosexual in the world of heterosexual men whenever he wanted to pass—be so careful about the process of getting at the surprise inside a box; it seemed to me to be like what straight men go through when they are with new and beautiful women for the first time or what gay men experience when sex becomes love.

"You've got a lot to learn about opening presents, Jake! Tear into it, man!"

He just looked up at me and smiled and continued at his own pace. When he finally got inside the box and lifted the bound volume out, he stared at as if he were seeing a rare nocturnal animal that he'd heard about but never seen anywhere other than in pictures, an animal soft, delicate, fearful, and easily killed if handled inappropriately. He touched the leather gently like touching a newborn, letting the tips of his fingers feel the ridges and valleys of the leatherworker's cuts and grooves. He ran his forefinger over "for Jake" like a blind man reading Braille, and when he was done, he lifted and turned the binder to see and touch the spine and the back, felt it like electrical signals were finger-walking up the nerve ends of his body to the pleasure centers of his brain.

When he had lifted the cover and laid it gently onto its face on the table, he approached the pages of text in much the same way he had treated the binder as a whole, feeling the crispness of the shiny paper, feeling the print as if it were somehow raised, feeling the space where I had typed, "Compiled and edited by Robert J. Wilson for Jake M. Davidson with love." Then, he raised his head and looked at me through some tears before he got up and came to me. I stood up to take him into my arms and held him as he wept against my neck and shoulder, and eventually said, "I'm sorry," as he tried to pull away, but I held him fast.

Telling him, or almost any man, not to be sorry for crying was a waste of words better spent on little boys before they have been indoctrinated into the cult of masculinity where crying is a subversion of the natural order of things—the masculinity of men, the connection to the warrior brotherhood. Were he to think about it, Jake knew how absurd it was to perpetuate the myth that men don't cry; yet, even he was sorry, not because I had seen him cry, but because he couldn't stop himself from being sorry. And I played my role by saying nothing more than, "It's okay," while I held him and refused to let him go as he dealt with his feelings, felt him burst into sobbing as he clung to me in ways he had never done before. I held him and waited for his body to calm; when it did, he nuzzled the side of my face and my neck with his face and then pulled away, picking up his napkin to wipe away the wetness. When he had summoned more control, he joked about getting my shirt wet, wiped my face and neck with his large hard hand, and then went back to his chair and sat down. He wiped his hand on his pants often as he looked through the book, gently turning the pages to take in all of it: table of contents, sectioning, page numbering, drawings, and neatly typed print... saying numerous times how beautiful the book was and offering his thanks. "This is the coolest thing anyone has ever done for me, Rob."

"It was worth it just to watch you open that box and to watch your face, man."

Jake wiped his eyes again with his napkin.

I gave him a moment and then went on: "You know? I still don't know what to do with it beyond giving it to you and sharing it with the history center and with Tina down at the Annex ... which I've done, by the way. I feel like I know Nathan Sanders, maybe too intimately, or as intimately as anybody can who has only newspaper stories and testimony to go on. I've done a hell of a lot of thinking about him and the case."

"And?" Jake asked in his inimitable way to provoke a summary judgement from me about the topic of the moment.

"Honestly, as far as the murders, I think he was guilty as hell, but I don't think he did it all by himself. It just doesn't seem possible he could handle all three of those people without help, especially the two women. But can I do what those people back then couldn't do and prove it? I wanted to give you answers, all I've given you is what has been recorded, a lot of what you already kind of knew. But there are a couple of surprises you'll find."

I set the book down on the table in front of him and turned to the first page I wanted to show him."

"Look at this. Look at the date. Your family has been on this land for a long time." I pointed to a copy of a legal document:

Emberland County, Ohio Deeds, Recorded April 17, 1837.

Know all men by these presents that I, Thomas L. Dishong, in the County of Emberland and State of Ohio for, and in consideration of the sum of one hundred and thirty seven and a half dollars to me in hand before the unsealing hereof well and truly paid by Charles Reed of Emberland in the County and State aforesaid the receipt whereof is hereby acknowledged have given, granted, bargained, and sold, and by these presents do freely, fully, and absolutely give, grant, bargain, promise, release, convey, and confirm unto him, the said Michael M. Davidson, and his heirs and assigns forever all that real estate situated in the Town of Emberland in the County of Emberland and State of Ohio known and described as lots numbered 115, 116, 117, 118, and 119.

After he read it, he said, "So a Davidson was here then ... when Sanders was lynched."

"Yes," I responded. "Look at this:" I turned to another page where I had made a family tree going back to his great-great-grandfather. Using resources at the local history center, I found the Davidson family, named the wives, marriage dates, and children down to the time of Jake's own birth. I pointed to the name "Orville Davidson" (son of Michael) who had ownership of the property at the time of the Trent Murders. As best I could judge from old records I fished from the courthouse basement, he had previously leased the quarry property to a company that extracted stone slabs and gravel for building materials.

"We can date the opening of the quarry right around 1850-55. But what I get from what little I had to work with was that the lease had ended sometime prior to the murders.

"Now look here." I pointed to Orville's name on the family tree. "He had three sisters. one of whom was named 'Grace. Through a bit of sleuthing, I learned that Grace had married a Mr. Clyde Trent in 1855."

"Oh, my God. It fits," he said with excitement. She was some kind of an aunt. Right?"

"Great grand aunt. And don't ask me about your relationship to the daughter. Get me into cousins x-number of times removed, and I go nuts."

"This is amazing."

"That's not all," I said as I turned to a map I had found that showed Jake's quarry in relationship to what was then the town of Emberland. The quarry was at the far back end of his property, only a mile or so from the town "as the crow flies"—as I had learned country folks talk about straight lines going over hilly areas. I told Jake that I was curious about that. "What if the people who had worked the quarry made a temporary road for getting the materials to the railroad station? It would have cut a couple of miles off the trip we currently drive to get there, saved time, effort, and money getting the product to the town and the railroad.

"I just didn't know how to find out if that was the case. I thought it might answer the question of why the lynch mob went to the quarry to do its dirty work." My point was that a trail would make the lynching site relatively close and private. "If Orville wanted to avenge his sister's murder, it would make sense that he might want to choose the spot where Sanders was going to die."

As he looked beyond me into space, pondering the possibilities, Jake said, "You're a hell of a detective, Slick."

"Maybe. But we're no closer to the truth. We just have more to speculate about. With what I see, I don't think we are going to get any closer to what really went down."

Jake thumbed through more pages, looking closely at maps. Then, he looked up at me and said, "I had no idea. But now lots of things make sense."

"It's not proof, Jake. Still a lot of 'ifs' and 'maybes.'"

We spent some time talking about his family, wondering about how the story might have played out in the lives of Orville's heirs over the next couple of generations. Jake talked about his father, the long silence of the man taking secrets with him into his grave.

Somewhere in a brief space between our give and take of talk, Jake asked, "What about you? Did you find anything in all that work that you can use? Any way to make some money out of your work."

"Who knows? Maybe someday, but I still haven't found the nugget in it all."

When he asked me what I meant by "nugget," I had to wrestle with my own thoughts to explain it. *Nugget*, I told him, was "one of those words that's hard to chew but easy to spew." It was a deliberately ridiculous statement that sounded homespun and sappy—an attempt to return to the foolish fun we had experienced earlier. I broke into laughter.

Jake threw the palm of his hand at his forehead hard enough to leave a red spot behind as he faked a laugh like a braying donkey before saying, "That is really bad, Slick! One of your all-time worst."

Trying to own up to my embarrassment and create the opportunity to tell him something that mattered, at least to me, I said, "It did suck, didn't it? I guess what I was trying to say is that I haven't found the essential thing, the one thing that makes the story worth telling for me."

I reiterated that there's nothing wrong with the Trent Murders story itself. It was sensational in the original meaning of the word. It could be written into a fictional account. But, for me, I joked, "It hasn't crawled into bed with me and made love to me."

"You're getting weird again, Slick. Sex with a story?"

"I'm a writer. So, yeah, weird. Get used to it, buddy!"

I tried to explain that I hadn't found the click that drives me into the story: the image, word, sound or feeling.

"There's something cooking in me, Jake, but it hasn't clicked yet. Maybe part of it is in the Sanders story, but there's more to it than that. When it comes, it will bring along some kind of clue as to why I'm here on this fucked-up planet with all these other humanoid creatures who drive me crazy.

"Nothing like setting manageable expectations, Slick! But I guess that's what makes you a good writer."

"The word *good* might be a bit over the top. But I want to be."

"You are, Shakespeare."

PART 3

27

Several days later, I was asked to do a shift at Fannon's from 3 to 9 p.m. As usual, I drove to the side lot furthest from the entrance door. It was where Nancy Tryger had told all of the store's employees to park so customers had more access to the prime spots out front; I simply complied with her request and didn't mind the fact that it was not well lit at night and required walking a distance. Amongst the many younger workers, it was a bone of contention; apparently, walking wasn't something they liked to do, and I guessed some of them felt a bit unsafe going out there in the dark. The perception seemed to be that there were perfectly good spaces much nearer the door so they could run in and be only two or three minutes late rather than five and could run out immediately after work to get to a party or maybe get laid or drunk or whatever might be of most importance to them on any given evening.

I supposed part of the issue was based in a notion that lots of people—including the regular customers—seem to have: they should all be able to own the closest space to the front door, but, if they couldn't, they should be entitled to have whatever space was next closest and were angered by being in second-best parking because someone had stolen "their rightful spot" and, God-forbid the thief was another person lower in rank (determined by the make or model or condition of the vehicle or an actual sighting indicating the driver's age, appearance or projected level of threat if confronted); it was one of those curious American things about being important—each person needing to be at the center of the universe, each believing that anyone who was not them wasn't worthy of having what they should have. It was a microcosm of the dynamics of Americanism and Capitalism. And whenever I thought about it, I could imagine an article in the *New York Times*: "Foundation for Fascism in Parking!"

Few employees—young or old—followed Nancy's rule, and the employee parking lot was often far less than half full. She had no way of enforcing a parking policy, and they knew it.

On that particular day, I had arrived thinking about a possible storyline. I still had fifteen minutes before I had to go on duty, so I sat behind the wheel imagining a couple of men in a saloon where the bartender has a shotgun hung on the underside of the bar. Perhaps he had hung it there to grab quickly if a thief should enter or a rowdy customer needed to be frightened into obeying his orders to leave. But what made it interesting came to me in the form of a question: What if the bartender didn't really need or want a shotgun, and it had been part of the bar when he bought the business and he hadn't bothered to remove it or he, himself, had hung it there for a reason I hadn't yet worked out, and, over time, had forgotten about it, never put shells in it, didn't even own shells for it, didn't have any interest in guns? My brain was racing through scenarios in which there would be a sudden occurrence where the gun came into play out of necessity, but it is in the hands of a customer, someone who knows nothing about guns other than what he has seen on TV. He believes the gun is loaded and lethal and is the only means for protecting himself and the bartender from a man—another customer—set on attacking them. I had all kinds of images going on in my head all of them related to making a statement about the January 6, 2021, insurrection and the immediate consequences of that event: the attacker as a stand-in for Trump's assault on democracy; the bartender and the man with the gun representing "difference" and the moral values of equality and fairness; A TV behind the bar showing non-stop images of Trump's supporters ransacking the Capitol Building; and the bar itself representing an appreciation of art and history even as it is in danger of being destroyed by an angry and violent customer.

I was lost in thought until the alarm I had set on my phone insisted I get into the building and work. Reluctantly, I tucked my story idea into a fold of my brain, hoping I would get back to the point of feeling the excitement about a worthless gun in the hands of a hapless patron taking on a bad guy. I jotted the last of my ideas in the little notebook I kept in the glove box and walked quickly toward the store.

It was a Friday night, and I was working at aisle one, which was long with impatient customers who had moved over to me out of frustration with Lacy, who was on aisle two. She had one speed and only one, and she was obviously not happy about working a Friday night shift and was cranky with the customers. When my cellphone went off in my pocket, I reached robot-like to it, pressed the off button, apologized to the customer I was serving, and quickly returned to scanning items. Often in checking products, I had to slow down long enough to manually press cash register keys and record items the scanner wouldn't recognize by their bar codes—a constant problem with the aged technology we had to work with. I knew there wouldn't be a break for some time, and whoever it was who had called would have to wait until I could get to the so-called "break room" (basically an open space in the stock room) and sit in an uncomfortable, hard, plastic chair provided by the company for employees who went there to escape work for their ten-minute breaks. When I finally got to it during a lull in grocery checkout, I tried to choke down a quick cup of the now almost-burned coffee from the rarely washed coffee machine. After a couple of sips, I dumped what I called the "coal tar" into the sink and sat down. It was then that I remembered the call. I pulled out my phone and listened to the message:

Rob, Just found out the Lidons—the store owners I told you about that "our friend" was shaking down—they died last night! Looks like suicide, but don't believe it. Won't know for sure for a while. I'm feeling real bad about it. I'll tell you more about it when I get home. In the meantime, just be careful.

Jake couldn't take personal calls while on duty, and I had no way of knowing when his next break might come along, so I sent a text that he could check whenever it came:

YOU AREN'T RESPONSIBLE regardless of whether they did it or it was done to them. Don't take on that load! Anyway, deaths might be unrelated to "the case." I'll be careful. You do the same!

It was a puny response; texting seemed wholly un-satisfactory for dealing with the thoughts and emotions I suspected Jake was experiencing. And he was trying to protect me. If Harridan had something to do with the Lidons' deaths, there was good reason to believe he was a much more dangerous threat than I had allowed myself to think. Killing the Lidons would scare off other people who might have been willing to testify against him, particularly other merchants he might be shaking down. He had already used me—at least I believed he had—to get to Jake. My mind was racing through questions of my vulnerability and concern for Jake's safety. I tried to convince myself that there was no point in going too far down the road of fear." I whispered, "Just be careful," repeating Jake's words and thought, "Okay ... whatever the hell that means."

Despite his cop's intuition about Harridan, Jake knew better than to jump to any conclusions, and I was deter-mined to do the same. Jake was a believer in evidence, and he would ultimately let that guide his thoughts about what happened to the old couple; still, old Mr. Lidon's last words to Jake over the telephone were attempts to blame him for setting them up, and though they were the words of an angry, fearful old man, Jake had heard them as a plea for help—help that he had no ability to give. And I knew the deaths would weigh heavily on his mind.

28

My shift ended a few minutes after nine o'clock by the time I served my last customer. In the breakroom, I remember pulling the spare pens out of my pants pocket and returning them to the blue apron, hanging it on its assigned hook, and then punching out at the time clock. Before leaving, I checked the work schedule posted on the door to the business office as I always did. All our first names were there in bold letters on the dry-erase board showing Sunday through Saturday of each week. I confirmed that nothing had changed, and I was to be on duty again the next day from 3 to 9 p.m. Knowing myself, I probably wasn't in any great hurry to race out of the building. Jake would be working until midnight. With the punch of the time clock, the story line I had turned off on arrival, turned on again. I was imagining a scenario, characters, pulling in as many thoughts as I could to carry me home where I could get them into my computer.

I barely recall the act of walking from the store. Like so many things in my life, it had been a rote task. Had I thought about it, back then, I probably would have said the walk was good for me, gave my body the opportunity to move and stretch after sitting in my car or standing for long periods of time at the register, provided time to think about things other than canned soup, pork chops, rice, and beans. In the big scheme of life, the walk wasn't all that long. From the exit door, the walking distance extended almost the full length of the building—the length of a football field—and then across a sidewalk, an access road for tractor trailers delivering shipments of food and supplies, another sidewalk and then the distance to wherever the car was parked. Admittedly, it wasn't a pleasant distance to walk if the weather was bad and I hadn't dressed appropriately for it or had forgotten to carry an umbrella.

Though I had heard Jake's warning, it didn't occur to me to be in any way concerned about making my way to the car. I was lost in thought. When that happens to me, the external world escapes me until I find myself suddenly aware that time has passed or that I have arrived somewhere without any recollection of how I got there. My body had made the trek on its own. If I had looked at the cars still parked in front of the building or the gum on the sidewalk, or looked at the bushes I already knew needed tending, I don't remember. My brain was engaged in the story making its way toward something I wanted to write. At the car, my brain and body reunited with the realization that I had to open the door, get in, and drive home. Exactly what happened in the seconds after that may never be fully clear to me. I vaguely remember walking between my car and another vehicle and pulling out my keys. Then there was the sensation of pain as my muscles and bones collided with the car's steel as powerful hands pushed me with enough force to make me feel my ribs would collapse. Whatever it was that stung my neck made me drop to my knees and then pass out.

Perhaps I just needed to believe it after the fact, but I have thought many times since then that I had a brief moment of trying to fight against whatever it was, wanting to rise up, feeling the muscles in my face pulling my lips back to bare my teeth, my reptile brain taking over and turning me into a fighting creature with fists flashing like fire against whatever it was. Even now, I find that the fantasy protects me from the probable reality that I could do nothing as the world went dark and deadly silent for a while.

29

Hands were touching my eyelids, my shoulder, but I couldn't see them. I heard a beeping sound from a machine. My tongue was thick and slow to react. It took time for me to study the blurred face above me and find words that came out in a mumbled whisper, "Where am I?"

"You're in the hospital. You've been hurt," the distorted voice said as if speaking from behind a heavy curtain.

Somebody touched me again. I tried to say, "Don't!" but the sound came out dull, barely audible even to me.

"You're safe. I'm your nurse. Nobody's going to hurt you. Can you tell me your name?" the voice asked.

I had to think for what seemed a long time before I could conjure, "Robert ... Rob Wilson." I thought I had said it. But then there was another voice, a strong male sound, and

and I was afraid of it. "Don't!" Again, there was no power behind the sound I was making.

"I'm Officer Lanning ..."

The name crawled slowly through a layer of sludge to come into my consciousness.

"Can you tell me your name?"

I must have told him, because after that he referred to me as "Rob." At some point as I tried to find words and make them more audible, I must have said something about Jake.

"Jake who?" Who are you referring to?

"Davidson ... cop."

Then he disappeared for a while. The room disappeared. My life disappeared, and then I was alive again feeling hands on my body, seeing flashes of light, hearing clicking sounds and voices floating over me.

"Jake?"

Then I disappeared again. And then I hadn't. I asked for Jake. People were asking me questions, and I was trying to answer. Then the male voice I had remembered was there again, his voice reminding me of who he was.

"Rob, Jake is on his way. Tony Angelino, our dispatcher, called him. He's been out looking for you most of the night."

"What time is it?" The words came slowly one at a time like speaking in the discovery of each word in an anagram.

"It's eight a.m. You've been here for a while. At least since midnight." After a brief pause as if waiting for me to absorb the time and make sense of it, he went on: "We want to catch who did this to you. Do you feel like you can talk to me about what happened?"

My mind was clearing, and I must have remembered that Jake had talked about Lanning in the past, talked about him as a good cop. But I didn't care at that moment that he was "good" or a cop or a friend of Jake's. I didn't want to talk to him, didn't want to tell this stranger anything, didn't want to talk to anybody but Jake. As my brain cleared, the pain in my body increased. I wanted him to go away. I wanted to be angry at somebody!

"Rob," the man said, "may I call you that?"

I looked away from him and said, "Yes" in what came out as a "no" voice. Jake would want me to say yes, but I wanted to rise and punch someone, pick him up bodily as if I were a hero in a 1950s western throwing a bad guy through the saloon windows during the inevitable bar fight. I wanted to be angry with him for being a cop, make him a representation of Harridan, make him another homophobic straight man who would think that I got what I and all other gay men deserved, and wishing he didn't have to be dealing with me. So, there I was, stereotyping this man not all that differently from the ways that many people stereotype gay men. He had done nothing but his job, but at that moment I was incapable of caring for his well-being as I lay in pain and humiliation, fuzzy-minded, and frustrated in ways I didn't know how to control. Yet, despite my thoughts, I found myself not wanting to alienate a friend of Jake's.

"Do you remember anything about how you got to the hospital, Rob?"

My voice was lifeless, even to my own ears as I tried to get this interview over with; I tried to talk: "Laying on concrete ... cold ... people covered me with something ... siren ... lights ... I can't remember."

I was beginning to see through the clouds that had hung between me and the people in the room: officer making notes on a pad, nurses in white and another man leaning into my line of site and out again. There was the sound of the door bursting as if broken by a bull coming out of a chute for *la corrida*. When Jake reached my bedside and could see that I was aware of his presence, he calmed and laid his hand on my face as lightly as if he were afraid the weight would crack me open. Then he let his fingers and palm slide to my neck as he looked me in the eye like a man saying goodbye to his dying child. He bent down over the bed and laid his arm over my chest and pressed his cheek against mine, and whispered, "I'm so sorry," into my ear. I tried to get my bandaged arm up off the bed to touch him as best I could, but the muscles felt flabby ... rubbery and heavy as hell.

I whispered, "I've been waiting for you," said it as a complete thought.

"I got here as fast as I could."

"I'm sorry," I said and maybe something else, and I couldn't think of why I was sorry or whether I was repeating the statement he had whispered in my ear. Perhaps it was the drugs I'd been given or a reaction to what I had experienced that I hadn't yet remembered, but it seemed important to say it.

"Never!" he whispered, and I wished I could remember what I had said. He disappeared and reappeared a couple times more. At some point, someone must have felt that I was in a better state of mind. Jake lifted his face from mine, stood up and spoke. "I need to let you talk to Jim here, Officer Lanning, so maybe we can catch the sons o' bitches who did this to you." As if I objected or had tried to stop him, he patted me on the arm and said, I'm not leaving, unless you want me to."

Speaking to Jake, my voice had risen above a whisper as I said what I hadn't been able to think until that moment. "You know ... what they did to me?" I asked, feeling like my life with him was on the line.

It felt like it took a long time for him to respond, like the room turned dark for a while, and then he was there again, Lanning beside him.

"Doctor told us, we had to know, Rob ... the investigation ... DNA test ..."

I remember saying something like, "Oh, my god!" and saying, "I'm sorry" over and over and trying to yell and not being able to hear my voice. People came and went in a blur, faces looking down at me and I didn't want them to, and then there was only Jake touching my face saying, it wasn't my fault several times as he wiped my face with a cloth.

After a while, he asked if there was anything he could do to make me more comfortable. Suddenly, hell-flash anger arose in my chest. I wanted to scream, "How in the hell am I ever going to feel comfortable ever again?" But I couldn't find the strength or the presence of mind to put all of those words together at the time. Instead, I looked into his eyes like he was Satan incarnate for just a moment before turning my head away, staring at the wall, feeling naked in a room of fully clothed and prudish strangers.

Jake and Lanning waited patiently, their very presence an irritant, an imposition, a demand that I get past my anger and tell them something they could use to begin the manhunt. To hell with shame. Not even a Catholic, I was locked in a confessional with a stranger for a priest knowing I'd done something wrong that I couldn't call to mind.

Lanning' voice slid in under my confusion. It was the voice of a father better than mine or a brother I never had. "Rob, I'm sorry for what has happened to you. Truly am. I'd like to catch whoever did this to you. If it helps, I feel like I know you. I've known about Jake ever since he's been on the force, and he's talked about you a lot with me: All good things. If it needs to be said, I have no issues with you guys at all. I'm happy you've found each other. What I have a problem with is people who do things like what you went through, and I would love to make them pay for what they've done."

As he talked, I found my hand reaching out, and he took it and held it gently as he asked, "Can you recall anything about who did this to you, where you were, things you saw or heard?"

I remember feeling caught between the confusion of trying to remember, the pain I was experiencing, the effects of the medications I had been given, and the clawing desire for silence, escape to hide in a dark space to heal like a wounded animal. The rational part of my brain had to make its way ever so slowly through the muck of my thoughts to remind me that Jake was with me. He trusted Lanning. Inevitability, I was going to have to talk if there was any hope of catching the men who had put me in the hospital, put me in moment-by-moment fluctuations between anger, fear, and disconsolation. My attempts to talk, to remember, to not get lost in the mudwrestling between my various feelings caused me to choke up often during the interview. I remember Jake putting his hand gently on my shoulder, letting the fingers and palm slide back and forth trying to soothe, then lifting his hand and touching my head, pushing the hair out of my face back toward the hairline.

At some point, I said to Lanning, "I don't want it to hurt Jake. Don't want my name ..."

Lanning reacted with, "I don't see any reporters in here, Rob, and I'm not going to give it to them, and nobody that I know of wants to violate your privacy."

"They already have ..."

I must have gotten emotionally charged at the thought. Jake and Lanning were trying to calm me. The nurse who was in the room watching over me during the interview asked if I would like to have the victim's advocate in the room before I said anything else. Perhaps I imagined it, but at some point in all the probing and prodding by the doctors and nurses earlier I was sure I had already heard someone talking to me in my drug-saturated state: "You did nothing wrong," "It wasn't your fault," and all of the other cliches people like or are trained to say. Imagined or not, the thought of subjecting myself to it was like eating unripe fruit soaked in a bitters bath. Had they been tangible, I would have hurled the goddamned platitudes at the wall, making them shatter into glass shards that would fall hard on what I assumed was a linoleum tiled floor. All I wanted was for Jake to take me out of the room and make me well so I could find the people who did this to me, capture them, humiliate them, make them feel what I was feeling and then kill them. As the thought slipped out of me like spittle behind a raging tirade, it became repulsive even to have thought it. Then I wanted to just say, "Screw this," get up and walk out of that room away from Jake and Lanning, find some place to scream into a pillow for hours on end, didn't want anyone around me to feel sorry for me. But Jake and Lanning stood there waiting patiently for me, ignorant of my thoughts.

Lanning asked if I'd rather he came back another time. My first instinct was to say, "Yes." Yet, for whatever reason, as I looked up at Jake at my bedside and saw the suffering in his face as he looked back at me, I found myself wanting to reach up to wipe the pain from him as gently as he was trying to wipe the tears from my cheek. Despite the absurdity, I was back in that locked confessional, an atheist awaiting absolution from a ghost on the other side of the booth.

"Let's get this over with," I said in a voice that fit somewhere between a whisper and a soft vocalization as my

energy drained from me; the room darkened, my eyes
wanting to melt into sightlessness; and it became difficult
for me to sort out what I was thinking, what I needed to say,
and then whether I was actually saying anything I wanted
to say. I listened to my voice speaking from somewhere
outside myself as if in another room down the hall. It came
out slowly, logically, and deliberately laying out the particulars for Jake and Lanning. Occasionally, it wavered, tore
itself away from the story line, mocked me and exploded in
bursts of anger, moments of weeping, and declarations of
shame, and, at other times, moments of silence as I tried
to remember. Several times, Jake broke into my consciousness to remind me that I could stop if I needed to, but the
voice found itself again:

"No. I've got to say it. If I can't say it now, I don't know
if I'm ever going to be able to say it again." I told them
about my leaving work and the experience of the scuffle and blacking out. I told them that when I came back
into something resembling consciousness after the car
scuffle, my head was inside what felt like a bag. I couldn't
see anything, and yet I could breathe even though I had
something stuffed in my mouth held in place by something
tied behind my head so tight that I felt like the sides of my
mouth were stretched to the point of splitting apart. My
head was throbbing with pain—a pain that I could only describe as being like what people say they experience with
a migraine when it's so overwhelming that they can't open
their eyes, so painful that even the individual hairs on their

heads hurt with the slightest movement, every pulsation of blood going deep into their brains as fire.

Lanning looked at me through eyes that weren't eyes, but sometimes windows, sometimes flickering candles, sometimes pools; Jake held me tight, wiped my eyes, clasped my hand, said I didn't have to tell what I wasn't ready to tell.

Lanning was a lot like Jake, I was later able to recognize, in that he tried to ask questions in multiple ways to trigger memories that might help pull out further clues the cops might be able to build on.

"When you gained consciousness, did you see, hear or smell anything that you can remember?"

I couldn't remember any of those things, and I was feeling like I was failing the interview, but Lanning said, "That's all right, Rob. Maybe something will come to you later. Go on with what you can remember."

A strange face came between Lanning and me. A doctor, I assumed. White coat. Little flashlight in his hand. He pulled my eyelids open, flashed the light in my eyes. He turned to Lanning and said I had had enough for a while, but I stopped him, and said I had to go on. He checked the tube carrying the liquid from somewhere above me into my vein, and for the first time I was aware that I had a needle and tube taped to the back of my hand.

When the doctor left, I tried to give details: "Right side of my face was pressed to a flat surface. Chest, too. Like a table, a big table. Bent over at my waist. Bare feet were cold, like standing on concrete. I was tied down. Arms stretched out in front of me. I was tied at my ankles and wrists. Must have been trying to break free," I said as I felt the skin rubbed raw. "Couldn't lift my face to shift the strain off the side of my neck. Wire, I think. Hood on me whole time. Wire cutting into my neck when I tried to move. Men's voices laughing.

"Any sounds or smells you remember?"

"Cold. Musty smell—maybe the hood. Movement, words I can't remember—at least three different voices."

Methodically, just like Jake would do it, Lanning said, "I know this is painful, to talk about Rob, but can you tell us what happened next?"

My chest muscles tightened; my hands clenched, somehow it became more difficult for me to breathe.

I started doing my best version of shouting at Jake as if he were somehow to be punished for what had happened; I was saying something like, "You want to hear details? What they did? You really want the words, truth, reality? You want to own the reality, fix it forever in your head?"

Jake didn't take the bait: "It's not what I want, Rob. It's what needs to be known. If you want me not to hear, I can step out." He insisted on being reasonable, thoughtful, un-provoked, as tears bled from his eyes and quivering lips caught the salty water that rolled down his face faster than he could wipe them away with the back of his hand. Then, he turned away from me briefly, away from Lanning to a place only Jake knew—a place deep in the shadows of his mind like the land he owned, its history that had risen up to writhe around his legs and then crawl up into his heart.

Jim Lanning saw Jake disappear in plain sight, saw how emotionally charged I had become and said we needed to take a break. He went to Jake, put his hand on Jake's shoulder; they stood quietly together until my voice spoke as it came up out of a cavern of overwhelming shame and grew into panicked hostility: "You both know what happened! They raped me! Three of them! Three different men laughing, cheering each other on! Laughing! And I couldn't do anything, say anything, stop anything." My voice sounded loud in my own ears—as loud as I could manage under the circumstances. "And all I could do was wait for them to stop. Is that what you needed to hear? You happy now?" Then I was sobbing.

Jake moved quickly to me crying, "I'm so sorry. It's all my fault."

I forced my hand up to put my palm over his mouth and missed. "*Sorry* isn't going to fix it!" It was the voice from hell that rose up within me and blasted in his ear as I tried to make him get away, fought him as he held me, tried to get my hand to come up off the bed to punch him as my body writhed beneath him ... white coats, blinding light ... consciousness slipping away from the screaming, flailing, trying to escape the demon of a horrible dream—a dream melting into the rush of nurses coming through the door barking and growling like mad dogs.

30

When I awakened again, Jake was sitting off to the right of the bed on the front edge of the chair's aqua blue Naugahyde seat cushion. Jake's hand was on my hand, and he was squeezing gently as he saw me break through the haze of the medication and back into the room where he was waiting for me. His eyes were red; sagging skin had accumulated under his eyes.

"You look so tired, Jake," I said guiltily.

"I'm fine," he said though we both knew it wasn't true, couldn't be true. He faked a smile as he said, "Let's worry about you right now. Okay?"

I started to say, "I'm sorry," but I stopped myself, and not really sure I wanted to know, asked, "How bad off am I?"

"It's going to take a while for you to heal. I'm going to take care of you." A tear rolled down his face to his chin; he tried to catch it with the back of his hand.

"They raped me, Jake." I had said it like a confession of sin and had not thought about how the words themselves brought it all back and I wanted to escape them, pretend I hadn't said them and somehow stop the gushing tears, the emotional tsunami that was coming at me. Then I felt him lay his head against mine as he leaned over the bed, our tears intermingling as he said several times, "I know," like someone at a funeral with nothing to offer but the humanity of trying to console the unconsolable.

After a brief time, he stood upright and wiped his eyes with his free hand and tried to gain control over his emotions. He took my hand into his and squeezed gently as he struggled to find a way to stop crying.

"Why did they do that to me?" I asked, trying to talk through the phlegm that had built up in my throat and the nasal clogs that made my voice blubbery. I asked him as though he should have an answer, or at least a theory, that would take away the ugly memories in my head of the men's voices, their use of my body as they pleased for a pleasure I couldn't comprehend.

"I don't know, man. I really don't know," Jake responded quietly as if anything worth saying had been said long ago.

When I asked if Harridan had been part of it, Jake tried to divert my attention, talk about my getting better, talk about resting and saving that conversation for another day when I was stronger, but I wouldn't be dissuaded and demanded answers as best I could through the fog of the drugs and the pain of knowing Jake knew what had happened to me. I demanded louder to know.

He recognized I was not going to settle for less than an honest answer and replied, "I don't know if he was backing it, but I know he was at his house when it happened to you."

I must have asked him how he knew that because he told me he had tried to call me and got no answer, went to Fannon's, found my car, keys on the ground and ... my mind was drifting away from me again.

I remember saying, "You shouldn't have gone there" and then feeling the weight of what had happened to me, the shame I felt, the sense of being something Jake could never love again, and then flailing, trying to punch something, trying to make my legs kick the bed out from under me as the space above me went blank.

No one told me how long I had been out. I only know that there were nurses and doctors in the room bustling about, checking monitors, putting their hands on me, trying to sound soothing as they went about their tasks. Jake was at my side, I looked up at him and said, "I've put you through hell, haven't I, Jake?"

"I think I'm the one who's put *you* through hell."

***

Jake took as much time off from work as he could to care for me and to keep me from the dark and dangerous backrooms of my mind where my captors waited to take me again. When he couldn't clear his work schedule, he called in a part-time nurse friend of his to stay with me and take me to my many appointments with doctors. He made sure that during the first week he personally took me to my almost daily visits with Dr. Crawford, the psychiatrist

I was referred to. He waited patiently in the waiting room or in his truck for the sessions to end so he could take me home; he listened patiently to my renditions of what I was discussing with my "shrink"—my summary word for Crawford, who I liked and grew to trust and would see weekly after that first week until I could manage on my own for longer periods of time without falling apart.

During the first few days of my convalescence, Jake wouldn't talk much about anything more in-depth than what he was making for dinner, what movie we could watch together, how I was feeling, and the weather. We made a few attempts at our customary banter without much success. Whenever I asked questions about Harridan or the investigations, he would say, "Let's not talk about that right now; we'll get to it." When I asked about the Lidons, he told me that detectives could find no evidence that it was anything other than a suicide, and that was the extent of addressing my questions. When I asked about the DNA test, he said it could make a real difference when and if a suspect could be identified. He held me when I became afraid, when I couldn't control my sadness or rage, and told me nothing was going to change between us, even though he and I both knew it already had.

The pain in my body eventually subsided until it became mysteriously unnoticed like the dead branches of the sycamores out at the edge of our yard, branches that fell in the night, their carcasses scattered about waiting for me to notice, pick them up and toss them into the woods. But the putrid thoughts were another thing altogether and were going to take more effort to get rid of. For what seemed like many, many weeks, I lay awake at night beside Jake, staring at the maple tree in silhouette beyond the window. On dark moonless nights I stared into the abyss of the bedroom, thinking I wanted to leave, escape, get in my car and drive in any direction for as far as the car would take me before rotting out from under me or its mechanical parts dying for lack of care; when that time came, I would get out and kick the door hard enough to push it all the way into the console. I wanted to become just another relic of humanity taken into the flotsam and jetsam of life in a strange place, know no one beyond the necessity of making a living, do nothing other than write stories and poems no one would ever read and burn them each morning upon awakening and then write them again, and repeat the process day by day until I too died in a pile of rust and lack of caring.

Sometimes I thought about wanting to meet Nathan Sanders at the hanging tree, ask him as he dangled there by his neck, what he had done and why he had done it and who had hanged him, but I knew he would open his eyes and answer with a look of contempt. There would be nothing more, and he wouldn't even follow me with his eyes as I walked to the pond to drown. And when I couldn't drown in water, I drowned in other forms of fantasy and horror. When I cried out from my sleep or found myself shivering beneath the covers, I had pulled up over my head in the night in fear of confronting my own mind, or when I would throw back the covers to escape the bed, Jake was awake, asking if I was alright, asking what he could do for me. There were times when I hated him for caring while simultaneously wanting him to hold me and protect me from the hauntings.

Despite all of the ugliness going on in my head, Jake and I found moments of non-sexual intimacy where we enjoyed one another's company, found a few things to laugh about and things to discuss in detail, and we found time to hold and be held and talk about our fears and hopes. However, there were nights when we would get into bed and Jake would bring his naked body up against me, and I would panic. The thought of sex terrified me. Though he had done nothing to show that his intention was to initiate sex, I would find myself angry and tell him abruptly, "No. I can't." We tried to talk about it on a couple of occasions when we were both awake and able to think clearly—not that I was actually thinking clearly at all—and each time, he said we would wait until I was ready. Sometimes I told him I wanted to be ready soon. Other times, all I could say was, "I'm sorry. I just can't." For a while, I convinced myself that he'd never think of me again as I had been before the rape, and he would leave me like Matt had, and I would deserve it.

I talked with my shrink about it, told him I was afraid. Every time I thought about sex, I felt dirty, like what those men had done to me had destroyed something inside me: I was a disgusting version of my former self, something unworthy of Jake; they had taken away what belonged only to Jake and me, and we would never be able to cleanse

ourselves of their stain. Jake would grow tired of waiting
and leave me, I was sure. Dr. Crawford did his best to remind me that I was still early in my recovery, and maybe I
was selling Jake short, and that, with time, Jake and I could
find a way back to intimacy.

In my various mood swings, I went from believing
Crawford to believing I should just get out of Jake's life and
let him find someone better to be with. I thought about
returning to Chicago but saw Matt's face come into focus
and knew it wasn't what I wanted. I wanted to stay, leave,
stay, drop out of life, run, stay ... all of them simultaneously
competing for a decision that I couldn't make.

Whether I talked in my sleep, or he just sensed my state
of mind, Jake seemed to know the feelings I was struggling
with about him and our relationship. At one point, he sat
down opposite me in the living room, and said sincerely
and thoughtfully, "I need to say this once and for all, I'm
not Matt and I have no desire to leave you or to believe you
really want to leave me even though you're going through
hell at the moment. You need to get this through your thick
skull: I'm not dumping you. If you decide at some point you
don't want to be with me for some reason, I will have to accept that; but I'm in for the long haul." As he was saying the
words, he came over to me, crouched on the floor in front
of me, laid his hand on my leg and looked up at me like an
initiate before a cross. I wanted to believe him. I hated my
own thoughts that were eating cancer-like at my life while
he waited like that maple outside the bedroom window

standing its ground, accepting as easily as breathing in air the constantly changing landscape into which it was born.

"But what if I can't get better?" I asked.

"You will!" His voice was confident as if there was no doubt in his mind and all he had to do was get me through the immediate crisis.

After a couple of weeks, I convinced Jake that I was getting better and could drive myself back and forth to see my shrink. In truth, I was only sure about my ability to drive myself, but I wanted to remove the burden of him paying someone to hang out with me and drive me around. He accepted my decision though I suspected he was worried that I might do something to harm myself in the time required for me to get past the initial stages of healing. His only request was that I have my cellphone on me at all times so he could check with me during his breaks and so I could call him in an emergency.

***

Approximately two months into therapy, Dr. Crawford had suggested to me that I write out the anger and frustration I was experiencing as an exercise and then attack it with logic and/or fantasy. At first, I wanted to resist the suggestion. I didn't want to think about that ugly event anymore; then, he reminded me that everything I was telling him was suggesting that I was thinking about it almost constantly, and if I was going to think about it, it might be good to deal with it on paper or on my computer screen, giving full force of my thoughts to the writing without any restrictions on language, subject matter or concern about a reader. His directions were clear enough: "If you wish, you can bring whatever you wrote with you for our next meeting, and we can talk about it. And if you don't want to show it to me, that's okay too. If you try it and can't do it, that's fine. If you do only a little bit of writing, even a word or two, that's fine too. Whatever you do with the assignment, if you do anything with it, I'd like to hear what the experience of writing it was like for you."

"Dealing with anger is so much easier when you can put a fist in somebody's face," I wanted to say in reply to him. "And your assignment is stupid, and I'm probably not going to do it." But I didn't say any of those things. I just said I would try to do the assignment and wished him a good day. It was obvious enough what he was trying to do with trying to get me back into writing, and it didn't take much effort to decipher the assignment as a way to break the trauma down to bite-sized pieces that could be confronted and reperceived in less threatening ways.

As I walked out of his office, I was reflecting upon what I hadn't said, and I heard the caged rage that was in me and thought of the violence that men resort to, thought about my frustration with the world of rapidly expanding hatred, and for a moment, once again, I wanted to kill Mike Harridan. Even if he hadn't been personally present at my attack, he was responsible. I was certain. And I wanted to kill something else that I couldn't name. As I held my white-knuckle grip on the steering wheel as I drove home, I let loose the entire litany of vulgarity I had in me as though my shouting those words would somehow take away the desire for destruction. When I was done, I felt worse.

I couldn't do the assignment in the seven days between sessions. It was closer to a month before I felt I had done the assignment to my own satisfaction. In the long hours of Jake's absence while he was at work each day, I wrote the hell out of my anger, poured bile onto page after page, destroying Harridan and his gang: popping him like a blood-filled tick; running him headfirst through a gigantic meat grinder; tying him and all his buddies together in a huge, inescapable net, taking them up in a huge helicopter and dropping the sack over a rock-filled canyon from a thousand feet up. On one occasion, I dressed Harridan and his amorphous collection of lackeys all in red and forced them out into an arena filled with angry bulls; and over time, I came up with large numbers of varied brutal, ugly deaths that I could conjure. I wrote until I couldn't think of any other way of mutilating Harridan and his sycophants.

I knew I was getting better when I found myself writing about Harridan appearing in a courtroom arraignment accused of assault and battery, murder, rape, hate crime, and, of course, extortion. When I got to the part in my writing where I had Harridan and his gang in custody and heading to a trial, I realized that, even though I would create a dazzling, well-spoken, nationally famous lawyer filled from the bottoms of his feet to the top layer of his scalp with legal knowledge and an ability to persuade juries, he couldn't win a case without proof.

At some point in the many meetings he (the lawyer) and the client—both, some version of me—my Superman-of-an-attorney-main-character said, "I believe you! There's too much coincidence with all that has happened. Everything points back to Harridan! But all you've given me is coincidence. What are Harridan's lawyer's going to say to that other than, 'Where's the proof? You can't send a man to prison based on coincidence or conjecture.' And that defense attorney would be right. I can't make a case for circumstantial evidence based on what you've given me to work with. We need to put him at the scene of these crimes or get somebody to rat him out, somebody who can give details that lead to proving our case. Eyewitness, DNA, a confession ..."

An impotent main character probably wouldn't sell well, I decided, and tore my lawyer creation apart and threw him into the waste heap. I was exhausted thinking about it all, tired of thinking about revenge, tired of living in the fantasy that people ultimately pay for their sins, tired of thinking there is such a thing as fairness in the world.

One morning before heading to Crawford's office, and after Jake left for work, I took my stack of vicious, violent mutilation papers out into the driveway, crumpled the sheets one after another until the wads were piled like odds and ends twigs gathered from the woods for building a campfire. I pulled the matches I had taken from the kitchen and lit the edges of the bottom-most wads and watched the white paper and ink turn to black and then disintegrate into tiny embers that rose above the flame, float briefly in the air, and fall lightly back to the ground as ash when the heat would no longer suspend them.

***

Crawford smiled when I told him I wanted my life back, that I had been blaming Jake for having enemies that ultimately took their hatred out on me and that I needed to come to terms with the reality that he didn't deserve punishment from me for something he could not control any more than I could control what was done to me. I told Crawford, that I wanted to be intimate, that I wanted to find a way to believe in myself again, I wanted to trust again and that I loved Jake and didn't want to lose him. Dr. Crawford and I talked about how I might help Jake understand that it would take a while for me to recover and that there was work I would have to do, but that I wanted him to be a part of the healing, and I wanted to help him deal with it too.

***

Jake had known what I was doing with the writing assignment Crawford had given me. Sometimes I read my stories out loud to him, and he would add some further way to make the destruction of the villains even more destructive, and we would talk about how far words could take us when there would be no consequences for doing anything with them other than say them to one another. When I told him about my burning of the stories, he was surprised that I could discard all that work; disappointed, it seemed to me. I'm not sure he totally understood the spiritual significance of the gesture as a letting go—an attempt to say I knew I was going to survive.

"But all that writing!" he exclaimed.

That he had such regard for my writing that he felt every word should be preserved was great for my ego and I loved him for it. It took some time for me to explain that I didn't see the act as one of destruction but something more like a religious ritual.

"The words did what they needed to do."

"But you've still got the files on your computer," he said.

"No. Trashed them too. I needed to let go completely. It was too heavy for me."

"But what about the people who did it? Are you saying you forgive them?"

"Hell no, Jake. If they can be found, they get whatever the law says they get. I'll never forgive them. I needed to forgive myself."

"But you didn't do anything wrong, Rob. You didn't cause that to happen."

"I know that, but I felt guilty, beat myself up for not being able somehow to make them stop, not being able to at least do something to defend myself ... and for becoming someone you couldn't love anymore."

The end of that sentence completed itself without my controlling it and caught me by surprise, and it stung like the moment when I told my father I was gay, and he backhanded me and knocked me to the floor.

When I recovered from the gasp I had dropped into the space between us, Jake said, "But you know I've never stopped loving you." He took me into his arms and held me tightly.

Through a flashflood of tears, I said something like, "I believe you, Jake. I do. But I had stopped feeling worthy of *anyone* loving me. It was me; not you. Do you understand, Jake? I lost myself for a while. I lost my drive to make a difference with my life, let them take that away from me." As I was speaking the words, I was imagining my name or just my initials chiseled into a rock, my name lying beneath a layer of dust among stacked court documents in a musty old courthouse basement, my books and stories scattered amongst the debris after a "friends of the library" book sale. "Worst of all, I haven't been able to get past my own emotional state to show you that I love you and don't want to lose you."

Jake listened carefully as I tried to apologize to him for all that he had gone through with me: the mood changes, the nightmares, the moments of anger and hostility. He tried to stop me to say that he had never given up ... but I cut him off, telling him I wanted intimacy again ... he had waited long enough ... I wanted to get better for him as well as for me ...

He stopped me, told me he loved me, and held me as he confessed his own sense of guilt and responsibility for what had happened to me ... it was he who "they" wanted to get to and he had failed to protect me ... they had succeeded in the worst way possible by using me ... he was responsible ... sorry .. capitalized, italicized, underscored ... face wet, sobbing.

***

As we fell together on the bed, we wrestled with our clothes, shedding them like man sweat from the pores of our skin. His body enveloped me, felt like velour as he pulled me against him face-to -face and let our flesh align. As we kissed, his body's midsection began to move gently and made small circular motions against my now pulsating flesh. Arousal was almost instantaneous. He reached down to my buttocks and pulled us together as his movement shifted to combinations of circular and up-and-down motions, our bodies working like two colors of paint swirling on a canvas, touching, twisting, playing. We were moving to the rhythms of our bodies, the sounds of skin on skin, an occasional moan or passionate remark, my telling him how much I wanted him as my hands slid all over his back and down to his hips and buttocks, all of his body muscles flexing in response to our pleasure; his "Mmm" and "Oh, yeah." For a while I was so caught up in pure joy that I had forgotten my traumatic ordeal, and then as Jake shifted his position and released me momentarily, I felt suddenly cold, remembered, and gasped. He felt the hesitation, heard the sound of my voice, put his hand on my face and asked me if I wanted to stop. For a moment I couldn't decide ... and then I did ... consciously decided I didn't want him to ... until there was nothing left of us but sleep.

***

It took us a while to come back to earth from our trip into the cosmos as the alarm went off for Jake to get up for work. In the little time we had, we talked about how good we felt, how much we had enjoyed each other and our commitment to getting through the healing process together.

Over coffee, Jake asked me a strange question: "Do you feel the need to be famous, Slick?"

I asked him where the question came from, and he mentioned times I had expressed a need to have something of myself live beyond me. At first I called up times when, if I were honest, I had felt the desire, that I liked the notion of people thinking of me as someone who was worthy of note, though the thought of seeking fame made me uncomfortable. For a moment, I struggled to put the question into the context of what I had said the previous evening about having lost the desire to make a difference with my life. As I thought about it, I realized I had not been clear in the ways I talked about the concepts—not even clear in my own head. I told him that fame and making a difference were two different things altogether, and I had confused them at times.

"Fame would be a great perk if it happened," I said, but I hope that's not really what I want. "But I do want my life to be about trying to make a difference."

In an attempt to explain, I talked about my belief that not everyone can be famous, but that anyone should be able to make a difference if she or he makes that a priority. On one level, continuing the species makes a difference, but there was more to it than that for me. Whether or not I said it well at the time or not, I was trying to say that fame only allows a handful of people to be in the world well beyond their own lives because they created or did something in their lives too precious to ignore or hide in a closet: Shakespeare, VanGogh, and Abraham Lincoln, for example. For the rest of us, life is ephemeral: We drift into the twilight as names in a ledger or on the back of an old photo or somebody's Ancestry.com account and, then even those things are gone... all of our ambitions and struggles don't matter to anyone anymore. "I would like to write things that add to the world while I am here and are of value after I'm gone, words that ease some of the pain of living or help us all understand who we are and what we could be. Most of all, I like thinking that when I get to the end of it all, in that last conscious thought of my life, I can say I did some good."

"The role of God may be a reach even for you, Slick!"

"I'd turn that job down even if it was handed to me; I hate to even think about how I'd clean up the mess my predecessor made. I just want to love you and to write, maybe get a few people to behave better in their lives than they might have had they not read my stuff.

"But you won't be here to know what happens with your work after you're gone. Isn't the point to live now as completely as we can and as honestly as we can with whatever we've got at our disposal to work with? Enjoy our existence while it exists?"

"I think that's part of it. What you're saying might be the only answer there is, Jake, but I feel like there's one step beyond that that I can't fully articulate, can't quite bring into focus. It has something to do with taking action of some kind, doing something to encourage others to be their best selves, maintain the drive to keep pushing humanity to do better. I'm trying to be the best writer I can be, the best artist I'm capable of being, and to be honest, I hope desperately that my art will outlive me, but you are right: whether or not it does, becomes irrelevant to me when my life ends, but it doesn't change that belief that there is more to existence than that."

As I said the words, I thought about the way I said them and the implications of meaning them. Taking action is a political act, a determination about what would be a better life, better thought, better for the future development of the species. But what is "better" depends upon so many variables and the awareness that my beliefs and commitments are coming from my education, reading, discussions with knowledgeable others, weighing of facts, and looking at ideas from multiple points of view, and yet there is doubt, and there are so many others who see the world differently. I tell myself there's something more that I've got to find—some way to find that something that is universal and free of the limitations of my own life experience... something that has eluded others or only came to them in the moment before dying, never to have been recorded because it is too profound for understanding before that point.

"I know what I'm saying sounds like I'm looking for something that isn't there. Maybe I'm going nuts! I don't know, but I can't stop trying to find whatever 'it' is. I suppose it could all amount to my indoctrination with God talk that has been pushed at me—most of us—almost from birth and reinforced in thousands of ways over a lifetime. Groupthink. God. The great myth of life after death. We've been fed that shit since we were born, and even though it is logically ridiculous, it has provided an excuse for human beings to resolve the problems that come sneaking out of the ages and their own times to lay claims to power and wealth. It's a cop-out ... no pun intended. It doesn't work for me."

Jake had sat quietly opposite me, looking at me as I spoke, waiting for whatever might be said next. I imagined him breaking the long silence between us in a soft voice like prayer in a chapel: "Maybe we have to accept that what people call God is nothing more than the conglomerate of unanswerable human questions."

He might as well have asked me if I was looking for a holy grail that never existed in the first place.

"You may very well be right. A quest. But it holds me together, makes me want to wake up each day and write, and if there is nothing more to life than seeking the answers, then that is as good a thing to be doing as anything else."

"Man of La Mancha," rolled off Jake's lip and splattered on the floor.

"Right, Sancho!"

After a chuckle, I tried to explain how I've never been able to settle into life without the turmoil that drives stories—all writing really—and makes me question everything from a hundred different angles and find every answer suspect. At some point, I said something like this: "Sometimes it feels like I've got steel balls rolling around in my brain ... like in a pinball game ... and wherever they strike, a whole new part of my brain is set into motion before it bats the balls off to new places." In my head I could see the score-point lights lighting up, the scoreboard going crazy, and felt the sudden loss of ability to control all the simultaneous actions. Too many things to watch and not enough good reflexes, my brain going into overload while all I can do is watch the balls roll back to 'home' to lay back against the spring-loaded launch rod which I would pull repeatedly. "I'm not sure I can ever find the serenity you talk about; I'm not sure that I want to. I'm afraid sometimes of what it might do to us, whether I might make you as crazy as I am."

"I love you for who you are. All of you, even the crazy part."

"Weird dude, right?"

"Well, there's that too!"

31

Writing about the months of my life after my abduction was in many ways therapeutic. Painful too. Necessary. I read back over the notes I could stand putting into words, tried to make myself think of it all as story rather than reality. Deal with it all through characters, let them withstand it. When I came to the night of the attack—the part Jake played as my support and empath—I realized that he had never given me any details about what happened when he went out to Harridan's looking for me and found him sitting in his living room watching TV. I had assumed that he just saw him, turned around and left. Then it dawned on me that at the time he was telling me, he was not giving me details about much of anything as he tried to protect me from the effects of the traumatic events I'd been through.

When Jake came in after his late shift and we sat together talking about his day and mine, I eventually came around to talking about my writing and keeping track of the Harridan story and asked him if there was any more to what he had originally shared.

"It's not too painful for you to talk about?"

"It's how I am handling it ... move it out of my brain into words in print that I can manipulate, make things come out the way I want them to. It's my way of fighting back."

He took me at my word and began talking. He said that he had parked his car down the road from Harridan's house and walked into the yard, where he could see through the curtainless living room window Harridan sitting in front of a TV. Jake walked around the garage and a small barn on the property, listening for any sounds of life, and then trying to look through windows and opening doors to the barn and sheds. When he satisfied himself that I wasn't tied up to a post or hiding behind a bale of straw, he walked up to the house and knocked on the front door to confront his suspect.

Not expecting anyone, and not knowing that it was Jake, Harridan turned on the porch light and pulled the heavy oak door open wide and looked through the glass storm door. He was standing there in a loose-fitting T-shirt, blue jeans, and a pair of white socks—no shoes—looking shocked at seeing Jake. He pushed the storm door open and stepped out onto the stoop.

"What the fuck are you doing here? Get the fuck off my property."

Jake told him that I was missing, and he wanted to know where I was.

"How would I know anything about it? Get off my property."

When Jake didn't respond, didn't move from where he was standing, Harridan started making threats about launching a physical attack on him, settling their differences right then. He backed down as Jake unlatched the strap holding his gun in place. Jake said again that he wanted to know where I was, and Harridan laughed at him. He laughed again when Jake said he was holding him responsible for anything that happened to me.

Sneering, Harridan responded, "You aren't going to do shit! Get the fuck out of here."

It was a cliched TV episode written by a tired writer: Jake saying something like, "I'm leaving, Mike, but you and I are going to have our day, and if I find out you are in any way involved in Rob's disappearance, we're going to have another meeting, and you won't like the way it turns out."

"What if we're wrong, Jake? What if all the stuff that has happened really is all about coincidence? I mean, that's a possibility, right?"

"I'm not a believer in that many coincidences happening when all of them play to Harridan's hand. Coincidence only works as a defense until proof comes along. The more he tries to get even with people and cover up his role in all of the things that happen, the tougher it gets for him to control the coincidences. He thinks he shut down all possibilities of the store owners in town testifying against him by killing off the Lidons. He needed a way to get at me for ratting him out, him losing his job and his 'extra' income, and my willingness to testify against him." When the beating his boys gave me didn't stop me, he had to find another way. That's where you come in."

"But how would he know anything about us ... that's what I can't figure out."

"Who knows? It's what he's good at: knowing things and using what he knows to control the people he knows about. All it would have taken was for someone to see us at the diner together a few times, or out buying groceries, or going to the gym together. Putting two and two together isn't all that difficult particularly if you're looking for something to use against someone else."

"But, Jake, there's no evidence for any of it, even the murder of the Lidons—if it was a murder."

Jake told me how a so-called suicide could be faked forcing the couple into the car's trunk, the murderers stepping outside after starting the car, letting the car run long enough to kill the couple, and then going in with masks on, turning the car off, lifting the bodies out of the trunk and setting them up in the seats of the car and turning the car back on before leaving. All the murderers had to do was to wear gloves so as not to leave any fingerprints. On the other hand, if it was, in fact, a suicide, it might have been because it was the Lidons' only way of avoiding the punishments Harridan and his minions were threatening them with; it was still murder as Jake described it.

Despite my best efforts to reassure him that he wasn't responsible, Jake still carried some guilt about the Lidons, believed that, in a round-about way, simply by asking them a few questions, he had inadvertently set them up—lit the fuse of their fears—caused them to make mistakes in judgment. Perhaps they told Harridan what he didn't need to know about Jake's questioning even though they hadn't given Jake anything meaningful to use as evidence. Jake had talked about the Lidons many times before their deaths, said he hoped they were alright, said how awful it must have been for them to be old and powerless to stand up to Harridan's potential for brutality, said he wished there was a way to help them despite their not wanting it. And then they were dead, apparently killing themselves to escape the fear of living. The city prosecutor's assessment of Jake's involvement in the case stabbed his chest and twisted as he thought about the old couple now lying in their graves.

"Don't think for a minute that the merchants he was shaking down aren't aware that Harridan was behind the Lidon's deaths even if it can't be proven," Jake said. "They got the message loud and clear. I know it as surely as anyone can know anything in this world that Harridan is at the heart of all of it. Count on it."

"But there isn't any proof, Jake, and passion can't deliver a verdict on its own."

"Proof will come."

"Like it did for Nathan Sanders? Is somebody going to be trying to figure this one out 150 years from now?"

"The chief must have something on him, or he wouldn't have been able to fire him—at least something serious enough that it violates the contract. There haven't been any lawsuits from Harridan's lawyer to try to reinstate him in the department; that tells me he knows the chief had enough on him to keep him from getting into a court battle. Chief's not stupid; he knows Harridan is the connector between all the dots. I trust Cooper, believe he's looking in every nook and cranny. But he's got his hands full. I hear Harridan's attorney is running interference on everything Cooper does. The lawyer is trying to make a case that the police are harassing his client. That might be part of the delay. Best I can figure, Cooper just doesn't have enough solid evidence for Boyle to take into the courtroom yet."

"Jake, Harridan had to know that all of the things that we think he's part of would point back at him. I mean, he's the obvious choice for a villain in these cases. Why would he call that much attention to himself? If he's at the heart of all of it as you say, you'd think he would want to distance himself from attention."

"He thinks he's smarter than everyone else and he can't lose. It's a game to him. And that's what's going to do him in. He *will* screw up! I told you a while ago, they all screw up eventually. It's just a matter of when. For all we know, he could have dozens of illegal operations going on out there, lots of people working for him. He just might piss off one of those folks and make that person want to get even, maybe drop a hint to somebody who could nail him. At some point, he'll forget to take care of a tiny detail that will break him!"

"I just don't get what's in it for him."

"You don't know how it is with people like him. This is a guy who doesn't think like you and I do. He wants control of other people; needs to feel important. Power and control are way more important to him than money. He likes people kowtowing to him, fearing him, and he doesn't like it when people say 'no' to his commands. You saw how he was with you at the store. In a sense, you said 'no,' to him; you weren't going to let him bully you. That triggered an even greater need to control you. That word, 'no,' was just an indicator that you would need some more powerful persuasion to convince you to run away from me. He was trying to control our relationship, control me, make you afraid to be with me."

"Well, he failed." And when I said that, for the first time since the abduction, I felt my muscles flexing ready to get up and move, felt light coming into my eyes, could almost hear the blood pumping through my veins. Jake saw my reaction and smiled.

32

It was a sun-filled Sunday in late May when Jake, Jim Lanning, and I went to the quarry to take our first swim of the summer. Jim had come to the house several times prior to that day just to spend time with us and do some shoptalk with Jake. Listening to them talk, it was obvious to me that there was increasing tension at the station; it was related to the interviews the chief had been conducting over the past six months with various members of the force and staff and the presence of state investigators attending and taking part in those interviews. Up until that Sunday, Jim had been careful not to share specific details. However, on that day, as we all sat on the rocks after a quick dip into the still-cold water, me sitting between them, Jim started talking by first of all saying, "You didn't hear this from me, but... a lot has happened in the last two or three days behind the scenes at work. A lot of the guys at the station are nervous, hoping they aren't going to get sucked into the Harridan investigation."

Speaking directly to Jake, he said, "You might have noticed that the chief had you out on assignments all day yesterday. It was because he wanted to keep you out of what was happening at the office." Lanning was too good a cop to tell everything he knew specifically, but he felt comfortable sharing what had leaked out at the station that Weller had confessed to luring Jake into work on the night of the beating. Rumor had it that he also had set up the timing of the phone call that took Jake out to the old church. "Have you noticed that Kyle Avery hasn't been in, and Tony and a couple others had to do extra time to cover for him? Turns out, the chief got Avery too. We all knew that the chief was going through copies of logs and phone records from the day of your beating as well as the day before and after. When we asked the chief what had happened to him, Chief just said, 'He's done.'"

"I knew if the chief looked, there wasn't going to be any traceable record of an incoming phone call from someone making an anonymous call," Jake responded. Then, he went on to run through his recollections of that night, certain that everything had been a set-up ... all too neat. He had barely arrived for work; everybody else was already out on the street—maybe physically closer to the church than he was at the station. "I'll bet anything that either there was no anonymous call or the log was faked." With all of the back-up systems in place at the station and the phone company, the chief should have been able to track the source of the anonymous phone call if it was made—even if only to find it was called in on a burner phone. The whole case should easily show that timing and opportunity were well planned and coordinated to get Jake alone in a vulnerable situation totally reliant on Avery to provide backup if he called in for backup. The area behind the church was secluded, dark, no one could have seen what was happening; houses around it were all student rentals and well removed from the churchyard. "I knew goddamned well that the chief would be able to see the record of my work phone and the time I called in for back-up and it didn't come."

Jim Lanning's guess was that the chief scared Avery, maybe threatened him with some jail time. Avery squealed, admitted Weller asked him to call Jake in, and it was Weller who told him what time he needed Jake to be assigned to check out the church. From what I was gathering from listening to Jim and Jake talk was that Avery was either fired and told he would be charged as an accessory to a crime and was likely hiding somewhere safe until Weller—and probably Harridan, too—wouldn't be a threat to him while the chief got more evidence.

"These are things the chief could have found out about a long time ago!" Jake was suddenly agitated. His voice got louder, angrier as he said, "Why in hell did it take so goddamned long?"

"Whoa, partner," Lanning said as he and I reacted to Jake's momentary outburst. I too was surprised. "Chief might have known for a while. You know the game, Jake. Sometimes you have to balance lots of pieces. Maybe he held back for good reason, maybe didn't want to tip his hand until he had better cards to play ...."

Trying to help Jake calm, I cut Jim off and said, "Maybe Cooper has his eye on getting Harridan for other crimes we don't know about. Who knows? You said he knows what he's doing, Jake!" As I said it, I realized that this had been the first and only time Jake had wavered in his trust in the chief.

He took a moment to collect himself and then acknowledged that he was overreacting. "You're both right. Sorry I reacted like that. It's just that I can't do anything to help him. I'm not good at being on the sidelines."

33

From the beginning of our relationship, I loved to hear Jake talk about his work. He gave me many strange and interesting stories. Because of the personal nature of it, I was especially intent on hearing anything related to the ongoing Harridan case. I wanted it solved as much as he did. When he talked about it, I asked him all kinds of questions and then wrote in my journal what he had said as best as I could remember it. Many days there was nothing much to write about. Though I worked on other projects, sold a couple of stories and articles, and continued to work on a play, I sometimes took time and responsibility for sorting and organizing my thoughts about what he told me, imagining conversations, creating details about locations and space. Expressing mood and emotional reactions was mine.

"What if there's no story, Rob? He gets off scot-free?"

"That might be part of the story; I don't know yet. It will end however it ends. Anyway, that's not *the* story."

"What is?"

"I'm not sure yet." When I said it, I knew that it was a coy response, but better than a lie.

Jake just shook his head from side to side, smiled, and rolled his blue eyes in that way that comes with wanting to understand something that is not ready to be understood even to the person who controls it.

***

The story. That little word, *the*, carries so much weight, demands so much of my time and thought no matter what I write. There is always the conflict between the story and the truth, the desire to create meaningful reading for someone else and finding the essential truth—the essential meaning—of the story. It was difficult enough trying to deal with Nathan Sanders and the paucity of truth, but then came love for Jake, the story of Mike Harridan and his hatred for Jake, and my own experience with the world of brutality in my personal life and in the world I live in. They were all intermingled in my mind, but I had concluded that somehow they were meant to be part of a larger whole that I couldn't clearly see at the time. I continued to write out of a hope and belief that all of my note taking, drafting, and revising would add up to a book.

The best and worst part of it all was that I was getting much of my information through Jake: best because he was careful to state what he gathered from his interactions with people in the story; worst because I couldn't be with him and pick up on all of the details that are needed to bring characters to life or to put what he told me into the context of a space, human interactions, verbal and non-verbal language, tone, emphasis; I couldn't know what he forgot or misperceived. Other than what I experienced my-self, I was working in a world of Jake's making and trans-lating impressions—both his and my own. Neither of us could be certain about much of anything we talked about except that we talked. Jake couldn't remember verbatim everything he said to others or heard from them, remem-ber specific phrases, or tell me things that he didn't hear or see. And yet, to tell *the story*, I needed details that made sense to fill in around what he was able to give me and what I had seen and heard for myself and then tried to capture in notes—which were always translations of what we *believed* we saw, heard, or experienced. And yet, good reading is created by the inclusion of details, details that happened whether we see and hear them or not and with-out them, telling *the* truth can be ever so boring.

***

Monday morning, the day after talking with Jim Lan-ning at the quarry, Jake went to Mark Cooper's office after roll call, closed the heavy door behind him, and said with a level of seriousness and command, "We need to talk." Cooper had known this day would come, the day when Jake would demand answers and he would have to find a way to dance around their friendship and decide what he could share about the ongoing work of trying to get at the connections between Harridan, Jake's ambush at the church, and my abduction and abuse.

The chief motioned for Jake to sit in the scarred chair where they were separated only by the corner of the chief's steel desk. Jake leaned forward, placing his forearm on the faux wood desktop and told Cooper that officers had been talking openly about firings and arrests within the department. He had just heard some of it before roll call. In his matter-of-fact way, Jake said, "It's time you level with me and bring me up to speed ... at least as far as you can go without jeopardizing the cases."

Cooper was clearly uncomfortable, made some comments about cops not being able to keep their mouths shut, worse than AA members promising not to tell what they hear in meetings, worse than school children keeping secrets about who is in love with whom. He asked what Jake had heard and reluctantly confirmed what Jake had been told.

Jake knew that Cooper liked him. Soon after becoming chief, Cooper saw how Jake had been singled out by some of the officers and knew there was bad blood in the force. As he got to know his officers, the chief took Jake under his wing to the extent that he relied on Jake's good judgements and loyalty to the laws and codes that guided their work. The chief headed off several conflicts within the department that would have involved Jake clashing with the Harridan group. The chief had told Jake at one time that he reminded him of his own enthusiasm, dedication, and desire to learn in his own early days on the force. As a result, Jake felt that he could be frank with him without it resulting in a contest of wills.

Maybe a little too boldly, Jake said, "I'm struggling to understand why it has taken so long to get to this point and why I'm the last to know what everybody else seems to know. You and I talked about the logs and phone records right after the beating I took. You led me to believe you were going to be all over this case. I've stayed out of it like you asked. But now I find out about where things stand through the grapevine. What's going on?"

Obviously, perceiving Jake's words a challenge to his friendship and leadership, the chief fired back, "First of all, the people who are flapping their jaws know very little about what's going on! And if you think I've been sitting on my ass all this time, you're wrong."

Jake's interpretation of the chief's demeanor was annoyance, discomfort, shakiness, not like himself at all. Cooper was avoiding eye contact, fidgeting with a click pen, rocking in his swivel chair. Clearly, something wasn't right, and Jake began wondering if the chief—his friend— had lost his commitment to the case, and maybe to Jake as well. As they sat together, Jake's mountain-stream-blue eyes fixed on the chief, making it more difficult for Cooper to dodge them. It was Jake's technique for drawing people out. It wasn't hard staring. In fact, his eyes were soft and kind and yet he could create an intensity within them that made it clear he wasn't interested in playing games. It was a technique that worked well on those with guilty consciences and secrets.

The chief knew their relationship well enough to understand that Jake would not turn away or allow himself

to be distracted by the behaviors he—the chief—was showing. He looked into Jake's face and put his hands into the
air as if giving up and said, "I can't do this!" As soon as
he spoke, the rigidity and nervousness of Cooper's body
began to abate. "I guess this is as good a time as any. I
couldn't ... wasn't allowed to share anything. I've wanted
to. And Boyle will chew my ass for talking to you. What do
you want to know?"

"Everything you're willing to tell me."

The chief made Jake promise that he wasn't going to
play TV cop, go rogue, interfere in the investigation or leak
information that might affect the case. After Jake agreed,
Cooper said that he had studied the logs and phone records immediately after the event. He had questioned
both Weller and Avery, heard their initial lies and denials.
He had been forced to use the city's detectives to interview several people who were thought to know something
about the handling of records and people who might have
an inside track to the motivations of the men in question.
Clearly, the chief believed it had been one or both of the
detectives who leaked information.

Particularly interesting to the chief was that each of the
men—Weller and Avery–early in their separate non-man-
datory interviews, asked in exactly the same way, "Do I
need to have my attorney present?" as if they suspected
trouble just being asked to answer questions about the day
of Jake's beating. Both men were consistent in denying any
part in a crime and said they would not answer specific
questions without their attorneys present. And with that,

the game began: the lions were to be turned loose in the arena, and any sign of fear on Cooper's part, any failure to follow the letter of the law would be an opportunity for the attorneys to slash his body with their claws, many slashings before they moved in for the kill. They would gnaw on the long history of his predecessor's bad judgments, the long period of time it was taking for him to rid the department of incompetence, and his "obvious desire" to use anyone he could "to satisfy his vendetta against a former police officer."

According to Jake, on the morning after the chief's most recent interviews with Weller and Avery where he told them they were suspects in the crime against Jake and were on paid leave until further notice, he—the chief—got a call from Dan Engler, a county commissioner asking for a 'favor.'"

ENGLER:	*"Mark, Ken Engler here. You on vacation?" He asked with his faked, "haw, haw" as a follow up to show he was joking.*
CHIEF:	*"What do you mean?"*
ENGLER:	*"I heard you were on a fishing expedition, haw, haw."*
CHIEF:	*"What do you mean?"*
ENGLER:	*[Any hint of joking left his voice.] "I heard you might be mistaken about a couple of officers you've been talking to.*
CHIEF:	*"Mistaken, how?"*

ENGLER: "Some of us think you might be better
           off not bothering those guys."

CHIEF: "What is that supposed to mean?
           What's your interest in this?"

ENGLER: "Let's just say, for the sake of the
           city, you might want to do something
           else with your time if you catch my
           meaning.

CHIEF: "By the 'city,' do you mean you,
           Commissioner?"

ENGLER: "You might want to remember that
           elections are coming up next year
           and you'll need some friends in your
           corner."

CHIEF: "Friends like you, Commissioner?
           Before you say anything else, I want
           to give you a quick heads up that all
           phone calls coming through the main
           line are recorded. Do you want to
           continue?"

Engler hung up and Cooper called Carolyn "Hard" Boyle to fill her in on what had happened. She was furious when the chief told her Engler had gotten involved in the case. Later, she looked at the evidence the chief had pulled together about the office log and phone records and listened to the recording of his phone conversation with Engler. Then she told him to go ahead with arresting the officers for falsifying records and leave Engler to her.

"*I might as well tell you now,*" she said. "*I brought the state into the case several weeks ago to do some behind-the-scenes investigation. Quite interesting what they've found.*"

"*Why didn't you tell me, Carolyn? Why the secrecy?*"

"*Because I want to know what in the hell I am getting myself into and who I can trust. And I don't like surprises.*

"*You thought I was part of this mess? You know what I've gone through. I inherited the police force I have, and, as you well know, I have to live by the contract and state employee/employer laws. I can't just fire people as I please. And, just in case it needs to be said, I've got some excellent officers, one of whom you didn't want on the case!*"

"*Chill the anger, Mark. It's not that simple, and it's not just about you and your officers. I wanted to know how far Harridan's racket goes, who's on the inside and who's on the outside and who knows the secrets that will get us beyond a bunch of suppositions about Harridan and his henchmen. Your detectives have given us nothing. I wanted some people with no personal stake in the people involved who could collect and assess evidence. You, unfortunately, are handicapped at the moment.*"

The words stung Cooper, felt like a face slap. Before he could react verbally, Boyle was doling out new information he needed to hear. State investigators had gained access to Harridan's bank records. He had been making significant cash deposits in several bank accounts for a long time and not accounting for them in his annual taxes. The state was building a case for tax evasion.

"*The Attorney General's office has done just enough to let it be known they are looking into Harridan's affairs,*" *Boyle said. "I want him to be nervous, nervous enough to make a mistake. And I want to make his pals nervous enough to make mistakes. I am not settling for tax evasion. I want to get him for corruption, intimidation, rape, and murder if I can." That's why I want you to arrest Weller and Avery Friday evening—tomorrow night—when they are less likely to get an attorney to come running to their aid. Let them cool their heels in a jail cell for a while.*

The theory was that allowing the officers to spend some time in a jail cell was a first step in encouraging them to loosen their tongues. The thought of prison time can be a powerful motivator—each of the men knowing full well the fate of an ex-cop amongst prisoners if he were to be found out; and hints could be dropped that other prisoners just might find out. Though she wouldn't personally do such a thing as setting prisoners—ex-cops—up for abuse or death, she and Cooper both knew the intimation of such a thing might be enough for them to consider cutting a deal.

A few of the braver merchants had intimated warily to the state investigators that they might be willing to testify in court that their "donations" to Harridan were coerced if they could be sure they and their families would be safe. The city's detectives, on the other hand, had failed to secure even a single potential witness.

"Your detectives aren't very good at what they do," she said.

"*I tried to tell you that ... water over the dam ... Sorry. And they're likely afraid to do a good job and face Harridan's wrath.*"

"*What in the hell is his power over these people?*" Boyle asked.

"*He's a blackmailer and a bully,*" Cooper said. "*My guess is that he finds things out about people and uses that information to his advantage—an affair, some sexual proclivity, illegal activity, etcetera—and takes ongoing payments to keep quiet. If that doesn't work, he intimidates them, convinces them that he can protect them from all kinds of conjured external threats or his own threats of violence.*"

County Commissioner Engler had long been rumored to be into what the older townspeople called "kinky" sex. What that meant and to what extent it might affect his reputation, marriage, and social standing if it were known to be true, might have been reason enough for him to make the call to Cooper that morning. Given Boyle's obvious annoyance with the commissioner, there may have been any number of factors about his political dealings or personal finances that brushed the edges of the law.

Boyle admitted to Cooper that in her estimation he had been handed a mess when he took responsibility for the department, and she believed only a major house cleaning was going to resolve the majority of issues. She implied that she would do what she could to get the city's attorney, the mayor, county commissioners, and city council to work with him to do what was necessary for him to get the officers and staff he had been asking for and needed. With the information Cooper had just brought to her, she said she was upping the ante for all involved by asking state investigators to look into Harridan's potentially undermining both the police department and city and county politics.

If Avery and Weller talked, the merchant witnesses could be made to talk, Harridan's bank records could be used, and Weller's corroboration, an extortion case would be what Boyle called a "slam dunk." Tax evasion. Extortion. Harridan's days were numbered. However, both she and the chief were holding back from arresting Harridan in hopes of getting him for the assaults on Jake and me, and the murder of the Lidons.

***

As they talked, Cooper told Jake that he was right about the Lidons. The coroner's report had shown postmortem lividity consistent with the bodies lying on their sides. The state investigators found trace evidence in the trunk of the couple's car: fibers from the clothing they were wearing that day, and fresh light scratches on the inside of the trunk lid that the city's detectives had missed ... information inconsistent with the couple having been found sitting up in their car. As Jake told it, there was more than enough evidence to figure out it was murder, but he couldn't pin it on anyone in particular with the evidence he had. He couldn't count on his own detectives, and he had been pushed into the role of assistant to State Investigators who were taking over.

***

When Jake paused in the telling of his interactions with the chief that morning, I thought about the Lidons:

The TV program the elderly couple watched was of no interest to them. It was simply the least uninteresting show they could find to watch—a nightly monotony to escape monotonous work dealing with customers, and vendors, as well as various organizations begging donations for good causes.

Nearly fifty years married and near as many working side by side in pursuit of the "dream"—that fantastical belief that had barely carried them from one day to the next living as close to the good life as a chained dog wanting to break free, barking and begging for something it would never have. They had nothing worth saying to one another or anyone else that had not been said ad nauseum. Instead, they talked to the TV, told the images what they should have said or done, or chastised characters for not using Lidon logic for making sense of a world that had been created by someone other than them, someone who allowed the actors to strut before them indifferent to their curses and corrections.

The bang, bang, bang at the door made the picture window on the opposite side of the room vibrate, caught their fears, broke their attempts to influence the outcomes of a story, their imaginations of living other people's lives, having power as they pursued and conquered thieves and murderers and human stupidity. They looked at one another, one of them saying, "Jesus Christ! Who's that at this time of night?" *Each of them hoping whoever was at the door would not see that the lights were on in the apartment or hear the TV blabbering away—it's inanity as it gained volume with the advent of a commercial. As the knocking continued, each of them hoped the other would take on the laborious task of rising and going to the door to see who was there.*

It might have occurred to one or both that it was the police coming to tell them once again that someone had broken a windowpane or had defaced the front of the building, something they could do nothing about at midnight. Old man Lidon, seeing his wife would outwait him, struggled to lift his heavy wrinkle of a body up out of the straight-backed chair that had succumbed and conformed to forty years of his weight. His body took time to adjust to standing, time to get the stinging pains of old age out of his knees so he could walk. The pounding came again, the windowed upper part of the door banging against the door frame, the deadbolt clanking against the strike, the insistence of the intruder who easily could have broken the glass, reached through the open hole and turn the lock knob counterclockwise.

In the seconds it took me to imagine the plight of the Lidons, Jake had moved on talking about the breadth of information Cooper had shared. It must have been obvious that he lost me for a moment. He stopped talking and looked at me from beneath the fall of his upper eyelids and the almost imperceptible fog that was entering his eyes to replace the fading gleam.

"Detectives have found the woman—prostitute—who played damsel in distress at the church. I'm hoping she's got something worthwhile to share."

He put his hand on my knee and said, "Unfortunately, still no clues helpful to take any action on what they did to you. I'm sorry."

We paused for a moment, sitting in the wasteland of "I'm sorry," each of us sorry for what the other had had to endure, sorry that the human race wallows in its own filth so much of the time. I thought of Nathan's limp body being cut from the tree to be thrown into a hand-dug hole, earth dropping over his face, the long decay reducing him to the good he could be—maybe the only good any human can be after it's too late for saying "I'm sorry"—as nutrition for deep-rooted trees.

Breaking the momentary silence, Jake went on, his cop-brain pursuing the flow of information: "Weller was in deep with Harridan, and he's likely going to be the key to getting him, and maybe to finding out who got to you. He's facing some criminal charges for setting me up, and I suspect he's going to get a lot of pressure over the next few days to squeal on Harridan."

At some point after Jake finished with his summary of the many things Cooper had shared with him, I asked if the chief had explained how he had fired Harridan without it ending up in a lawsuit or some politician coming to his rescue. As it turned out, Harridan and a rookie cop, Mickey Stanley—who had only a couple of months on the job— were on patrol on a weekend evening. During a routine check of a beverage distributor's warehouses, the two officers came upon an unlocked door. Apparently, there were cases of whiskey in clear sight as Harridan shined his flashlight into the interior. The two men entered, scanned the huge, stocked shelves and stacked pallets, but found no intruders, nothing amiss-- Nothing other than what Harridan did next. I'm guessing it went something like this:

HARRIDAN: *"Kind of like being a fox in a henhouse, eh?"*

STANLEY: *"What do you mean?"*

HARRIDAN: *"Any kind of whiskey a man could want. Right here for the taking."*

STANLEY: *(Trying to treat it like a joke.) "Yeah. Sure is."*

HARRIDAN: *"You know what? Nobody but you and me knows for sure that somebody didn't come in here before us. Somebody comes in here, helps himself to a few bottles. That's all. Company accepts a bit of loss, says they're glad it was no worse. End of story."*

STANLEY: *"So, what are you saying? ... Hold it just a minute, I just got a text." (As he said this, he pulled his cell phone out of his shirt, glanced at it, clicked a button, and returned to the conversation.) "Sorry. It was nothing."*

> *HARRIDAN:* "I'm just saying, nobody would know
> better, and you'd have yourself some of
> the best whiskey a man can drink."
> *STANLEY:* "And you?"
> *HARRIDAN:* "A couple of bottles for you, a couple
> for me, nobody's the wiser."

In my scenario, Stanley said he didn't want to be any part of a theft. Harridan had argued that it wasn't a theft, exactly. It was a deserved bennie for cops who are overworked and underpaid; and he asked how anyone could possibly know the liquor hadn't been stolen prior to their arrival; all the boy had to do was keep his mouth shut. When Stanley refused once again, Harridan called him a "pussy," drove him back to the station and said he should keep his mouth shut for his own good.

What Harridan didn't know was that Stanley had seen for himself what Jake and others suspected—the frequent stops and being told to wait in the car, the unequal treatment of suspects if there was an implied agreement between them and Harridan for favors. The rookie also knew the talk around the station about Harridan and didn't like or trust him. When it was clear what he was being asked to do in the warehouse, he had effectively made a quick decision to fake an incoming text message and use his phone to record the rest of their conversation, including the threats on the way back to the station.

The next day, Stanley walked into Cooper's office, played the recording, allowed the chief to copy it, and then turned in his badge, saying something like, "I know what happens around here to people who cross that son-of-bitch; if I stay, I'll be a target. No, thanks." He shook hands with the chief, said he was sorry he couldn't stay, and left without giving the chief time to try to talk him into changing his mind—the few minutes it would take to convince the young man that he was exactly the kind of officer needed on the force.

According to Jake, the chief called Harridan into the office later that day and played the tape for him, recited the section of the policies and procedures Harridan had violated, and fired him.

"I know you're extorting money from some of the merchants, and when I can prove it, you'll be hauled into jail like any other common criminal to get the justice you so richly deserve. Until then, you are fired. Lay your gun and your badge on the desk and get out of my office."

I suspected that it probably wasn't smart for the chief to have shown his hand on the extortion case, but he did, and that's maybe what kicked Harridan's rage into motion; now he was going to have to work on multiple fronts to avoid getting caught.

"Maybe the chief wanted to push Harridan to panic, push him to move out of fear. Just like I told you, Rob, they all make mistakes, and the mistakes are linking up to become the big hammer that's coming down on him soon."

I hoped he was right, stood up, pulled him up out of his sitting position, and hugged him, told him I was glad

Harridan's days were numbered, glad life might get better for Jake at the station, glad that we could begin to put the ugliness of what had happened to each of us into lockable boxes we could bury in the back yard and cover the spaces they had taken up in our lives with warm blankets to cover us when we were cold.

"Don't get too excited yet, Slick. Harridan's not going to go quietly or gracefully. By now he knows the walls are closing in, and when a dangerous man sees that all his alternatives for escaping are about to disappear, he becomes like a wild animal and at least twice as dangerous."

***

After Jake had fallen asleep, I was still writing the story of the Lidons in my head. It took a while for me to accept that I couldn't hold the thoughts until morning, and since I couldn't sleep, I got up and wrote. By the time Jake came down the stairs that morning, I had made my way through a rendition of what happened to the Lidons.

When the old man got to the door, he looked out the window into the dark. "Who is it? What do you want?"

The unrecognizable voice simply said in a confident voice, "Open up! Harridan sent us to talk about your protection.

"I don't know what you're talking about. Protection? Who are you?" The old man's voice was shaky, fearful.

The voice on the other side of the door said something that the old man, or maybe the old woman who had come to his side, understood as a threat better managed by opening

the door than calling the police. Two men, strangers, entered the room, looking about. One of them, the taller of
the two, a man with a square face and dark brooding eyes
told them they were going to take a ride. When the old
woman started weeping and pleading, the man touched
her shoulder, told her not to worry; she wouldn't be hurt;
it was just a ride; Harridan needed to talk to them about
some things they shouldn't be saying. Just a chat. Nothing
more. Then back home. That easy.

"What if we say no. Then what?"

"Well ... that would be downright unfriendly. Wouldn't
go over well. Probably best to just come along, chat for a
few minutes and then come right back home."

The old man tried to convince her everything would be
fine. She continued to cry. Mrs. Lidon turned off the TV
and the table lamp, pulled the door shut after the second
of the two men came out. Over years of habit and without thinking, she locked the door and then pushed against
it while turning the knob to be sure it was secure. At the
bottom of the stairs, the man who was doing the talking
said, "I think it's best we take your car. You don't mind, do
you? Mine's been a little sluggish lately; don't wanna risk
anything happening on the road. You understand, right?"

Befuddled, the old man reached into his pockets. Realizing his keys weren't there, he told his wife to give them
hers after she unlocked the side door to the garage. Mr.
Lidon went through first and reached toward the button
that would open the garage door but one of the men took
his wrist and held it, told him to turn on an overhead light

and wait while Mrs. Lidon was escorted through and the door pulled shut. The silent man stood blocking the door while the other went to the trunk of the car and used his key to unlock it and look in. By this time, the old lady was sobbing, and a gun appeared in the hands of the man who had stood guard at the door.

Old people don't easily crawl into the trunk of a car. Old bodies don't move like young ones. It was easier to put guns to their heads to ensure their silence, tie them up wrists and ankles with the rope pulled out of the younger men's jackets, put gags in their mouths before picking them up and dropping them into the trunk as their bodies tried to find a kick, a two-fisted punch, or a twist of the torso that would somehow save them from their unsavable situation before the car started and time came to an end.

34

Over the next few weeks, many pieces started coming together. Each of the three county commissioners was interviewed by State Investigators who showed them phone logs of their calls to and from Harridan. They all tried to pass the records off as part of their jobs dealing with a citizen, who, like lots of other citizens, called too often with complaints about one thing or another. However, when Dan Engler was confronted with the chief's affidavit and a transcript of the phone call to the chief, he simply admitted he had acted inappropriately and was sorry; he had done so based upon the concerns of citizens who had called him (citizens not to be named) and hadn't intentionally threatened Cooper. It was all a misunderstanding. He vehemently denied that Mike Harridan had anything to do with the call and denied Harridan (or anyone else) was extorting him. In other words, he was hoping investigators would buy his "stupid" defense and would see enough ambiguity in what he had done to decide he wasn't worth pursuing. If he had shut up at that point, he was probably right. Unfortunately for him, he went on to say that if the State tried to use his phone records in any way, he would sue—based on "principle" of course. The red cape had been splayed and swirled before the raging bull.

"What's the connection with Harridan?"

"Could be anything. But you can bet money has got something to do with it if anybody cares to look. Either the two of them have got some kind of scam going on or Harridan is blackmailing Engler. There's a connection. It just comes down to figuring out what it is and how big it is."

"Engler's a politician, Jake. He'll duck and weave until the case is so old nobody cares one way or the other anymore."

"Well... that kind of depends on how interested the newspapers might be in the story once all of this comes out. And if the papers don't pick up on it, they might need to be invited to pick up on it by some good citizen who wants the public to know about the people they voted for and put into office. Know any good citizens like that, Rob?"

"I might."

Judging by what I was hearing from Jake and by my perceptions of Police Chief Cooper and Carolyn Boyle, it was clear that there would eventually be a trial for at least some of Harridan's crimes. I could picture him sitting at a table beside an attorney and doing his best performance of innocence while the prosecutor did everything in his power to provoke the defendant to react to witnesses, maybe lose control, maybe rise to fight or make threats, show his true nature.

He would not be, could not be a Nathan Sanders sitting quietly and patiently amidst the proceedings as his lawyer battled to keep him from the gallows:

Nathan Sanders seemed more a sculpture than a man. There were no indicators of what he was thinking or feeling as he sat quietly beside defense attorney, Radcliff, who represented him. Sanders let happen whatever was to happen, had seemingly forgiven the attorney—or at least accepted the man who had once offered passionately to prosecute him before the judge ordered him to serve as the lead defense attorney.

Each day, the young man in ankle and wrist chains made his way into the courtroom walking between two guards who would lead him to the chair behind the defense table beside Radcliff and remove his chains. One of the guards would remain throughout the day, sitting directly behind the prisoner. The other guard would return at noon to rechain Sanders and assist in taking the defendant back to the jail for lunch. The pattern would repeat itself in the afternoon. There would be no outbursts, attempts to cause a scene; Sanders did what he was told and offered no resistance whatsoever.

If Sanders was listening to what anyone was saying on the witness stand, he gave no indications. His clean-shaven face was present, but his eyes appeared absent like the eyes of a dreamer so far gone into the pleasant rooms of his brain that all of the blather of human talk simply disappeared. There was one exception: his mother taking the stand to tell the jurors of her son's oddities as a child, his desire to be alone, his rejection of potential playmates, his inability to learn, her frustration with trying to help him overcome lack of all ambition until he grew old enough to run off on his own, find alcohol, women, anger, violence, brutality ... all so different from the sweet little boy he had been, his mother's sweet boy ... something wrong with his mind that she couldn't touch ... something no one seemed to be able to access or fix. Nathan watched his mother cry. His one moment of emotional response came and went with a quick wipe at his eyes as she descended from the witness stand and crawled back into her cave of despair to wait for whatever the attorney told her son to accept, guilty or not.

***

Harridan would be more fairly judged than Nathan Sanders had been and wouldn't face the community hysteria that led to vigilante action against the monster the young man was perceived to be. However, his freedom, his ability to wreak havoc on the world could end all the same depending upon a jury and their impressions of warring lawyers engaged in a battle—lords of *Prosecution vs. Defense* performing as knights fighting for the honor of their avowed and oppositional versions of truth.

I hated everything about Mike Harridan: what I believed he had done to me, to Jake, to the Lidons, to his co-workers, and probably many others. Had I been around when Nathan Sanders was alive and somehow been a target, I might have harbored similar feelings about him ... but

I didn't really believe I would have. So much depends upon the time and distance between oneself and other humans. I felt no hatred for Nathan Sanders who was more than likely equally guilty. With Sanders, I found myself somehow in sympathy with what I perceived to be his youth, his simple-mindedness, his little-boy approach to playing adult. Perhaps the difference was only time and lack of information, but I held a shred of hope for Nathan that maybe he wasn't the guiltiest person in the gruesome, impossible-to-be-proven-beyond-a-shadow-of-doubt   murder to which he would be linked until history is dissolved. I held no such sympathy for Mike Harridan.

As I sat writing and wondering about such things, I did a quick search, found, and pulled up one of the newspaper reports written about Nathan Sanders that I had saved. It dealt with his trial and his demise. I had read it several times previously, but I needed a touchstone as I pondered the ways "truth" is used and abused to lead a jury and the public to make deadly decisions about the value of a man's life when facts are damned and bias and unexamined perceptions make the final call! Distort facts enough, whip people's fears to a frenzy and it—collective fear—becomes *fact* enough for retributive slaughter. How little things have changed, I thought.

***

The defense had argued that the confession of an accused man who was drunk at the time he gave a confession, and who bordered on being simple-minded, couldn't be relied upon for conviction, particularly since little evidence corroborated the things he had confessed. In various motions Radcliff cited case law and precedents to countermand the use of circumstantial theories without corroborating evidence. Like a bantam rooster scraping and scratching at logic, Radcliff paced before the jury rail using his most confident, boldly spoken words to insist that at least two men <u>must</u> have taken part in the murder; "it was clear" as he had "proven." He was determined that the jury <u>must</u> see that it is plausible that Sanders had simply watched as he said he had. He went so far as to point a finger at the judge and state that the judge himself in a statement in the courtroom expressed doubt as to whether the actual murderer had been found.

The prosecution responded to defense motions by pulling out its shield of case law proving exactly the opposite of what Radcliff had stated. In front of the jury, the prosecuting attorney stated with theatrical gesture and voice that they had proven Sanders had committed the crimes without help from anyone. They claimed that even if some minor discrepancies were somehow worthy of notice, their version of the story was logical. They had proven beyond any doubt that Sanders was guilty of murder in the first degree, and the jury's job was simply to acknowledge that truth.

As a result of the arguments and "truths" thrown at them and the overlong explanations by the judge as to their duties, the jury members readied to begin their *deliberations the following day, only to learn their services were appreciated but no longer needed.*

Wishing somehow my computer would cast my thoughts backward through unimaginable concepts at the time of fiber optics, radio waves shouting back and forth between towers, satellites bouncing words across the planet to race through phone lines, cable lines to brain paths of those who might have cared, I said to a deaf and earless screen: "So much for Truth, Justice, and the American way."

35

Aaron Weller probably hadn't liked spending the week-end in what guys like him referred to as "the slam-mer." Perhaps, at first, he had been defiant, believed that no one was going to have enough evidence to do him much damage. On the other hand, he knew full well what he had done and how things could go for him if evidence became known that would incriminate Harridan. No doubt, he spent some of that time thinking about people who might have fingered him or could finger him in the future—peo-ple who would sell him down the river to save their own as-ses. Having helped to put many people in jails and prisons, he had to know that how he dealt with what was coming at him could affect decisions about whether or not he would be amongst them. If he couldn't cover his own ass in lies, he would have to take some kind of a deal or gamble that the chief was bluffing about having evidence. And he had to have been thinking about what prison life would be like. If he had to do time, he would be living among other pris-oners who thought of cops as beetle dung, laying beneath an overcrowded container of slithering vipers. All it would take was one word from the outside to almost any prisoner that there was an ex-cop in their midst, and almost every prisoner in his cell block would be waiting for a perfect time to take him.

As I thought about Weller sitting in a jail cell, I painted a picture in my head of him sitting at a chow table by himself until some big 300-pound Bubba with tattoos all over his neck and arms and a tattooed teardrop at the corner of his right eye came up beside him carrying a tray of bread and mostly-flour gravy with a huge scoop of gray peas slopped up against the bland glop of bread, grease, and white ooze with bits of hamburger crumbles for effect. As the Bubba took the chair beside Weller, he dropped the tray onto the hard plastic table with enough force to send some of the peas and gravy splattering into Weller's space and tray and with enough noise-making power to turn the eyes of all the men in the room toward them. Bubba put his hand on Weller's shoulder, holding him in place while he sat down. When the big man had squared himself to the table and released Weller's shoulder, he let his thick thigh rub Weller's leg; when Weller tried to remove himself, Bubba leaned over and whispered, "Yer a dead man, cop!" Then, Bubba hunched his upper body over his food and covered it from each side with his arms—a vulture—pushing huge chunks of the gravy-soaked bread into his almost-toothless mouth as he continued talking: "Didja notice, ain't nobody here wants to sit beside you but me cuz they know 'bout you. I'd drink that coffee you got in front of ya if'n I was you.

Never know when it might be the last cup ya ever have. Who knows?"

In my telling, Weller's tough guy image started falling apart as soon as he realized there were too many of "them" and only one of him. I could imagine him toying with the notion of becoming somebody's *bitch*, maybe Bubba's, in return for protection, thinking about whether he could do it or preferred to die at the point of a shiv coming up beside him in that unknowable moment when the right guy had the right amount of cover to stick him.

"Jackal." That's what Jake called him. Cunning. Sneaks around in the background waiting for his moment to tear at the flesh of someone else's prey, takes his share and slinks off into the brush. Cage him, and he'll spend his time pacing endlessly back and forth frantically seeking a way to break free and run.

Weller and his attorney must have been hit with enough evidence that, a few days after his arrest, he was looking for a deal. The murder of the Lidons was a step too far even for Weller—a blunder—the murderers too stupid to do the job right. Before he was released on bail, he was informed that the prostitute who had lured Jake into the churchyard had ratted him out, said he had set up the trap for Jake and used her to help. He had to know that the walls were closing in on Harridan and anyone associated with him and his criminal activities; somebody would break, and whoever that was would likely get the best deal. Apparently, he sang an ugly song.

36

Jake and I were in his truck twelve miles outside of town heading for Columbus where we intended to pick up the bathroom fixtures as well as the special-order floor and wall tiles we needed to renovate our ancient upstairs bathroom. We had already cut out a portion of the roof and the corresponding rafters and joists below it; we had braced the injured supports with "headers" and "uprights" to maintain the roof's ability to handle winter's heaviest snow falls, spring's rains, and the weight of people making roof repairs—should that ever be needed. Jake was masterful in making his measurements so that the skylight fit perfectly above the boxed in space between the slope of the roof and the ceiling below. We had joyfully torn out mildewed flower-faced drywall and marveled at the wide, hand-hewn upright planks that had been hidden behind it. As if looking upon ancient Egyptian antiquities, one of us declared, "You rarely get a chance to look at bones like this—very old bones—or get to touch and feel their makers' presence." I picked up my phone and took pictures of each of the bared walls for posterity and Facebook. We installed new copper water lines and PVC drain lines where the old galvanized and cast-iron fittings had been, ran new electric lines, installed an exhaust fan and overhead light, and, finally, put greenboard on the walls and spoke of grief at letting the bones fall back into their graves for future archaeologist-minded-homeowners to rediscover.

We had worked side by side getting sweaty and dirty, exerting our muscles, and testing our stamina; sometimes, we worked into the early morning hours when we should have been sleeping, but we were enjoying one another and the work too much to stop. We had fallen easily into the rhythm of men united by physical work and taking opportunities to play, make jokes, laugh, enjoy the touch that happens with men—even heterosexual men—who work closely with other men, reaching over one another's bodies to hold things in place, or to put tools into hands, or to protect one another from falling in dangerous situations.

In the short distance we had driven, we talked about what was left to be done, when we might do it, and how we could be finished with it in a few days if we kept at it and weren't interrupted by unexpected calls for Jake to cover hours for other officers. We had every incentive to get the job done: we were both tired of sponge baths in the downstairs bathroom and shaving at a too-small mirror propped up at an angle behind the faucet. Back and forth we shot comedic comments about our contrived listings of inconveniences we had endured dealing with the doorless bathroom, the clouds of plaster dust, the grit of sawdust in our pants and shoes. And then Jake's cellphone went off.

Tony Angelino was calling from his personal cell phone. Jake hit the "accept" button on the dashboard's Bluetooth and said, "Hey, Tony! What's up?" I almost laughed out loud when Tony asked, "Jake, is that you?" It had always struck me as funny that some people needed to confirm and reconfirm that they were talking to whomever they had called on a cell phone. I thought it would be hilarious if Jake had responded with, "No, Tony, I'm lying. I'm not me. Somebody else is answering my cell phone" or "No! I'm not me, you must have the wrong number." But the message spilling out through the speaker quickly wiped the smartass grin from my face.

Tony, who tended to talk slowly in his everyday speech had gotten hold of something that prodded that voice like a racehorse out of its chute. "Lot going on; want you to know; state police went out to Harridan's to arrest him; soon as they got out of the car, shots came from the house; hit one of them; other one got clear and called for back-up; somebody called the station and told Chief; SWAT team on its way out there; and probably every available Trooper in the state. Chief and Lanning are heading out there now—"

Cutting Angelino off, since it didn't appear he was going to be taking a breath, Jake spoke in a loud and authoritative voice, "Tony, Listen! I'm heading out there. I'm away from home and don't have my weapon with me. Call Cooper and tell him to get his shotgun out of the trunk for me; and tell him to let the troopers know I'm coming so they don't hassle me when I get there." As he was spewing commands to Tony, he found a place to do a U-turn on the four-lane highway, spun around in a fury, pressed the gas pedal to the floor, and sped upwards of 90-miles-per-hour toward what I hoped would be the inevitable denouement.

Jake knew Tony Angelino had a great fondness for the chief and tended to worry about his safety; it was his nature to worry about all the officers who went out on potentially dangerous assignments. Jake reassured Angelino that he would do everything in his power to make sure nobody else got hurt and Tony needed to stay calm and focus on his job. "Don't worry, man. Everything's going to be fine," Jake said assertively. And then he hung up, looked over at me, and said, "There's no time for me to drop you off somewhere. This could get really ugly, Slick, so you've got to do exactly what I say."

Jake had mentally put on his Supercop cape and started barking orders from the side of his mouth as he dodged potential problems with traffic and individual cars he would come upon and pass. The gist of his orders was that when we got near Harridan's place, I was to jump into the driver's seat and take the truck back to the house; he would call me when whatever was going to happen was over; he would ride back with the chief and Lanning or some other officer he might know. His mind raced through back-up strategies as well: isIf somehow anything occurred before I could safely leave, I was to get down on the floor of the truck and not come out until he came and got me. And most importantly, "Don't do anything stupid. You're not a cop; let us handle this." His body was tense; he was clinging to the steering wheel as though he expected any second something monstrous would attack the truck and topple it. His blazing eyes darted back and forth as he checked the rear-view mirror and dodged the lines of seemingly slow-moving vehicles that held the place between him and his destiny.

The road that would take us to Harridan's turned out to be little more than one lane of gravel-covered dirt. Ditches on both sides of the so-called road limited the opportunities for making any mistakes when meeting another car coming from the opposite direction. A couple of driveways spanned the deep gouges that carried water away in heavy rains and floods common in Southeastern Ohio. Those driveways were few, and almost all of them just around the corner from the main road; and then there was only the long narrow road and an occasional entrance to a field or privately-owned woods, the fences marked with loud, "NO TRESPASSING" signs.

As Jake completed his instructions to me, I said, "Alright! I don't have any desire to die, Jake. I'll do what you say, but how in the hell am I not supposed to be worried about you?"

"You probably can't! You're just going to have to trust that I'm good at my job. I'm not going to take any unnecessary chances or be stupid. Anyhow, the troopers might have this thing wrapped up by the time we get there."

But they didn't. As we pulled up, there were police cars seemingly everywhere that a vehicle could be parked out front of Harridan's home. There were men behind the vehicles with guns drawn. I could see the chief and Jim Landon hunkered down behind their unit. Jake stopped abruptly some distance from the other vehicles, threw his door open, told me to keep my head down and slide into the driver's seat and remember what he told me. I was barely able to get the words, "Be careful," out before he was gone and running to where the chief was waiting with a pistol in one hand and a shotgun in the other. When I saw that Jake was behind the squad car, I started backing the truck up. It felt like I had been backing up for a considerable time and distance on the narrow country road searching for a space wide enough to turn the truck around and avoid the ditches that now looked more like empty moats than drains. My arms were shaky. My ability to keep the vehicle straight on the road was unusually difficult as I grappled with fear for Jake. I was within a short distance of a manhunt that had already caused at least one officer to be shot. It could get worse. Much worse. The image of Nathan Sanders ran across my mind's eye and then Harridan's image pushed him aside; they were running, running, looking back over their shoulders and nowhere to go. And I didn't want to think about either of them, let them run! Get away! I wanted Jake to be safe.

The fear in and of itself was bad enough, but I hadn't had much experience driving Jake's truck—or any truck for that matter. I had to stop many times just short of going off the road, pull forward to straighten the wheels and return to driving with my head wrenching my neck as far back as I could make it swivel to see what I was doing. Though it hadn't been a great feat of driving, I was eventually able to find a lane that lay over top of a concrete pipe that let water flow through and vehicles to cross safely. It was one of a handful of entrance paths I had seen on the way up from the main road, what I assumed were access points to farmers' fields. It provided approximately ten feet of space in front of a steel gate. With some maneuvering to grasp the turn ratio of the truck, and with several adjustments, I was finally able to get the vehicle heading away from whatever drama was taking place behind me and look out of the windshield and give my neck the opportunity to quit complaining about the torture I had been inflicting upon it.

Though my eyes were looking forward, my brain was still behind me with Jake and producing all kinds of scenarios where Jake ended up hurt or killed. I hadn't gotten far down the narrow road before I saw a moving figure ahead of me and couldn't imagine why; I conjured farmer, school boy, vagabond, just someone out on a walk on a lonely road to think without the distractions of traffic, or maybe it was some local who had seen the police cars racing up the road and wanted to see for themselves what all the commotion was about.

It hadn't crossed my mind that the figure standing there could be Harridan, but as I got close enough to see him, there he was, poised in a police shooting position with a gun aimed at the windshield of the truck and at my head. When the recognition hit me, I instinctively put all my strength into my legs and tried to push the clutch and brake through the floorboard to stop well short of him so I could flee backwards once again. The tires screeched and slid sideways on the gravel refusing my attempts to control the momentum as the passenger-side tires dropped into the ditch, the truck chassis screamed through the steel crunching beneath me as the tires spun against asphalt and stone, the road itself crying out in agonizing pain as the engine balked and died, the vehicle now tilted low on the passenger side. My body weight pulled against the seatbelt that kept me from falling headlong across the seat and sliding hard into the downhill door. Harridan, still at some distance, was running full speed toward me. Fighting gravity, I restarted the engine, punched the clutch, and put the truck in first gear, pressed the gas pedal hard, and released the clutch. I wanted magic—my only recourse as thought dissolved in the chemical soup of my brain screaming at me, "Escape!" Driver side wheels up above the pavement; passenger side wheels hanging free above the ditch; the entire vehicle suspended by the chassis balancing on the road's broken edges; beneath me the engine screaming at the tires to find something to push against before it died once again.

The seatbelt catching my waist and shoulders felt like it was going to cut into my flesh, making me want to succumb to the inviolable gravitational force of nature. And then Harridan was standing on the truck's running board holding the barrel of his gun against the window at face level commanding something like, "Roll down that window, or I'll blow your fucking brains out." When I did what he said, he put the open mouth of the barrel against my temple and said, "Well, this is my lucky day! Davidson's girlfriend arrives just in time. Get your ass out of that truck."

As something resembling thought started finding its way back to my brain, I felt myself imagining a way to react to his snarling words with a cannon shot of fist through the window into his face. But then, there was the gun. Since there weren't many options that I could think of in the panic of those initial seconds, I said, with as much courage as I could muster, that I would do what he said, but I had to get out of the seatbelt, and I couldn't get the door open with him on the running board. "It will be easier for both of us if you let me get out the passenger side."

"You just do that, and don't try any heroic crap. I'll be into the truck bed and on top of you so fast, you won't know what happened just before you died. Got it?"

"I've got it," I said as he watched me struggle to unlock the seat belt and slide down the seat slope using the steering wheel to keep me from moving too quickly or crashing against the interior door handle or into the glass of the side window. By the time I got to the passenger-side door, Harridan was already across the truck bed and was watching me through the rear window. I unlatched the door. Gravity and the weight of the door swung it open with enough force to pull me out and drop me into the grass and mud-covered ditch. As I picked myself up, I could feel the burn the rough grass had rubbed onto my face as I rolled, the pain of dropping to the ground and catching my fall with my shoulder and hip. I had barely arrived at a standing position when Harridan, already behind me, grabbed the back of my shirt practically lifting me off the ground, and threw me forward a step or two, then pushed me past the nose of the truck and up out of the ditch.

As we moved up onto the pavement, I could hear muffled explosions from up the road ... found myself yelling at Harridan. "What did you do? What's happening?" Then turning toward the continuing explosions and screaming, "Jake!"

The gun barrel stuck against my ribs and pushed me across the hot tar toward the shrub-faced, wooded area opposite the truck. My brain was racing, trying to think of a way to break free and run, get to Jake; flailing arms, arhythmic twisting and tremoring of my body, giving away my intentions.

"Calm down!" he yelled. "The dumbasses are shooting tear gas and smoke bombs into the house. Wasting their time. Now move!" He pushed the palm of his hand into the space between my shoulder blades and shoved me forward with enough force to make me stumble. He grabbed the back of my shirt and held me as we stepped off into the thick brush that tore at my pantlegs and arms. "Won't be long before they figure out that I'm not there. Dumb Asses. You and me, we've got some traveling to do."

"Why would I go anywhere with you?" I yelled as I tried to dig in my heals against his powerful pushing at the back of my neck. As I said it, I heard a braver version of myself not so much asking the question as demanding an answer. Defiance spoke for me in a voice more like Jake's cop voice than my own, a voice that said, "Don't mistake me for someone who is afraid of you." And I realized that, despite the danger I was in, I was now more angry than frightened, and I was alone and had to make choices about how I would stay alive. It wasn't something I could have named then, but looking back upon it, I had chosen a strategy of keeping him off balance and slowing him down.

"Because I say so, that's why," he spoke loudly, his voice snarling. "Unless, of course, you want to die right here, right now. This could've been easy. But no, you had to go and ditch the truck. Now, you're going to be my shield if they catch up to us. You and me, we're going to take us a little walk through these woods to the highway, get us a car. We'll see where things go from there."

As he pushed me forward, I tried to resist him, walked as slowly as I could to slow him down, made him work to move me around, dragged my feet to leave a trail in the leaves for Jake to follow if he came looking for my body, find ways to make it miserable for Harridan to escape, but not so miserable that he decided he would be better off taking his chances without having me for a hostage. He was onto me almost immediately, used his muscles and his gun to keep me moving as best he could while I tried to think of something I could use to keep him off balance psychologically. And all I had to work with at that moment were my words and the resistance of my body.

I started talking, talking fast and annoyingly. "Pretty clever the way you slipped out from under the cops, Mike. Slipped out right after you shot the trooper, Right, Mike? Can I call you 'Mike'? Never mind. Since you're likely to— how would you say it?—plug me anyway, I'm going to call you 'Mike.' So, yeah. Pretty clever. You're a smart man. You duck out right after you plugged the cop, Mikey? Put one of them down and run out the back door and into the woods to the road to hustle a car while the other cop calls in the cavalry?" I threw every question I could think of at him, kept hitting him with diminutives of his name, and talking to him like he was a two-dimensional character in an old B-rated mobster story.

When I annoyed him enough, he pulled my shirt collar tight against my throat and spoke through clenched teeth, "You figured it out Dick Tracy. Now shut the fuck up and move your ass." Again, he thrust me forward as he released the grip on my shirt.

I was getting to him, could feel his increasing agitation. I added some repetition to the repertoire of nearly ceaseless words. "I wish I could be smart like you, Mikey. I probably wouldn't be out here right now with a gun in my back. I have to admit it, you are one smart guy. Those cops were morons. Right? Most cops are. Right? That's how you got powerful! Right, Mikey? Mike Harridan, Master Police Officer! Right? Except ... I hate to say the obvious, Mikey, but you screwed up somewhere along the way. You've been found out, and now you're on the run. But you'll outsmart them all, won't you, Mikey? You're smarter than all those other criminals you helped put away, aren't you?"

"Shut up and keep walking." His voice grew angrier each time he spoke. I suspected had he not needed to keep me alive for the moment, he would have dropped my body from his misery right then. I was perfecting my routine of non-stop talk, irritating him, and relying on the hope that he needed me at least until he could find a vehicle. Somewhere in the back of my brain were all the clichéd TV episodes I'd seen where I and everyone else watching knows in advance how this week's episode is going to end. But then, I wasn't a main character and there was no TV show. Harridan *could* easily blow my brains out and make a run for it on his own. And there might not be that moment where the cops arrive and find the villain standing in an open space totally exposed and waving a gun until he succumbs to an endless barrage of bullets spued from the overwhelming number of guns firing at him by the cops who have managed to be in exactly the right place at the right time. The alternative scenarios might have been something like the cops arriving and watching this guy killing me just before sending the cascade of bullets at his body; he fights to continue standing until the one bullet gets to his forehead and he collapses; or maybe he lets me live so he can hide behind me never guessing that a sniper will eventually blow his brains out and splatter his gore all over me, or some hero—Jake maybe—says just the right thing to him to make him believe "we can work this out. This doesn't have to end this way," so he lays his gun down, steps away from me with his hands in the air and willingly faces the prospect of prison rather than the sentence of death he knows is coming from officers ready to blast him into oblivion.

"Kind of like a bad movie. Isn't it? They're closing in on you, Mikey. All this trouble. Shaking down merchants, beating Jake up, killing the Lidons, getting your so-called straight boys to take me. And you a cop," I said sarcastically. "You had to know, Mikey, that you'd slip up somewhere; all criminals do. Too many dishes spinning, Mikey ... balls in the air. Too many weak people knowing too much. Tell me, Mikey, did you put the Lidon's in the trunk first or find some other way to get them gassed to death?"

Again, he told me to shut up and pushed me forward.

"What difference does it make, Mikey? You can tell me. You're going to kill me anyway. Did you kill the Lidons? Did you have Jake beaten? What about me, Mike? Did your boys do it? Just say 'yes' or 'no.' Can't you give me that much? Let me die knowing the truth. Okay? Give me something worth knowing before I die: a 'yes' or 'no.' 'Yes,' you did all of it. Or 'No,' you weren't behind any of it. Let me have that. Will you?"

"Shut up or I'll drop you right here and now. I can't see how Davidson puts up with your endless mouth. I don't want to hear any more from you!"

"Alright, Mikey. Whatever you say." Hey. Can we take a quick break? I've got to go, man. You've got me so nervous I can't hold it much longer. Can we do that, please?"

"Just keep moving. You'll survive."

A barrage of words exploded from my mouth about urgency, not wanting to embarrass myself, being desperate as I performed the dance of profound need.

I accepted the punches at my back, kept talking until he finally gave in, "Jesus Christ! Do it!" He stopped pushing, then stood and waited. "But you make one false move..."

"Yeah. Yeah. I know. You're going to plug me. The cliches are getting old, Mike." I could feel his eyes on me as my hands moved toward the front of my pants and the realization that I might actually have to produce something worthy of his annoyance with me. "I can't go with you watching me, Mikey. I know you'd like to see it, but I just can't do it with you watching."

Harridan pulled his eyes off me and looked beyond me into the trees.

"Hey, can I ask one more question? Can you tell me, was Weller in on all of your fun, your criminal activities? Who else?"

He was looking at me now. "Like what you see, Mike? You do like it, don't you."

"You've had plenty of time to finish up. Let's move."

"Does he like being with other men, Mikey? I mean ... in his spare time."

"I don't care what he does. Now pull it in and let's move."

"No, you don't care," I said as zipped up. "Is that what you liked about him? Was he into you? You two into each other? I know you like men, don't you? Jake told me all about you."

The punch at the side of my head knocked me to the ground. The kicks against my stomach and ribs took my breath away, caused me to writhe in pain before he picked me up again by my collar and told me to keep my "lying, filthy mouth shut."

It took me a moment to get my legs under me and make them carry my body without wanting to fall down. The sounds of sirens grew behind us, and there was the faint sound of a hound howling and moving toward us from the direction of Harridan's property.

The beating had changed my earlier anger into the fear I had previously denied. It took me some time to find words. In truth, they found me, came through the throbbing pains of my head and body, carrying forward the attempt to fight with what little I had to work with. The boldness of my voice wasn't there for me, but the words were, though they seemed to be far from my hearing and halting, "They're onto you, Mikey. What do you think? Coming for you."

"Once and for all, shut the fuck up!" He kicked at the back of my thighs, but it lost much of its force as I stumbled forward ahead of his plan for his shoe to connect.

I could feel my body becoming numb, my mind struggling to find words, and yet they came, fell out of me like water from a spilled glass. "I'm nervous. When I'm nervous, I talk a lot. It's who I am." Defiance began rising again out of wherever it had hidden itself for a short while within me and leapt over the fear and the sudden gut-awareness of a critical moment coming. "Let's take a stand right here and just get this thing over with. What do you say? I'm not going any further." I stopped walking, took the blows to my back, the kicks at my legs. When he pushed me again, I deliberately fell forward into the dry leaves of last year's autumn and said, "Shoot me right here if that's what you are going to do. I'm telling you, I'm done!"

"The hell you are!" As he said it, he was bent over me and had his hand around a section of my shirt above the shoulder. As he started to lift, I instinctively felt the earth under my feet, felt the push of my crouched legs shooting straight up and driving the top of my head up under his chin. More animal than man, I spun to face him and swung my right arm with all the force I had in me remembering what Jake had told me about fighting in a life and death situation: "Don't think about punching the face; that's weak! Think about your fist reaching all the way through it to the back of the man's skull."

Harridan obviously hadn't considered the possibility that a "fag" would fight, or even that I was capable of fighting. When my fist landed, his jaw dropped, leaving his mouth an open hole and his eyes bulging as he caught himself reacting to the pain, humiliation, and shock. He was reeling—his body staggering backward off balance, his hand uncontrollably releasing the gun, letting it fall to the ground. And while he was staggering, I unleashed as many punches as I could land—at least two more solid punches to his face and an uppercut to his jaw—before he overcame his shock, felt the blood running down his chin, and gained control of his body. When he did, all his training as a police officer kicked into gear. Rage seemed to rise up from his toes, through his torso and into his face as he took a classic fighter's stance, left foot forward, right foot back, chest turned at an angle to minimize the opponent's target areas, his left fist raised just below his jaw line, elbows tight to his ribs, his right arm and fist lowered slightly as he hunched to cover his midsection. When my last attempt at a punch had gone wild to the left, he cocked his right arm and threw a punch that was more aluminum baseball bat than a human fist and not just any aluminum baseball bat: it was a bat swung by a revered Yankees slugger who was the terror of the ball field. I wasn't aware that I had fallen or that my mind had vomited all sensibility momentarily until I landed on the gun, its hard steel cylinder sending pain up through my chest—pain that demanded my brain kick back into action. At that point, there was only survival. There was the gun. And there was whatever luck that might come to me. I had the gun in my hand, managed to roll onto my back and have it pointed right at the gut of the man who was hovering over me, casting his shadow on me as he readied another sledgehammer punch until he saw the barrel and my finger on the trigger. He pulled the punch with him as he instinctively backed away two or three steps, suddenly frightened by the shifting of power between us.

"Whoa. Hold on now. Hold on," he was shouting.

"Hold on, my ass! Back off! Now!" I demanded.

My body was shaking as I got up off the ground and tried to clear my head. My hands were quivering as they joined upon the gun, one below the trigger assembly to steady it and the other on the handle, my finger shaking against the crescent of the trigger.

As Harridan put his hands up of his own accord, I shook my head and tried to dislodge the thunder and fear rattling there and tried to keep my finger steady as I leveled the barrel toward the flat surface of his chest, but the shaking of my hands was altering second-by-second the insertion point or the total miss for the bullet if he attacked or I accidentally pulled the lever.

"You don't want to kill me. You know it." Harridan was trying to sound fatherly, play on some belief that he could get me to rise to a moral code of behavior that he, himself, didn't have. "You know it. You wouldn't be able to live with yourself. You'd go to prison for a lot of years. You'd lose your boyfriend. Everything."

Immediately countering him, words came loudly into my consciousness: "He's not going to let you take him. He knows you're frightened. He's playing you. Keep him scared."

I heard my rendition of a "Jake-in-command-voice" saying firmly and in total control, "Mikey, you have no idea how much I'd like to kill you right now, and you don't know anything about my moral values. Now get down on your knees!"

When he refused and said I wouldn't shoot him, I fired a shot into the ground just slightly off to his left. Since I had never actually fired a handgun, I was lucky it went where I thought I was aiming. He dropped to his knees at once. I could hear many people crashing through the woods—people I assumed to be police officers—years of leaves grating upon one another, saplings breaking as the rush of humanity overcame them.

Though I wanted to turn to see them, I did not. I ordered Harridan to put his hands behind his head, lock his fingers together, and not move as I walked around behind him with the gun pointed at his body and staying out of his reach. "It's going to be a pleasure killing you, Mikey, in the name of the Lidons, in the name of all those you stole from, in the name of everyone you ever took advantage of, in the name of Jake Davidson, in the name of Rob Wilson—me—the man who is going to make you pay. I am now going to do the world a favor and put you out of its misery. And since I don't give a shit whether or not you pretend to be religious, you've had all the time I'm willing to give you to... "

"Just take me in. We'll let the law do its thing."

"No, Mikey. I'm not the law. This gun is the law right now. And you're going to tell me what I want to know, or you are going to die right where you are."

"You've got me all wrong, I was ..."

"You're about one second away from meeting your maker."

"Wait! Wait! You don't want to kill me, man! Don't kill me," he pleaded. "The cops are going to be here in a minute. They'll shoot you down, you having that gun and all."

"That may be. But they're also going to find your corpse alongside mine unless I hear you say what you did, all of it, and you'd better be goddamned convincing. And I have no interest in waiting any longer. Three ... two ..."

"All right! All right! What do you want to know?"

"I told you. I want to know it all. Admit what you did!"

He knew I was nervous. I was sure he was hoping to catch me off guard and regain control, but I was out of his reach. I saw him looking around for something he could use as a weapon.

"You so much as blink wrong, you're dead. Got it?" I warned. Obviously, he thought I was bluffing. When he tried to draw his leg up as if to lunge forward, I fired another round into the ground just left of him. He dropped back to his hands and knees, threw his hands out as if begging

"Okay! Okay! I took protection money from merchants."

"And you killed the Lidons. Why?" I demanded.

"Because they were old and stupid and told Davidson about me."

"I've got news for you, you stupid son of a bitch. They didn't!"

I could see his lower jaw fall open and then his whole head dropping his chin onto his chest. He had been surprised, knew that despite his best efforts he had made the mistake he hadn't expected to make.

"Now tell me about setting Jake up," I said through clenched teeth, my mouth still leaking sarcasm.

"He was going to rat me out. Just wanted to scare him off. I don't like him."

"Come on, Mikey, that's so lame. I know about you. You liked him plenty. You wanted his ass, and he didn't want you. Let's be real for a minute, just you and me out here in the woods, two gay men, nobody around. You wanted some man-on-man action. Then you wanted to make him pay because he knew you for what you are, what you couldn't admit about yourself. Let's hear it.

"I can't."

"Three, two ..."

"Alright. Alright. I wanted him. Okay? You happy?"

"Not yet. There's the little matter of you setting me up with your boys. Was that because you were jealous that I had Jake and you didn't?

"I told Weller to scare you. I wanted to make Jake afraid to talk. I didn't know Weller and his guys were going to do what he did. There. I told you everything. How 'bout you put that gun down."

"Do you really think I'm that stupid?"

"I'll confess it all in court if you don't kill me."

"I don't think you're worth the cost and hassle of a trial."

"If you're going to kill me, at least let me stand up and take the shot like a man."

"Mikey, you barely qualify as a man. You stay right where you are while I decide whether you are going to live or die. If you move, you're the one making the decision for you to die. Got it?"

In my peripheral vision, I could see Jake and other police officers lined up to my right and behind Harridan, almost all standing with guns pointed at Harridan and me. Then, Jake walked forward holding the other officers back with his arm raised and his palm turned toward them in the command stop/wait position. He shouted, "Rob, listen to me! You don't want to do this. Don't throw your life away for him; he's not worth it."

"Then somebody better get his ass up here and take this son of a bitch," I shouted as I turned briefly in his direction without moving the gun from its focus on Harridan's head. "Come get him; then I'll put the gun down. Tell them, Jake. Tell the others I mean them no harm. You and Lanning come up here. I'll turn this worthless piece of shit over to you two. I'll give you the gun. But I'm not taking it off him until somebody has him in cuffs."

The two men came up quickly, pushed Harridan face down with great force, causing him to cry out in the pain of his face hitting the hard earth beneath the sandpaper leaves that offered no cushion. Saying nothing, they pulled his hands behind him and cuffed him, and still I stood there poised to shoot even as Harridan was dragged aside and no longer in front of the gun. Jake came up beside me, tried to remove the gun from my hands, but I couldn't let go of it. I wanted to, but as I watched him, it was like watching him remove fingers or a hand, a physical extension of the body of another person. He slowly and gently pushed my arms toward the ground, then pried my fingers one-by-one from the metal and took the gun from the still-clenched fingers. He lifted the gun over his head for the other officers to see. They quickly filled in the space around us, lifted Harridan up, and four or five of them started him on the march toward the squad cars beyond the woods. My body began to shake, my eyes clouded, and I felt like I didn't want to think anymore, didn't want to remember anything, didn't want to function, just wanted to feel safe again. Jake wrapped his arms around me, pulled me into him like the first time we had surrendered ourselves to one another.

I whispered into his ears as the tears began to roll out of my eyes and onto his shirt. "I was afraid, Jake," the words felt haphazard, gushy, and uncontrollable, "that you wouldn't come. That I couldn't hold him. That he would kill me. That he would get away. I made him confess, Jake. He did it. All of it. He confessed."

He held me tighter and whispered, "We all heard him, Rob. You were a hell of a cop out here today. I'm so proud of you." I could feel the blood returning to my fingers and they began to move at my command and found their way around him as I felt the muscles of his back as I held him as tightly as I could, not wanting to let go.

"I was scared." My voice came out as staccato notes: "He beat the hell out of me; he was going to kill me."

"But you got him, man. You beat him."

Pulling myself together as best I could, I pulled my head back so I could look him in the eye. Surprisingly clearly, I said, "I wanted to kill him. I wanted to kill him for you and me. I really wanted to. I thought he was going to make me kill him, Jake, or I wouldn't be able to stop myself. I wanted to kill him."

"You were surviving, Rob. I knew you wouldn't kill him."

"No, Jake. I wasn't just surviving. I wanted him to be afraid of me, if even for a few minutes. I wanted him to know what it feels like to be at someone else's mercy. I wanted him to have just a few minutes of the terror I had when his buddies took me and took away every defense I had. I wanted to make him suffer and then make him die."

"But you didn't kill him, and that's the difference between you and people like him."

"Am I going to be arrested for telling him I wanted to kill him?"

"No judge is going to convict you for trying to save your life. You did nothing wrong. Hell, Slick. You're a hero."

Mark Cooper appeared from somewhere out of the haze of relief that was enveloping me. He and Jim Lanning stepped toward us. Jake swung sideways so we were both facing them. The chief put his hand out to me, took mine in his and gripped it solidly as he said, "I don't know how you did it, but what you did was a real act of courage, my friend. You're a good man, Rob. After all you have been through, it took a lot of control not to pull that trigger and keep him in custody." I remember faking some kind of smile as the chief turned to Jake to say, "You've got a good one here; don't screw it up." Jake laughed and said he had no such intentions.

Cooper turned back to me and said, "I need you to come to the station and give a statement for the record. Not today. Tomorrow. You've had a hell of a day. Tomorrow if you can. I 'm looking forward to hearing how you managed to get the drop on a guy like him." The chief put his hands on our shoulders and patted them in a fatherly way. Then, he dropped his hands and stepped aside. Before he walked away, he said, "By the way, I'll be getting a DNA test done on Weller as soon as it can be done."

Jim Lanning stepped in close and wrapped his arms around our necks and pulled our heads against his face and upper chest and whispered, "I am so glad you are safe." Then he squeezed us tighter before whispering, "How about we all go skinny dipping this weekend."

In an attempt to respond in the midst of the confluence of fleeting fear, flooding emotional responses to the notion that I could have taken a life, verbal tokens of heroism being thrown at me, and the profound warmth of human touch, I found myself saying mechanically and jokingly, "You think I want to see your naked ass again?" I couldn't think of what else to say and found myself stumbling around with, "Actually, I would like that."

"Let's see how Rob is feeling in the next day or two, and we'll go from there," Jake whispered.

Jim stepped back and looked me in the eye and said, "You're a hell of a man, Rob." Seeing the bruising that was coming quickly into my face from Harridan's punch, he crinkled his face to a smirk and said, "By the way, when anybody asks you how you got that shiner you're going to have, you can say, 'That's nothing. You should see the other guy; he had to be picked up off the ground and hauled away!' ... Now, how about we get out of here?"

Maybe I was just talked out, too tired to pull my thoughts together, too confused to decide whether or not anything was worth saying until the words rolled out of their own volition as they moved beyond the myopia of my muddled brain: "We're going to have to catch a ride, Jake. I'm sorry about your truck."

"No worry. The guys will help me get it out; that's what cops do: help each other out. The good ones, anyway. And if it won't run, we'll get it towed. Let's worry about that when we have to."

As Jim and the chief started walking, I found myself asking about what had happened to the cop Harridan had shot, "Is he alive?" My voice sounded strange, distant, like that voice I once had when I was in the hospital trying to make people hear me and knowing they couldn't and wouldn't have understood if they had.

"Not too badly hurt. He'll come through," one of them said over his shoulder.

As we started walking, I began to feel a queasiness rising up lava like out of my stomach, a reflexive shudder suddenly taking over my whole body, my face throbbing with pain, my brain flooding with images of those moments in which I expected to die. I could feel Jake wrapping his strong, sinewy arm around me as he helped me stumble out of the woods and into the road where the truck stood waiting behind a trooper holding the keys out to us. I remember Jake helping me into the seat and nothing else from then until I woke up at home in our bed, the last of the afternoon light wiping its hard-calloused hands on our bodies.

37

A few weeks later, we set off to spend a few hours at the quarry. As we neared it, I told Jake that I wanted to take a detour to "the hanging tree." As soon as we got to it, I started climbing up as if I had done it many times and knew exactly where to set my feet and take hold with my hands, and Jake followed, both of us working ourselves out onto the thick almost perpendicular limb that once held the dangling neck-stretched body of Nathan Sanders. We sat side by side looking out over the landscape, the quarry walls, and the scrub brush that had taken over what were once grasslands for feeding wandering cattle.

As we sat there, I was thinking about what I had told Jake when he came home from work the night before. I had gone to visit the local historical society staff earlier in the day to discuss their desire to use my materials to print a short factual accounting of the Trent case. During our time together, I had expressed my disappointment with being unable to answer the many questions that lingered about the Trent murders. When I told them about my suspicions there had once been a way into town from the quarry but couldn't prove it, they asked me if I had checked the Sanborn maps to see if a trail had been noted where it came into town. Since I had never heard of a Sanborn map, I was ready to be educated. They pulled some out of their files. It turns out that Sanborn maps had been used widely to map changes in towns for insurance purposes. On the earliest rendition of the Emberland map, we found an arrow pointing off the map with the word "quarry" beneath it. It didn't show the quarry or the trail itself, but it showed there was one. Like so much of the story, it wasn't conclusive ... but suggestive, anti-climactic.

"He's not here anymore, Jake." The words came out of me almost as if they had sneaked out, dodged any foreknowledge on my part, more like ghost words than real.

"Where is he then?"

"I don't know. I just know he's gone," I said as if I somehow had power over ghosts. "He doesn't need us anymore."

"Did he ever?"

"I think he did."

"For what?"

"A shot at redemption."

"Guess I'll have to take your word for that, Slick. Do you think he got it?"

"No. Never will. But he got a fair hearing from us. And maybe that's the best he was ever going to get anyway."

We sat there for a few minutes as we took in the smells of the wild, watched the slight motion of new leaves reacting to the tiniest of breezes. Then, almost deciding simultaneously, and without discussion, we climbed down and walked away, leaving the tree behind us as if forever. We spent several hours at the old quarry, swimming, sunbathing, eating the lunch we had packed, playing child-like ... it was a day much like the day I first came to it. But there were differences too. I had become accustomed to the place, to Jake, to the feelings that other people from out of the past still gathered there, spoke, laughed, teased, and played. At one point, I thought I could almost hear them singing above a fiddle that provided the accompaniment. It wasn't the mournful tune I would have expected had I thought about hearing any sound from the past, and though I couldn't make out the words, I felt happy at hearing it. I asked Jake if he could hear it, and he said he often did, but he couldn't right then and that was okay. Before we left, I turned to the quarry, ran my eyes over the multi-colored walls and thought about finding a way to add my name there. "Maybe one day soon; maybe just my initials," I thought as I turned to Jake and started walking home.

That evening we sat side by side on the living room sofa—my head on Jake's shoulder as we talked—and enjoyed the cool summer night's cleansed air flowing into the house through the window screens, over us and into the corners of old rooms to chase out the musty smell of time and the generations of families and their unnamable visitors, lovers, friends and enemies who had come and gone. Jake was stroking the hair on the side of my head lightly with his fingertips. We talked about our plans for remaking the house our own, about our work, and about our dreams of life together. I found myself reminding him about a time early in our relationship when I was describing for him what it was like for me as a writer who needed to find that "something"—that nugget; what I now called my "truth"—that grabbed me and demanded I write it even when it wouldn't name itself and I didn't know where I was to be taken by it—that something that waited until the last word was written to reveal itself to me or sometimes refused to reveal itself in words at all and that I accepted through unexplainable responses of my mind and body.

"It's not all that different from trying to figure out what it is that makes a life worthwhile," I said as I twisted my neck to look at his eyes. "I remember you saying something to the effect of 'It's all about living life honestly and trying to be as good a person as you can be and that's enough.' But I couldn't accept that then, Jake; and I told you that I thought there was something beyond your words I needed to find. And we talked about the beyond, the beyond of our living and our deaths. And you said something like maybe we just have to accept the questions because there may not be answers. Do you remember all that, Jake?"

"I remember," he said softly into my ear as he continued to stroke my hair. "Have you figured anything out since then? Come up with any answers?"

"Maybe. And maybe it just falls under trying to be the best person I am able to be just like you said, but it feels like it's more than that. Nathan Sanders and Mike Harridan led me to it. I've written the story, Jake—not the story you wanted me to write way back when we first met.

I wrote the story of loving you and being loved, learning from you what it means to be real. I want you to read it. You're in it, I'm in it. Together, we've made a good story, a story that lives beyond us.

"Slick. I want to read it."

He not only wanted to read it; he wanted to read it right then. I lifted the weight of my upper torso from him and pulled myself up off the sofa to go upstairs to my writing desk where I took a copy of this manuscript that I had made for him out of the drawer and brought it to him minus these last few pages that could not be written until this moment arrived and drifted into our history. I promised him they would be written before he got to them in his reading of the manuscript. As I put it in his hands, I could feel that old exciting sense of trepidation and pride wrestling one another in my chest to the inevitable draw that would be the end result. I suggested he take as long as he wanted to read. But before leaving, I told him that he had no obligations; he could talk about it if and when he was ready or never as he wished. As I began walking toward the door, I had a momentary sense of mourning; I had given the creation its first occasion to step out on its own. And though I knew Jake would be kind, I hoped I hadn't failed him.

Much like the fire I had once built of paper scrawled with rage—a fire to cleanse me of the bile I had felt, I pulled off my shirt, dropped my shorts, pulled off my socks... all in a single heap and walked out to bathe in the moon beyond the maple that stood waiting for this time to pass into memory.

www.ingramcontent.com/pod-product-compliance
Lightning Source LLC
Chambersburg PA
CBHW030336120726
47901CB00007B/1806